Penguin
Random
House

MW00427229

A NOTE FROM THE AUTHOR, CHRISTINA LYNCH

Dear Reader,

A murder mystery for adults about a pony that's also a hilarious and poignant story of love, loss, courage, and redemption? And it's a retelling of *The Odyssey*? Yes, genres were bent in the making of this novel! Let me explain:

In a moment of insanity in 2018, I bought a pony named Floraa. I am a full-size adult, so Floraa is a large pony, but still very much a pony. A pony, to be clear, is not a small horse. Horses are generally kind and sweet and just the tiniest bit dumb (sorry, Seabiscuit!). They do what they're asked. Ponies are a different creature altogether: they do what they want. If you are in the way of that, you might get bitten, kicked, or launched into space. At the same time, they are endlessly adorable and deeply funny—my pony (who lives right outside the back door) makes me laugh every single day. A lot.

When the pandemic hit, you can guess who my quarantine buddy was. She also became my muse. I thought about all of the ponies who are deeply loved by kids and their families, but are then sold when the child grows a few inches. The pony who grabbed the pen on the very first day I sat down to write *Pony Confidential* had an even bigger personality than Floraa. He shocked me at times with his acid critiques of humans—delivered with comedic flair. But at its heart, *Pony Confidential* is a love story. The pony is desperately searching for Penny, the one little girl he truly loved, twenty-five years after he last saw her. At the same time, law-abiding Penny is arrested on her doorstep and jailed for a murder she didn't commit—and only the pony can prove that.

Our bonds with our pets reveal a lot about ourselves. My hope is that the story of the pony and Penny will help readers find a deeper connection with the animals—and people—in their lives.

And did I mention there's a goat named Circe in it who has some choice words for you?

I hope you're intrigued enough to take a ride with *Pony Confidential*!

Happy trails,

PONY CONFIDENTIAL

PONY CONFIDENTIAL

Christina Lynch

Berkley

New York

BERKLEY
An imprint of Penguin Random House LLC
penguinrandomhouse.com

Copyright © 2024 by Christina Lynch
Penguin Random House supports copyright. Copyright fuels creativity, encourages diverse voices, promotes free speech, and creates a vibrant culture. Thank you for buying an authorized edition of this book and for complying with copyright laws by not reproducing, scanning, or distributing any part of it in any form without permission. You are supporting writers and allowing Penguin Random House to continue to publish books for every reader.

BERKLEY and the BERKLEY & B colophon are registered trademarks of Penguin Random House LLC.

Permission for use of lines from the poem "Instructions for the Journey" (*The Weight of Love*, Negative Capability Press, 2019, p. 70) by Pat Schneider is granted by her family.

ISBN: 9780593640364

An application to register this book for cataloging has been submitted to the Library of Congress.

Printed in the United States of America
$PrintCode

Book design by [TK]

For all the ponies I have loved,
and for Addie, future pony girl

The greatest obstacle to the study of animal emotions is the common objection that "we cannot know what they feel." While this is undeniably true, we should realize that it also holds for fellow human beings.

—Frans de Waal, *What Is an Animal Emotion?*

PONY CONFIDENTIAL

PROLOGUE

PENNY MARCUS OPENS her front door to find Ed, the local sheriff's deputy, on the doorstep. It's a bright sunny spring day and it never crosses her mind that something is amiss, partly because she saw Ed at the coffee shop just this morning, as she does every morning before she heads off to teach third grade in the little California mountain town where they live. They're both latte people.

"Hey, Ed," she says, opening the door with a smile and smoothing the front of her light blue linen sundress with lemons on it. "Your little girl aced her math quiz today."

"Hi, Penny," says Ed. He seems a bit apologetic as he says, "Can you stick your hands out for me?"

She laughs. Ed is a little bit of a prankster. He had a role in their local theater production of *Arsenic and Old Lace* last year. He was hilarious as the cop who is always one step behind the murderous old ladies.

Penny plays along and sticks out her hands and Ed snaps handcuffs on her. "Ha ha ha," she says. "What are you auditioning for now, *Murder, She Wrote*?" She hefts the cuffs a couple times. "Hey, these things are heavier than I thought." She adds pointedly, "And kind of tight and uncomfortable."

Ed doesn't smile. "You have the right to remain silent. Anything you say can and will—"

"—be used against you in a court of law. Yeah, we've all memorized it. Very funny, but I have to get back to grading the kids' homework. The spelling bee is tomorrow. Can you take these things off now?"

"You have the right to an attorney. If you cannot afford an attorney, one will be appointed for you."

Her stomach begins to churn a little. "Ed? What is this?"

Almost apologetically he says, "You're under arrest for murder."

Penny blinks. "Murder? Ed, excuse my language, but I have no effing idea what you're talking about. Murder of whom? Who died?"

He checks his phone. "Doesn't say. You're being extradited to New York."

Penny just stares at him in shock. "New York?" Her mind is whirling. "When did this supposed murder take place?"

He looks at his phone again and counts on one hand. "Um, just about twenty-five years ago."

"Ed. Twenty-five years ago I was twelve years old. Twelve. A twelve-year-old little girl."

Ed shrugs. "I'm sorry, Penny, I can't say more. I'm just doing my job. You'll have to come with me." He checks his watch, which Penny knows was a gift from the town to honor his first ten years of service. She herself had contributed ten dollars to the purchase of that watch, had even lobbied for the thick brown leather band instead of a blue nylon one that she worried would chafe his wrist. Now it's her wrists that are chafing.

"Come on, Ed," she says. "This is crazy. Please. Let me go."

PART ONE

A Taste for Revenge
(and Carrots)

1

PENNY

ED HAS BROUGHT Penny to a courthouse in Fresno where a lawyer she met thirty seconds ago is talking fast. "Okay, so because the crime was committed in New York and you left the state, you're considered a fugitive from justice."

"But I wasn't accused of a crime at the time I left the state. Which was twenty-five years ago!" Penny is trying to remain calm, but it's not easy.

"It doesn't matter. For the purposes of the law you're considered a wanted fugitive."

Penny has a flash of her face on a post office wall. "This can't be happening," she says.

The lawyer has thick black hair and kind eyes, and Penny has a vague recollection of seeing his face on a billboard alongside the highway next to a walnut orchard. She can tell he's trying to simplify it all for her, but it's still feels like he's speaking in a language she can't understand. He says, "Also, because you were only twelve at the time, you could be tried in juvenile court."

Penny thinks of the elementary school where she teaches, with little child-sized desks and chairs and drinking fountains. Is juvenile court like that? Tiny handcuffs and miniature gavels? Will she be like

Alice in Wonderland in an orange jumpsuit, her head and feet sticking out of the bars of a playhouse-sized jail cell?

"But if found guilty you would serve your time in regular adult prison," the lawyer adds.

"Prison?" Penny is trying to focus on what the lawyer is saying, but she's also still waiting for someone to tell her this is all a joke. It's not April Fool's, but there's gotta be a punch line here somewhere, right? Does this prank come with a TV appearance? A check? At this point she'd settle for an apology and getting dropped at the bus stop.

"In juvenile court you won't have the right to a jury trial or bail," says the lawyer. "I would advise you to waive the fitness hearing when you get to New York and go straight to adult court. You do have the right to an extradition hearing here, but it would only be a delaying tactic."

"I don't want any delays. I want this straightened out right now," Penny says.

PENNY SITS IN the back of Ed's police car, staring out the window on the way to the airport, marveling at the strange twist her day has taken. To avoid conversation Ed has put a country music station on loud, so Penny is treated to a series of songs about heartbreak, tequila, and Chevys. He takes pity on her when a song called "Way Too Pretty for Prison" comes on, but when he spins the dial it lands on Taylor Swift crooning "No Body, No Crime." Ed meets her eyes in the rearview mirror and turns the radio off, but the silence is even more excruciating.

Surely the next stop will be a restaurant full of people shouting "Surprise!" Won't it?

Penny tries to distract herself by examining the vehicles they are passing, guessing where the people inside are going. The truckers are taking their loads to big box stores, the commuters are racing home after a stop to shop at the big box stores. It's central California, so there are trucks full of tomatoes headed for sauce, and oranges headed for juice. They pass a huge semi labeled *Bob's Racehorse Transport*, and Penny catches a glimpse through the windows of sleek Thoroughbreds wearing halters with fluffy sheepskin padding. She wonders what the horses think, zooming down the highway in a metal box. Not many vehicles later comes a gooseneck rig emblazoned with names of roping championships and a pair of sorrel quarter horses napping inside. They don't get to choose where they go, she thinks. Nor what they eat or wear. It's all out of their control.

More trucks of tomatoes, more oranges. They pull alongside a little rickety 1940s-era two-horse straight-load trailer with an open back and sides. Hand painted on the trailer it says *Magical Unicorn Rides* and an 800 number. Penny presses her nose to the car window and peers out. A white pony inside the trailer turns its head and stares back at Penny. The pony's mane and tail have been dyed bright pink. *Not my choice*, says the pony's expression. Penny blinks, and the pony blinks back.

"I had a pony when I was little," says Ed.

"Me too," says Penny.

"Mine was a pinto. What was yours?"

"The color of the sun."

They are both quiet for a minute.

"Happiest days of my life," Penny says.

"Yeah," Ed agrees.

Penny shifts, trying to position her handcuffed hands in a way that doesn't hurt. The white pony continues to stare back at her.

As the police car finally leaves behind the pony in its rattling metal box, Penny is left with the vision of the too-tight halter cutting into the pony's nose, and the expression in the pony's large brown eyes. *I don't know where I'm going. I don't know what comes next. But I'm pretty sure it's going to suck.*

"Yeah," Penny says.

2

THE PONY

I AM A PONY. But not just any pony. I am a pony who is bent on revenge. I am the Iago of ponies, a furry Fury. I am both adorable and devious, and, until I get what I want, I'm going to make every human I meet pay for your collective crimes. I am a tiny, mop-topped demon, and I am coming for you.

PICTURE A RIDING stable. If you haven't been in one, a row of horses hang their heads over their stall doors, gently bobbing to escape the flies, pricking their ears when a human appears who might have a carrot or a peppermint in her pocket.

In the riding arena, a sandy rectangle outlined by a white wooden fence that could use a coat of paint, there's a small dapple gray pony named Boo Boo carrying a girl named Kimmie over a row of low jumps under the watchful eye of Phee, her instructor. It's all so sickeningly sweet, right? Boo Boo looks happy, lifting his forelegs and sailing over the crossbars in a perfect arc, his tail a lush banner in the breeze. Kimmie and Boo Boo come to a stop near Phee, who is very tall and wears tan jodhpurs and tall black boots and a ball cap. The pony gives a happy sneeze, knowing he has done his job well. Kimmie takes her skinny legs, folded at the knee like a stepladder, out of the stirrups and they hang down below the edge of the pony's belly.

"We've got to lengthen those stirrups," says the instructor. "You'll get a cramp."

Kimmie frowns. "The judges won't like it. And my feet are going to hit the poles. It's fine."

Kimmie's mom calls out from where she's leaning on the fence, holding the leash of a Labrador retriever who is sniffing for crumbs. "She looks big for the pony," says the mom, removing her sunglasses and squinting from under a straw hat. "Is she getting too big for him?"

"Mom," says Kimmie, "he's such a good boy."

"I know, but you look ridiculous," says the mom.

"I don't want to sell him."

"Well, we can't afford to keep two animals. If you want to keep riding, you need to move up to a horse."

Kimmie slumps forward like a rag doll and throws her arms around the pony's neck. She will never agree to part with her beloved pony, the pony who has carried her safely and dutifully over hundreds of obstacles, through rivers, up and down mountains, in parades, the pony who did not protest when forced to wear antlers at Christmas, bunny ears at Easter, and large wings at Halloween. Surely all that is worth more than—

"Can I get a Thoroughbred?" Kimmie asks.

NOW TURN YOUR gaze back to the stable nearby. Inside that stable there's another pony. A heck of a pony, if I do say so myself. I was once, like Boo Boo, a good boy. Not anymore. Fifteen summers ago, I had my own little girl just like Kimmie. Her name was Penny. Penny and I did everything together. Then one day out of the blue she up and sold me. With no warning she kicked me to the curb like an old bicycle or a Slinky that no longer slinks.

After Penny cast me adrift, I floated from home to home, islands in the sea of life. I was eventually bought by Phee for children to take riding lessons on. (A lucky few kids will end up owning their own ponies, but most will ride lesson ponies until they either discover romance or get tall enough to ride horses, or both.) Phee is not a bad person—she's quiet and sensible, like an oak tree, and she gets along with all the children and parents by never contradicting them, at least not out loud. (I have been privy to some muttering.) Despite the dislike for humans that simmers in me thanks to Penny, I dutifully carried the children Phee trains and coaches for years on end, circling the damn arena, trotting over crossbars. I'm getting older now, and I figured Phee would retire me at some point soon and let me live out my final years in peace and quiet in the pasture behind the barn. If well cared for, ponies can live to thirty or even forty years old, and after twenty years of being a fairly good boy, all things, considered, I felt I had some well-earned leisure coming my way.

Then last week, in a deeply, deeply tragic misunderstanding, my reputation and my retirement plans went permanently south after I dumped one too many "future Olympians" into the dust of the riding ring.

In my defense, Peacock Lastrigon had it coming. Peacock's family owns a chain of burger joints, the Hungry Cannibal. At age ten, Peacock has an astounding faith in his own wonderfulness. All of us should have a day of walking around in Peacock's skin, just to experience what total self-confidence feels like. As you might expect, he is oblivious to any evidence of his shortcomings. When he fails a test, it's the teacher's fault. When his friend Tip shunned him after Peacock called him stupid, Tip was too thin-skinned and couldn't take a joke. When Peacock tripped and fell on the playground, it was the playground's fault and his family demanded it be repaved. In short, Peacock is a monster. In stories, people like Peacock get punished. In life, they get prizes.

Peacock loves to win horse shows. This means that Phee trains me, schools me, grooms me, cleans my saddle and polishes my bridle, and drives me to the show location. There, ringside, pug-nosed Peacock is hoisted into the freshly oiled saddle. We go into the arena, walk and trot around, maybe jump a little obstacle or two, then line up for the judges. Peacock is usually awarded a blue ribbon, further proof that he's *better* than everyone else. The *best*. I get nothing. Phee gets a crisp white envelope from Peacock's parents and drives me home.

We were ringside at a huge showgrounds that fateful day. The wind was up, and flags were flapping in the breeze. Hundreds of horses and ponies milled around, their hair in tiny rows of braids like mine, riders in black coats and helmets. Everyone looked serious, like this all mattered a lot to them. The loudspeaker called our class. Phee whispered to me before Peacock got on. "Be good," she said with more urgency than usual. After all, it was cool and breezy, which has the same effect on a pony as a tequila shot on a college freshman. I should have listened to her, just toughed out the three minutes before Peacock would dismount and I would get my hay and go home. But as Peacock bounced on my back, spurred my sides, and yanked my mouth, a rage began to simmer and then boil inside me. Must the Peacocks of the world always win? I thought about Penny, and how much I wanted to make her pay for discarding me like a bag of trash all those years ago, the primal wound that changed the course of my life forever. Must she, too, remain unpunished for her callousness?

As Peacock kicked me toward a brush jump, I saw my opportunity. Hundreds of people were watching. I headed for the fence, then at the last second took a sharp left. The crowd groaned. Unfortunately, Peacock had an iron-fisted grasp on the reins and he didn't come off, but he did shift his center of gravity in the saddle. Feeling my chance, I ducked my right shoulder and gave a buck, then a twist while I was in the air. Honestly, in a gymnastics competition I would have scored a perfect ten. The crowd gasped at the unexpected rodeo. Show ponies never behaved like this, dutiful little drones that we are. I like to think I heard an undercurrent of joy, if not admiration in that gasp. And that last twisting bronco-style buck did it—Peacock came off with a thud, and a small cloud of dust rose around him. The crowd was on its feet, waiting to see if he was hurt. His face as he sat there was red, red, red and then an *AHHHHH!* burst out of him like a pimple erupting. He continued screaming in rage as he leapt to his feet. The crowd clapped politely. Phee rushed toward him pulling the signed release form up on her phone, as did his parents, speed-dialing their lawyers. I was caught by a judge and escorted from the ring.

I can't describe how good it felt to leave Peacock in the dust, howling. I wished he were Penny, but close enough. However, it's possible I was too clever for my own good, because now no one wants to ride me. Phee's lawyer has advised her not to use me for lessons. I thought maybe this would simply move up my retirement date, but apparently Phee thinks she can still get some money for me.

Money.

That's what I am to you humans. What all we ponies are. You make us think we're beloved family members (I'm looking at you, Penny!) and then you put a dollar sign on our heads and send us off with anyone who coughs up the cash.

To add insult to insult, Phee has shut the stall door and I can't see over it. All I see are four bare walls and the sawdust on the floor. It's like a prison cell. And the empty hay rack! The hay rack is full for two painfully brief periods each day. It only takes eight minutes for me to vacuum it clean again. Pathetic. Cruel. They say it's so I don't get fat, but I tell you I'm wasting away inside this deceptively plump, round body. I eat, then I'm bored for the next eleven hours and fifty-two minutes. This has given me a lot of time to plan my next steps. And now I'm putting my plan into action.

Starting today, I am going to really get back at you humans.

Especially you, Penny. Peacock is bad, but you are the worst. Enough with the Gandhi-style passive resistance in which I just refuse to do what people want. I'm going guerrilla. From this day on, I am devoting my life to finding you, Penny, and confronting you for selling me all those many years ago. You couldn't even look me in the face and tell me why you did it. That's what I want from you. An explanation. And an apology. There is no statute of limitations on your crime. Yes, you seemed to be a sweet little girl, but who better than an adorable pony to see through that ruse? I know what you are and I am going to make you pay for it.

If a person happened to be standing outside my stall, they would hear scraping, banging, and chewing, as if a master carpenter is at work—please do not compare this sound to that made by a large rodent. Then, after an hour or so of this noise, they would see a small nose with two delicate nostrils (my princely ancestry is evident in my nose) appear at the top of the half door. Then they would see the door push open from the inside. Ta-da! Here I am! I'm drinking in the sight of the surprised horses, the clean-swept barn aisle, and sturdy Phee, who has her back turned to me a few feet away.

I am exactly as you imagine me. Small and furry. I'm the color of the sun itself, a blazing incandescent gold with crème brûlée and burnt cork accents. I do not want to hear you describe me as "beige," "toast," or "tan." And I've got a lotta hair. I'm not ashamed to say I'm proud of my hair, a thick shaggy mane that breaks even metal combs and a tail that sends flies into the next county with a single swish.

They call me Houdini here. This is my superpower. I can escape from anywhere. I successfully chew the latch off the stall door and hold it in my teeth. I drop it to the ground with a clatter that makes Phee turn. She has one glass eye, but the expression in the real one is priceless: shock and anger. I bolt at top speed not away, but *toward* her, messing with her head, which outrages her more, and I run past her as she yells at me to stop. Yeah, right, sister. I run down the stable aisle, under the belly of a big dumb Friesian horse so huge he barely notices me. I knock over a ten-year-old boy named Thad who dares to try to stop me, and just for good measure, I also kick over a manure cart. Two foofy Thoroughbreds named Sandalwood and Lioness are on crossties being groomed to a high shine and are spooked by my ruckus. They rear up, the whites of their eyes showing. A black Labrador flees, tail between his legs. I pause just long enough to grab a carrot from outside the stall of an uptight and ulcer-prone Arabian gelding named Jiffy as I bolt past. I carry the stolen carrot in my teeth, like a matador with a rose, as I burst out of the barn and flee for the territory ahead. I delight to hear the cries of Phee: "Loose horse! Would someone grab that darn pony?"

I run around a corner, hell-bent on getting out of there for good and hitting the road to find Penny, but instead I find nirvana: an expanse of green grass. Why have I not been shown this before? Why am I not here *all the time*? My anger at the rank unfairness of the world cools briefly as I settle in for a good snack. After all, I will need strength to complete my quest. I snatch huge mouthfuls of grass as fast as I can. It's hard to chew with that much grass in my mouth, so I spit out a wad and start over. I position myself under some trees that will be good for scratching once I have eaten just seven or eight more bites. Maybe ten. Then I will hit the road. Insects buzz around me. The sun warms my back. Life, dear reader, is good.

Phee comes out of the barn with a bucket of grain. I need to leave, now, but I am powerless to resist her. Oats are my Achilles' heel. I follow her back into the barn. She locks me in the stall. A familiar sign is tacked to the door. PONY FOR SALE.

3

PENNY

PENNY LOOKS OUT the window of the airplane. That way she doesn't see the other passengers staring at her, and especially at the handcuffs still cutting into her wrists, one of which is numb. She can imagine her husband at work, listening to her voicemail, the one phone call that she was allowed to make. *Hi honey, something happened today and I won't be home for dinner . . .* She shivers in the linen sundress and needs to use the restroom, but she is handcuffed to Ed, who is asleep, his mouth open and a tiny bit of drool rolling down his cheek.

I'm a law-abiding wife and mother! she wants to shout at the other passengers. *I've never even had a speeding ticket! I drive a Prius!*

This will all get straightened out, she tells herself. It will all get fixed.

But what if it doesn't? People get jailed all the time for crimes they didn't commit. You hear about it on the news. *Man released after forty years in prison when new evidence exonerates him.* Even she knows that once you're in the system, it's really hard to get out.

She thinks of all the articles she's skimmed about how broken the justice system is. Articles that seemed too depressing to spend time reading on a sunny Sunday morning. She flipped past them to the crossword, those long stories of people wrongly accused, framed, corrupt police, rushed investigations, botched DNA tests, unskilled lawyers, aging judges well into senility. Now she wishes she had paid closer attention. She didn't because before today, those things only happened to other people.

The flight attendant is coming down the aisle. "Nuts?" she says.

Penny looks up at her. "It certainly is."

4

THE PONY

PHEE SENDS ME to a dealer who sells me on to someone new. And then those people sell me. And so on. I don't find Penny, but I learn things that only intensify my desire for revenge on her and all humans. I have many homes, and many jobs, and many Christmases. Christmas has a whole different meaning for ponies. Every Christmas children all around the world wish for a pony. Rich, poor, urban, rural, boys, girls, it doesn't matter. Ponies are cuddly but fast, huggable yet slightly dangerous. They're like a motorcycle whose hair you can brush. As the marketers say, they hit all the quadrants. For the lucky kids, that wish actually comes true. A period of bliss ensues, months or even a couple of years long. Pony and child go on trail rides, jump obstacles, and explore wild places. There's hugging, petting, carrots every day. Then, inevitably, comes a growth spurt and the day when little Johnny or Janie's legs start dragging on the ground. The pony is now deemed "too small," instead of the blame being placed on the child for growing "too tall." The pony, no matter how beloved or loyal or wonderful, is—you guessed it!—sold. Just like Penny sold me. I don't know why I believed her lies that we would be together forever. All ponies get passed around like a stomach virus instead of getting to live out our years as adored pets like those lesser animals that are basically useless sacks of fur. You don't hear about people selling Fido or Fluffy, but somehow selling a pony is just fine. It's *expected*.

And you wonder why we turn mean?

Some of my Christmases are pretty good, like the single mom who brings me home before dawn on Christmas Day and ties me to the mailbox for her six kids to wake up to. Alice, Astrid, Angela, Aaron, Anna, and Anthony all give me Life Savers and carrots and pudding from their lunches, and take turns riding me. They don't have much themselves, but they make sure I have what I need, even though I am pretty nasty to them. Then little Anthony, the youngest, outgrows me, and I am passed on to another family, and another. Some Christmases are less good, like the grandparents who buy me so their icky spoiled little grandson can win leadline classes, which are the dumbest thing ever. An adult holds the leash while the kid sits on the pony and does nothing except look cute. Okay, if you say so. I try to spice things up a little, show off for the judges by rearing up like a circus pony. Exit stage left in disgrace.

Then I *am* a circus pony, which is fun, running in circles with a beagle on my back in the middle of a bunch of saucy Andalusian stallions who tell each other off-color jokes all day as we roll across America in an air-conditioned sixteen-wheeler. Then the husband of the couple running the circus sleeps with the contortionist, who is married to the strong man. Everyone gets divorced, and all of us are sold. I still miss those foul-mouthed stallions.

Though it's now been more than twenty years since I last saw her, my anger at Penny has not faded, and my search for her is not over. I could try to bond with the new kids, but why? If humans are not going to get attached to me, I am not going to get attached to them. I'm older, pushing thirty now, and more clever in figuring out ways to do less and eat more. You know, quiet quitting. That's pretty much what my life has become—where once there was passion and joy and energy and connection, then a burning desire to leave a trail of terror and debris in my wake, now there is only a selfish urge to do as little as possible, fill my belly, and take a nap.

Early one morning I find myself watching out the window of a horse trailer as a pink balloon rises up against a blue sky. It sails over a suburban house that I don't need a crystal ball to know is occupied by a kind and loving family who does not realize they have too much stuff. (I have just ended a gig as an emotional support animal for a college student who has strong opinions about the future of the planet, while also flying home across the country every other weekend to see her therapist. She took me on the plane with her once. Let's just say that my career as a flying pony was cut short when I discovered that airplane seats are delicious.) The parents I am about to meet will care about the environment, yes, but not enough to stop heating and cooling a house that could sleep four additional families (or forty ponies), driving a car that guzzles gas, and flying around the world on vacation. They have not, I am ready to bet, even cut down on their paper towel use.

Without having met this family yet, I am pretty sure the love of their life is their daughter Binky, or Betsy, Ashley, or Katrina, who is turning five today. They say they would do anything for her, but that apparently does not extend to switching to sustainable bamboo toilet paper so that the planet has a chance of continuing to be hospitable for Binky and her future children. That would be too much to ask. They mistake objects for love, and put their own physical comfort and convenience above everything else. This is something I have seen over and over in my travels. Part of me understands their weakness—after all, I like good food and a soft bed. But it still feels crazy to me, like eating yourself to death. Animals never destroy their habitats. It just wouldn't make sense.

But here I am. Binky's party will be fun for everyone. Most everyone. There will likely be a bounce house operator who would prefer to be elsewhere. There will be a table with balloons tied to it, a huge cake decorated with a unicorn, and a bowl of sweet pink punch. A flock of little girls in sparkly tulle-skirted party dresses and boys in shorts and collared shirts will dart and swirl like a school of fish.

I do not love my job.

An older man in a purple satin suit and top hat and a tired-looking woman in fairy wings unload us from the trailer. The other pony is white as snow. Thanks to a dye job this morning, both of us have startlingly bright pink manes and tails. Yes, doubting reader, this is a true detail. Pink manes and tails.

"Wait," says the woman as the man starts to lead us toward the house. She pulls out a tube of glue that smells terrible. I watch as she puts the glue on the forehead of my companion, whose name is Violet. Violet flares her nostrils and blinks but stands still as the woman then presses a plastic horn onto the glue.

"What the—?" I say. I have done plenty of parties, but this is new to me.

"It doesn't hurt," says Violet, who is a pony of few words.

The horn may not hurt, but the smell is as outrageous as the idea of it. I am *not* a unicorn. Not a mythical creature of any kind. I am intensely real and, I would like to modestly say, perfect as nature made me. I do not need a pink tail or a plastic horn.

I widen my eyes and snort but stand still as the woman glues the horn to my forehead. Violet is really cute and I don't want her to think I'm a chicken. No one likes chickens, not even other chickens. I speak from experience. "He's got a scar here," says the woman, fingering the raised crescent I got while breaking out of a stall a few years back. "Someone gave him a heckuva bang to the head."

Violet looks over at me questioningly.

"You should see the other guy," I say huskily. Violet's eyes soften in sympathy. I plan to tell her the whole story later, with plenty of gory details that will make her fall in love with me. She's cute, and she's available. It's just us in the makeshift stable in the garage behind the couple's house in the city. Definitely not up to code, but who am I to call city hall and report them? These two are bringing joy to little children or at least alleviating the guilt their parents feel for not buying them enough stuff, even though they buy them all the stuff.

The man in the purple suit leads Violet, and the winged woman takes my lead rope.

"Come on, Sequoia," says the woman kindly. That's what they call me here. I guess it's meant to be a joke, given that I am not, shall we say, tall of stature. Not laughing. I follow her toward the backyard. As we round the corner, I see the swarm of children. I am on high alert. Is Penny among them? Many rotations of the sun have happened since I last saw her and it's possible she looks different now, even though I look exactly the same. Still I feel I will recognize her even though sight is not my strongest sense—I have about the same visual ability as a human who is color-blind. Not terrible, but not great. I do, however, have excellent hearing, and I strain to hear her voice. I sniff the air, pulling it into my large lungs through my perfect nostrils. Our sense of touch is also extraordinary—we can feel a fly on us even through a thick winter coat, but our strongest sense is not one that humans have quantified or recognized: our ability to read you like a book. We know everything about you at a glance—your heart rate, your cortisol levels, your mood, your intentions, your energy. If you are a bad person, we know it.

"She's not here," I say to Violet with a sigh.

"Who?" she asks. Damn she's cute, even with that stupid horn sticking out of her face.

"No one. Just another bunch of kids—sticky-fingered octopuses."

Violet looks horrified.

"I mean, kids, yay." She doesn't buy my halfhearted about-face.

"Hey, kids, who wants to ride a *unicorn*?" calls out the man in the purple suit.

We're surrounded by loud children who are heaved on one or two at a time. To impress the lovely Violet, I dutifully carry them around the backyard, only grabbing the occasional mouthful of grass. After a half hour of this, I realize everyone here loves to party but me and the bounce house guy. He vomits quietly behind a hedge. No such catharsis for me.

I make a few more rounds of the backyard, a child or two sitting on my back, others crowding around. I have had enough. Penny may be my intended victim, but in a pinch, any kid will do. I make one small, unobtrusive move with a hoof.

"Ow! That pony stepped on my foot. Mom!" A tiny tot points to me. I prick my ears and look adorably innocent.

"It wasn't on purpose, honey," says the mom. I turn to face an imaginary camera over my shoulder, one eyebrow raised.

The man in the purple suit says quietly to the woman in the fairy wings, "Let's wrap this up." To the children he says, "One at a time, little elves. Violet here is friendly, but don't put your fingers near Sequoia's mouth. He's part unicorn, part dragon." The kids back away from me. I drop my head to graze.

LATER, WE ARE dehorned and loaded back into the little horse trailer with a sign on the side that says MAGICAL UNICORN RIDES and an 800 number. The man in the purple suit turns to the woman as she removes her wings. He points to me. "That one is not working out."

She nods. He's not wrong. We all know it.

Still, I sigh in frustration. This gig allows me to meet a whole lot of kids, and one of them one day will be Penny. I just have to go to enough birthday parties and I will eventually find her. I didn't even bite anyone today, though I desperately wanted to. What's a toe or two when you have ten of them? These kids need to learn boundaries, and I am a great teacher. I look over at the lovely Violet, quietly eating hay from the manger. I realize that Violet loves her job. The kids, the cake, even the horn. I find it all insipid. Violet will, too, one day. Someday, maybe just a year or two from now, she will be riding down the highway to a birthday party, wondering where her life went wrong. I mean, how many times can you hear the "Happy Birthday" song before you just want to bite someone? For me, the answer is once.

You can blame Penny for that. I do.

PART TWO

Loneliness and the Smell of Despair

5

PENNY

PENNY CRANES HER head and stares up through pouring rain at the massive red brick bulk of the Sticks River Correctional Facility for Women. The unmarked white van transporting her cruises through a gate in the tall razor-wire fence. The castle-like crenellations do have a certain Dickensian charm, she thinks as she is removed from the vehicle by waiting guards and led to intake, though circling vultures and bats would not feel out of place.

WELL, I CAN *never again say I haven't been deloused.* She is given a short-sleeve dark green shirt and matching pants that remind her of the uniforms that her park ranger neighbors wear back home in California, minus the Smokey Bear hat. The material is scratchy and stiff against her skin and she immediately realizes why the other prisoners wear long-sleeve cotton T-shirts underneath. Except they're not called "prisoners," she learns in a brief orientation delivered via a VHS tape that has been played so many times it looks and sounds like it was recorded underwater. She is a "pre-trial detainee." Others here are "inmates," although apparently there is a self-actualized group who call themselves "convicts" that she gets the sense she should avoid. She will be called by her number—170333—not her name. "If a shot is fired you will lie down on the ground immediately. Anyone still standing will be considered a threat and appropriate action will be taken."

She has nothing to put on under the scratchy uniform other than the sleeveless light blue linen sundress with lemons on it, which was apparently washed and dried on high heat while she was doing her paperwork, and which has been returned to her as a pale green shriveled softball.

As she is shown down a cement hallway to her cell she is told by a stout female guard with a strong New York accent that the jail has been home to some very famous murderers.

"You know the Scarsdale Diet killer and that chick who shot Mrs. Joey Buttafuoco? They were here."

Ever the people pleaser, Penny raises her eyebrows and nods as if the jail is suddenly more appealing to her. "And when do I meet my public defender?" she asks.

The guard shrugs. "They're really overworked," she says. "It could be a while."

"Okay, but it's just that there's been a mistake and I'm not supposed to be in here. I didn't kill anyone."

"That's so weird," says the guard sarcastically. "I've never heard that before!" They reach the cell and the guard shoves Penny inside. "Room service will be by to take your breakfast order and you can ring for a maid any time."

Laughter echoes down the hallway as the guard says, "You are so adorable," and slams the door shut in Penny's face.

6

THE PONY

ISN'T HE ADORABLE?" A woman with gray braids and a kind smile stares at me. It's three days before Christmas. Something tells me I'm getting closer to Penny. Yes, it's been many winters since I last saw her, but my anger keeps the memory of her sharp. After all, it's her fault that for all these years I have been at the mercy of the Peacocks of the world. The birthday pony man, who is more than ready to be rid of me, tells the woman I am indeed adorable, and very well behaved. The woman with braids has a soft leather purse, and nice shoes. I can see the hope in Birthday Pony Ride Guy's eyes.

"Are you buying him for a child?" he asks a bit tentatively. "For Christmas?"

Birthday Pony Ride Guy's question to this woman really sets my teeth on edge, and I have a lot of teeth. He can guess and I know how many children I have bitten, stepped on, and sent into orbit, even before my latest offense. I would like to point out I haven't actually hurt any of them, and one could argue that I taught them how to keep their hands to themselves or fall off safely, very useful lessons indeed, but this has moved me from the "Intermediate" to "Advanced" end of the riding pony scale. Above all, I sense Birthday Guy does not want me coming back to him. The lawyers have spoken.

"No, he's for me!" the woman exclaims theatrically, with a laugh.

She has large rings on her fingers, and earrings that sway as she moves. I can't decide how I feel about her—I haven't really met a lot of humans like her. But maybe she will lead me to Penny.

"Oh. As a lawn mower?" Birthday Guy asks. "Yes, a lot of people these days use animals instead of gas-powered devices to keep weeds down." I consider this. Being a lawn mower on a rural property is seen as a good life for a retired or lame equine, as long as the attending humans understand the care the equines need, which can be summed up as the three Fs: food, friends, freedom. We're simple creatures, equines: all we need is quality hay and grains, some other equines for company, and a large area to roam—at least an acre per horse, please, with large shade trees and a windproof shelter and a flowing stream would be nice. Oh, and no mold in that grain or hay, and we need shots and worming and sometimes a chiropractor and a dentist and let's not forget, hoof trimming every six weeks and custom shoes and a well-fitting saddle. Daily fly spray. Vitamin supplements. Not too much grass in the spring. And could you fix the fencing when we scratch our butts on it? Thanks. As I said, our needs are simple.

"I am looking for a pony as a companion."

Birthday Guy pauses. "Have you had horses or ponies before?" He glances over at me, and I can see that he is now suddenly feeling a little sorry for me. As much of a pain in the behind as I have been, he doesn't want me to end up starving to death in some tiny yard. I am with him on that one. I feel a sudden fondness for him, this top-hatted entertainer, purveyor of unicorns, and I affectionately rifle through his pockets with my nose. He swats me away.

"My previous companion pony just passed away. He was my best friend. He lived to be forty-two. The vet said he lived a happier life than any other animal he treated."

Birthday Guy nods. He almost doesn't want to ask more. He is content to know this much. I have some more questions, but no way to ask them. "Good luck, and be good for a change," Birthday Guy whispers to me. "Merry Christmas."

———

I'M NOW CALLED "O." It's the shortest name I've had. I'm guessing previous pets were "M" and "N." I'm wary of all new situations—I've seen a lot in my life already—but this one feels especially odd to me. Where is the happy child? Where is the barn? Where are the other horses? Still, I am on a mission. I sniff the air for traces of Penny. The woman speaks softly to me, which calms me a little as Birthday Guy's sparkly trailer pulls away, leaving me in front of a huge glass house surrounded by green lawns. Lawns! I forget Penny for a moment and I'm all about the lawn, and drag the lady toward it so that she will see how useful I am.

"No, O," she says. "I don't want you walking on the grass. Your little hoofies will leave marks in it." Huh? She pulls me instead toward the house, talking all the while. She's going on about how cute I am, and what good friends we are, which seems to assume an intimacy I'm not sure I'm comfortable with yet. We get to the glass building. I have been around long enough to know the difference between a house and a barn, and this is definitely a house, which is a barn for humans. She leads me up a couple of steps and opens the front door. The floor inside is white and smooth. I snort at this. This does not seem right to me. I like to be outdoors. I pull gently back to the lawn, but she shuts the door, still talking nonstop about how adorable I am and what fun we're having. My skepticism is growing. I study the doorknob. It looks tricky, though I am something of an amateur locksmith.

She leads me into the very spacious "kitchen," as she calls it. I scan the place. No sign of Penny here. The lady shows me a gleaming stainless steel dish of water. Okay. Next to it is a gleaming stainless steel bowl of hay pellets. Yes! They are situated in a beautiful wood table so I hardly have to bend my neck to eat and drink. I head right over to the dish and start vacuuming up those pellets. Delicious! How lucky I am! Skepticism vanishes with the pellets.

"This is your dining table," says the lady with the gray braids. I'm not really listening. I can barely hear her over the sound of my own chewing. I'll get back to looking for Penny right after dinner. I catch a hint of molasses, and a whiff of clover in the pellets, which are the most delicious I have ever had.

"I have the pellets specially made by a shaman-slash-animal-nutritionist," she tells me. "They are nutritionally perfect." She launches into an explanation of the pellets and where they're made and how she drove to get them and everything she saw on the way.

I suppose I could like this lady, if these pellets are a regular thing. She talks a lot, like a human fly buzzing around me, but I've made peace with insects before. After eating these pellets, I'm going to go out and get to work on that lawn. Instead the lady leads me into a room with a lot of cloth objects in it. I usually only associate cloth with saddle blankets, horse blankets, and human clothing. Am I going to have to jump these things? It's a lot of work, jumping, especially when you can so easily walk around things. But these are not shaped like things you jump. I taste one, but it is flavorless. The room smells like flowers, which I like to eat, but I cannot find them.

"This is the living room," says the lady. "This is where we will watch TV." She starts listing all the things she likes to watch on TV and why, but I am already learning to tune her out. She hands me a baby carrot from her pocket, so it's all good. I've got a little buzz going from the hay pellets.

She leads me to another large room, this one with a wide horizontal cloth surface in it, and a padded mat on the floor. "This is the bedroom, where we will sleep," she says, then proceeds to tell me the fabric content of every object in the room and where she purchased them from and what she paid. Thread counts? Discounts? She is seriously overestimating my interest in her spending habits. In all her habits, really. Why do people think we animals care? All we are thinking about as you speak is when the next meal is coming down the pike.

She leads me to a door to the outside made of plastic that she pushes open with her hand, then invites me to push open with my nose. I've done this in trail training before. Humans love this weird stuff. Sometimes I say no, but this time I want to go outside, so I push open the door. It leads to a small fenced dirt area that smells of antiseptic. Not appealing to me.

"This is the bathroom," she says. "This is where you will go poo and pee. Every day the gardener will come clean up after you."

Being a pony, I have always just performed my bodily functions without shame or care. Where I am, there I go. The lady's words mean nothing to me. Humans clean up after me. That's why I think of them as my "staff." The lady feeds me another carrot. She stares at me, smiling softly and talking about something she saw on the news about organic farming and the minerals it adds to the soil. I just stand there, looking over the wooden fence toward the lawn beyond. The lawn looks so good I can hardly stand it. I nod my head toward it, to show her what I desire. *Take me there*, I order her.

"No," she says. "You are an indoor pony now. You are my companion."

Her words make no sense to me, yet there is something ominous about them. She continues to stand there, smiling, talking, encouraging me to do something without saying what. She's very intense, I realize. I continue to stand there, scheming how to get over or through that fence and have a chomp and a roll on that lawn and then hit the road and keep on searching. I feel a twinge of worry in my belly.

Then that twinge becomes something else, the pellets and the carrots move through me, and I feel nature's call. I lift my tail and out comes one of the more than twenty deposits in the Bank of Poo that I proudly make each day, each individual poo-let perfectly round, dark brown, and shiny.

"Good boy!" she says. "Good boy!" She gives me a treat. I have never been rewarded for pooing before, and I like the idea. "This is where you will go from now on," she says. "Not in the house. Here." She says it twenty more times, in a singsong voice. Okay, whatever. I have no intention of doing as she says.

She leads me back through the soft plastic swinging door into the house and unhitches my lead rope. "Let's watch TV," she says.

She holds out a carrot, so I follow her into the living room. She turns on the TV. It's a box that flickers. Humans are so odd. To ponies, if you can't eat it and it's not going to eat you, it's not interesting. "What do you want to watch?" she asks. "How about a western?" To me, "western" is a kind of saddle. She tells me all about which westerns she likes and which she does not, because they are too violent. I'm confused.

More flickering lights. The song is all about rawhide, and there is the sound of a whip, which makes me uncomfortable. I am briefly interested in the sounds of hoofbeats and neighing, but no other equines appear in the room. I feel lonely all of a sudden. All my life I have been a little bit nasty to the horses and ponies I have met, because that's just who I am, but now I miss all of them. Even Jiffy, the Arabian who made fun of me for being short. But I am a herd animal, and a human is not a good substitute for another equine.

I go to leave the room, and the lady calls after me. "O, don't go. Your job now is to be my companion. My heart was broken when my last pony died. Let's watch a Christmas movie."

Although I do not understand every word she says, I understand more than you might think. As I said, we equines are very sensitive animals. I totally get that the lady is also lonely. She has kind, sad eyes. Needy eyes. Intensely needy eyes. She never shuts up because she wants what we all want—a connection. She wants to be known, and still to be loved. Humans are really bad at that one—that I know from experience. That's why they like us animals so much. We appear to be way less judgmental than humans, though speaking for myself, appearances are deceptive. I have figured out that if I let this lady pet me, and talk to me, I will have all of the food I want. This could be the retirement I have been hoping for. I will sleep on a soft bed and have a cashmere blanket with a floral pattern. I'm not stupid—I grasp all of this. I can see that seven or eight years will pass in a heartbeat. I can see that all of my physical needs will be satisfied here, I'll get my shots and worming, and I can make lonely Mrs. Calypso happy. I also realize I might never see Penny again, after all. She is out there somewhere, but

I don't know where, and it has been a long time. Maybe I should let go of my revenge fantasies, stop looking for her, and make peace with the human in front of me.

I reach down over the lady as she sits there watching TV, and nuzzle her braids, then her shoulder, making her giggle. And then I bite down, hard.

7

PENNY

THERE IS A very particular smell in the jail that Penny decides is ten percent sweat, ten percent disinfectant, twenty percent canned fruit cup, and sixty percent despair.

At six a.m. her cell door opens and guards herd them to the cafeteria. It's like being back in middle school, a slow-moving line, a plastic tray, lunch ladies—other inmates, Penny realizes, on work duty—in hairnets ladling beige food from steaming vats.

Penny finds she can't eat. It's not a hunger strike, she just can't get herself to swallow. She lifts the piece of toast to her mouth, takes a little mousy nibble, and chews, but she can't seem to remember how to start the process of sending the food down to her stomach, so she ends up passing a scratchy paper napkin over her mouth and spitting out the bits, folding the dissolving warm napkin, and leaving it on the tray to be dumped into the trash.

As Penny sits and waits with her eyes down until it's time to leave the cafeteria, two young women nearby begin to scream at each other. One hauls off and whacks the other, as if the green plastic tray is a tennis racket and the other woman's head is the ball. Guards begin to shout. Penny is frozen in place, but everyone else knows the drill. Line up against the wall, hands in the air. Blood streams from the corner of the attacked woman's mouth, and the sight takes Penny back in a rush, sucks her straight to that night. She can taste blood, feel the sharp pain on her cheek where the whip cut into her skin.

They are all herded back to their cells. The guards are on alert the rest of the day, their electric batons out and ready.

THAT NIGHT THEY are fed in their cells: oatmeal that isn't quite cooked enough, and crunchy naked spaghetti that looks like hay and smells like glue.

She hasn't eaten in about thirty-six hours and is beginning to feel light-headed and shaky, yet she is repulsed by the idea of putting anything in her mouth. She thinks of her pony, the way he would snatch stolen mouthfuls of grass on the trail. What would he make of this meal?

She closes her eyes and becomes him, all hair and attitude and glorious appetite.

She opens her eyes, leans over and sniffs the oatmeal, licks it tentatively, takes a small bite, then wolfs it down until the bowl is licked clean.

She finds her full stomach to be a comfort. Just being him, the pony, is a comfort. She no longer feels afraid. Wary, but not afraid. A little pissed off, but not unhinged. There is room now in her brain to notice the spider in the corner of the ceiling, waiting for a hapless fly.

Penny curls up and settles into her box stall to await whatever other people decide comes next.

8

THE PONY

MRS. CALYPSO WASTES no time in getting rid of me. In fact, only moments after I bite her, she calls the gardener in. He's holding a chainsaw.

"Take him out of my sight and get rid of him," she says. Her voice is cold and harsh as a winter gale on a shaven tummy. I eye the chainsaw nervously.

"You want me to . . . ?"

"Not kill him," she specifies at last, and the gardener and I both exhale. "Just take him away."

The gardener calls his uncle, who comes with a slightly askew battered white truck loaded with rakes that lean to the left, and an ancient slatted red open-topped trailer that leans to the right and smells and tastes like hedge trimmings. I get into the trailer and the green lawns and Christmas lights disappear behind me. We drive for a long time. I stare out over the sea of buildings and cars like I am helming a ship, my forelock blowing in the breeze. I sniff and scan the world for traces of Penny. I see rows of houses and lines of cars, and I smell diesel. I make a mental list of my favorite things: carrots, peppermints, grass, oats, anger. I reorder the list, putting oats and anger higher. I promise myself that I will try to be nicer to other animals, who are so much better than humans. I see a donut shop, and a Thai place, and smell butterscotch

PONY CONFIDENTIAL

coming from a candy factory. People look up as I sail past, and some cars honk at me, kids wave from the back seat. Maybe it's just the wind in my nose, but I feel optimistic, like life is still full of possibility. I will find Penny, and the satisfaction I will feel when I confront her with her crimes is palpable. We pass a fairgrounds, and I can smell cotton candy and motor oil and stuffed animals.

Eventually the journey ends and I am unloaded at a house on the outskirts of a city. I sniff. I don't recognize the smell, but it's strong. Not Penny, but maybe not that far from Penny, either. It's like I'm sniffing an ocean that Penny swam in one part of. Like she's there, but not there at the same time. A footprint in the sand of scents that waves of more scents keep washing over. I'm closer. I know it.

Palm trees are silhouetted against a pinkish sky. There are telephone wires and empty lots and the whooshing sound of a distant highway. Nothing green is visible, not even weeds. I'm led down a short concrete driveway into a bare dirt backyard surrounded by a tall wooden fence. I see a scraggly lemon tree in the corner with a large sleeping dog under it who barely opens her eyes when I arrive, and a purple car up on blocks. A screen door leads to a beige house that needs a paint job. Bars on the windows. In the middle of the backyard is a plywood doghouse. And on top of that doghouse is . . . a large white goat. My heart sinks as I take in the sight of that goat. Man, those things stink.

Still, I vow to make friends with the goat, as per the promise I made to myself in the trailer.

"Madam, you have lovely horns," I say. But the goat, who tells me in an imperious tone that her name is Circe, is having none of it.

"Ponies stink," she announces.

My optimism dissolves. Penny is not here after all.

Days go by. Weeks. Months. Every morning, the screen door opens and an old, old, bowlegged man with deep creases in his face and a black cowboy hat jammed down onto his head angles down the two cement steps like an action figure whose legs don't move anymore. He makes his way silently past us to the door at the back of the yard, which

37

leads into the garage. From the garage door comes a forkful of hay flying out, and then another. Then he crabs his way back across the yard and turns on the hose to fill the metal bucket by the back door. He drops a cup of kibble into a metal dish for the dog. Then, in audible pain, *oof, oof, oof*, he climbs the back stairs. The screen door slams and that's it. There's no petting. He doesn't even make eye contact with us. Circe clambers down from the doghouse, the dog stretches and groans and ambles over, and we eat.

I sigh.

"What's your problem?" demands the goat.

"No problem," I say.

"Good," says the goat. "I don't like complainers. Or whiners."

"I'm not complaining. Or whining."

"Stop sighing."

This is my life now. I spend all of my time sniffing and scanning for a trace of Penny. Sometimes I catch what seems like her, but then it's gone. Is she driving by? Is she out there on the sidewalk? I know I will feel her energy when she is close.

Other than the few minutes when we're eating, Circe spends almost all of her time standing on top of the doghouse berating me. It's hard to imagine what she did before I arrived to give her life focus. Maybe she yelled at the dog, which would explain why the dog looks so tired all the time, her long ears drooping. If I chew audibly, it's too loud. If I chew silently, she says it's creepy. She claims she can hear me shedding. Nothing I do or say is ever good enough for Circe. I have the sense that unless I magically transform into a handsome billy goat or a bucket of goat chow, I'm always going to be bad in her eyes, and she's always going to be happy to narrate her dissatisfaction all day and all night.

So here I am, trapped in the backyard of this small house, somewhere, with a purple car up on blocks, a white nylon clothesline, a black and brown hound dog named Caya who has fleas (Sally and Wayne), and Circe the ill-tempered goat. Sometimes I can hear auto racing at the fairgrounds and smell burnt rubber. Sometimes I can see the lights of a Ferris wheel, hear the merry-go-round, and smell the show cows and their fancy shampoos. Mostly the fairgrounds are empty and silent, yet there is one scent that is always present.

"I now know what the smell is that I could not identify the day I arrived here," I say out loud in the middle of a long afternoon. "It's despair. It permeates this place—the air, the people, the soil, the plants, and us."

"I don't know what you're talking about," says Circe. "I'm perfectly happy. Caya's perfectly happy." She glares at me until I look away.

I can only practice patience (not something that comes naturally for ponies). I wait for another scent of Penny. And I dream of all the ways I will make her pay for discarding me.

9

PENNY

PENNY IS AWAKENED early the next morning.

"Hands out," says a young female guard. She seems nervous, and Penny wonders if she is new to the job. It must be scary to work here.

"Where are you taking me?" Penny asks.

"Shut up and do as I say," says the guard.

Penny puts her hands out and the guard snaps cuffs on them. The guard attaches a chain on the cuffs like a leash and leads Penny like a prized poodle down the hallway. She passes Penny's leash off to another guard, an older man with gray hair and a paunch.

"Am I being released?" asks Penny.

"Hope springs eternal," says the guard.

They go down in a noisy elevator, walk through a tunnel underground, get on another noisy elevator, and emerge in the middle of a bustling hallway. A man and a woman in gray suits pass by carrying leather briefcases, and a jacketless young man pushes a gray plastic trolley filled with boxes marked EVIDENCE. Lines of shackled men in blue jumpsuits are led past her.

"Is this a courthouse?" Penny asks.

"It's a zoo," says the guard.

"Am I going to see a judge?"

"A magistrate."

"What's that?"

"Cross between a judge and an air traffic controller."

Penny is left in a crowded hallway shackled to a metal rail for several hours. She feels like a pony at a horse show, waiting to be called into the show ring. The hallway smells like burnt coffee and vanilla body spray. A copiously tattooed young man in a blue jumpsuit sits mansplayed across from her, shackled to the rail on his side of the hallway, staring at Penny. She tries to keep her eyes anywhere but on him. She is falling asleep staring at her foot when another guard finally comes and unchains her and leads her into a courtroom lit with really unflattering fluorescent lights. The magistrate, a woman in her sixties, is in the traditional black robes and has bifocals riding down her nose. Penny wonders what it must be like to see, on a daily basis, the worst humans alive. Penny remembers a survey she took online that asked whether you thought most people were basically good or basically bad. She wonders what this magistrate would answer.

"State your name, please," says the magistrate without looking up. She sounds tired and irritated. Penny doesn't realize the magistrate is talking to her, and the guard gives her a shove.

"Oh, oh, sorry! Penelope Marcus."

The magistrate says, "Oh Oh Sorry Penelope Marcus? Or just Penelope Marcus?"

"My name is Penelope Marcus. This is all a huge mistake. I—"

"Save it," says the magistrate. "This is just the arraignment. I don't need a plea yet. This is where I look at the facts and see if there's probable cause to move ahead."

"There isn't," says Penny.

The magistrate looks at the paper in front of her for all of three seconds and then says, "Charge is second degree murder. Probable cause is established. Defendant was a minor when the events occurred but is now"—she glances again at Penny—"an adult. I understand you want to waive your right to be tried in juvenile court?"

"Yes."

"Then you will be tried by a jury of your peers. Do you have counsel?"

"It's been twenty-five years. Isn't there a statute of limitations or something?"

"Not for murder. Do you have a lawyer, Ms. Marcus?"

"No."

"Would you like the court to appoint a lawyer on your behalf?"

"Um. Yes?"

"County public defender's office is appointed. Your lawyer will be in touch. I see you're a resident of California?"

"Yes, I live—"

"Flight risk. No bail. Your lawyer will represent you at the preliminary hearing, which is when you will enter your plea. We'll have the preliminary hearing on . . ." She flips through a calendar, muttering, "Memorial Day, graduation, Fourth of July, vacation, civil, civil, Labor Day, Rosh Hashanah, surgery . . ." and then names a date that sounds very far away.

"I have to stay here until then?"

"Enjoy your time in Ithaca," says the magistrate.

PART THREE

The Dull Ache of Remembered Joy

10

THE PONY

W HO IS THE worst human you ever met?" I ask Caya the hound dog. She has a furrowed brow and long jowls, our lady of perpetual exhaustion. She doesn't answer. She just lies there, as she does day after day, rising each morning to eat the kibble the old man dumps in her bowl, then trying to squat as discreetly as possible behind the junked car to do her business. The man is in too much pain to make cleanliness a high priority, but once a week he listens to the neighbors' complaints about flies and fills a trash can with our waste.

People drive past this place all day long and they don't care. No one slows or stops or questions why animals live in a tiny pen next to a highway, and never leave it. It never crosses their minds that we deserve anything more than a life sentence behind concrete and chicken wire. If we're not starving to death, then we must be fine. No one cares about our mental or emotional health. Can neglect be mental? Is boredom abuse? Caya chews on her own feet. I find myself weaving back and forth just to have something to do. Only Circe seems unharmed by her life here.

Caya sprawls panting on the concrete in the sun, some flies buzzing over her nose. Circe is standing on the doghouse, staring into the distance at something I can't see, pretending not to listen to me.

"I know who the worst human I ever met was. Her name is Penny. Penny has reddish brown hair the color of . . . betrayal."

"Betrayal is a concept, and as a concept it is colorless," says the goat.

"I beg to differ. If jealousy is green, betrayal is reddish brown."

The goat looks at me. "You are reddish brown."

"No, I'm not. I'm honey blond."

"Green is the color of grass, not jealousy. Everyone knows jealousy is a clear liquid." She swallows a beetle. "You want my story? I was born a goat, and I plan to die a goat."

I ignore her and address my comments to the dog, who hasn't moved. "But to really tell you about how bad Penny is, I have to start the story earlier than that, and tell you about Silla," I say. Caya's nose twitches, which I broadly interpret as encouragement. "And to tell you about Silla, I better start at the beginning." I take a deep breath and shake my mane a little and sneeze to clear my nose. "I was born at Happy Pony Farms in Ithaca."

Circe snorts from atop the doghouse, where she stares into infinity. "There is no such place. And no one cares. Shut up. It's horse racing day at the fairgrounds and I have a bet with a rat on a nag in the third race."

I prick my ears and can faintly hear the clang of the starting bell and humans shouting in the distance. There are hundreds of people there, and the wind carries their sounds and smells to me. I filter the scents, looking for one individual human. I zero in on something. Is it her? It smells like Penny. But it's faint, and it's not coming from the fairgrounds. It's just on the wind blowing by, maybe from a hundred or more miles away. Then, it's gone. After a minute, I sneeze. She's not near here today. Maybe tomorrow.

Instead I vacuum in the smell of racehorses. I've met a few retired Thoroughbreds at riding stables over the years. They've told me about life on the second-rate circuit, far from the Kentucky Derbys of the world. The horses race, they get loaded in trucks and driven hundreds of miles to the next fairgrounds, and then they race again, over and over, all across the country.

"Will your rat bookie place a bet for me?" I ask.

"Do you even know who's running?"

"If there's a pretty chestnut mare, I'll put a handful of oats on her."

Circe fastens her yellow eyes on me briefly. "I'll take that bet. Prepare to lose, sucker."

I choose to ignore her and keep going with my story. "Well, Caya, since you asked, my colthood was uneventful, and I thought life was all about green pastures, stone walls, and red barns."

The goat bleats, "I know this story. Ginger dies."

I ignore the infernal goat and push on. "This idyllic time came to an end when, at age three, I was sold to a woman named Silla, who trained me to ride and pull a cart, and used me for lessons." I pause to chew some hay and think about those times. Clouds scud over us, and a siren wails in the distance. I can faintly hear the horse racing. I'm surprised when, after a few minutes, Caya lifts her head and fixes me with her rheumy eyes, one brown and one blue.

"Is that where you met Bad Penny?"

The goat groans, "Don't encourage him!"

I raise my head, arch my neck, and turn to face Caya, who has cocked an interested ear. "Did she pet you?" Caya asks softly.

"Oh, she petted me all right," I say.

"Get to the reddish-brown part," says the goat.

11

PENNY

PENNY'S PUBLIC DEFENDER appears to be about sixteen years old, a shy girl with long dark hair parted in the middle who introduces herself as Lisa.

"Forgive me for saying this, but you seem very young to have a law degree," Penny says. They are in the "conversation pit" in the jail, which is a wall of plexiglass booths embedded with chicken wire. There are very strict rules about what visitors can and can't bring in, and everything has to be checked in and inspected by guards.

Penny gauges that Lisa, like her, isn't much over five feet tall. They can barely see each other over the partition. They are talking across the plexiglass on old-fashioned gray plastic handsets that crackle and pop.

"I'm not your public defender, I'm an intern in the public defender's office," says Lisa.

"Nice to meet you," says Penny mechanically, feeling fear creeping back in. Her case is being handled by a child. But this is out of her control. She cannot afford a private lawyer. She must take what they give her. Submit to the process, but also make it work for her. Where has her pony self gone? She needs to summon his bravery, his sass.

Lisa says, "I just finished law school online and I'm waiting to hear if I passed the bar exam."

"Do you think you did well?" asks Penny cautiously.

Lisa frowns. "It was really hard. I'm on a trial period in this job, so I want you to know I am totally committed to helping you. My whole career depends on it. Gonna slay."

"Great," Penny says, ignoring the murder reference. She thinks of how the pony would pull her toward the field behind the barn, how it was almost impossible to stop him because his will was so strong. "You're going to clear my name and get me out of here," she says to Lisa. Not a question.

Lisa blinks. "Or get you a really good deal."

"Deal?"

Lisa's voice is hardly more than a whisper, and Penny strains to make out the words. "Well, most cases don't actually go to trial, you know? The lawyers make a plea deal, where you plead guilty to a lesser charge so you don't take the risk of going to trial and being found guilty for the worser thing."

"I'm not guilty," Penny snaps, the pony in her rearing up. "I didn't kill anyone."

"Okay," says Lisa, a little taken aback. Penny tells herself to be nicer, or at least appear to be nicer. This young woman is all she has, and she has said she is going to do her best. *I have to trust this girl*, she thinks, *the way the pony trusted me. I don't have a choice.*

Lisa says, "Um, let's start with what happened that day. Okay if I take notes?" She waves a pink flowered notebook. "Oh, and before you say anything, just know that all of our conversations here are monitored. They can use whatever you say in court."

Wow, Penny thinks. But there is no time to ponder the right of privacy and what it feels like to lose it.

Even though she has run the movie of that day in her brain a million times, she struggles for a second to find the right starting point.

"When I was little, all I ever wanted was—" Not right. She starts again. "I begged and begged and finally my parents gave me riding lessons at the end of fifth grade."

"Horseback riding?"

"Yes, well, I mean, I rode a pony."

"Like a baby horse?"

"No, a pony isn't a baby horse, it's a smaller animal."

"Oh. Didn't know that." Lisa writes in her notebook. Penny sees she has written *PONY.*

"I really loved that pony," says Penny.

Lisa's phone beeps, and Penny realizes how ridiculous she sounds. A *pony.* Like she was some little princess. Lisa must be inwardly rolling her eyes.

Penny says, "My parents weren't rich, this wasn't their world, but the lessons were like a gateway drug. I was hooked, and I had to have more." Penny stops again, realizing she is leaning too heavily on the drug metaphor, given her current circumstances. "Anyway, they tried to say no, but I promised to get straight As and work at the stable to defray the cost, and eventually they agreed to buy a pony for me from the owner of the stable."

"Mm-hmm," says Lisa. Penny can tell she is losing her interest. She wonders who Lisa's other clients are—she must listen to these stories of bad decisions and wrong turns all day.

"Are you an animal person?" Penny asks.

Lisa shakes her head. "My mom is, though. The joke in our family is that she loves the dog more than us."

Penny decides to stick to the facts. "The stable was owned by this woman, Silla. I was so afraid of her at first. Everyone was."

12

THE PONY

I T WAS A beautiful fall day, blue sky and sycamores going gold. The riding stable was small and neat, a white barn with a stone foundation, stone walls around the fields, and brightly painted striped jumps in the sand arena. "I'm supremely confident that we have built you the perfect wall, ma'am," said a short man in a red plaid jacket with a Maine accent, while the other one, very tall and skinny in overalls and an orange hat, added, "and would you like a water jump as well?"

"We've never done a water jump," said the Mainer. He sounded skeptical. I was standing nearby, my reins held by a ruddy-faced woman. Silla. She interrupted them. "Enough with the engineering. Get out of the way."

I liked her brusqueness. Choleric and prone to wild displays of emotion, she would have made a great pony. Silla used me for lessons, for leadline classes at the local showgrounds, the occasional cart ride, and I had even taken one genuinely petrified child fox hunting. Silla's farm was on the edge of a hardwood forest, and she occasionally hired these so-called handymen to work on building a course of natural obstacles in the field. She had dreams of a team of child-pony eventers, international competitions, rows of blue ribbons and trophies in the tack room. These dreams had been thwarted by a combination of her own off-putting style, her location on the outskirts of a small city struggling economically, and the general dislike most children have these days for cutthroat competition. And also by the fact that another riding stable—a very fancy one—had recently opened and stolen most of her business. High Rise Farms was run by one Frank Ross. The children Ross trained were winning ribbons, and their parents were telling other parents, and now no one who could afford High Rise's prices wanted to ride at Silla's.

She looked at the fences the handymen had built, nowhere near as fancy as the ones over at High Rise, and grabbed the closest child, a tear-stained, snot-nosed little boy named Neddie, in one hand and thrust him onto my back against his will. "Go jump that wall," she told him. "Go on. Put the pony toward it and go."

I trotted as dutifully as I could toward the wall. Neddie fell off before we even got there. I dropped my head and grazed. She shouted to Neddie, "Get back on and try again. Now!"

The children were all terrified of her. Her voice's volume button was stuck on high even when shouting endearments at her vicious Jack Russell terrier, Ribs. Her skin was stained in varying shades of scarlet and purple from the sun and the bottle of whiskey she hid behind the fly spray in the tack room. She kept up a constant stream of shouted acid criticism from the center of the arena as we ponies circled around her like electrons, each topped by a panicked child wearing a giant black helmet.

I loved her mindset, which was that a pony could do no wrong. Everything bad was the child's fault. If Tinkerbell darted around the crossbar, little Junie had not kept a strong enough leg on her. If Pepper grabbed the bit and bolted, it was because little Alicia was not soft in her hands. The parents who had stayed loyal to Silla loved her because she reminded them of everyone in their lives who had tortured them and thus shaped them into the perfect embodiments of human virtue they were today. No participation awards at Silla's stable, just humiliation and despair in the pursuit of ever-elusive excellence. Also, lessons cost less than half what they did at High Rise Farms.

"WHEN YOU SHOUT at me like that, does it mean I'm not invisible?" asked a new little girl named Penny one day. It was Penny's first lesson, a sunny afternoon in June. She had whispered to me at the mounting block that she had been begging for a pony since she was three. The constant asking had finally paid off with a punch card for ten lessons at Silla's. Penny hummed with excitement as the group lesson began, and her enthusiasm zapped into me, too, as if I were the ground wire to her high-voltage power line. We walked in a swirling, churning whirlpool around Silla, as we always did.

Silla shouted at the children to put their heels down and their heads up, their thumbs up and their hands light and responsive. Knees against the saddle flaps, eyes ahead, never down, except for the microsecond you were allowed to check your diagonal, to make sure you were rising at the trot in sync with the pony's outside shoulder. Silla was bellowing hoarsely as she always was, Ribs napping at her feet. I was jogging along, dreaming of the carrots I had smelled in Penny's blue flowered backpack when she set it next to my stall.

"What's that?" Silla said in surprise to Penny's question. I had never heard a child speak to her during a riding lesson before. In fact, rarely did children speak in her presence.

"I'm really trying to disappear," said Penny in a clear, high voice like a chickadee. She pulled me to a halt and turned me to face Silla. "I know riding is all about fitting in, about erasing our individuality. We all have to dress identically, make our movements nearly invisible. We're silent. Becoming one with the animal. It's a perfect metaphor for the erasure of self."

Silla stared at her, dumbfounded.

"I want to fit in," Penny continued. "It's all I want. To disappear."

Silla was silent, still staring. Ribs sat up and yapped once.

"I just want you to know that I love this," said Penny. "I want to get it right. I want you to tell me everything. Don't hold back."

Penny gently moved me back into the line of ponies and squeezed me into a trot.

Silla was silent for a moment, and only the muffled thrum of hooves on sand broke the quiet of the afternoon. "Boy in blue," Silla barked at last. "Head up. Girl on Samson, heels down. You're not in ballet class." Then she said, "Penny. Your toes are clenched. Release them, wiggle them inside your boots, and let your leg from the knee down drop and become elastic."

This was the first time I had ever heard Silla call a child by its name. I didn't think she knew their names. For the rest of the lesson, she gave the other children the basic commands we had all heard thousands of times about seats and heads and heels being wrong, wrong, wrong. But to Penny she gave more specific and insightful feedback: "One half squeeze of the reins like a sponge you don't want fully dry," "Raise your left shoulder one inch as you ask for the canter," "Breathe out as you bring him down to the walk." Penny did these things, and they sent tiny signals to me that provoked involuntary muscular responses that made me relax and stretch my back and collect under her. I had always seen my riders as opponents in a wrestling match. The objective was to get them to the mat. But with Penny I saw there could be a different goal.

Penny talked to me as she led me to and from the stable, and then more when she eventually talked Silla into letting her help with the chores. She told me she was only two and a half pounds when she was born, very premature, and had lived in an incubator for the first months of her life. Her parents had always been worried about her. They had followed her around constantly from the moment she could walk, terrified that she would fall (she did, uneventfully), bump into things (ditto), or wander into the street (never). They checked on her while she slept and followed her when she rode her bike. Their perpetual expressions of worry drove her nuts. Sometimes when they stood over her, thinking she was asleep, she would hold her breath, just to mess with them.

The more they tried to keep her close, the more she longed to escape, coming home later for dinner, or leaving before breakfast. Adding to their concern was that at eleven she was still very small for her age, looking more like an eight-year-old, so they were always envisioning the worst, locking themselves and her into a cycle of worry, rebellion, and anger. Penny had been drawing horses, reading about horses, and dreaming about horses her whole life, but her parents had always told her she was too small for riding lessons, or it wasn't safe, or it was too far away. Finally, she blew up at them one night and screamed that she felt like she was living under a microscope. She told them she would pay for her own riding lessons by selling homework at school—or worse, leaving them to imagine what "worse" was—if they didn't give her a set of lessons for her birthday.

Riding lessons made Penny supremely happy. She hummed and practically levitated as she walked into the stable. She started coming more often, even on days when she didn't have lessons, just to hang out with us ponies and watch other kids ride. Of course, Silla put her to work, grooming, cleaning tack, polishing bits, rolling polo wraps. This gave Penny credits for more lessons, which made her even happier. Joy intensified, like an opera singer's voice going up a pitch.

After coming one day and finding another little girl, Ellen, bouncing on my back, making me wince, Penny asked her parents to buy me from Silla. It was a prolonged negotiation, involving promises of straight As and clean rooms. They hashed out clauses, subclauses, footnotes, strikethroughs, and forces majeure and mineure. The deal closed at last on Christmas Eve. Penny came that night and threw her arms around me and fed me carrots. "It's official. I'm your person," she said. "Your one true person."

I cannot describe to you how happy this made me, except by saying it was like tasting carrots all the time, or the joy you get when you chase a dog out of the pasture. Every day from Christmas on, Penny trudged through the snow to pet me and feed me, even when it was too dark and snowy and muddy to ride.

One afternoon Penny sat in a pile of hay in my stall and read to me while a blizzard raged outside. "*Whether I shall turn out to be the hero of my own life, or whether that station will be held by anybody else, these pages must show.*" The story of the human kid, David Copperfield, wasn't all that interesting, but I pondered that opening line. Up until then I had just assumed that everyone was the hero of their own life, but the more I looked around, the more I saw ponies and people just going with the flow, doing what was easy.

When the snow stopped, Penny led me out of the barn into a startlingly white landscape under an azure sky that made us both gasp, my hooves sinking into the fluffy white, her boots squeaking on the crust. I smelled pine and woodsmoke. I flipped my tail up into the air and leapt, then threw myself down into the snow to roll, then leapt up again, snorting and bucking. Penny laughed and laughed and threw snowballs at me.

Winter turned to spring, the blue eggs in the nest above my stall hatched and became robins, and Penny was there every day after school. We would hack out into the forest and walk down narrow paths between the trees, squirrels doing acrobatics overhead, and birds singing to us.

I thought I was at eleven on the happiness scale, but the bliss just intensified when the school year ended. Penny glided into the stable at dawn every day that leafy, sun-dappled summer, a tiny figure in riding tights, jodhpur boots, and a striped T-shirt. In silence she would take the huge wheelbarrow and wrestle it down the aisle and start cleaning the stalls. When every single pooplet was gone from every one of the stalls, she maneuvered the heaping wheelbarrow down the aisle and out the door, manure towering over her head, and somehow dumped it onto the steaming pile behind the barn where Ribs liked to burrow. She then swept the barn aisle perfectly clean.

Then she would go to the tack room and grab the handle of Silla's polished wooden box of brushes. It bore a brass label declaring CHAMPION—GROOMING AND STABLE CARE, TROY PONY CLUB. Penny would carefully set it down in front of each stall in turn, duck under the webbed stall guard, and give us a thorough scrubbing, rubbing, brushing, polishing, combing, and fluffing. Some of the ponies were ticklish and didn't like to be brushed, especially on the belly, and with them Penny was very light in her touch, rubbing her hand on their necks in reassurance. I loved a good massage, so I leaned into her palm in the rubber mitt—oh, the rubber mitt!—almost knocking her over. I sighed as she whisked the dead hairs and wood shavings out of my coat, then finished with the flick of the body brush that lifted the last dust motes, bringing me to a lustrous shine. I can still smell the tarry scent of the hoof oil she used, and the menthol tang of the liniment. At the end of each grooming session she would press her lips into the soft indentation on the side of my nose just above my mouth and below the nostril.

Silla would appear, crusty eyed and blinking with a hangover. She'd inspect Penny's work, find some imaginary flaw that Penny would nod and correct, and then the cars would start to arrive and the children shuffle in for the day's lessons.

"Promise me one thing," Silla said to Penny one day.

"What?"

"You'll never hurt a horse."

Penny's face flushed. "I would never."

"Good," said Silla. "Remember that."

Penny had to be home by dark, but she always stayed until just before sunset, wolfing down a sandwich from her backpack at lunchtime, crunching an apple and saving the core for me (seeds removed). She tacked and untacked the ponies for the lessons, fed us and turned us out in the paddock for a roll. At the end of the day when the stalls were picked out again and the feeders full of hay, she would pedal home on her bike, racing the sun to the horizon.

Caya, I was so happy. It wasn't like with Princess or Ray-Ray, pony mares at the stable that I had crushes on. This kind of happiness needed a different word to describe it. My world got brighter when Penny walked into the barn each day. I was a better pony with her, a better version of myself than I had ever been. My gaits had an elasticity I didn't know I possessed. I felt the smallest movement of her legs, hands, seat, and shoulders, and responded smoothly, willingly. Okay, every now and then I surprised her with a buck when she asked me for a canter, but it was out of joy, not naughtiness. The sour heaviness of my life lifted. I didn't recognize the pony I saw in the water trough. I worried that I had gone soft. But at the same time I didn't care. Oh, life, that submerges us in this sweetness, as a fish swims in a pond on a summer afternoon, frogs happily kicking past, insects skittering on the surface, the sun warming the water, lucky fish who is unaware there is any other way to be, who thinks this is all that there is, all that there ever will be.

13

PENNY

LISA IS TAKING notes, and Penny pauses to let her catch up. She thinks about a Pat Schneider poem she used to read to the pony. *"Wash your own dishes, let cold water run between your fingers."* She'd lie on his back, her head on his broad rump, her legs swinging at his sides. It seemed like the skies were blue every day back then. She loved reading to the pony. He probably wasn't listening, but she imagined he was, that he was learning from what she read to him. She had to maintain straight As in order to keep the pony, but that wasn't the only reason she read so much. She liked books. The pony seemed skeptical of these useless inedible objects she shoved in her backpack, but he liked it when she took him into the meadow behind the stable at Silla's and read to him there. At first she would lie in the grass as he ate around her, nudging her legs aside to get choice tufts. After she found a tick on her arm she instead liked the relative safety of the pony's back.

It's easy to lose this tenderly
unfolding moment

14

THE PONY

Look for it
as if it were the first green blade
after a long winter.

That's what Penny was for me. The first green blade. She awakened me from years of torpor. She wasn't prettier or smarter or lighter or stronger than any other child. But when she put her foot in the stirrup or, more frequently these days, swung up onto me bareback, I felt calm and interested in what we would do together. Go for a trail ride? Swim in the river? Jump some fences? Laze around in the meadow? Yes.

"STILL WAITING FOR the bad part," says Circe.

15

PENNY

"AND THE MURDER?" Lisa is looking at the big clock on the wall.

Penny realizes their time is almost up. Like an idiot, she's been waxing on and on rhapsodically about her pony and the daily routine at Silla's. She almost forgot why poor Lisa is having to listen to all this.

"I called my parents to tell them I was going on a trail ride," Penny says. "I didn't have a cell phone back then, so I called them on the phone in Silla's office. I told them it was with some other kids and their ponies and horses, because I didn't want them to know I was riding out alone with Alex. I knew him from school. He was a year older. We weren't really friends, but I knew he lived at High Rise Farms, the fancy barn up the road from Silla's. I told my parents I'd be back by dinner."

16

THE PONY

PENNY SADDLED ME and led me out. She climbed on and we rode out across Silla's property and out the back gate into the forest. We trotted down a trail to a junction and waited a few minutes under a broad oak tree. I heard hoofbeats and a big chestnut mare trotted up, all flashy with a white blaze and four white socks.

"Hello, gorgeous," I said with a little whinny.

The mare gave me side eye and said nothing. Some horses are just like that. Snobs. On top of the snobby red mare was a male human I guessed as being about Penny's age, maybe a little older. I felt Penny sit up straighter and drop her heels lower in the stirrups.

"Where are the others?" he asked.

"They couldn't come," said Penny. "Want to ride to the old house?" We rode out there sometimes. Personally I'm not that interested in houses unless they are made of carrots.

"What old house?"

"It's in the forest. Come on," Penny said. There was an edge to her voice I hadn't heard before, like she was showing off.

She kicked me into a gallop but we were quickly overtaken by the long-legged mare, which I thought was really rude. There was a lot of hooting and hollering from Penny and the boy as we clattered down the trail through the forest. I had the sense Penny wanted to go hell-for-leather, but I stayed in a controlled canter so I didn't trip over tree roots and send both of us sprawling.

We eventually caught up to the boy and the snobby mare in the darkest part of the forest, where the vegetation was thick and I usually liked to spook at every noise. Today I was playing it cool with the pretty red mare, whose name was Arete, like I wasn't afraid of anything.

"It's over here," Penny said to the boy.

"What is?"

"The old house. Head over that way," Penny ordered him.

The boy urged Arete off the trail, and she picked her way daintily over logs and around bushes. I was significantly shorter than the mare and some of the logs were a bit of a challenge for me, I am not ashamed to say, but I soldiered on, uncomplaining.

"Farther?" asked the boy over his shoulder.

"Just a bit," Penny said.

We crested a hill and there was a dense tangle of vines and underbrush in front of us. A raven cawed nearby. I had been there before, but today I could smell something unfamiliar. I wanted to snort, but I restrained myself, still playing it cool in front of the pretty lady-horse.

"You're a really good rider," said the boy. "You should come ride some of our horses over at High Rise."

Hmph, I thought. Penny would never betray me that way.

"You could show them for us," the boy added. "A lot of the owners don't ride, they just want to watch their horses win. You wouldn't believe these horses they buy. Some are from the racetrack here at Saratoga, but some are from Ireland and Germany. Half million bucks and up."

Penny and I both turned in shock. I found putting a price on an animal extremely distasteful, though who doesn't want to be highly valued? I'd met some of those off-the-track horses from Saratoga and didn't think they were all that. Based on them, I estimated my own worth in that moment at around five million dollars, give or take.

"How would that work?" Penny asked.

"You'd get paid to ride them, both in training and at shows."

I waited for Penny to tell him she already had her one perfect mount, but instead she said, "Let's tie up here. The abandoned house is just ahead."

The boy dismounted and tied Arete to a tree. Penny did the same. I felt anxious, and I couldn't tell if it was just that I was bothered by their conversation or whether there was real danger here. I snorted and when the mare wasn't looking did a little anxiety dance to tell Penny this wasn't a good idea.

"Just stay here," she said to me a tad more dismissively than I would have expected. "I'll be right back." I could smell that she had a carrot in her pocket. I tried to will her to give it to me immediately, but she pushed my nose away. "After," she said.

She disappeared into the underbrush, and I could hear her crunching footfalls on the dry leaves. I neighed at her.

She stopped and turned back and called to me. "I'll be right there," she repeated. I could hear impatience in her voice. "Come on," she said to the boy. She and he disappeared into the trees.

The mare looked at me. "You talk to your human?"

Boy, that mare's little dishy face was pretty. "Of course," I said with élan, savoir faire, and je ne sais quoi. "Penny doesn't understand the words, of course, but they get the tone. I've trained her with voice commands. When I nicker, she gives me a carrot."

"Mine is untrainable," sighed Arete. "I can't get Alex to do anything I want."

"I've trained Penny to give me treats when she gets on and off, and to rub my ears, and scratch under my chin. She's pretty smart for a human."

The mare snorted. "Lucky you. Does she beat you?"

"Beat me?" I laughed, startled by her question. "No," I said. "She definitely does not beat me."

We waited, shifting our weight from foot to foot and stretching the lead ropes as far as we could in search of blades of grass.

"This moss isn't bad," said Arete, licking the tree trunk.

A cloud of blue butterflies danced around my head. "Hello!" I said to them and got hundreds of tiny "hellos" in return. Butterflies are one of the few things I like that aren't edible. Their wings were silvery blue with little semicircles of black spots that had orange dots inside them.

"We're called Karner Blues," they said. "We're rare and beautiful."

"Join the club," I said, tossing my mane. The dancing butterflies made me calmer, but I also felt a little bored. And mischievous. With all this talk of Saratoga racehorses and pricey show horses, maybe Penny needed a little reminder of how much I meant to her. I could go hide behind a tree and make her think I ran off, and then reappear as if by magic. Penny and I loved playing these kinds of pranks on each other. I turned to the mare. "Hey, you know what I can do?"

I leaned over as far as I could and pulled the end of her lead rope, which was tied in a slipknot. It came loose, as I knew it would.

"Oh my God," she said, standing there with her lead rope dangling. "You're a magician! Can you do yours, too?"

"Of course." Penny knew I could do this, so she tied the rope in a special way, but come on, I'm a pony. I had my own rope undone in two seconds.

"Let's go!" said the mare, turning and trotting a few strides.

"Um. No? Wait. We can't leave our humans here. Let's just hide over there and wait for them. Hide and seek."

"Are you kidding me?" The mare's tone was all contempt. "I'm outta here. But I don't want to go alone. There could be wild animals. You gotta come, too." She raised her head high and swiveled her ears, listening for danger.

"You're scared of wild animals?" I pretended I didn't know what she was talking about, even though I had jumped sideways at the sight of a squirrel only the day before.

"Wild animals are scary," she said. "And they're everywhere. I see them all the time, even when they're not there, just in case."

"Well, yeah, I do that, too. But I can't leave Penny here."

"You can't leave me to be eaten by bears and lions and chipmunks. It's the equine code. We stick together. Come on."

I hesitated, torn. It was the equine code. She was right about that. And she had long legs and beautiful eyes. "But how are they going to get back?" I asked.

"They'll walk on their ridiculous two legs. And besides, that will give them more time together."

"Why would they want that?"

"He's a boy, she's a girl. They like each other."

"They just met."

"That's all it takes. One look. You heard Alex. He's invited her to ride at High Rise. Soon she'll stop riding you altogether. She's at that age. You'll be forgotten. And sold."

"Hey. That's my Penny you're talking about. She's not going to sell me, ever. We're going to grow old together. When she's too big to ride me I'll live in her backyard, under an apple tree. She and I have talked about this."

"Dream on, shorty. I'm leaving. I smell grass."

I sniffed. I smelled something, but it wasn't grass. Something ominous.

She galloped off, leaping the logs and crashing through the leaves. I was all riled up, my mind churning. Now I was all alone in the creepy dark wood that smelled like death.

And it was almost dinnertime.

17

PENNY

ALEX AND I came out of the abandoned house and my pony and
the horse were gone. It wasn't that unusual—he could be quite
naughty—but I was embarrassed. Alex said—"

Lisa's cell phone rings. "One sec," she says, and hangs up the gray
phone for a second. Penny watches Lisa listening and nodding. Her
makeup is artfully applied and Penny wonders if Lisa does it herself or
has a sibling who does it for her. Penny's daughter Tella loves to do
Penny's makeup, though sometimes it's a bit goth for a teacher of third
graders and Penny has to remove most of the eyeliner in the car on the
way to school. Finally, Lisa hangs up her cell phone and picks up the
gray plastic receiver.

"Good news," she says.

"They're dropping the charges?"

"The public defender gave me a bunch more cases to investigate. So
amped! He thinks I'm doing a really great job. Anyway, I gotta go."
Lisa starts to pack up her notebook.

"But I didn't finish telling you about what happened."

"I'll be back as soon as I can. You could maybe write it down for me
in the meantime?"

"How do I get paper and a pen?"

"I'll make sure you get that."

"Wait. What changed?" Penny asks Lisa as she's about to hang up the gray phone. "I was questioned by the police when the murder happened. Why are they arresting me now, after all this time?"

"I'll find out," says Lisa.

PENNY IS ONCE again escorted back to her cell. She walks laps between her bed and the wall, unsatisfied. She has been wanting to tell someone her story, to have someone listen and say, "Oh my God, that's so crazy." She wants someone to acknowledge how absurd this all is, see that they have made a big mistake in locking her up here. Everyone keeps acting like this is normal.

How is it possible that she can never get away from one terrible hour in her life? How is it possible that all of the other hours in her life, hours spent caring for others, teaching little children, taking care of her daughter and husband, flying home to look after her parents as they aged and died, how is it that all that doesn't count? How is it possible that people can't see that she's a good person? Isn't that just apparent to them?

Clearly, it is not. She may be a "detainee," but really Penny is just another prisoner. A number. A crime.

She thinks about the aftermath of that night, when she thought she had escaped with nothing more than a broken rib and a concussion. Penny's parents had yanked her out of school and moved the family away because they didn't want her to be "the girl who everyone thinks killed that guy." Penny was furious to be ripped away from her life. It was only later that she understood her parents' decision, when she was a parent herself, understood her mom and dad's fear that whispers in the schoolyard would cling to her and define her and shape her life. "Don't talk about what happened, okay?" her dad had said as Penny stood in the hallway of their new apartment in Chicago in new beige corduroys and a new blue sweater and new white canvas sneakers, heading off for her first day in a new seventh-grade classroom. So much new.

So she didn't talk about it. Didn't talk about anything. Didn't make friends. She was the new girl who sat by herself in the cafeteria, read books in a corner of the playground. She went to school, went home, did her homework, and went to sleep, her mouth and heart firmly shut. Her only rebellion was to draw ponies in the margins of her homework until Mrs. Smeriglio gave her an F and made her rewrite her essay on the Gettysburg Address. Except for the occasional glimpse of a carriage horse on Michigan Avenue, everything equine disappeared from her life.

For the rest of middle school and high school she was "the quiet one." She wasn't so much bullied as steered clear of. Ignored. Picked last. In class, she didn't raise her hand, but if the teacher called on her, she knew the answer. She didn't tell her college roommates what had happened to her when she was twelve, didn't tell Laus when they were dating or when he became her husband. Why tell them? It was all so long ago.

DAYS PASS. LIKE a dutiful horse, she is fed, exercised, has her teeth examined by the jail's dentist, cold fingers in her mouth. The guards lead her back and forth down the hallway exactly like riding horses are led from their stall to the arena and back again. She doesn't want to be a polite and docile horse. She wants to be a naughty pony. But she sees the guns, the Tasers, the dogs ready to subdue anyone who steps out of line.

The guard locks her in. She waits for the next meal.

IN HER FIRST days at Sticks River, which sounds comically like the name of a golf course gated community, she felt reasonably certain this mess would be straightened out and she would be back home soon, but now she's not so sure. The wheels of justice don't seem to turn as smoothly as she was led to believe in sixth grade civics. In the cafeteria she has overheard stories of women who were framed, or killed their

CHRISTINA LYNCH

abusive husbands in self-defense, or to save their children's lives. They're in prison for decades, sometimes for life.

Penny lies on her bunk in her cell and tries to pretend she is anywhere else. She closes her eyes and wills herself to leave her body and fly away.

She hears a voice, and it takes a second for her to realize it's not coming from inside her own head. "Hey? Hey? You got kids?" Penny stands and goes to the little grate on the front of her cell. When she arrived at Sticks River she had to laugh despite her horror—the interior of the place looks exactly like the elementary school where Penny teaches third grade. The same white-painted cinder-block walls, the same waxed gray-and-white tile floors, the same blue metal doors inset with a skinny vertical rectangle of tempered glass, the same fluorescent lighting. Except instead of classrooms, the doors lead to narrow cinder-block cells, like college dorm rooms at a state school whose budget has been slashed. Besides the skinny window, each cell door has a small grate in it so you can hear the guards, and an opening that looks like a mail slot but is actually for you to put your hands through so a guard can snap handcuffs on before they unlock the door.

She locates the voice as coming from the woman in the cell next to hers. She's new. Arrived yesterday, but Penny doesn't know why or from where. No one here ever asks what you're in for. This is the murder wing. From their cells, which they are locked in twenty-three hours a day, they can hear each other through the small grate but can't see each other. Penny did see the woman being led down the hallway when she arrived. She's twice Penny's size and thus scares her, but then so does everyone here, even the women who are small like her. Penny has been keeping her mouth closed and her eyes down since she arrived. She's lonely.

"Yes," she says against her better judgment, staring through the tiny grate at the fire extinguisher across the hall from her cell. "My daughter is thirteen. You?"

"A son. Six. I can't figure out how to handle it. You tell her you're here?"

"Not yet. She was diagnosed a few years ago with an anxiety disorder. She's at a boarding school for girls with mental health issues."

"Boarding school," says the woman, and Penny realizes she thinks she's rich.

"That's why I can't afford a lawyer," Penny says quickly, the words tumbling out. "My husband and I raided our retirement account and drained our savings to send Tella there for a year. We took another mortgage on the house. Tella was having a really hard time. It was . . . necessary." She doesn't elaborate.

"Tella. Pretty name. You're a good mom to give up everything to help her," says the woman. "Your husband come to visit you?"

"He's in California. We're sort of separated. I mean, nothing official. We were actually going to have dinner the night I was arrested." She gives a little half sigh, half sob. "He's a good dad."

What has Laus told Tella about all of this? She hopes he's said nothing. But Tella must be wondering why her mom hasn't called. Phone calls are very limited here, and the rules are complicated. It's the same on Tella's end, too, at Arcadia. It's a beautiful place out in the country, but the rules are strict. The school philosophy is to wean the girls off their phones and get them to connect with nature, animals, and each other. She hopes Tella is happy there. Maybe even making friends. She just wants Tella to feel better.

Penny has only been able to talk to Laus once since she got here. He was flabbergasted, of course, to have his completely law-abiding wife hauled across the country and put in jail. He offered to fly out there, but she told him to stay in California. They need his income—Laus has told the school where Penny teaches that she has a personal emergency. She's already used up her personal leave time dealing with Tella, so now she's not getting paid. And the principal must be so irritated with her, disappearing without a word, leaving them hanging. Laus said he was keeping things quiet back home, that he'd implied her absence was an emergency with Tella, but Penny did wonder if word had leaked out. Theirs was a very small town and Ed had likely let it slip to someone where Penny was.

71

She pictures the parents of her third graders getting the news that their kids' teacher has been arrested for murder. It's such a shocking and juicy piece of gossip that even she has to laugh. They must be clucking like hens at pickup. "I totally knew something was off with her! The way she kept the scissors in the locked drawer of her desk," she can imagine them saying.

Arrested for murder. A murder she supposedly committed when she was twelve, like she was some kind of demon child.

Penny wonders if there is a part of Laus that thinks she might have killed someone. She can see him, too, buying into that cultural trope about the oh-so-nice wife and mother who finally snaps, male paranoia at its best. He's probably rewatching *Fatal Attraction* and counting his blessings she didn't kill *him*.

You're not being fair to him, she tells herself. What if the roles were reversed? But she's still angry with Laus for so many things. And at the same time she misses him. She does wish he were here, nearby, and could come see her. Would he? Maybe it's better not to know. Does he still love her? Lately Penny wonders if she even knows what love is. Is making dinner what love is? Being polite to someone day after day? A mutually beneficial partnership—is that love?

Penny longs to talk to Tella, too, to see her, to hug her and say that everything will be all right, even if she isn't a hundred percent certain it will be. They are both in institutions against their will, she thinks. At least Tella's at a good facility with caring staff. Hopefully she's come to like it. Penny thinks about the last time she saw Tella, the day she dropped her off. Tella was crying, screaming, angry, hysterical. The staff said that was normal. And so Penny just drove away.

Penny stares through the skinny window at the fire extinguisher across the hall from her cell. "I'm worried she thinks I abandoned her," she says aloud.

18

THE PONY

PENNY NEVER CAME back to the stable. I never saw her again. One day I was the most important thing in the world to her, and the next day she couldn't even be bothered to say goodbye. Within a couple of days of that trail ride, Silla sent me to a horse dealer, and that was that. Sold, like a pound of pork chops." I look at Caya and Circe. "That's why I hate Penny."

Caya howls mournfully. "Noooooo . . ."

"She could have just treated me badly from the beginning. Then I wouldn't have become attached. But she showed me that humans can be different. And then she took that away from me. She left me for a boy."

"That's so wrong," says Caya.

I nod. "Wherever I went after that, I could only be lost. Penny was my lighthouse, my home, and suddenly there was no lighthouse, no home, just lies and open sea."

I turn and see Circe's yellow slit-eyed pupils fastened on me.

"Staring is rude," I say.

"Sucker," she says. "You fell for the human's lies."

I hate baring my soul to a goat, but I have to agree with her. "Yup," I say. "I've spent every day since then plotting how to get back at her. To practice for that day, I've made a lot of humans unhappy."

She gives me the goat equivalent of a high five, which is a head butt. "Humans don't have emotions and thus deserve nothing but pain and suffering," she says.

"No, no," says Caya, looking actually fierce for the first time since I got here. "You're not getting what I'm saying. You're wrong, pony."

"I'm wrong about what?"

"You're an idiot," growls Caya.

I stand up to my full height. "I beg your pardon?"

"You. Are. An. Idiot."

"Why do you say that?"

"You just told the story. You left your person in the woods and ran home without her? And you're mad at *her*?"

I feel a little defensive all of a sudden. "It was just a prank. Apparently she couldn't take a joke. She turned around and *sold* me, for crying out loud. Total overreaction on her part. Cold and cruel."

"And you call yourself a domesticated animal? You *left* her. Anything could have happened to her." Caya is growling and snapping at my nose.

I pin my ears at her. "I'm sure she was fine. She was with the boy. Alex. The boy she liked better than me."

"Oh my God!" howls Caya. "I don't even know where to begin. Do you even know that she came out of the woods? Maybe she's still there, waiting for you!"

"What?" I'm confused.

"You abandoned your person!"

"No no no. Weren't you listening? She abandoned me. I was sold . . . I was owned by a million people . . . I bit and kick and dumped and bolted and . . . for years and years and years . . ." My words trail off. I can hardly form the syllables, but they come out of me anyway in a whisper: "I abandoned my person."

I fall to the ground.

"Are you making fun of fainting goats?" says Circe. "Because that is not cool."

I moan. Softly at first, then louder. I am lying on my side, stretched out, eyes open. *Grooooooaaaaan.*

I hear a clatter of hooves and the pad of paws. From the corner of my eye I see Circe's yellow eyes and Caya's brown and blue eyes staring down at me.

Groooooaaaaannnnn.

"You messed up," says Circe.

Caya nods.

"All this time," I whisper. "I was surviving on anger. I felt so . . . justified. So enraged. So strong."

"Anger is empowering," says Caya. "It's a dangerous emotion. It's addictive."

"You've been living a lie," says Circe. Then adds, "Ha! Stupid pony."

They turn their backs on me. Caya goes and curls up facing away from me. Circe resumes her post atop the doghouse listening to the horse races. I continue to lie there and moan, until Circe tells me to knock it off and Caya gives a little snarl. Then I lie there in silence.

Day turns to dusk and then to night. I do not move. I lie there and replay the events of the day that I last saw Penny, and every day in between. Caya and Circe are right. I am so stupid.

Day dawns and I am still lying there, cold and stiff and miserable. I hear the sounds of the neighborhood waking up around me, sparrows chittering, flies buzzing, the sound of the garbage truck backing up: *beep beep beep.* At some point, I think, I will die. Though I have a lot of meat on my bones. Starvation could take a while.

"Is this shame or guilt?" I ask. "Because I have never felt either before, and I want to know what I'm going to die of."

"Guilt is about something you did," says Caya.

"And shame is about who you are," says Circe.

I ponder this, still facedown in the dust. "I'm going with guilt," I say, and close my eyes.

"You have to go back," says Caya at last.

I open my eyes. "Back?"

"You have to go back to Penny."

"I'm a pony. I only go where I'm taken."

"You have legs, don't you?"

"They're more decorative than functional."

Caya puts her face in my face and growls. "If I had a human who loved me, I would do anything to get back to her. That kind of connection is rare and magical."

"Mmmmmagical?" Circe starts laughing in a not-nice way.

I look at Caya and say as sweetly as I can, trying not to hurt her feelings, "Ponies don't really believe in magic. We're very practical animals when you get down to it."

"You don't believe in *magic*?" Caya is amazed, and I'm amazed at her amazement.

"You *do*?" I ask.

"She's a dog," says Circe. "They live too closely with the humans and their heads are filled with nonsense as a result."

"Maybe you don't call it magic, but you believe in love," says Caya. "I saw it in your face when you talked about Penny."

"She fed me. She was nice to me. Isn't love just a word humans made up for something that doesn't really exist?"

Circe chimes in, "I hate to say it, but the pony is correct. There is no such thing as magic *or* love. There is only relief that someone is not beating you, starving you, or eating you, or pain and fear if they are." Circe struts back and forth, lecturing us. "Domestic animals are reliant on humans to feed and care for them, and the humans are reliant on the animals who are useful to them in some way, either physically or mentally, such as the ones who give them 'unconditional love.'"

If you've never seen a goat do air quotes, it's impressive. Circe goes on, "It's a mutually beneficial relationship, not love. The proof of that is that humans don't care about any of the other animals that are not useful to them. Humans have animal hierarchies—some animals are useful and thus good, worth caring for and protecting, but almost all other animals are to be ignored or outright killed, even eaten, driven extinct. That's what I hate about humans. They play favorites. I ate a psychology textbook once. Learned a *lot*."

Caya and I absorb all this.

"Pop quiz for you idiots," Circe says. "If humans love us, then why is there no word in any language for their bond with us? They're all about language. If we really mattered to them, they would have created a word for that. Right?"

The screen door bangs open and the old man bowlegs his way down the stairs and across the yard to the garage without looking at us. He dumps a scoop of kibble in Caya's tin bowl, and tosses a half flake of hay to me and to Circe. Then he tops up the water dish and bowlegs back up the stairs and goes back into the house. Slam, the screen door bangs shut again.

"Stop expecting more," says Circe, wagging her horns in the direction the man went. "Nobody else wants us. That man is not our jailer. He's our savior. He doesn't always have enough food for himself, but he still feeds us. Everyone else would just kill us without even blinking, but he's keeping us alive."

We pause our philosophical discussion to wolf down our food, and then Caya lies down flat on her side in the sun. "I'm not contradicting you," she says. "Everything you say about the humans is true. But I still believe in love. I've never had a human who loved me, but I believe it exists, even if there's no word for it in their language."

"Even if what you say is true," Circe says to Caya, "even if there was a person named Penny who in theory *was* better than every other human and actually cared on some deep selfless level about this stupid pony, he wouldn't deserve her. He abandoned her. He deserves . . . this." She waves her horns in a circle around the empty yard.

There is a moment of silence, and then I say quietly, "You're right. I let her down."

"We can't escape our fates," says Circe.

"I don't believe that," says Caya, sitting up. "We have flaws, yes, but we can choose to overcome them and change our destiny."

"A domesticated animal who believes in free will?" says Circe. "Now I've seen everything."

"Well, I don't know where the forest of the blue butterflies is," I say. "So it's kind of a moot point. That's that."

A red-throated hummingbird buzzes around my ears. "I know where it is. I'd calculate that it's four days' flying from here."

"What's that in walking-on-short-legs time?" I ask.

The hummingbird pauses, humming, then spits out a number. "Five."

"Five days?"

"Five months. If you trot the flat stretches. And avoid winter in the Rockies."

"Too far," I groan.

Circe says, "Even if you could find her, Penny is an adult human now. I'd bet good money she doesn't *want* a pony anymore. Have you considered that?"

"The goat has a point," I say to Caya.

"I've heard enough!" Caya barks, startling me and the goat. She sticks her face in mine and growls. "Start walking," she says. "Because you're not staying here."

"Okay, okay," I say, swishing my tail and shaking off the dust. "I'm making a plan." My mind clicks and churns, running through all the things I know about how animals get from place to place. They fly, they swim, they run, they—

I hear a scampering on the fence. I look up and see a rat there. Big glossy fellow with a long tail. Circe is passing him some oats that he's stowing in his cheek. "Damn rats always win," she mutters.

"Hey, rat," I say. "You hang around the racehorses, don't you?"

"I might," says the rat, cagey. "Who's asking?"

"Are any of those racehorses really nervous types?"

The rat snorts. "Do fish swim?"

"And do those nervous racehorses ever go to a place called Saratoga?"

The rat fastens his beady eyes on me and his nose twitches. "They might. What's it to ya?"

"A lot."

"That's a relative term and I deal in specifics."

"If you get me there, I will split my grain with you the whole way. Halvsies."

"No cheating?" The rat's whiskers twitch.

"If you promise not to poop in the bucket."

"Can't make any promises, but I'll try. Is it a deal?"

"It's a deal," I say.

"Okay. Come with me," the rat says, scampering along the fence.

I walk to the gate and unlatch it in about two seconds flat. It swings open to reveal the alley. Trash cans, an old sofa, and battered garage doors.

"Good luck, pony," says Caya. "Trust in the magic."

Circe fastens me with her yellow goat eyes. "You'll be eaten by wolves within two days."

19

PENNY

PENNY IS A little more ready for the preliminary hearing than she was for the arraignment. Lisa has told her what to expect, that she will not give evidence herself, but that probable cause will be evaluated more thoroughly than at the arraignment and that the case could be dismissed.

"I would be released?" she asks Lisa.

"Yes. But if probable cause is found, your case will be bound over to a trial court, and we'll have to wait for a trial date to be set. I just want to caution you that the court system is very backed up. That's why the plea deal is such a common choice for people."

FOR A PROCESS that seems to involve a gigantic amount of waiting, Penny is shocked by how quickly the preliminary hearing proceeds.

Lisa introduces her to her public defender, Steve, a man in his twenties in a not very flattering tight gray suit and a buzz cut who is on his phone. Steve gives her a smile and a wave and a "give me a sec" hand gesture, but that sec doesn't come and suddenly he is talking to the judge on her behalf.

"They have nothing on my client," Steve says.

The prosecutor and Steve look so much alike that Penny has trouble telling them apart, like a chess set where all the pieces are gray. Is there a law school that churns out identical arrogant young men? Yes, she thinks.

The prosecutor says, "We have a confession, Your Honor."

A confession? she wants to shout. She looks at Steve and frantically shakes her head.

"Bogus," says Steve to the judge.

Penny is dying to talk, to demand to know what this supposed confession is all about, but Lisa has told her to absolutely keep her mouth shut. Lisa steps up alongside Steve, who gives her a nod. Penny imagines Lisa is nervous, since this is her courtroom debut, yet she projects strength with her tailored blue suit and black stiletto heels.

Lisa asks the prosecutor, "Do you have a witness to this confession?" Both Penny and Lisa clearly expect that the answer is no, and that this will prompt the judge to dismiss the case.

"Yes, we do," says the prosecutor.

The judge says, "The defendant is bound over to the district court for trial."

PART FOUR

Grief

20

THE PONY

FOLLOW THE rat down the alley toward the fairgrounds. He scampers above me along the telephone wires, leaping onto rooftops and tree limbs. It's getting dark and fortunately the humans are all inside. I pass their lighted windows and see them watching their screens. One woman with a dachshund is coming out of her front gate and the dachshund barks and the lady's eyes get wide when she sees me, but she's afraid and yanks the dog back and I cross the street and trot off and she doesn't run after me. The rat and I turn left into a quiet street and I trot along another sidewalk, and then the sidewalk ends and I walk along the edge of a road, avoiding headlights. Fortunately it's quite dark now and the races are over for the day so the fairground and the big dirt parking lots all around it are empty.

The rat knows exactly where there is a pony-sized hole in the fence and we slink through the chain-link entrance to the fairgrounds. "I gotta give it to you rats. You really are the smartest animals. I've never met a dolphin, but that's a battle of wits I'd like to see."

"You ponies are no dummies, either. How are you going to convince the humans to take you to Saratoga?"

This is where I spring on him what my superpower is. "I'll make it seem like it's their idea."

The rat doesn't seem as impressed as I'd hoped. In fact, he chuckles.

"Humans. They always think something is their idea, even when it's totally set in motion by us."

"No, really. This is something I've been practicing for years. I haven't perfected it, but if I stare at a human intently, sometimes I can put an idea into their heads."

"Interesting. What kind of ideas?"

"To give me food, usually."

He laughs, which takes some of the wind out of my sails. "Rats have been working on that one for a while now. Take the invention of the kitchen cupboard. Totally designed by rats to keep our food clean and dry, but built by humans who thought it was their idea."

"Okay, that is kind of impressive, but—"

"And the subway system? A way for rats to travel underground efficiently and easily. The humans think it was their idea and we just happened to take to it. Same for dumpsters. We put the idea into their heads and then they build it. Easy peasy."

"I'm going to show you. If I really concentrate, I can make them do what I want."

"I can't wait to see you in action," says the rat.

I can smell the horses in the barn now. They do smell high-strung. "Have any of the horses going to Saratoga recently lost an animal companion?"

"Yes. One of the colts lost his chicken. It was eaten by a hawk."

"Perfect. Point me in that horse's direction and I will work my magic."

The rat leads me to a big barn. I head down the center aisle. The rat is scampering along the electrical wire that runs the length of the barn above us. A tall man in a cowboy hat who smells like tobacco frowns as I walk by.

"Where'd that pony come from?" he calls to another man, who is short and has a checkered shirt and smells like soap. I stare at the man who smells like soap and form the idea that I was dumped here by someone who didn't want me. I send that idea to the man's brain.

"I don't know. Maybe someone dumped him here," the guy says.

I gasp. "Oh my God, it's working," I say to the rat. A shiver runs over me.

The long barn aisle has that fairgrounds feel to it, like it will all be disassembled tomorrow. But right now it's a series of wood and metal stalls with tall horses sticking their heads out in curiosity. Some of them ignore me, but others call out as I walk past.

"Howdy," calls a gray horse.

"Hey, short stop," calls a bay mare. I give her a shake of my forelock.

"The next one is him," calls the rat, but I already know this. I can smell it. Grief. I stop in front of a stall. It's the only one that doesn't have the Dutch door open.

"That's weird," says the shorter man, who has come up behind me.

"It's like he knew," says the man who smells like tobacco. He unlatches and swings open the top half of the stall door.

I see a huge chestnut colt pawing and pacing in the stall, clacking his teeth together in frustration. He's worn a path down to the dirt, and all the fluffy white shavings are piled up on the sides around him, as if watching the spectacle of his displeasure. Christmas music plays from a small radio next to the wheelbarrow outside the stall. Without looking at us, the big colt reaches out a delicate hind leg and cracks his hoof against the plywood of his stall.

"Rat?" I call out. "Rat? I don't like the looks of this. Any other horses headed to Saratoga?"

"Just him," says the rat.

The chestnut colt rears and paces in his stall.

"Change of plan," I start to say, but the tall man has grabbed my halter.

I send the thought *This is not the pony we want!* as hard as I can into his brain. *Let's let him go!*

But the tall guy keeps holding my halter and says to the other man, "If this doesn't work, we'll call Animal Control and see if someone reported a lost pony. If it does work . . . finders keepers."

You think ponies have fungible ethics? Have you met a human? They can rationalize *anything*.

"Help, rat, help! This horse is going to kill me!" I say.

The rat thinks this is funny. "Do your Vulcan mind meld, dude."

Now the tall man and the rat are both whispering to me at the same time. Their words merge in my head so I can't form any thoughts of my own. "Listen, pony. This horse was strangely devoted to Freddie the Chicken. With Freddie by his side, the colt slept, ate, and ran fast. Freddie was his best friend, pacifier, and guru from the day they met at the stable where the big colt was foaled. Freddie traveled with him everywhere he went except onto the racetrack itself." The man pauses and pets my neck. The rat adds, "Plus Freddie was a hoot—he and I liked to make a wager or two. And I warned him about teasing that hawk, but . . ."

The big red colt pins his ears back. "He doesn't look very friendly," I say.

"Since Freddie passed, he's slid downhill. We're all afraid he's going to hurt himself. The humans have tried a goat, a dog, a radio, a TV, and they even made one of the trainer's assistants put a cot in the stall and sleep there, poor sucker. The horse will not settle."

I'm terrified, but I also feel bad for this big sad horse. "He needs to go home to his farm and be out in a pasture with a herd of other horses so he has time to process this loss," I say. "He shouldn't be under pressure to race while he's grieving."

The rat rolls his eyes. "I don't think you're getting through to them. To them the big horse ain't a family member to be nurtured, he's an investment. And to you, he's a ticket to Saratoga. Don't lose your focus. Didn't you say you gotta find that Penny person?"

"Yes," I say. My body gets a little jolt from her name, as if I have touched an electric fence.

"Do you love her?" asks the rat.

"Love?" I shake my head as if a fly is on my ear. As I tried to say to Caya, I don't understand all the hoopla around the word *love*. I love carrots because they taste so good. But love something other than food? Makes no sense to me. I say to the rat, "I just . . . I can't explain it, but I have to make things right with her. Then I can go back to just being myself. The way it was before, just thinking about food."

The rat nods.

"His season will be over if he comes up lame from all this pacing," says the trainer, and the other man nods. I get it. The subtext is no more racing, and no jobs for this down-on-his-luck trainer and his assistant.

"The pony is our last hope," says the short man to the tall man.

The giant red horse cavorts around, nostrils wide.

"Hey, big guy," I say, trying to keep it light. "What's up besides the price of hay?"

The horse stops leaping and comes over to me, sticking his head and neck over the half door and looking down at the top of my head.

"Freddie?" the big colt says, as I reach my nose up to his.

"You can call me anything you want," I say soothingly. "I know you're grieving. I'm sad myself."

The big horse stares down at me, stock-still. "You don't know what grief is," he says at last.

"I've suffered some losses," I say.

"My friend died."

"I know. Teased the wrong hawk, right?"

"Do not blame him!"

"I'm not. I'm commiserating. You feel sad, I feel sad."

"Don't even compare your feelings to mine. You have no idea."

This guy is getting on my nerves. It's like he's offended at the idea that anyone could feel pain other than him. Like he's got a monopoly on sadness.

"Others have felt what you're feeling. I knew a duck whose entire clutch of eggs got eaten by a raccoon. It gets better."

"Things will never be right again. My life is a disaster."

"Well, you're living in a nice barn, and you got a massive bucket of oats there."

The big horse lets out a long, very long, eardrum-piercing neigh, almost a scream, and stares into the distance.

"I agree. Humans are selfish. It's not convenient for them to recognize us as emotional beings. Though I see they've padded your stall," I say before I can stop myself. "But you're just sad, you're not . . . crazy, right?"

The horse thrashes around the stall. "I'M. NOT. CRAZY!" he neighs so loud that my forelock and mane blow back.

"I don't like to judge—" I whisper to the rat.

"I hear you love to judge," says the rat.

"Okay, I do love to judge. I love it, but I am trying to be a better pony. Mental health is a gift I am blessed with, and others are not so lucky. This guy was probably hypersensitive, narcissistic, and anxious before his friend died, and now he's having a full-blown nervous breakdown. This is what happens when you breed animals for speed and not temperament. It's sad, but also annoying."

"Sar-a-toga," sings the rat to the tune of "Oklahoma."

The big horse snorts in my face.

"Okay, okay, settle down, champ. I didn't mean anything by it."

"I want Freddie," neighs the horse again.

"Put the pony in there," says the tall trainer.

"Whoa, whoa, whoa," I say, even though I know the man will not understand me. All the trainer hears is a throttled squeal as I try to back away down the barn aisle.

The Thoroughbred leaps and churns in the stall, wild with grief and loneliness, his hooves four sharp weapons. Reason, logic, and empathy are absent in his brain. I definitely do not want to be in there with him.

"There must be another way to get to Saratoga!" I shout to the rat.

"We could rent a car, I guess," says the rat as the trainer's assistant opens the door and together the two men shove me into the stall.

I press myself as close to the stall door as possible as hooves fly around my head. I close my eyes and shrink even smaller in size. The big red horse rears and bucks and kicks until he's covered with lather. Finally, there is silence. I open one eye.

"You done?"

The horse pants, puts his ears back, and shows his teeth. "You're not Freddie."

"Maybe I'm better. Give me a try. You're not Penny, but I'm willing to get to know you. You gonna eat that?" I take a step toward the oats in the feeder. "I mean, c'mon, it's Christm—"

Thwack. I'm thrown back against the stall door. I have just enough time to mutter "asssss" before it all goes black.

21

PENNY

LISA IS TALKING into the gray phone and staring at Penny through the chicken-wire glass. It's really important that Penny concentrate on what Lisa is saying, but the phone is doing that snap-crackle-pop thing, which is adding to the fact that what Lisa is saying isn't making any sense.

"It was your therapist," Lisa says again. She looks down at her floral notebook. "Dr. Resa? She said you confessed to her that you killed Frank Ross."

"What?" Penny needs to start counting the number of times she has been gobsmacked since the day of her arrest. Is this just a bad dream? Some kind of crazy hidden-camera reality show? Because it keeps getting weirder and weirder. "I never said that." Penny feels rage course through her. "Can she just do that? Say that I said something I never said and get me locked up in jail?"

"Therapists in California are mandated reporters, so she's under a legal obligation to report any crimes to law enforcement. I guess she told the police that you said you killed Frank."

"But I didn't. Why would she say that?" Hot tears of frustration fill Penny's eyes.

Lisa looks as comforting as someone can through an inch of cracked plastic. "I'm sorry," she says. "So this doctor is lying?"

"Yes, she's lying. Or maybe she misunderstood? I don't know. Can you look into that? I mean, who is she?" Penny tries to think about everything she knows about this therapist who was assigned to her by her health insurance. Zoom therapy. It was supposed to be such a great option for busy families. She knows nothing about the woman, she realizes. Nothing.

"What was the context in which you talked to her about the death of Frank?"

Penny tries to remember details. "I started seeing her about a year ago, when we were deciding whether to send my daughter Tella away to Arcadia, a facility for girls with mental health issues. I was really upset, of course. I felt like a failure as a mother. Why couldn't I make my kid better, right? We did some family therapy, and Tella did a lot of one-on-one. But I talked to Dr. Resa on my own, too, you know, just to try to sort through everything I was feeling. She seemed really helpful." *God*, Penny thinks. *I trusted her completely.*

"Did she ask you about Frank's death? Or did it come up organically?"

Penny tries to remember. "She asked me about my own childhood, my relationship with my mom and dad, what kind of parents they were. I told her about how devastated I was when they sold my pony, how I resented them for years after that. She asked why my parents and I moved away from Ithaca so suddenly, so I told her about Frank's death and why I never got to see the pony again."

Penny remembers telling Dr. Resa about how furious she was with her own parents when they uprooted her and plunked her into a new city, a new school. She was afraid to do that to Tella. She recalls telling Dr. Resa how it was only when she was a mother herself that her mom and dad's decision to move started to make more sense. *I mean, as a parent myself, the idea that one night you get a call to come to the hospital and find your twelve-year-old daughter there covered in blood, surrounded by police, a person of interest in a murder case . . .*

Lisa nods and takes notes. "I can talk to her, ask her if she was mistaken."

"I just don't get why she would say that," Penny says. "Maybe she's crazy. Maybe she wants to hurt me." Her mind races, all the things she'd said during their sessions. Had the woman been crafting her plan all along? Waiting for some way to attack? Penny felt so stupid, so dumbly trusting, like a lapdog.

"Listen," says Lisa as loud bells ring, echoing through the room. They ring all the time, but Penny still jumps. "The good news is that we're scheduled to go to trial in December."

"December?" That's good news?

"But I just want to warn you that it's pretty common for these things to get postponed."

"For how long? How long am I going to be in here?"

Lisa took a deep breath. "I just read about this for an online class I'm taking. It's pretty depressing. About four hundred thousand people are currently awaiting trial in the U.S. Most cases take about seven to eight months to go to trial."

Penny just sits there in shock.

"It's not ideal, I know," says Lisa. "But that does give us time to prepare your defense. Take statements from witnesses on your behalf, find holes in the other side's case."

Penny's voice is quiet. "You're getting me off, right? This therapist's word isn't enough evidence to convict me, is it?" She feels hollow inside.

Lisa doesn't smile. "Steve is very good, but he has a lot of cases right now. He'll definitely come talk to you before the trial, though, at least once."

Oh my God, thinks Penny. *This is the American way of justice?* And also a new realization. *Everyone thinks I'm guilty.*

She wants to roll into the fetal position but knows that will only get her kicked and beaten and carried back to her cell.

Lisa goes on. "We need some character witnesses who know you well who can say that you definitely did not do this, that you would have told them if you did."

"My husband."

"It's better if they're not relatives. You're a teacher, right? Would your principal, maybe other teachers, if we sat them down in a deposition, say that you're an amazing, nice person who would never in a million years do this? Have you won any awards? Teacher of the Year? Neighbor of the Year? Anything that would help show the jury that you are just another upstanding person like them?"

Lisa is going to call up her boss? Her neighbors? "Does everyone have to know about this?"

Lisa looks pained. "It's been covered in the press already. A cold case like this, crime solved after twenty-five years, people think it's kinda fun."

Fun. *Killer Tot Nabbed after Secret Life on the Lam? 3rd Grade Teacher Unmasked as Former Demon Child?*

Lisa raps a knuckle on the glass to get Penny's attention. "Who should I call who will testify on your behalf?"

Penny sighs. "I'm kind of a loner."

Lisa flinches. "Don't use that word, okay?"

"I mean, I'm a private person. I'm a good teacher, they would definitely say that. But with Tella's illness . . . Maybe I haven't always been as warm and fuzzy as I should have been. I've been so tired." Penny can't stop herself from crying again. "It's just a lot," she says. "I know you're trying to help me."

"It's okay," says Lisa, and her eyes are indeed kind. "I can't even imagine what you're going through. I'm going to do some digging and come back soon, okay?"

PENNY HAS BEEN curled up for hours, weeping. Regressive crying, Dr. Resa called it. She's completely exhausted but her mind is racing. She stretches out on her bunk and thinks about her conversations with Dr. Resa. She seemed so nice. Perky. Chirpy. Supportive. Why is she lying? Penny remembers reading that people with mental health problems are drawn to being therapists. Maybe she told her deepest feelings and fears to a psychopath. Maybe Dr. Resa is really crazy.

She reminds herself not to use that word. As the parent of a mentally ill child, she knows it gets thrown around way too much. Perhaps Dr. Resa has some mental health challenges. Or maybe she just misheard. Maybe she has another client who murdered someone when they were twelve and she mixed them up? Penny tries to remember how their last session went. It was right after she came home from dropping Tella off at boarding school. Laus had moved out. Penny felt so at sea, like such a failure. Broken. Dr. Resa asked her when she was last truly happy.

"With my pony," Penny had said. It felt shameful to admit that, but it was true. It was the last time she had felt whole. Honest. Calm. Confident. Strong.

"That's a long time ago," said Dr. Resa.

"Twenty-five years." She'd suppressed a little sob, tried to swallow the lump in her throat.

"Close your eyes. Let's do some breath work. Tell me what the pony meant to you," Dr. Resa said.

Penny had begun the deep breaths Dr. Resa had taught her. Time slowed. It felt hypnotic, dreamlike, like she was in two places at once, the past and the present. She remembers coming out of it and saying, "My pony was my best friend. And then I was ripped away from him. It was agonizing. Like my arm had been torn off. More than an arm. Like half of me. Half of my brain and my heart and my stomach and a lung and a kidney and a leg."

She opened her eyes and Dr. Resa just kind of said, "Hmm," like maybe she was thinking about what she was going to make for dinner.

Penny had kept talking anyway. After all, the shrink was getting paid to listen. "And I couldn't, you know, call him up, write him a letter. Find out how he was doing. Tell him I missed him. The idea that he was just out there somewhere . . . Anyway, it was like a torture to me. I cried a lot."

Dr. Resa said, "So you never looked up old news stories about the murder? Little internet sleuthing? Whether the police caught the person who bashed that guy's head in?"

Penny remembers staring at Dr. Resa's image on-screen for a second. The shrink's eyes were not on the camera. They were slightly to the left. How did she know how Frank died? "Are you looking it up right now?" Penny asked her.

PART FIVE

Insecurity

22

THE PONY

THAT'S HOW I end up on the Thoroughbred racing circuit. The big red horse, after nearly bashing my head in, does sort of accept me as his new emotional support chicken. Well, who he really takes to is the rat, so I'm kind of just the third wheel. The horse needs the rat, and the rat needs my oats, and I need to get to Saratoga, so we all make do. The rat has to stay out of sight of the humans, who really spend a lot of time brushing and combing and worrying about and cleaning up after equines, but they kill rodents on sight, which makes no sense since rodents are smarter and cleaner and would make great racing animals, but who am I to complain?

The horse's name is Burning Flames, but I call him Burnie. He and the rat have long conversations—this horse really likes to talk about himself—and I eavesdrop on them. What choice do I have? We are all stuck in a small space together. The horse was foaled in Kentucky but wasn't quite fast enough for the stakes races. He doesn't say that—"I chose not to humiliate the other horses by going top speed," he says—but I read between the lines. A claiming race here and a claiming race there and Burnie found himself with the tall trainer, whose name is Joel. The shorter man is Mike, the assistant-trainer-slash-groom. They're very good with Burnie, who's kind of a nervous wreck. They are always patient and kind, even when he flips out at a flying plastic bag or panics in the starting gate. Not all humans are like that, let me tell you.

They've got a story, too, of course, as everyone does. I'm not super interested in them except at mealtime, but the rat is fascinated by everyone, it seems. "Joel is married to Nancy," says the rat as we are lying in the deep shavings one night. The horse, tired from the day's workout, is sound asleep and snoring. "Nancy's back in Ohio with the kiddies and keeps bugging Joel to send money, which is understandable, because I get the same complaints from the mothers of my children. 'Send more cotton for nest material. Can you drag home a slice of apple pie for Junior's birthday?' Anyway, Nancy doesn't know that Mike and Joel are in love. She knows they travel back and forth across the country together for eleven months of the year, but she thinks they're just coworkers and friends."

"What does this love thing look like?" I ask the rat.

"It's obvious. I've had my share of migration affairs," says the pigeon in the rafters above us.

"I've been trying to convince Joel to find the courage to tell Nancy," says the rat.

"Just out of curiosity, how are you going about that?" I ask. This rat is something else.

"You could use your mind powers on him," the rat teases.

"I only act out of self-interest," I say.

"Be that way. I keep taking the photo of her in his drawer and leaving it out on the kitchen table. Near it I leave things I've chewed out of newspapers and magazines and other things in the trash that seem relevant. Horoscopes that say 'tell others the truth this week,' and yesterday a review of a new book about overcoming fear and shame. I even replaced his shaving cream with one I found called Pride."

"Why are you doing that?"

"Mike and Joel are ashamed of who they are, insecure and afraid of what others think."

"That's because humans like to kill each other and us," I point out. "They hate and fear anyone who is different."

"We can't live our lives ruled by fear. Mike and Joel are going to be so much happier when they come out and live their true selves. But we can't rush them. People need to grow at their own pace." This rat should have his own daytime TV show.

"You actually care about all of this?" I say. "You spend time thinking about these humans?"

The rat laughs. "Get real. I'm working the angles. Joel is popping antacids like candy and his temper is short and he feels stressed all the time. He's transmitting his anxiety to the horse, and that's keeping Burnie from running at his best. Right now every animal in the barn thinks Burnie is an anxious self-defeating loser and they're betting against him. I plan on getting him in top form on the sly and then cashing in." He calls into the rafters, "You keep your mouth shut, pigeon, or I will eat your eggs for breakfast."

The pigeon flutters in fear.

"Phew," I say. "I thought for a second you actually gave a crap about some human 'love' story." Now I'm the one doing air quotes.

"Shoot me now," he snorts. "I'm in it for the money."

The rat gives the horse pep talks every morning before his workouts. "Feel your strength. Feel your power. It's a fire within you. Contain it until you need it." Every week on Saturday Burnie runs a race. He usually comes in second or third, fast enough to make some money, but not fast enough to win the top prize. Joel and Mike console each other over a beer or two and talk about some unnamed future time when they'll have a stable full of winning horses.

Sometimes I watch them when they're in the barn together, to find evidence to show the rat that love is not a real thing. I study the way Mike looks at Joel as he rolls the polo wraps, and the way Joel looks at Mike as he oils the saddles. I'm a grown pony and I've seen plenty of animals in the throes of the mating dance. That's there between Mike and Joel, but I have to admit, there's something more to it. They remind me of a pair of swans I knew who lived in a pond in a city park near the Birthday Pony Ride Guy's house. One day a drunken boater rowed up and tried to grab the female swan. The male swan, who could have just avoided the action, threw himself between the human and his mate, to save her. The human strangled the male swan, right there in cold blood. He was going for the female, too, when a park ranger grabbed him. The female swan, Bridget, was unharmed but inconsolable, swimming around making these sad squeaking sounds. Even though there were other very attractive swans she could have paired off with, she raised the cygnets on her own and once they fledged she just stopped eating and died.

"Mike and Joel seem to have that kind of pair bond where they would do anything for the other person," I say to the rat with a dismissive snort. "Like the other person makes life worth living, more than even food."

"Stupid, right?" says the rat, eyeing me closely.

"Sure is," I say, not sure why I am avoiding the rat's gaze.

"That's love, you know," he says.

"Hope I don't catch it," I say, staring at a spiderweb in a corner of the stall.

"Amen, brother," he says. "Love will mess you up."

Every Sunday we all pack up and climb in the trailer and hit the highway to the next race meet. By Monday or Tuesday we're there, and we unload into another temporary stall and Burnie gets a few workouts on the track and runs a race and the cycle starts again.

"He's almost ready," whispers the rat to me. "Saratoga is where it's going to happen."

"He's going to win?"

The rat nods and puts a paw to his lips. "Keep that on the down low."

The rat tells me that the horse is owned by a man who has never seen him in person.

"I thought he was owned by Joel?"

"You gotta pay closer attention, pony. Joel is the trainer. Mike is the assistant trainer. Larry is the owner."

"Who's Larry?"

"I just told you. The owner." The rat overheard Mike and Joel talking about Larry one night while stealing tortilla chips from their kitchen and placing a photo of Elton John on the night table. "Larry's some kind of medium big shot in the human world, or thinks he is," the rat tells me. "He likes to brag about his racehorse. Mike and Joel send him videos of the horse all the time. His share prices are going up and down apparently, and they're worried he's going to cut them loose."

"What are share prices? Is that like us, how we share our food?"

The rat shrugs. "The humans value certain pieces of paper and their plastic cards the same way you and I value food and a warm place to sleep. Makes no sense to me, but to each his own."

The rat continues to psychoanalyze the horse. I doze as the horse talks about himself for hours, all his insecurities, all his feelings of envy at the speed of other horses, their confidence, their shiny coats and fluffy manes and tails.

"Is this really adding up to anything?" I ask the rat when the horse is out for a workout.

"It's all about getting him to recognize his own innate worth," says the rat. "That's the source of his insecurity, that he doesn't see himself as worthy of being loved for himself. He thinks it's all about winning. Paradoxically, he won't win a race until he doesn't care about winning anymore."

"Maybe he shouldn't be a racehorse. He's only three years old. Still a baby. If horse breeders had ethics he'd still be back where he was born, racing nothing but other colts in green pastures. His bones aren't even done growing yet, much less his mind, and he's racing every other week at three hundred racetracks in forty states."

"He lives for it," says the rat.

"He gets ulcer meds every day and lives in a box."

"It's a hard-knock life," says the rat. "You can't insulate yourself from stress. You gotta learn how to cope with it. Instead of wishing for a perfect life, live the life you have. Be happy now." When he finishes talking, he takes an extra mouthful of oats from my side of the bucket.

"Hey!" I complain.

"I'm worth it," he says.

23

PENNY

THERE'S A COVID case in the jail and they abruptly cancel visiting hours and recreation and group mealtimes. The inmates are locked in their cells at all times, with no way of knowing how long this will last.

Penny feels fine. She wonders if there even is a COVID case, or if this is just a break for the staff. Keeping inmates in individual boxes is much easier on them. It's why most people don't keep horses in herds, even though that's the natural way for them to live. Out in a pasture, horses battle for supremacy, bite and kick each other, stick their feet in squirrel holes, get career-ending sprains or even fatally break their legs, run through fences, and get into unimaginable amounts of trouble. In stalls, they are clean, separate, still, eating prescribed amounts of food. And most of the time, miserable and bored as hell.

"I'm Dawn," Penny hears one day. It's the woman in the cell next to hers. They've spoken about their kids but never introduced themselves. "Like Tony Orlando's backup singers."

Penny hasn't said her name to anyone in here. "I'm Penny," she says through the grate. "Like the coin. I'm sorry I can't shake your hand."

"Put your eye up against the window." Penny does, and Dawn sticks her fingers out of the grate on her own cell door and waggles them at Penny. Penny sees rose pink fingernails. Penny does the same with her own stubby fingers, each topped with a bitten-down, colorless nail. "How is your son?" Penny asks. "Did you get a chance to talk to him?"

"I decided to let my mom handle it," says Dawn. "She says he's good. But I miss him so much."

"Same. I don't think I ever understood how hard this is, being locked up. I know that sounds dumb."

"A little," says Dawn. "I mean, it's jail."

"I guess I thought, 'well, at least in jail you don't have to cook your own food or choose your clothes or make any decisions.' Like somehow that might be a relief. It's not a relief."

"Nope."

"I have no purpose here," says Penny. "My life is completely empty of meaning."

Dawn, who seems to have quite a bit of previous incarceration experience, gives her some advice: "Think of a really good day and then go visit it in your head, you know, like the day your daughter was born."

She doesn't tell Dawn that although she loves Tella with every fiber of her being and would die to protect her, if she's being honest, her *happiest* memory was from before the onset of adult responsibilities. Pick a day, any day with her pony. The feel of his warm furry body under her, the smell of his skin in the whorl under his mane, the sensation of flying, of being out of control, having to trust that he wouldn't kill her, the sound of him neighing for her when she came into the barn, the way he came running when she called him, the way she would reach down and scratch the itchy spot under his belly or the base of his tail, the way he would in return tickle the nape of her neck with his stubbly nose. Every single day with him was hilarious and fun and thrilling and wonderful.

That was why she'd wanted to find him so badly.

That was why she'd gone back to Ithaca.

24

THE PONY

S O WHY ARE you trying to find this Penny person?" asks Burnie as we are speeding down a highway that looks like every other highway we've sped down. Burnie has a fancy leather halter with sheepskin padding and partitions to lean against and a window to look out and a giant hay bag. The rat and I are sandwiched between some hay bales and aluminum trash cans filled with grain. They are inconveniently padlocked and bungeed into place, but Joel and Mike are not stingy with the rations, so I'm not complaining, even though the rat always seems to end up with the lion's share. If I rear up and put my hooves against the side of the trailer, I can just barely see out the window.

I realize in our months together, this is the first time Burnie has ever asked me about myself. It's the first time he's ever shown genuine interest in anyone other than himself.

"Well, it's complicated," I tell him.

"We've got six hours until our next stop," says the red colt. "It's this or license plate bingo. So what's Penny to you? Do you love her?"

"Don't be gross."

"Love doesn't have to be about mating," Burnie says, giving me a little nip. "You can truly deeply love someone just for themselves. Because they're wonderful and you can see that."

Horses are so dumb, and this one takes the cake. "I just need to find out if she's okay."

"Is that your job?"

I think about this. The question says a lot about how the horse views the world—in terms of purpose. His purpose in life is simple—to win races. I haven't really thought about myself this way before, but I try. Was my purpose to carry Penny around? I think about the days we spent lounging under the big oak tree, when she braided my mane and read me poetry.

> Like the sweet apple which reddens upon the topmost
>   bough,
> Atop on the topmost twig,—which the pluckers forgot,
>   somehow,—
> Forget it not, nay; but got it not, for none could get it till
>   now.

"Well. I guess my job was to be her best friend, and I failed at it. So yeah, it's just a work thing, not about feelings or anything like that."

We hit a pothole and all of us—me, the horse, and the rat—are tossed in the air for a second, then land back where we were. The rat, nested in my haynet, doesn't even wake up.

"I used to think my purpose was to win races," says the big horse kindly. "And so it drove me crazy when I lost. Like the other day at Fonner Park when that big gray nosed past me at the finish line. But then I realized something. My purpose is to run as fast as I can. It's out of my hands whether the other horses run faster than me or not. All I can control is my own effort."

I have to admit I'm impressed by the work the rat has done on this horse.

"It's okay," the horse continues. "You'll try again. You'll find Penny and try again."

I wonder if he knows that one day his racing career will come to an end, that he will have to find a purpose other than running fast. He's so young and strong and happy and confident in the feel of his lithe, agile body—I can't tell him that this particular joy will cease someday, that his body will fail him, but there might be other joys, other purposes beyond it. He won't be able to imagine that.

"Do you ever miss nature?" I ask him. "You go from the truck to the stall to the track. Do you miss green fields and fresh air and just being loose?"

"I can't remember that," he says. "So I don't think about it. I'm just trying to enjoy what's happening now. I'm trying to be more observant and appreciative of what's good in my life. The connections I'm making with people like Dr. Rat and Mike and Joel and you."

The brakes squeal as we get to our exit and the rat is tossed out of the haynet onto the shavings as we decelerate. He stretches his arms and yawns.

"Next stop Saratoga Springs," says the rat. "In my home state of New York."

I'M FILLED WITH excitement as we unload from the trailer and Joel and Mike lead the big horse and me to our assigned stall in the historic barn area called Horse Haven. "This racetrack dates back to the Civil War," says the rat.

"What's the Civil War?"

"I don't know, but the humans always say that. It's old, I guess."

I neigh hello to all the horses hanging their heads out of the stalls, but mostly I sniff and sniff and sniff for the scent of Penny.

"Big day tomorrow, buddy," says Joel to the horse as he pats his shiny copper neck. The horse snorts and shakes his head.

Trotting along behind them, I start chatting up the sparrows swirling around the barns. "Have you been to the forest with the blue butterflies?" I ask over and over. Finally, one little sparrow swivels its head and says "Yes!" I stop and she swoops down to talk to me.

"Where can I find it?"

Mike yanks on my lead rope. "Come on, Sidekick," he says. That's what Mike and Joel call me. He yanks again. Humans are so bossy. I try to compel him to stop for a second, but he just keeps dragging me along.

"I'll show you," calls out the sparrow. "But I'm going to bed now. Get free tomorrow and meet me by my nest under the grandstand. My name is Fifi."

The big horse and I are closed into our stall for the night with our hay and grain rations. The rat drops down from the pipes overhead and lands in my feed bucket.

"Penny's close by," I tell him. I can hardly contain myself. I'm so excited I can barely eat, though I make myself eat because I need strength for whatever comes next. I want to go to the sparrow right now, but if I bust out of here and get waylaid by humans, I could blow the whole thing. Plus, birds get really pissed off when you bother them at night. "I need to wait for the right moment to exit the stall and go to the grandstand and find her," I say, thinking out loud.

"Tomorrow," says the rat. "During the race when Mike and Joel are busy. That's your best moment to slip out."

25

PENNY

"YOU BEEN TALKING to Dawn," says a guard to Penny one day. The guard is a tall woman with a platinum blond crew cut, red lipstick, and huge biceps. She's standing outside Penny's cell and looking at Penny through the narrow window. "She's out in the exercise yard now," the guard adds.

"We've talked a little. Is that okay?" says Penny. Has she broken a rule? Bad things happen when you break rules.

"Suit yourself," says the guard. "But you should know she's a real frequent flyer. Back in here this time accused of something really awful."

"I don't want to know," says Penny.

"Been in and out of the system for almost forty years."

"Forty years?" Penny can't fathom that number. Forty years of staring at cinder-block walls?

"Yup. If you ask me, she's certifiably crazy."

"I don't like that word," says Penny reflexively. The guard gives a little eye roll and moves off, and Penny worries that she's offended her. There could be consequences for that, like a pony who bucks off the wrong little rider.

Penny thinks about Tella and her heart aches. People are often compassionate when someone has a physical issue that affects their heart or lungs, but they cross the street to avoid someone who is struggling with their brain, which is just another organ. Penny would get furious when other children ostracized Tella when she heard things they didn't hear, or when a teacher lost patience with Tella's outbursts. And yet Penny herself often struggled to connect with Tella. Tella hated to be touched and would recoil from Penny, and had once said that the sound of Penny's voice was like razor blades in her ears. Penny told herself Tella didn't mean it, but it still hurt.

And a year ago, when Tella was twelve and Penny suggested other ways of behaving, Tella accused her of trying to change her.

"You don't love me as I am!" Tella had shouted. "You only love this imaginary person you think I should become. This *normal* person! You love your imaginary normal daughter, not me."

Penny had been silenced by this, because it rang true. A wave of guilt passed over her. She did imagine them finding some path forward, some treatment that would turn Tella into a confident, calm young woman. A normal young woman. But that didn't mean she didn't love Tella. She remembers standing in the living room of their house, trying to find something to say. Tella's hair was flying around and her eyes were intense, like a fox.

"You don't want to change?" Penny finally asked. "You're okay with living like this? Because if that's true . . ."

"What?" Tella said. "You'll kick me to the curb? Put me out with the trash?"

"No. I'll figure out how to build a life for us where you can just be yourself." Penny pictured moving somewhere remote and letting Tella live however she wanted to. She could run wild. Far from the constraints of civilization, where people expect you to make eye contact and not talk to yourself. "We could move to Alaska," Penny said.

"Mom, those movies always end with people being eaten by grizzly bears."

Penny laughs, and Tella actually laughs with her. Then Tella turns her beautiful face to Penny and asks a heartbreaking question. "Do you think people can change?"

"Of course," Penny says. "We're all changing and growing all the time."

"No, really," Tella says. "Do you think I can be different?"

26

THE PONY

RACE DAY DAWNS and everyone is excited. Mike grooms the big red horse with a series of mitts, brushes, and cloths until he shines like a copper—

Penny.

I can think of nothing but how close I am to finding Penny. Finding her will make the guilt that's like an ache inside me go away so I can just focus on eating again.

Mike saddles the horse, who's so keyed up he dances. "Calm down, Fred Astaire," says Mike softly. "Save your energy for the race." We all like Mike the best—he speaks in little more than a whisper most of the time and usually has a pocket full of mints he's willing to share.

Joel appears with Burnie's saddle over his arm and hands it to Mike. "That's one shiny horse," he says admiringly.

"I wish it wasn't a claimer," says Mike. "He looks so good today."

Joel nods. "Wasn't my choice either," he says, petting the horse's neck and letting his hand stray to Mike's for a second before he pulls it away. "But we've taken chances before and no one's claimed him."

Mike whispers, "So Nancy's going to be here soon, huh?"

Joel averts his eyes and nods.

Mike brushes a final speck of dust off the horse. "I'm just gonna . . . be up in the grandstand." He hands the saddle back to Joel.

Joel takes it and nods. "Thank you."

Mike walks away down the barn aisle alone. Joel kicks a hay bale.

There's a lot of pain in the air, and the horse stamps his foot. "I don't like it," he says to me. "I don't like it at all."

"Focus on yourself," calls the rat from overhead. "Let them work out their own problems."

"I hear you," says the horse. "But Mike should be by my side today, too. We should all be together. I want you there, too, pony."

Joel goes to lead the horse out, but the horse thrashes and rears.

"Whatsa matter, buddy?" asks Joel. "You've been so good lately and now today you're causing problems?"

The horse neighs for me. "I want you there!" calls the horse. "If I can't have my rat because of these stupid rodent-hating humans, I want my pony!"

I look up at the rat. "I have other plans. You know that. That bird could fly away at any second. Or get eaten by a hawk."

The rat puts his little hands together. "Please. He needs you. I need you."

"I am a pony and we are by nature selfish and mean," I remind the rat.

"People can change," he says. "Empathy is painful and inconvenient, but it also can bring us a much deeper joy than material things, even carrots."

I sigh and say, "This does not constitute agreement," as I open the stall door and trot over to the horse, who instantly calms down and gives me a big sloppy lick on the ear.

"Eeew," I squeal.

Joel watches all this in wonder and confusion. "Would you look at that?" he says.

The three of us—me, the horse, and Joel—head for the track, the rat calling encouragement from the rafters. "I'll be watching!" he calls to the horse.

The horse stops and turns back. "I love you!" he calls to the rat.

I turn and see the expression on the rat's face. Ears up, eyes wide, mouth open. I knew it. He's become like those damn swans.

I turn back to study the horse. He waits for a second, then turns back toward the track, a shadow in his eyes. Love is such a precarious thing. I want no part of it. Pain and grief are the price of love, and that's just too expensive in my book.

Still, I feel for the big sap of a horse, having lost his heart to a rat. "You caught him off guard is all," I say to the horse. "You know how he is."

I STAY WITH Joel and Burnie until the jockey is up. Then Joel hands the horse off to an outrider on a big black-and-white pinto named George. Each one of George's feet is five times the size of mine.

I realize it's up to me to give the horse the final push he needs. And you know how I feel about helping someone other than myself. Not my bag. But I make an effort to imagine what might help the big red horse.

I canter alongside giant George. "Go run your heart out," I tell Burnie. "Don't even look at the other horses. Just have fun out there, friend."

Burnie nods and prances next to the lumbering George. "I will, friend," he neighs.

"Take good care of him," I tell George as Joel leads me the other direction through a gate into the infield. Burnie looks amazing—rippling muscles under his copper coat. And the best part is, he's smiling.

How weird that I noticed that, and that it makes me smile, too. I gotta find that sparrow and get the hell out of here before I go all soft inside.

"He feels different today," calls the jockey to Joel.

"Yippeee!" calls Burnie. "I am loving life! Having a happy flash!"

Once we are on the infield, Joel finds a spot on the rail and leans on it while I nibble on some grass. Eating reminds me that I am still, thank God, a deliciously hateful little beast. Still even as I chew, thoughts of

Mike up in the grandstand by himself sneak into my head. He must be feeling very sad up there, I think.

Joel and I watch as Burnie is loaded into the starting gate. It's a beautiful day—crisp, cool, a little breezy. The bell rings and the horses bolt out of the gate. I jump a little even though I know it's coming, and everyone starts shouting.

"Come on, horse!" shouts Joel.

"Go, Burnie!" I neigh.

Burnie breaks well but gets boxed in behind a couple of other horses. His jockey is trying to steer him left to the inside but the hole is closing and Burnie goes right.

"Don't fight him," whispers Joel to himself.

"Just let him run," I whisper to myself.

Burnie accelerates on the outside and it looks like the other horses are standing still. He cruises past them and into the lead, and is in the lead all the way to the finish line. He wins by six lengths. The crowd is on its feet, screaming.

Joel is not a man who usually shows a lot of emotion, but he is jumping up and down. He hugs me. He and I duck under the rail and Burnie comes trotting right to us, his sides heaving and nostrils blowing.

"Did you see that? Did you see it?" says Burnie. He's so full of joy he could burst.

"Oh my," says the jockey. "He sure felt good today."

The stewards come and surround us and people are snapping photos and Joel leads the horse into the winner's circle. I follow. "You did it!" I tell Burnie.

"That was fun," says Burnie.

The jockey is weighed and Burnie gets a huge collar of flowers over his neck.

There are a lot of people around me all of a sudden and I stomp on a few toes to keep them back. "Give him space," I tell these annoying humans.

"Honey, that was amazing," says a woman who appears alongside Joel.

"Nancy," says Joel. "Thank you for coming." She has red hair and freckles and even though I want to dislike her, I can't. None of this is her fault, after all. She has a blue dress on and it looks like she got a fresh manicure.

"He was on fire today," says Joel in his low-key way. His eyes are scanning the crowd. I know who he's looking for. I can smell both guilt and shame on him.

Larry—for who else could be the monster in skinny black jeans who is holding the horse too tight?—snaps selfies of himself with Burnie. "Hashtag winning!" he crows, and I long to bite him. Finally he lets go of the bridle only to pop a champagne cork right under the horse's nose. Burnie blinks but doesn't move.

"You had every right to spook at that and run him over," I say to Burnie.

"I'm in a generous mood," says the horse.

"I'm in a generous mood," says Larry. "Here, you want a picture with this before I take it home?" He offers the big silver trophy to Joel.

It just doesn't feel right that Mike's not here. None of my business, I try to tell myself. Not important to my pursuit of Penny. But I could try to help, even though there's nothing in it for me. The rat said people need to grow at their own pace, but I am impatient and annoyed. I stare at Joel and concentrate and try to put a picture of Mike's face in Joel's head. He blinks. Is it working?

"Be right back," Joel says, and disappears into the crowd.

The announcer says, "Burning Flames has been claimed. I repeat, Burning Flames has been claimed. Will the track veterinarian retrieve the horse, please?"

"You're no longer the owner of the horse, sir," says a woman in a white coat and a stethoscope as she takes the lead rope from Larry. "He'll go under a one-hour vet hold and then if he's sound, he'll go to his new owner." The steward hands Larry a check for the claiming price.

"But . . ." says Larry. "He's worth so much more now. He won."

"I'm sorry, sir," says the steward. "That's how a claiming race works."

Joel has returned with Mike behind him.

I give a little neigh. I did it! I actually compelled these stupid humans to act.

"What the—?" says Larry to Joel. "What does she mean I no longer own the horse?"

"You told me to enter him in a claimer. I have it in writing from you." Joel holds up a piece of paper. "He got claimed."

"No effing way!" shouts Larry, even though this is a family-friendly racetrack. "Who the eff dared to buy my horse?"

"We did," says Joel. "Me and Mike. We bought him."

Nancy's eyes narrow. "You bought the horse? You and that guy?"

"Um, yeah," said Joel. "It's just a business thing."

"Yeah," says Mike. "Business."

I'm sick of this. I put my head behind Joel and give him a big shove so he hurtles into Mike. As they collide, Mike grabs him and they tumble to the ground together.

Nancy watches them, and I watch Nancy. It's like an opera on fast forward (Silla was an opera fan and I spent many Saturday afternoons listening to broadcasts from the Met on the barn radio). Her face is like *Tosca*: recognition, shock, denial, anger. And then a lot more anger. It all plays out in a matter of about three seconds.

"I knew you were cheating on me!" she shouts, and shoves Joel just as he's getting to his feet, which sends him stumbling back down again. And then she tries to kick Mike and calls him something quite nasty, even nastier than a very mean pony would say, adding, "You stole my husband!"

Larry shouts, "You stole my horse!" and punches Joel.

Then there is a level of diving, pushing, shoving, punching, hair pulling, and screaming that I have not seen since I accidentally wandered into a field of mares in heat.

Love, I think to myself. *No, thank you.*

My work here is done, so I slip out of the crowd and under the grandstand. There is a lot of trash under there. Humans are really disgusting creatures.

"Fifi?" I call. "Fifi the sparrow?"

"Here!" calls a little voice.

I wade through a confetti of tote slips, plastic cups, racing forms, plastic bags, diapers, foam containers, and more high-heeled shoes than I would have imagined.

I position myself under a nest of swirling twigs and soda straws that's angled into the corner of two beams over my head. A little brown bird is peering down at me.

"Can you take me to the forest with the blue butterflies?"

The sparrow doesn't even ask me for anything in return. Sparrows are so dumb! She helps me slip out of the racetrack complex. I dodge some humans and dart into a wooded area and race into some dense trees.

"How far is the butterfly forest?" I ask.

"About a hundred and fifty miles as the crow flies. Hundred and forty-eight as the sparrow flies. We cut corners."

I groan but start trotting. I manage to stay out of sight of the humans, away from main roads and houses. I hug the edges of the Great Sacandaga Lake, Peck Hill State Forest, and the ominously named Bear Swamp State Forest. To be honest, I don't care for bears or swamps, and I am on high alert the whole trip. I impress myself with my endurance and fortitude. I eat as I go, gobbling green grass and the tender shoots of willow trees.

"I'm tired," says Fifi the sparrow.

"I'm amazing," I say.

It's just before dawn when we get to the shore of Cayuga Lake. We're in the backyard of a big house that looks empty. The lake is vast and calm and black. My legs are tired from all the trotting and I stand in the cool water up to my knees, enjoying the icy tingle. The sparrow says, "Where you're going is on the other side of this lake. It's not very far across but it would be really far to go all the way around—the lake is long and skinny like a German shepherd's tail. Can you swim?"

"About as well as any other animal that's shaped like a barrel with very short legs and no flippers."

"Hmm. How do you feel about boats? Sometimes when I'm tired I hitch a ride on a boat." There on the shore next to us is a large wooden canoe. "Get in," says the sparrow.

I clamber into the canoe and immediately two of my hooves go through the bottom of it. "Flimsy," I sniff.

"Hmm. Try the paddleboard," says the sparrow.

As the predawn light begins to turn the lake a rosy pink, I stand tall on a paddleboard that's drifting slowly away from shore, my mane and tail blowing in a light breeze.

"What makes it go?" I ask.

"Wind. And the paddle you left on shore."

I stand there, teetering, getting farther and farther from the safety of the land while going slowly down, not across, the lake. "This was a stupid idea," I say, swishing my tail and pinning my ears. "I knew I shouldn't listen to a sparrow. Bird brain! You really messed up! Idiot!"

"You're kind of a jerk, aren't you?" says the sparrow, and she flies off.

"Wait!" I neigh. "I'm sorry!"

She doesn't return and I wonder if in future I should maybe not lash out at other creatures when something is my own dumb fault. *Ucch*, I think. I try to work up some anger and resentment, tried-and-true antidotes to the guilt and shame I'm feeling. Why can't people just accept me as I am? Penny did.

Penny. I wonder what she would think if she saw me now. I can hear the tinkle of her laugh and feel her arms around my neck. "Best pony in the world," she would say. It's not unpleasant, standing in the middle of a lake, silent and black, the sun not yet over the horizon, but I imagine soon the humans will start zipping around on boats and the sight of a paddleboarding pony will give someone pause. I can't afford to end up at Animal Control. I've got a microchip in my neck, and who knows which of my many previous owners I'm registered to? I really don't want to be sent back to any of them, especially when I'm only a few short gallops from the forest of the blue butterflies where I last saw Penny.

Waves roll toward me and the paddleboard begins to sway. I struggle to stay upright, and neigh in distress. "Helllp!"

One second I am alone and the next a flock of seagulls is circling my head. "Need a tow? Tow? Tow?" they shout. I don't really like seagulls much—they're very loud. But I nod my head.

"What's in it for us?" screeches one of the birds. These are not generous sparrows.

I think for a moment. "When we get to the other shore, I will open a dumpster for you."

"A big one?"

"Yes," I say. "A restaurant dumpster. There will be fish and chips, and bits of hamburgers and buns. And plastic!"

"We love plastic!"

"I'll hook you up. I'm really good with latches and locks."

They scream in delight and with their ghastly hairless feet pick up the rope at the bow of the paddleboard. And we're off! Picture this: a line of ten screeching, clamoring, arguing seagulls flapping their wings as hard as they can while discussing garbage and towing one small pony atop a paddleboard across a long, skinny lake. It's like *Washington Crossing the Delaware*, except I have all my own teeth. The only humans we pass are a group of very hungover frat brothers lying around on a speedboat that appears to be out of gas.

"Dude," says one of them to me. "Got beer?"

We land in a wooded spot. The seagulls are threatening to peck my eyes out if I don't make good on my promise, so in the parking lot of a lakeside restaurant I deftly unclip a dumpster top and peel it open. The gulls go wild, dive-bombing for scraps and assorted trash. One of them grabs a six-pack holder and the other a plastic straw.

"That's not—" I start to say, but they are already gone.

I can tell from the hum of distant cars that the humans are waking up, so I slide into the woods along the shore and stay out of sight. It's strange to be back in my old stomping grounds after so many rotations of the sun. The scent of the place brings back a thousand overlapping memories. My colthood at Happy Pony Farms, then the early days at

Silla's when I was young, optimistic, and eager to learn from the humans. Penny. I close my eyes and breathe in the scents of the fields we rode through together, nibble once again the moss on the old familiar falling-down stone walls. There is something so strange about returning to the place of early happiness. There's a sweetness, but also a terrible nostalgia.

I trot along the old trails, and before I know it I spot a blue butterfly.

"Hello!" I say. "I'm back!"

"Hi," says the butterfly quietly.

"Where are all your friends?"

"There's not many of us left," says the butterfly with a little cough. "I really wish people would stop using chemicals on their lawns."

"Agree," I say. "Gives the grass a terrible aftertaste."

I race down the trails. Everything here is the same—and my memory of it snaps into place over reality like a rubber glove over flesh, intensifying the experience. The roots in the trail, the twists and turns, the little stream crossing.

"Penny!" I neigh as I gallop toward the abandoned house. "Penny! I'm back! I'm so sorry! I came back for you!"

I jump the log where the red mare Arete and I had been tied up. I crash through the vines toward the house, half afraid it's going to have been turned into luxury condos on a golf course.

But it's there. Just as a I left it, although maybe a bit more decrepit. Thank the gods this part of New York State has not been discovered by the gentrifiers. I stride between the vines and push on the broken glass door. I have never been inside the house before. I step cautiously through the doorway. I startle as a pair of crows shoot into the air, complaining at top volume about being disturbed.

"Sorry!" I call.

The roof is mostly collapsed, small trees growing in what was the living room.

"Penny?" I whicker softly.

"Who?" says a voice above me. I look up. An owl is on a limb over my head. What is this place, an aviary? I think about how when the humans move out, everyone else moves in. And vice versa.

"Penny," I say.

"Not here," says the owl. Its yellow eyes follow me as its head swivels.

"I'm just going to look around," I say. "It's been a long time."

I sniff deeply. Even though years have passed, and hundreds of teenagers have gathered to smoke and drink here, I can still individuate traces of Penny. With each sniff, she comes alive before my eyes. The many times we came here are all layered over each other. Penny laughing. Penny reading me poetry. Penny giving me half her sandwich. Penny running and hiding behind a tree.

Scent is central to memory, and memory allows us to see the past. How sad that humans have such a pathetic sense of smell. I think they would be better creatures if they could smell what I do.

I sniff again, and again, vacuuming the earth in ever larger circles, drilling down through the layers of scents to the last day I saw Penny. I move away from the old house into the forest. Like a paleontologist scraping for fossils, I can carbon-date every scent according to number of summers that have passed. At last I find it. Penny, Penny, but also . . . the hairs on the tips of my ears stand on end. My whiskers vibrate. Death. I sniff more deeply. Someone died here. The smell of death and the smell of Penny, they're tightly intermixed, too tightly . . .

I drop to my knees in panic. Blood. I smell lots of blood. I keep sniffing, and the scene comes to life. Penny. The red mare. And a man. A very bad man.

27

PENNY

WHEN AT LAST Penny is able to meet with her again, Lisa is wearing a yellow dress that seems purposefully cheerful. Penny wonders if she has a date tonight. *What a day I've had,* she imagines Lisa saying while leaning over a candlelit table, her fork twirling in a bowl of pasta—*this crazy woman who's obsessed with ponies—ponies!—and clearly guilty as hell . . . What a waste of tax-payer dollars!*

Penny gives Lisa the names of neighbors back in California that Penny hopes will be discreet and who would be willing to be deposed under oath and say that she is a good person who, even after several glasses of wine, never once mentioned anything to them about killing anyone.

Lisa has finally gotten permission to give Penny a legal pad and a pen so she can write down anything about the case that might help. But when Penny gets the pen, it's just the flexible ink tube inner part. "People use the hard plastic outer part to make weapons," Lisa explains. "So it's not allowed. Also no unlined paper."

"Damn, there goes my new career as a forger of documents," says Penny.

"You also can't have spiral notebooks." Lisa makes a little stabbing motion. They both laugh and it feels like they're bonding. Over murder.

"Here's the other thing that's been on my mind," says Penny, leaning forward and peering at Lisa through the glass as she talks into the gray handset, which smells like disinfectant. "I didn't kill Frank Ross. So who did? I mean, couldn't we find out who did kill him so it's clear that I didn't?"

"I know that seems like an obvious path," says Lisa. "But our office has limited resources and personnel."

"It's my life we're talking about."

"It's really unlikely you will get the death penalty for this."

Gobsmacked again. "While that's of some comfort," Penny says carefully, "the idea of spending five or ten or twenty or forty years in prison is not super appealing, especially since I am *innocent*."

"I will do everything I can." Lisa's tone is apologetic but firm. She already seems older than she did the first day they met. Penny wonders what her life is like, whether she will stick with this job. "I filed a motion to get the police report, and I read it, and I think their case is pretty weak. I did some searching about your therapist. I checked with the company that she works for to find out if there have been any complaints against her, what her employment history is."

"And?"

"They wouldn't release any information, so I had to file paperwork to force them to release that to me. That's taking some time."

Time. So much time. Seasons are changing out there. Trees have flowered, sprouted leaves, absorbed a summer's worth of energy from the sun, shed those leaves, and are now holding naked branches high in autumn winds. Soon another generation of leaves will emerge from those same woody fingertips again. Children are going from crawling to walking and talking. TV shows are debuting and getting canceled. All while Penny sits here, waiting for justice to be served. She tries to stay calm. "Can we get anyone to try to find out who did kill Frank?" she asks.

"You could hire a private detective."

Penny sighs. "I don't have the money for that. Isn't that the job of the police?"

Another bell rings and Lisa gathers her notebook and pens. "It's pretty rare that they solve a cold case like this, so I think they're really hoping for a win."

THERE IS AN owl hooting somewhere outside Penny's cell window, and it gives her some comfort to think that nature is still out there, outside this cement-block, tempered-glass-and-steel nightmare. Ithaca is out there, this place that won't let her go, that keeps pulling her back. Her problem-solving brain keeps spinning on and on, unwilling to surrender. Yes, the police have a confession, so of course they have no incentive to find a suspect other than her. *I need a detective who will work for free*, Penny thinks as she lies in her bunk that night. But could a detective solve a crime that happened twenty-five years ago? A good one could, she thinks.

Hooo hoooo, says the owl.

That is a good question, thinks Penny. *Who* was in the forest that night?

PART SIX

A Hunger for Fame (and Kettle Corn)

PART SIX

28

THE PONY

AFTER CATALOGING EVERY scent in the old house and the surrounding area, I leave it behind and make my way back down the path that Penny and I took on the last day I saw her. I'm happy to leave that place behind. I never want to go back there again. It gave me no answers, only more questions. And the only person who can answer them is the red mare. Arete.

At the crossroads in the trail where I first laid eyes on Arete, I turn away from the path to Silla's and follow the trail to the stable the red mare and the boy came from. The path widens and sunlight streams down on me as I leave the forest and emerge on a groomed bridle path. Instead of rocks and roots, there's smooth dirt under my hooves. A large stable complex unfolds in front of me. Fancy. White board fences, green fields, arenas with jumps, huge barns, and long-legged horses grazing. Mares and foals. I hover in the trees at the edge of the fence line and study them, looking for Arete. I don't see her, but one of the mares spots me and lifts her head in surprise. She stares at me for a beat, then gives a cautious neigh.

The other horses lift their heads. The lead mare (there's always a bossy one) trots over with a huge swinging stride. She's massive and black, with a crowned H brand on her left hip. A Holsteiner. The others follow her but stay back a stride as she comes up to the fence and pins her ears in suspicion and warning. A set of gangly long-legged foals peek out from behind their mothers' rumps.

"Who the hell are you?" the black mare demands in a sharp German accent.

"Do you know a red mare named Arete?"

The mare squeals and kicks the fence.

I jump back. "Sorry. Just asking for a friend."

"Don't stand so close!" the black mare says. "I like my space." I do not point out that she has about twenty acres of space. "Who are you looking for?" she spits.

"A mare who lived here. Arete. Chestnut, four white socks and a blaze?"

"Hmmph, chrome," says the mare dismissively. "What's wrong with a horse that's all one color? People buy horses for their flashy coats when all they should be looking at are bloodlines."

I'm not going to take issue with this, although I really want to introduce some thoughts about behavior and adorableness. "I think Arete was with my person in the woods. Her name is Penny. It was a while ago."

"I'm only six," says the black mare. "I was imported last year." She swivels. *Wo ist Sabrie?* she calls out in German. "Sabrie?" she screams, then adds, "She's a little deaf."

An old, old mare makes her way slowly toward me. The black mare and the rest of the herd parts to let her through. "She's an Arabian. Thirty-three years old," says the black mare. "She's not as nimble on her pins as she once was, but she remembers everything."

"As we all do," I say.

The mares nod. An equine never forgets.

The bay mare called Sabrie has a thin white blaze like a lightning strike on her forehead. Her eye sockets are sunken and her face is flecked with gray. Her eyes are bluish with age but her expression is alert and curious.

"A pony!" she says. "How delightful."

I like her already. "Please, ma'am," I begin. "I'm looking for my human. Her name is Penny. I lost her in the woods a while back. She was with a mare from here. Arete. A red mare, the color called chestnut or sorrel depending on where you're from? And a man."

The bay mare takes a step back in fear and so does the whole herd. "Arete?" she gasps.

"Yes. Someone . . . died out there," I say. "Near the old house in the woods."

"I don't know who died out there," says Sabrie. "But I remember Penny."

"You do?"

"Penny saved a life. She saved Arete."

"She did?" This news brings tears to my eyes.

"It was many years ago," says Sabrie. "There was a full moon."

"Yes!" I say, recalling the night I waited in Silla's stable for Penny to return.

29

PENNY

AS SHE LISTENS to the owl, Penny thinks about how the question of who actually killed Frank Ross is not something she's ever really delved that deep into—Frank was a terrible person, and she didn't kill him, and she wasn't sorry he was dead, and that was all that mattered. Until now.

He was rich, and a grade A jerk. Lots of people must have hated him enough to kill him. What is it the TV detectives always say? Motive, means, opportunity. The forest was—is—a public place. Anyone could have been out there. She just has to find someone who will help her prove that.

She lies on her bunk with the yellow legal pad and the pen innards, trying not to let the precious ink leak onto her hand. Once again she replays the events of that night in her head. She tunes out the sounds of the jail—the bells, the clanging of doors, the footsteps echoing off cement walls and floors. She pushes aside her more recent visit to Ithaca, the encounter with Alex she doesn't want to think about, and makes herself go back to the forest, back to that night.

She and Alex had come out of the abandoned house to discover that her pony and Alex's horse were gone. The sunlight was fading, but she wasn't that worried. She had the beginnings of a crush on Alex, and this was a chance to talk to him more, to show him who she was.

By the time they got to the crossroads in the trail where one path led back to Silla's and one led to High Rise, it was nearly dark. Penny didn't have a cell phone or a flashlight.

WHEN SHE IS face to face across the chicken-wire glass with Lisa again, Penny waves a yellow piece of paper covered on both sides with her tiny neat print.

"I wrote down everything about that night I could remember for you," she says.

"Great. Leave it there and the guard will give it to me. I'm sorry that I have to run but school called and my little sister is sick. I have to go pick her up."

"You take care of her?"

"Yeah. She's seven. A bit of a handful."

Penny nods. She knows what those calls do to your day. She got them a lot. *Tella has a stomachache. Tella has a migraine. Tella has hives.* Tella was so sensitive—she flinched at every bell during the school day, every slammed locker. A million times Penny had wished she could trade places with her kid, take on all her pain, all her worry, all her . . . problems.

The guard comes in and takes the paper from Penny, looks at it to see if it really is indeed just a piece of paper, and then disappears with it.

"Your mom must be very grateful for your help," Penny says while they're waiting.

Lisa frowns. "Yeah, I guess. I have custody of my younger siblings. My dad died and my mom is . . . in a place like this."

"Oh," says Penny, aware of how inept a response that is. "I'm so sorry."

"I became a lawyer so I could help her, and people like her, like you, but law school—even the one I went to, that advertises on the subway—it was pricey. I better pass that bar exam, that's all I can say. Looking at my student loans, I totally get why people go work for those fancy thousand-dollar-an-hour law firms that make sure rich people never pay for their crimes."

"When do you hear about the bar exam results?"

"Few more weeks."

A moment later, the guard appears on the other side of the plexiglass and hands the paper to Lisa. She squints at it, then says, "The first line is a little smudged. What does this say?"

"Alex said, 'Walk back with me and I'll have my mom give you a ride.'"

30

THE PONY

"PENNY AND ALEX came back on foot from the woods. It was almost dark," says Sabrie.

Alex. Yes. That was the boy Penny was with.

"Frank was holding the red mare when they came back."

"Who's Frank?" I ask.

Sabrie shudders. "The man who ran this place. He . . . he had a temper. We all toed the line when Frank was around. He yelled at Alex for taking Arete out on the trail and letting her get loose."

"That was actually my fault."

"Alex said he was sorry and went to take the horse to put her away, but Frank said Alex was being too soft on her. He said Alex was spoiling her. Then Frank got on Arete."

A chill comes over me.

"He took her at a jump, but she wasn't ready and she refused. He grabbed his dressage whip off the fence post and told Alex to go clean the stalls."

I'm holding my breath, and so are all the mares who are listening. The foals stop nursing and prick up their little ears.

Sabrie goes on. "Alex did as he was told and left, but Penny was still standing there. Anyone could see that Arete was frightened, not recalcitrant, but Frank started to beat the horse. She refused the jump again.

She was panicked, covered with sweat and foam. Penny was just a little girl, but she stormed into the ring and tried to grab the whip from him. She held on tight to the end of it. He was enraged, shouting, but she wouldn't let go. As Penny pulled on the whip, the horse went the other direction, and Frank slid off into the dirt. Arete ran off, bucking. Frank jumped up in a rage and slashed Penny across the face with the whip."

All the mares and I gasp in unison.

Sabrie continues, "Penny put her hand to her cheek and started to walk away, and Arete ran to her. Frank shouted, but before he could do anything, Penny swung up onto the mare. The two of them were like one being. Arete jumped the arena fence and they disappeared into the woods."

I am rigid with fear, hearing this. Penny! I can feel the lash as it slices across her delicate human skin. Pain. Blood.

"Frank jumped on the ATV and chased them into the woods," says Sabrie.

I grit my teeth and swallow. "What happened next?"

"I don't know," says Sabrie, and she takes a bite of grass. "Arete came back the next morning by herself, covered with dried sweat and with her saddle half off. She was sold before I had a chance to talk to her. Last I heard she was in Florida on the jumper circuit. Based in Palm Beach, I think."

"But what happened to Penny?"

Sabrie lifts her head and looks me in the eye. "I never saw her or Frank again. Only Arete knows what happened in that forest."

31

PENNY

PENNY STANDS ON her bunk and stares out of the small high window. Through the bars she can see a parking lot. It's raining. It feels like it's always raining.

It's more clear to her than ever that she has to get herself out of this jail. No one else has the time, energy, money, or motive to help her. She is on her own. It's daunting, but also empowering—it's time to stop waiting for someone else to save her, and figure out how to save herself.

She catalogs everything she knows about Frank Ross.

He was the owner of High Rise Farms.

He was Alex's uncle, the brother of Alex's mom. Melanie. Melanie Kinsworth. They all lived at the farm. Alex didn't have a dad. He died when Alex was little, she vaguely remembers.

Frank Ross had a terrible temper and was cruel to horses. Penny had seen that firsthand.

She thinks about how Silla made all the riders at her barn take an oath. *Never hurt a horse.* It was drilled into them as deeply as *Head up, heels down.* Deeper. Every kid who rode at Silla's had to prick a finger and spill some blood onto *The Horseman's Bible,* even the little hemophiliac girl who bled all over the page on how to braid a tail. *I will never hurt a horse.*

Silla had told them that horses would test your patience, drive you crazy, make you furious, and that was okay, normal, to be expected, and they shouldn't feel ashamed, but you had to go kick and punch the hay bales, not the horse. After a lesson you'd see three or four kids out there kicking and punching the wall of alfalfa with their tiny gloved hands and little booted feet, releasing their frustration, tears of rage streaming down their faces. Then they would go back in the barn and tenderly groom their ponies and bed them down for the night.

Silla's rule had shaped all of them. It had shaped how Penny dealt with Tella when she was acting out as a toddler, when she was flying into a panicked rage now. Silla's rule had taught Penny not to be ashamed of an urge to shake or slap Tella, but to never act on it, not once, not ever. She never needed to. Instead she walked a few paces away and jumped up and down a few times. That always did the trick.

AS MOONLIGHT STREAMS into her cell, Penny recalls a time a few months before the Very Bad Night when she and Silla and the other kids had gone to a horse show. They had spent the previous day bathing and grooming the ponies, and then of course her pony had squirmed out of his blanket during the night and lain down in his own manure, leaving a big brown stain on his haunch. Penny was mortified. All the tack and grooming tools were already packed in plastic bins in the horse trailer.

"There isn't time," barked Silla, staring at the huge brown crust the shape and size of South America. "We have to go now."

The kids loaded their ponies into the trailer and Silla drove them a few miles to the showgrounds. They'd unloaded the ponies and tied them to Silla's ratty green livestock hauler with the flaking paint and wobbly floorboards. The other kids had groomed their ponies and then gone off to watch an adult jumper class.

Penny was still working on the manure stain with a stiff brush, Silla sitting nearby on a canvas folding chair, her Jack Russell terrier Ribs on her lap, when a huge, brand-new, gleaming white horse trailer pulled in next to them. HIGH RISE FARMS" was emblazoned on the side of the giant rig. Compared to Silla's trailer, it was like watching a megayacht dock next to a rowboat. Penny watched as lanky Thoroughbreds in clean monogrammed blankets were unloaded, their legs in pristine padded wraps, their braided manes secured with Lycra neck covers. They paraded past Silla's trailer and the mismatched assortment of ponies tied there like royalty past riffraff.

A tall, lean, tanned man with white teeth and thick, wavy, sandy hair emerged from the giant truck, also emblazoned with the High Rise Farms logo. White jodhpurs and tall black shiny boots. A yellow tie tucked into his white shirt.

"Silla," he boomed as behind him, a groom unloaded glossy wooden tack trunks and set up pens for the horses. He scanned the ponies, including Penny's, who chose that moment to let out an enormous fart. "That's quite a lineup you have there," said the man. "Do you need change so you can run them through the car wash?" He let out a huge laugh.

To Penny's surprise, Silla laughed, too. "Frank," she said affectionately. "Pull up a hay bale."

Frank remained standing. Penny remembers him smiling, handsome, a crop shoved in his perfect slim boot. He had a charismatic energy, and despite herself she felt drawn to him as if he were a movie star. She thought of what the kids at the barn said, and the kids at school. Frank was a famous rider who won at places like Madison Square Garden.

"Surprised to see you here," Silla said to him. "Thought you'd be at Devon this weekend. Isn't a schooling show a little lowbrow for your team?"

"We've got some green horses and ponies that need an easy confidence builder," said Frank.

"And parents who want their kids to come home with blue ribbons?"

"My team wins blue ribbons wherever they go." He gave her a wink.

Silla smiled as if she were immune to his arrogance. As if she enjoyed it. A woman appeared beside Frank. She was tall and tan and wiry like him, her blond hair pulled back into a sleek ponytail. Pearl studs and a gold bracelet dangling from her wrist, delicate and obviously expensive. Like Frank, she was in white breeches and shiny black boots, though she also wore a fitted black jacket. She was leading a bay gelding in a beautiful leather halter. She leaned over and greeted Silla with an air kiss.

"Melanie-darling," said Silla as if it were all one word. "Are you riding today? Who's this lovely boy?"

"My new hunter."

Silla studied the horse. "Very calm eye."

"He's a good boy."

Silla said, "Funny. The way his ears are drooping, he almost looks Aced." Penny knew that Ace was a drug people gave to calm horses down for medical procedures. It wasn't legal or ethical to give it to a horse in a show. "But I know you'd never do that," said Silla.

Melanie's smile was tight. "He's just very well trained. You know how Frank is a genius with difficult horses." She led the horse away.

Frank grinned at Silla and followed Melanie.

THE MEMORY MORPHS into later that same day at the horse show, when Penny was looking for the porta-potty. She had an equitation class in a few minutes, and she'd thought she could wait, but then realized she couldn't, and tied up the pony lickety-split and gone running. Dread. That was the emotion the memory was tied to in her mind. Dr. Resa had told her that memories were not videos, they were stories shaped by emotions, that the memory center in the brain and the emotion center were inextricably intertwined. If you wanted to remember something, you needed to conjure the emotion. She remembered that Dr. Resa had said that was part of her research in grad school.

Penny was darting between the horse trailers, looking for the porta-potties, which were so far from the show ring. She had come around a trailer and seen someone there. From the back. He was holding a palomino pony by the reins. The man lifted his left leg and kicked the pony hard once in the belly. The shocked pony spun around him, and the man saw Penny standing there. Frank Ross. He winked at Penny.

"Now you're awake," he said to the pony, and stalked off between two horse trailers, the wide-eyed pony following.

Penny felt the pee starting to come and ran for the porta-potty, which had miraculously appeared.

She remembered wanting to tell Silla what she had seen, but feeling confused, too. No one liked a tattletale. Silla was clearly friends with the man. Maybe it was Penny who had misunderstood what she saw. Maybe the pony had kicked someone and deserved to be punished. Kicking was the worst possible vice in a pony and could kill you, after all.

SHE COULDN'T REMEMBER seeing Frank again until the night he died.

So who else was in the woods that night with them? The police must have asked her that. Must have asked Alex, too, and Melanie. Where was she in all this? It was so long ago, and Penny had ridden that trail so many times. The woods were always full of people. She constantly rode past people out walking their dogs, teenagers making out. Hunters in camo. A man with a butterfly net. He was in the woods a lot. Had he been there the day that Frank died?

The police must have studied the crime scene. Must have looked for footprints, bloodstains, fingerprints, all the things you see on TV. What had they found, and what had they missed?

32

THE PONY

THERE'S SO MUCH I need to know. I leave the mares and the forest behind and head south. A house wren tells me I have a long ways to go and I'll have to cross through large areas that are densely populated with humans. I take about four steps before I am jumpy and on high alert. The smell of death is still in my nostrils.

I THINK ABOUT how to get all the way to Florida to find Arete. As I walk along a country road lined with stone walls and beech trees, I sniff and think, think and sniff, and process everything I know about the world, which can really be divided into two categories: food and food-adjacent. The answer finally comes to me, and I follow my nose for several miles and then turn left onto a busier street. A truck honks at me and I dodge a minivan and dart into a residential street. It's late afternoon and the grassy green lawns are calling to my rumbling tummy, but I make myself trot quickly down to another busy road, where I look both ways and make a run for another quiet residential street. As the sun sets and darkness hides the landscape once again, I cross through some backyards and a ball field. But now I have a problem. I can smell my destination—it's a few minutes' trot from where I am standing—but there is a giant highway in between it and me. Even though it's now nighttime when humans are supposed to be sleeping, I can see lots of headlights and hear the roar of cars and trucks. Although Penny often told me I was the Bravest Pony in the World, I am in truth a little afraid. Still, I have to keep going.

I study the situation. There are three lanes of traffic in each direction, which is terrifying, but there is a wide median in between them. I wait for a break in the traffic, then race toward the median. I have timed it well and I make it to the median safe and sound. Look at me— pony genius!

I am in the middle of the median when the ground under my feet starts to tremble. What the—? A herd of buffalo? Then I see a light coming right toward me. I look down. I am standing on a train track. The train horn screams and I scream and am frozen in panic and the train is bearing down on me and then finally my flight instinct kicks in and I bolt at top speed, without looking in both directions or looking at all across the other three lanes of traffic. I hear horns and brakes and the crunch of metal on metal but I just keep going, leaping the fence on the other side of the highway in a single bound like I am an Olympic show jumper. I land in a pile of leaves in someone's backyard and fall to the ground and just lie there for a second, panting, amazed that I am still alive and in one piece. My heart is pounding and my adrenaline is pumping, but as I lie there, I start to calm a little. *You are safe*, I tell myself. *The danger has passed*. Then I hear it.

Grrrrrrrr . . .

I leap to my feet and a huge pit bull is running toward me, fangs bared, aiming right for my jugular. I close my eyes and wait for death and . . .

"Hi!" She leaps onto me and hugs me with her paws and starts licking my face. "Hi hi hi hi hi!"

"Hello," I say with as much dignity as I can muster. I have never been tongue-kissed by a dog before. It's not unpleasant, except that it's a bit . . . invasive.

She continues to jump on me and lick me and shout greetings.

"Are you staying? Can you stay? Do you want to play? I have toys!"

she says. She runs and grabs a rope toy and offers it to me. "Tug of war?"

"No, thank you," I say. "I am incredibly grateful for your hospitality, but I'm afraid I have to go."

Her entire body goes from manic to droopy. Her tail droops, her ears droop, and she lies down and sighs. "That is so sad," she says at last. "I really thought I finally had a friend."

"You do," I say. "I am definitely your friend."

"You are?" She leaps up again and picks up the chew toy. I give it a tug, just to be polite. She yanks it out of my teeth with amazing force and then says, "Again!"

"I have to go," I say. "I'm really sorry."

She nods. "I guess you have to. But will you come back and play?"

"As soon as I possibly can," I say.

I let myself out of the side gate and close it behind me so she doesn't get out and get run over on the terrifying car/trainway.

"Bye!" she calls.

"Bye!" I answer. Why do people make animals live by themselves? Do they not think we feel loneliness? Or do they not care, because they are so lonely themselves with their piles of useless belongings and money?

I trot south on a four-lane road and turn right, passing a car wash. Next to a wig store is a chain-link fence topped with barbed wire. The smells that come from the other side of that fence are intoxicating. I know hay the way sommeliers know wine. With one sniff I can tell you the terroir and vintage of any forage, be it grass, grain, or legume. One bite and I can tell you the balance of starch and sugar, protein level, and moisture content. Here I'm smelling timothy hay from Canada, orchard grass from Oregon, teff from Utah, alfalfa from California . . . and yes—peanut hay. Bingo. I am swooning. And the grains—even through the bags I can smell sweet feed and balancer pellets and rice bran and oats and corn and . . .

Focus. I need to focus.

I strike the fence with my foreleg and it rattles noisily. Another dog starts barking. This one is an Australian cattle dog. He's alone, too, and racing around in the wrong direction.

"Hey, genius, I'm over here," I neigh to the dog.

"What?" barks the dog as he runs up. "What what what? You woke me up. You can't have any oats. I know what you ponies are like. You'll do anything for a snack." I love his accent. *Snack* sounds like *snik*.

"I don't need oats, although if you have any to spare, I have come a long way . . ."

"Sorry, no freebies. Boss's orders. I'm guarding these oats against the raccoons."

"You mean the ones that are over there chowing down like it's all-you-can-eat night?"

He turns and spots what I saw immediately—five masked bandits atop a pallet of equine senior shoving fistfuls of food in their mouths from the bag they've busted open.

"No no no no no!" calls the dog in a rage. He races over to the stack of bags and against the odds leaps and clambers to the top. Even though he is not a huge dog, he faces down the snarling raccoons and they finally retreat to the nearest tree and hiss down at him.

"Thank you!" calls the dog to me. "They're such terrible thieves. What can I do for you?"

"I need to go to where that perennial peanut hay comes from." You know those souvenir maps that show you the national parks or teams or flowers in each state? Sometimes they're printed on a dish towel? Well I have a very clear map in my head of the hay in each state. Peanut hay is from Florida. "Are you going south to collect peanut hay soon?"

"Sorry," says the dog. "We just got a huge load. We'll go again in a couple of months if you can wait."

"I can't wait. My person needs me." I know dogs, and this gets the response I expect.

"Oh no!" says the dog, ears up. "You got separated from your person? And she needs you?" It's like an episode of *Lassie*. Dogs are the

147

most loyal to the humans of all the animals, to the point where frankly it's pathetic.

"Yes," I say. "She's in danger."

"Has she fallen down a well?"

I hesitate. I'm really trying to be a better pony. But if the ends justify the means? "Yes," I say. "That is exactly the problem. She has fallen down a well. Only I can save her."

"Oh no oh no oh no!" barks the dog so loudly that the raccoons retreat higher up the tree. "You gotta go! You gotta go right now! You gotta save her!"

"I know. How can I get to Florida?"

"Uh uh uh let me think," says the frantic dog, racing in circles. "The show season is underway down there, but I don't see you as a show jumper . . . wait! I know!"

"What?"

"Pony races!" the dog shouts. "We deliver hay to a guy who does pony races! All around the country! His barn cat boasted about it. Man, I would like to bite that cat."

"There are *pony* races?"

"That's what the cat said. I accused her of lying, because well she's a cat, but she swore she was telling the truth. Said it was kind of a novelty act at fancy horse shows. If you can get on the pony racing circuit, you'll eventually end up in Florida."

"Thank you," I say to the dog.

"Go save the day!" says the dog, and barks directions to where the cat lives. "Now hurry!"

I start to trot away and then stop and call back to him. "You ever get a day off?"

"Yeah," he says. "Why?"

"There's a pit bull over on the corner of Gilbert and Mystic who is everything a dog could ever want."

"Does she like to play?"

I nod. "She has toys!" I call over my shoulder as I trot away.

Somehow I think those raccoons are going to get all the grain they want tonight.

FORTUNATELY THERE ARE no highways between me and the barn where the cat lives. I swing into the driveway a little after midnight. I can smell my own kind and make my way toward the barn behind the house. But it's locked up tight.

"How did you get out?" says a voice from the hay shed next to me. I look up to see an orange tabby swirling like liquid above me.

"I'm trying to get in," I say.

"Ponies never try to get in," she says. "Only out."

"Well, this pony wants in."

"You'll have to wait until morning. I'm not waking Robbie up. He needs his rest."

The barn cat and I hang out until dawn breaks. She tells me about Robbie. Robbie organizes pony racing around the country. When Robbie finally appears, he's a short man in a ball cap with a heavily muscled torso, like a wrestler. He has rough, calloused hands but he seems nice enough. He is perplexed to find me standing outside his barn, and when he rolls back the barn door, he does a quick head count and is still perplexed.

I fixate on him and plant the idea that I am his new racing pony.

"Pennies from heaven," he finally says, which I take to be a good sign. He ties me up and gives me some food and water and then loads me into a giant horse hauler where nine other ponies, each of a different color, neigh hello to me. I haven't been around this many ponies all at once since Silla's.

"Is this a good life?" I ask them as the truck starts moving.

"Depends on how you feel about running at top speed," says a cute little spotted Pony of the Americas.

"I like it," I say, thinking about Burnie. "I almost never get to do that." It was true. Almost everyone who rides ponies likes to be in control—which is silly. Why shouldn't the pony be in control—we're the ones whose legs are moving. Only Penny ever trusted me enough to give me my head and go belly-to-the-ground fast.

"Are you competitive?" asks a bay pony with a white face and four white socks.

"No," I say. "I've never really tried to win at horse shows, because it was more fun to crush the dreams of the humans."

"Welcome to the herd," says a brown-and-white pinto pony. "What do you want us to call you?"

"Lightning," I say.

"I'm Lightning," says a palomino pony.

"Speedy," I say.

"I'm Speedy," says a black pony.

"What's not taken?" Ever since Penny read me that first chapter of *David Copperfield*, I've been thinking about heroism. What does it actually mean to be the hero of your own life? I ask, "What about Hero?"

"Welcome, Hero," say the ponies in unison.

The barn cat, who is riding along with us on top of a bale of hay, rolls her eyes. "He named himself after a sandwich," she says. "Perfect."

Apparently I have arrived just in time. Robbie has a months-long schedule of appearances for us. They include county fairs, horse shows, and charity auctions. But our very first stop is a big fancy horse show in Ocala, Florida.

"Ocala! That's not far from Palm Beach!" I shout.

"I see drowning in your future," says the cat.

"Actually I'm an expert paddleboarder," I say. "But I plan to stay away from water from now on."

"I'm Cassandra," says the cat.

I roll that around on my tongue. "I will call you Cat," I say.

Robbie is not a bad man, the ponies tell me. He's a showman and a businessman, and we are his assets, so he buys us good food and treats us nicely. "But you gotta run," the black pony says.

"Or what?"

"Or they feed you to tigers."

"Tigers?" I don't like the sound of that one bit.

"At the cat sanctuary. It's where they send the tigers and lions that people keep illegally in their backyards, or extra ones from shows and zoos. Tigers gotta eat, too," says Cat. "And they prefer live prey."

I make a plan to run very, very fast.

After a long ride we're unloaded at a beautiful fairgrounds with white fences and white tents and green lawns we aren't supposed to walk on.

"Is this Ocala?" I ask a sparrow on the telephone wire.

The bird looks closely at me and then says. "I know who you are. Word gets around, pony. You're no friend of sparrows." It flies off.

I guess that stupid sparrow from Saratoga, Fifi, has been maligning my good name. *Whatever*, I think. Who cares what sparrows think anyway?

I find out from Cat that this is indeed Ocala. Robbie ties us in a row to the truck. The showgrounds are bustling with horses of every size and shape—huge black Friesians and Percherons, sleek leggy jumpers, muscled quarter horses wearing silver studded saddles, and dressage horses in white leg wraps. People walk up and down the aisles of the show barns inhaling the scent of fresh cedar shavings and oiled leather and admiring the ribbons hanging outside the stalls. In the distance a Ferris wheel turns, its lights blinking against the dusky sky. It makes me think of Circe and Caya. I wonder how they are doing. I am surprised to realize I miss them.

As I chow down on my hay I fall to talking to a mule in the stall next to me. Now, I am not a huge fan of mules for one reason: they are famous pranksters. People think ponies enjoy a good trick, and we do, but our ability to tease and joke pales in comparison with mules. Still, she happens to be in the stall next to me, and I have time before my race. This mule's name is Athena. She's the U.S. Army Military Academy's mascot. She's had about as many jobs as I have, but she loves her current job the best. "I live at West Point," she says, "but technically

I'm the mascot for the entire U.S. Army. I get to be in parades, football games, funerals, all kinds of events. Many people look down on mules, but not the army. They see us for what we are: strong, smart, and opinionated."

"Good meal plan?"

"Decent," says the mule. "Better than the army humans eat. So you're a racing pony?"

"For now," I say. I explain to her that I'm on my way to Palm Beach to find out what happened to Penny so I can locate her. "I left Penny alone in the woods. I'm so ashamed," I say, my cheeks full of hay.

"What did the pretty red mare smell like?" asks the mule, waggling her long ears.

I give Athena as detailed a description of the pretty mare's scent as I can remember.

Athena does a flehmen, which is when you lift your top lip high off your teeth when you're smelling something especially pungent.

"I think I know her," says the mule. "Before I became an army mule I was a lumberjane, and before that I was a pack mule in a national park. I think that mare was a guide horse there. I never forget a scent."

I am flabbergasted. What incredible luck. I describe the mare again, this time visually. "I thought she was a show jumper," I say. "Yay high, four white socks, white blaze? Name of Arete?"

"That's her!" says the mule. "Arete."

I see Robbie coming down the aisle toward me. It's time for me to go race. I might never see this mule again. "Hurry up! Tell me what you know about the mare and the man Frank who beat her and hit Penny and chased them to the abandoned house. What happened that night? Is Penny okay? Is Frank dead?"

"Yes," says the mule. "If I'm remembering the story, the man is dead. Penny killed him."

"What?"

"Or did Frank kill her? I don't remember," she brays. "Maybe it was a murder-suicide?"

I scream in alarm. "I have to get to Palm Beach to find Arete!"

"She hasn't been in Palm Beach in years," says the mule. "Last I heard she was in Chicago working as a carriage horse."

The mule's bray sounds in my ears as I'm led to Robbie's tack room and tied up alongside the other ponies. Frank was a bad man, but his murder would put Penny in terrible danger with her fellow humans . . . I've got to find Arete. She's the last one to have seen Penny.

I'm all amped up—which the other ponies take as excitement about the race. "I'm going to win tonight!" says Starlet, a dapple gray pony. "Eat my dust!"

"No way," says Lightning. "Tonight I am on fire."

"I've wasted all this time getting to Florida when where I need to be is Chicago!" I neigh.

A horsefly lands on my nose. "The Fates are with you. The pony races will go to Chicago right after New Orleans and Kansas City. In Chicago the ponies are invited to march in the Fourth of July parade," says the fly. "You'll go right down Michigan Avenue. Right past the kettle corn place."

"Mmmm . . . kettle corn," I say. "Is the kettle corn place near the carriage horse stand?"

"Very close," he says. "About four or five dumpster hops away."

"That's it, then," I tell myself. "All I need to do is stay on the pony racing circuit until we get to Chicago, then when we're marching in the parade I will disappear and go find the red mare and find out what happened and where Penny is." I might snag myself a bucket of kettle corn while I'm at it.

"*Bzzzzz*," says the fly, impressed.

Robbie brushes the shavings out of our manes and tails and polishes our coats. He puts a little saddle on each of us over a pad with a big number on it. I am #1. That feels like a good sign. Robbie gathers us around him—five of us on each side in prancing formation, and leads us to the main arena.

The crowd cheers thunderously as we are led into the arena. The lights are bright and it electrifies me to hear thousands of people clapping and cheering. This must be what Burnie feels, I think. No wonder he has a big ego. It's intoxicating. There are ringside tables with women in gowns and men in tuxedos, as well as stands packed with families. Banners with product names line the oval. I can smell money mixed with the cotton candy and popcorn. The announcer calls their names as eight boys and girls from the local pony club aged six to sixteen and wearing brightly colored silks enter the arena in a line, waving. They draw numbers from a top hat held by the ringmaster. Each child then marches over and takes his or her assigned pony, while a handler helps them mount and makes sure the chin straps on their helmets are tight. Some of the kids are little dots atop their ponies, while others' legs hang down below the pony's sides. I get a smallish boy who pets me and whispers in my ear before he mounts. "Let's do this," he says. In the past I would have bucked him off just for fun, but now I swish my tail approvingly.

Once the kids are on top, we walk in a circle nervously, chewing our bits and tossing our heads while the announcer explains the rules to the crowd and the riders. When the flag drops, we are going to leap forward and gallop around the racecourse twice, leaping two-foot-high brush and bar obstacles. First one across the line is the winner.

We line up in a row. Starlet paws in excitement. I stand stock-still, waiting, my heart pounding, my muscles tense, repeating to myself over and over: *Penny. Be alive. Be alive.*

"Beware of the thirst for fame," whispers Cat from the sidelines.

"What?"

"Fame is a form of greed. It's always the hero's downfall."

I have no idea what she means. Fame? Greed?

The announcer holds the red flag high, and the crowd falls silent, holding its breath. Then the flag drops and all of us ponies leap forward. The William Tell Overture blasts over the loudspeaker. I race toward the first jump, the boy on my back holding tightly to my mane and hanging on for dear life. The crowd screams. Are they laughing or cheering?

I leap over the jump at top speed just behind the white pony and the pinto pony. By the second jump I have made it into the lead.

The lead! I've never won anything before in my life. It feels amazing. Maybe I really am the pony that Penny thought I was. A hero! I run faster, straining my heart and legs and muscles harder than I have ever pushed them before. "Hang on, kid," I say as I gallop around the curve, even though he can't hear me. He doesn't even bother to try to steer or slow me—very wise. He just grabs mane and holds tight.

I see a kid fall off out of the corner of my eye but he bounces back to his feet, thanks to all the protective gear. The audiences cheer. Lightning comes up behind me as I race toward the last jump, trying to jostle me aside. My muscles are screaming and burning and I have no oxygen left in my lungs, but I really want to win. I race across the finish line—first! The boy slides off my back and hugs me, tears in his eyes. I see something on his face—joy, but also amazement, and I know this is a story he will tell his grandchildren. I can see him, a bent old man, whispering, "The pony flew over the jumps . . ."

I wait for the photographers, arching my neck and sashaying, but then a famous Dutch Warmblood who won the Olympics enters the ring and they turn away, mobbing him. I am ignored.

I am livid when I get back to the trailer. "Mr. Prancypants stole my thunder!" I squeal at Cat.

"Victory," she purrs. "I tried to warn you. It's what every athlete craves, but it's over in a second. It's a mirage. A dime-store form of heroism. You think you want it more than anything, that it's going to make you feel great forever, but it never does." She bats at a piece of baling twine near my chin. "Humans and ponies are good at anticipation, and bad at contentment. Wanting more, greed, destroys your ability to be happy with what you have, every time."

"You're wrong!" I say. "I could be happy if I'm only for once appreciated, for God's sake!" I am fuming and depressed. At least we're only a few stops away from Chicago.

Robbie gives us all fresh hay bags and a handful of grain. He rubs our legs with liniment that feels tingly. I wonder if I might get a little extra something for winning, but Robbie keeps it all fair and square.

"Nice work, new guy," says Lightning.

But the next day when Robbie unloads us at a county fair in Jacksonville, I stumble a little coming down the ramp. He frowns at me, worried, and puts the dapple gray in my place in the racing lineup.

"Toldja," snarks Cat.

"I'll be fine tomorrow," I tell her. "A day off is totally going to loosen me up."

But the next day I'm worse. I hobble along, favoring my left foreleg, which is hot and puffy.

Robbie kneels down next to me, fixing an ice pack to my leg. "Too bad," he says to me. "You've got heart."

I put my nose against his cheek and he rubs my forehead. *Please don't sell me*, I say to him. I try to put the idea into his head. *I need to get to Chicago to find out what happened to Penny.*

But he can't understand a word I say.

Robbie takes his phone out of his pocket. I assume he's calling the vet. I don't like vets because they poke you with needles.

"Hello," says Robbie into his phone. "Is this the cat sanctuary?"

33

PENNY

ENNY IS STARING through the grate in the door of her cell at the fire extinguisher and telling Dawn about how colicky Tella was as a baby. She doesn't care what Dawn did to get locked up over and over. All she cares is that she is willing to listen. "I tried to soothe her," Penny says, "but it seemed like nothing would make her stop crying."

She and Dawn talk all the time now, although all she can ever see of Dawn is her rosy pink fingers. It's such a comfort to talk to someone. At least they can hear each other, like horses in a barn, neighing down the aisle.

"It was the same with my little boy," says Dawn. "I felt like the worst mother ever."

Penny does briefly wonder if Dawn is *in legal terms* the worst mother ever, then banishes the thought and says, "I imagined Tella was screaming at the injustice of being forced to be born into this terrible world. I knew immediately that she got that from me, and my husband knew it, too. 'Chip off the old block,' he'd say with a pained smile as he handed her to me after rocking her in his arms for an hour trying to get her to go to sleep. From him she got thick wavy hair and good teeth. From me? The feeling that I get a lot of the time, that even on a nice day, even when things are going well, something terrible is about to happen, that it's all about to fall apart and I'm about to be plunged into Hieronymus Bosch–style hellish chaos. And look, here I am!"

Dawn laughs. "There are worse places than this," she says. "At least there are no rats here."

Penny is in that moment reminded that most of the women in here have not had her advantages in life, advantages that never seemed that numerous until she realized that "not bitten by rats in your sleep" was one of them. Poverty, mental health, addiction, abuse—these are the paths that for most of them led here.

Dawn says, "I just wish I could leave my son a million dollars so he could have a better life."

"Yeah. Anxiety, not wealth, is apparently my legacy to my daughter. She's amazingly sensitive. It's like she can hear and feel things that no one else can. When she was a baby I was in Chicago riding a bus with her in my arms one day and an old woman shrouded in black shawls told me Tella had special powers of communication."

"Really?"

"'Not with me she doesn't,' I said. The woman's stop came before she told me what she meant."

"That's crazy. What's Tella like?"

Penny pauses. "Worried. Through Tella's whole childhood her expression as she slept was troubled. She would sweat and churn the covers and cry out every night. I did everything I could to make her life as calm and pleasant as possible, played soothing white noise and was always smiling and patient with her, and always told her I was proud of her, but she was perpetually anxious, crying, angry."

"Was your husband around to help?" Dawn asks. Penny feels like she's talking too much, like she should ask Dawn more about herself, but it also feels like personal questions could be problematic here. *Forty years.* She definitely doesn't want to pry into anyone's business.

"He tried," Penny says. "But then one night when Tella was about eight he suddenly said, 'I didn't sign up for this.' After that he just kind of stopped trying, and left me to do all the parenting."

"Men. What did you say?"

"I tried to reason with him, even though I wanted to kill him." *Oops*, Penny thinks, but goes on as if she didn't just admit to murderous thoughts. "'Mental illness is hard,' I pointed out to him. I said, 'If she had a visible disease, like leprosy, you would not be like *I can't deal because my kid's nose fell off.* He didn't laugh. I thought maybe the one upside of sending Tella to boarding school was that Laus and I would have some time to try to remember what we loved about each other, but instead it gave us less in common, and he ended up moving out. And, you know, now I'm in jail three thousand miles from home."

"Hang on, I gotta use the powder room," says Dawn.

"Remember to tip the attendant," calls Penny. Each cell has what is basically an updated pit toilet in the corner. It emits a chemical stench at all times. When it overwhelms her, Penny tries to be her pony, who seemed to relish strong smells to the point of rolling in foul patches of mud.

As she stands there staring at the fire extinguisher across the hall, Penny remembers something Dr. Resa said about her and Laus. *Maybe you're just both reconnecting with yourselves and you will come together again when you've been able to do that important work.* Then Dr. Resa had encouraged Penny to go to Ithaca. *I think a trip back to your hometown will help,* she'd said. *When you get there, ask the local librarian about the crime you witnessed. They love local history and they can probably tell you what happened.*

Even in the moment that had seemed to Penny like a weird left turn on the shrink's part. Why was she so interested in Frank's death? Did she know him? Or just hate Penny? Dr. Resa had also had some sessions with Laus as well as Tella. Had she become fixated on Laus? Did she feel like she needed to get Penny out of the picture?

Penny decides when she talks to Laus next she will ask him what he thinks of Dr. Resa. Maybe he can find out something about her, some reason she's lying about Penny having confessed.

"I'm back," says Dawn.

"What about your husband?" asks Penny. "What's he like?"

"Dead," says Dawn. "I made sure of that."

———

THE NEXT MORNING Lisa comes back to see Penny. It's Saturday, and from her cell window Penny sees that the parking lot is full of family members bringing little kids to see their moms in jail. America: home of the incarcerated, thinks Penny. Girls in little white dresses with bows, little boys with shiny shoes and slicked hair. How many of their moms are innocent, she wonders. "Probably one in twenty," Lisa estimates when Penny asks.

Penny wants to ask Lisa more about her own mom, but it feels like an invasion of privacy. Lisa will tell her if and when she wants her to know.

How many women like her are innocent but stuck in jail awaiting trial because they can't afford bail? How many convicted women are guilty but are no longer a danger to society and could be let out? This system is so effed up, thinks Penny. She makes a promise that if she ever gets out of here, she will try to do something, anything, to change the system.

She can see her own reflection in the plexiglass when she sits down to talk to Lisa. She looks even more tired, if that is possible. Dark circles under her eyes, and her skin is blotchy and paler than before. The scar on her cheek stands out like a seam in her face. Lisa must feel like she's dealing with a monster.

"I talked to Melanie Kinsworth," says Lisa. "Frank Ross's sister. We don't always have success getting people close to the victim to talk to us, but she had quite a few things to say. She said you came back to Ithaca recently, that you went to High Rise?" Lisa sounds a little miffed, like Penny should have told her all this. But it just hadn't come up—all their conversations had been focused on the night Frank died.

"It was a couple of weeks before I was arrested. I was just visiting," says Penny, feeling defensive.

"Hmm," Lisa says, definitely pissed off. "I can't help you if you lie to me. I feel blindsided by this."

"I didn't mean to—I'm sorry," says Penny. "I should have told you," she says, leaving it at that. But how is it Penny's fault that she hasn't told her every detail of her life? Lisa is always on a tight schedule.

"Tell me everything that happened when you went back to Ithaca," Lisa says carefully.

"Okay," Penny says. "Here's everything. Last spring—"

"Can you write it down for me?" Lisa interrupts. Her cell phone beeps every couple of seconds and she seems distracted. "It just feels more efficient that way. That was helpful, what you wrote before. The more detail the better. You never know what's going to be important."

PENNY SITS ON the edge of her bunk and writes. *In April, a few days after dropping my daughter Tella off at a therapeutic school for girls, I went back to Ithaca to try to find my pony. I had no idea where he might be, or even if he was alive or dead, but that seemed like the logical place to start.*

34

THE PONY

Robbie takes pity on me and sells me on Craigslist instead of sending me to the cat sanctuary. He even drops me off at my new home on his way out of Ocala. I discover when I am unloaded into a rural Florida backyard full of treadmills, chest freezers, spools of metal cable, giant cement dolphins, and patio umbrellas that I have been bought by a fast-talking man with a mustache named Nestor.

"He will be the loved pony of my daughter," says Nestor. I know in that moment that Nestor has no daughter.

Robbie just nods, hands him the lead rope, and drives away as I neigh hysterically. I am locked in a dog kennel I can't get out of.

Nestor has no children, but he does have a thriving business on the internet selling stuff. He buys and resells everything he can, jacking up the prices as high as possible while still keeping them low enough to keep the merchandise moving. He sells me that same day to a very beautiful blond woman named Helen who flips ponies for a living the way other people flip houses.

I arrive at a tidy but slightly rundown backyard stable outside Orlando. Helen exudes sophistication, peppering her speech with French and Italian phrases, even though she grew up in a trailer in Dubuque, raising herself while her mom got high. (The day I arrive she is trying to get the people who produced *Tiger King* interested in her story, so I hear her practice her pitch multiple times.) Helen never finished high school, instead putting Dubuque in the rear-view mirror at age fifteen. After a series of bad boyfriends and rough times, she has created a nice little niche business for herself taking scruffy ponies like me that she buys cheap and then reselling them as top-class show ponies on the high-end show circuit. Show ponies, just so you know, can sell for upward of the price of a house. A nice house, in a nice neighborhood.

One gray pony of uncertain parentage I meet that first day at Helen's barn tells me she picked him up two weeks earlier from an Animal Control facility in New Hampshire for a hundred-and-fifty-dollar adoption fee, and has given him a good haircut, a pedicure, and some square meals. The next day I watch Helen sell him for thirty thousand dollars to a couple from Connecticut as a purebred Welsh. I stand there as he's loaded onto a trailer and taken away to a cushy new life. Another backyard find I meet at Helen's, an especially elegant and well-behaved chestnut with four white socks, gets forged German Riding Pony papers (who can read German?) and within twenty-four hours sells for a hundred thousand dollars. Some would say what Helen does is dishonest. Okay, almost everyone would say it is dishonest. But from my point of view, she simply adjusts the perceived value of the ponies. The ponies are always wonderful, even when starved and mud-encrusted. But most people can't see that, so she uses some smoke and mirrors to help them see the ponies differently. And let's face it, how bad do you feel for someone who can afford to drop a hundred K on a pony? It's practically a crime *not* to rip that person off.

Life at Helen's seems like it would be interesting, and the orange groves and palmettos are beautiful, but I am on a mission. I wait until the next time the barn is empty of humans, and slip the latch on the stall. I am halfway out the barn door when a flashy bay pony says, "Hey, didn't you say you wanted to get to Chicago?"

"I'm on my way there now."

"On foot?"

I nod. "These hooves are made for walkin'."

The flashy bay pony shakes his forelock. "Well, genius, you're less likely to be eaten by an alligator if you ride with us. The Pony National Championships are in Chicago this year."

"You're kidding." The prospect of not walking a thousand miles has a lot of appeal. I could ride in style and be fed on the way!

"Count me in," I say. "Thanks for the tip." I turn to head back toward my stall.

"You better up your game," says the bay, looking me over with a critical eye. "There are no scruffy backyard ponies at Nationals."

I am offended by this. "I love my natural look and think it's very endearing," I sniff.

"Whiskers? Hair on the inside of your ears? Your fetlocks? *Hmm*," sniffs the bay. "Honey, you need an Olympic-level makeover."

I snort right back at him. "I'm going to Pony Nationals," I say.

The next morning Helen, her eyes always hidden behind designer sunglasses and her neck swathed in a Hermès scarf, has her ten-year-old daughter Ines put me through a series of tests. Ines is an exact miniature copy of Helen, right down to the tweed jacket and shiny black riding boots. Most parents insulate their children from the truth about what harm humans are capable of doing to each other, but from my eavesdropping I gather Helen has never lied to Ines about what life does to women who do not stay alert and look out for themselves. From her energy I can sense Helen does this in the hopes that history will not repeat itself, but as a result Ines has the coldest eyes of any little girl I have ever met, and zero trust in any other human being, including her mother. She is, however, an expert rider. They measure me carefully (height determines which division a pony is shown in), and then Helen watches as Ines makes me stand still, walk, trot, and canter, then jump. They debate in which show category I will be most marketable—small working hunter pony, where style is paramount? Medium jumper? Large harness pony? Roadster pony? Pleasure driving pony? Gymkhana? Western pleasure? Reining? I know from the flashy bay pony that the next step is usually to take the new pony to a distant but important horse show, where Ines will ride the pony to victory, usually under an assumed name and with a freshly forged Euro pedigree (counting on the fact that no one speaks Dutch or Czech, either), and Helen will entertain cash offers from parents whose children have come second, third, fourth, or lower. I need to be so amazing that Helen and Ines decide to hold on to me and compete with me at Pony Nationals, where they are certain to get a better price for me.

When Ines first gets on me, I'm impressed. She has strong little legs and light hands, but I can tell she is not going to let me get away with anything. Some kids just have a force of will that makes you realize it's better to submit.

"How does he feel?" calls Helen.

"Can't tell yet," says Ines. "He's not afraid. He feels ready."

I am ready. I need to go to Nationals!

Helen watches as we walk, then trot, then canter in a circle.

"He gives to pressure," says Ines. "I think he's well trained."

I am, I concur. Or I can pretend to be when I want to.

"Try him over the straight bar."

Ines turns me toward a blue-and-white-striped jump. I have always liked jumping if the price is right. I gather my forelegs under me and try to sail over the jump, but I knock it down with a hind leg.

Ines pulls me to a stop. "He's willing," she says. "But stiff."

Helen nods. "That we can fix."

They lead me back to the barn. Helen studies the white hairs on my face, then brushes some dye on them. She stands back to admire her handiwork.

"He looks five again," says Ines.

Helen then gives me injections in my legs. I tend to climb trees when I see needles, but all I feel is a little prick. They body-clip me, touch up the dye job, and spray me with a silicone spray so I am sleek and shiny.

The next day, Ines gets back on and takes me over the jump again. I fly over that thing. It's amazing!

Back in the barn, I turn to a little piebald pony in the stall next to me whose legs are all wrapped up.

"That stuff is incredible," I say. "I've never felt younger. I could trot all the way to Chicago right now."

"You'll feel old when it wears off," says the pony.

"Why does it have to wear off? I want this feeling to last forever."

He shakes his head a little and stamps a hoof. "I know," he says. "No one wants to live in pain. But if you were only going to stand around all day in a field and swish your tail at flies, that would be okay. But you're jumping on legs that should not be jumping. I know. I bowed a tendon last week. Helen and Ines are evil."

"Not to me they aren't. They made me young again. Bring it on."

He sighs. "There's no fountain of youth, even for humans. When you try to act younger than you are, it bites you on the rear end eventually. Good luck," he says, hobbling over to the feeder.

That night I hear a gunshot. The next morning the piebald pony is gone.

"Where did he go?" I ask the gray pony in the stall on the other side of me. She says nothing, just keeps eating her hay. Instead, the gray barn cat answers, his tail forming a question mark, then an exclamation point.

"Cat sanctuary."

My heart stops. And, in proof that cats all have the same catch-phrase, their justification for eating songbirds, adorable little moles and voles and mouselets, not to mention a total absence of empathy, he adds, "Tigers gotta eat, too." Carnivores!

Helen briskly gives me one more round of injections and Ines puts me over a series of eight jumps. I try really hard, pulling my forelegs up high, but I knock two of them down. Helen frowns.

"Should we try the cart?"

Ines shakes her head. "Not flashy enough. Needs a higher action."

Hey! I try to plant the idea inside their heads. *I'm cute!* I start prancing for them, pulling my knees up as high as I can, arching my neck and lifting my tail.

Helen squints at me and cocks her head. "Hmmmm . . ." she says.

35

PENNY

"YES, I REMEMBER you. I have nothing to say to you," says Silla, my old riding instructor. Clearly she has a little dementia, which is not that surprising given that she is very old and, if the state of her nose is any indication, has been drinking steadily for most of her adult life. We're in her office in the barn, which looks like nothing has been tidied in the twenty-five years since I was last here. Or dusted. I loved this place when I was a kid, and I instantly love it again now. Faded ribbons and trophies, random pieces of tack, piles of horse magazines, grimy out-of-date calendars, laminated flyers for horse wormers and gastric supplements. It's heaven.

"Okay, well, I just want you to know that the happiest moments of my life were spent here, so I'm very grateful to you," I say.

She swings around in her chair and looks at me again. "Penny," she says, some light of recognition in her cloudy eyes.

"Yes. I'm Penny. I had a pony. I bought him from you. He was wonderful."

"He was. You two were magic together." She says it like that's a bad thing. "And then you sold him."

"Well, my parents did. I would never have sold him. They took me away. I had to live in a city and I never got to ride again. I was really depressed."

"You shouldn't sell a pony like that. They're very sensitive. Ponies don't like that."

She's still angry. She doesn't care that I hurt or why, only that I hurt the pony. "I think you're right," I say. "I really miss him, still."

"Anything could have happened to him. Ponies can be lent to other children but shouldn't be sold on, and they should be retired at home and allowed to live out their lives. It's cruel. Taking them away from their homes, their friends. There are so many bad people out there. People who hurt and neglect animals. People who don't understand that animals have emotions. That they feel things. That they can suffer mentally even if they are physically healthy."

She is a very angry woman, I can see that. Some people with dementia get this way, I know. The brain decays and only the angry circuits are left. "Do you have any idea who bought him?" I ask.

"For God's sake," she explodes. "Now? You wait more than twenty years and now you want to know where he is?"

My face flushes with shame. I sense there's no point in trying to explain that life got in the way, that at first I was a child, and then I was trying to hold down a job, then I was married and teaching and a mother of a child with serious issues. Still am.

Silla doesn't care about any of that. Silla cares about horses. *Never hurt a horse.*

"I'm in town for a few days. I'll come see you again," I say.

"Wait. Let me see," she says, struggling to get to her feet. "Let me just see."

I go to help her out of her chair but she pushes my hand away.

"I don't need help," she yells. I am reminded of how she would shout at us during riding lessons. How is it that being yelled at by a drill sergeant is the happiest memory of my life? But it is. She moves slowly through the messy office, an ancient Jack Russell at her feet. It can't be the same dog, can it? She pushes aside boxes, photos. This place is a time capsule. She sifts through tattered issues of *Chronicle of the Horse* and *Horse and Hound*. I love this office. I think of my own neat, sterile, lifeless desk.

"I want an office like this some day." I say.

"Do you?" she says. "Why?"

"Proof of a life well lived."

She yanks open a filing cabinet with a clatter. This makes the dog bark.

"Yes, yes," she shouts over the sound of the dog. "Here it is. Your pony went to the dealer over in Springfield. Hankins. They might know what happened to him."

"Thank you," I say. "Thank you!"

She seems mollified. "I always liked you," she says. "I hoped you'd come back some day." She slams the filing cabinet, which I see also contains a bottle of whiskey. She totters out of the office into the barn aisle and over to a stack of hay bales. She hands me two flakes and puts two under her arm. "My cart has a flat," she says. The hay goes down my shirt and makes me itch. I follow her out of the barn to a pasture where two very old horses are standing, and a llama that looks like it could use a shearing. The llama looks skeptically in my direction and I hope it doesn't spit at me. There are three strands of yellow electric fence tape to keep the horses in. I stand back from the fence, cautious of it.

"It's not on," she says, leaning on the electric fence with a gnarled hand. "They don't need it. Hasn't been on in years. Saves on the electric bill."

I toss the hay over the fence and the old horses amble over and begin eating. She rubs their ears and they sigh and shift so she can get to the itchy spots. The llama hangs back, wary.

"You think my pony's still alive?"

"He wasn't that old when you sold him, so . . ." She counts on her twisted fingers. "Could be. If a colic didn't get him or he didn't get sent to the cat sanctuary."

A barn cat curls its tail and spits at the dog, which begins barking again.

My pony could be out there somewhere. Alive.

"Hankins," I say. "Springfield."

36

THE PONY

THANKS TO MY inimitable sass and verve, Helen and Ines take
me to Pony Nationals to compete in the Open Non-Hackney Small
Ponies in Harness division. Helen is wearing a long black skirt and
a top hat. I'm wearing a gleaming black harness with blinkers and a
silver-studded browband and my mane is tightly braided into sleek
little knots. For the first time in my entire life, there is not one speck of
dust on me. Even my hooves are polished to a high shine. I am attached
to a cart called a viceroy with four big silver-spoked wheels. It's light
as air, even with Helen in it.

I am in Chicago!

We're stabled in the basement of an armory right in the downtown
of the city. It's very exciting—all of the ponies at this show are ex-
tremely beautiful or talented or both. I am in awe of them. There are
so many different classes the ponies are competing in—Green Pony
Hunter, Pony Hunter Under Saddle, Pony Jumpers Two Foot Three,
Two Foot Six, and Two Foot Nine to Three Feet, Half-Welsh Part-
Bred, Leadline Rein 4–8, Stock Seat Equitation, Short Stirrup and
Long Stirrup, halter classes for every age and size of pony, and the
carriage classes: Carriage Driving, Pleasure Driving, and Obstacle
Driving, where you have to navigate around cones. I am meeting so
many ponies, too! Welshes and Shetlands, of course, but also Hack-

neys, Connemaras from Ireland, Dales and Exmoors from England, Gotlands from Sweden, Highlands from Scotland . . . it's fascinating to see all the different sizes and shapes and colors and smells of pony.

Helen is all business. She already has the FOR SALE sign on my stall and is entertaining offers in the range of what luxury cars cost. I haven't been able to get out to find the carriage horses. I have sussed out the situation, though, and I know that there is a ramp that goes up to the ground level. The door to the street is a huge metal thing that rolls up when a human pushes the button. The door is of course kept closed and there is a human guard sitting there on a stool 24/7 as no one wants any ponies to get loose in downtown Chicago . . . do they?

Helen and Ines have several ponies in the show. Helen is tacking me up for my preliminary class when a large woman appears in the door of the stall. She has red hair and is wearing shiny black riding boots and a fierce expression.

"Hey," she says in a cold tone. "Helen. The pony you sold me at Devon was lame."

Helen doesn't reflect any concern, just continues putting the harness over me and fastening the straps. "I'm not responsible for what happens after I sell a pony. If you can't take proper care of them, that's your problem."

"The X-ray showed laminitis."

"You must have fed him too much rich food."

"You know perfectly well that you sold me a lame pony."

"I didn't."

I wonder if there is going to be a physical fight between them, but the red-haired woman stares at Helen for a minute, then says, "We'll see about that." She stomps off.

Ines appears from the next stall. "Mom," she says. "That's a problem and you know it. She's—"

"I know who she is."

"I told you not to sell her that pony."

"We have bills to pay, Ines."

Helen finishes harnessing me in silence. "You need to win this class," she says to me. "So I can sell you for a lot of money and get the hell out of here."

I don't dislike Helen and Ines. They do what they have to do to survive, like ponies do. Still, I know that if I don't attract a buyer, Helen will send me to the cat sanctuary without blinking an eye. That's the world she lives in. There is no room for feelings.

She harnesses me to the viceroy and leads me up the ramp past the big metal door, and then we climb to the level of the show ring. The stands are full of people—some entire family groups, but mostly a lot of moms and their daughters. The girls are of all ages and are wearing pony sweaters, pony socks, pony hats, and pony bracelets. There are vendors selling stuffed ponies, plastic ponies, pony phone bumpers, pony notebooks, and pony T-shirts. I am relieved there is no pony-flavored popcorn.

Helen climbs into the cart and we enter the arena. There are seven other ponies in the class. At first we circle the arena at a walk, and then at a signal from the judge we trot. I lift my knees high and push from behind. This is a good sport for me—the effort is not too great and it's a chance to really show off. I can't show off too much, though—I have to actually listen to Helen because I am judged on obedience as well as form. After we have walked and trotted and halted and turned around and done it all in the other direction, we line up.

I win the class!

A blue sash is tied around my neck and I trot a victory lap with the crowd cheering. As I prance in front of the adoring crowd, I keep in mind what the barn cat told me at the pony races about fame. I can see envy and resentment on the faces of the other drivers, and even on the faces of the ponies themselves. I think about what the rat taught Burnie. We should compete for the sheer joy of it or not at all.

Helen dismounts from the carriage and leads me down the ramp. As we pass the big metal door, I see that the guard is not there on his stool. There is a paper sign taped there that I am guessing says that this person is on a bathroom break and will be right back. This would be the ideal time to make a run for it, but Helen is holding me tightly.

"You qualified for finals!" says Ines, entering the stall to help un-tack me.

Helen smiles and grabs a Sharpie. She crosses out my price on the FOR SALE sign and doubles it. She hangs the blue ribbon outside the stall right next to the sign.

"The finals are at eight tomorrow morning," says Helen. "Let's give the pony some hay and get some rest. We'll get up at five and begin grooming."

I wait until all the ponies have been put away and the barn is quiet. My plan is to slip out and find the carriage horse stand. I know from a local mosquito I let feed on my inner ear that it's nearby on Michigan Avenue. I can picture Arete there, and she will help me find Penny.

I feel sort of bad about leaving Helen and Ines at this crucial mo-ment. I am supposed to save the day for them. Win my class, sell for a high price, and keep them afloat until the next champion comes along. Oh well. Not my problem.

I unlatch the stall door (humans never learn) and slink through the darkened aisles between the stalls. A couple of ponies nicker a little and I say, "Shhhhh . . ." I peek around the corner.

The guard is at the door looking at his phone. I only have to wait about five minutes before he heads off to the restroom.

I trot as quietly as possible up the ramp to the big metal door. I hit the red button with my nose.

The noise is deafening. The metal door rolls up very slowly with a grinding wail that could wake the dead. It is only about eighteen inches off the ground when the guard comes running back down the ramp from the upper level. "Hey!" he shouts. "Stop!" He's gaining on me, arms outstretched!

The door is so slow! I wait until the last second and then drop to my knees and scooch under the door. The guard grabs my tail and holds on. I swear I have no choice in the matter. I kick out with my hind legs, hear an "ooph," and I am free. I gallop down the sidewalk and around the corner, bucking in glee.

Following the mosquito's directions I make it to Michigan Avenue and I find the line of carriage horses. There are some tourists enjoying the evening out, and some of them start to take pictures of me. The drivers are amazed to see a loose pony, and they try to catch me as I trot along the sidewalk alongside the carriage horses. Gray. Bay. Bay. Gray. Where is the red mare?

"Hey!" I say, darting past a coachwoman wielding a big horse halter.

"Hay?" an old gray mare asks, swinging her head so she can see me around her blinkers. Her driver dives for me again but I step out of her grasp. The tourists laugh and clap. At least they're on my side.

"Do you know a red mare named Arete?" I ask the gray mare.

She shakes her head. "Never heard of her."

I hear a twittering over my head. "Hee hee hee. Stupid pony. I knew you'd show up here eventually."

"Who's there?" I call up into the trees, still dodging the coach-woman.

A tiny swallow voice laden with contempt spews down on me. "It's me. Fifi. You fell for it, pony. Arete isn't here. I bribed the mule to lie to you."

At this I am frozen. A fellow equine lied to me? The coachwoman's rope lands on me and I come alive again, shaking it off. I hear the *woop-woop* of a police car coming down the street. "What? Why?" I call to the sparrow, but I know the answer.

"You hurt my feelings. You called me an idiot. I was only trying to help you!"

I am so furious I could buck and kick and destroy this whole city. "But . . . my human. Her life could hang in the balance."

"Guess next time you'll be nicer to sparrows."

I want to cry with frustration and rage, but instead I think about how I can get this stupid effing bird to tell me what I want to know. I gallop away from the coachwoman down the block to the kettle corn place. It's easy to find because of the strong sweet-and-salty smell. I clatter into the marble-floored store. People scream and back away as if I am a shark in a swimming pool and not an adorably fuzzy pony. I grab a paper funnel of kettle corn from a shocked tourist.

"Come back here!" he yells as I dart back out the door and down the sidewalk.

Trying not to spill the kettle corn, I gallop back to the tree and call out, "Fifi! Fifi!" which is not easy with a mouthful of cardboard. I try not to sound angry.

"I'm sorry," I mumble around the edge of the cone of corn. I want to throttle this bird until she is a small pile of feathers, but instead I say, "I shouldn't have spoken to you that way. I have brought you a delicious cone of kettle corn to make up for my rudeness."

"Is it caramel and cheese?" Fifi folds her wings and fluffs her tail feathers.

I sigh and drop the paper cone, spilling the delicious popcorn all over the sidewalk, and gallop back to the kettle corn store, where people start screaming again and the owner tries to hit me with his tongs. "Shoo! Shoo!" he yells, flapping his white apron. I evade him, racing through the crowd of tourists in the store, shoving my nose into each bucket of kettle corn as I pass by. Truffle, chocolate, habanero, pecan-caramel, garlic, caramel and cheese. Bingo. I grab a huge cardboard bucket of caramel and cheese from an outraged five-year-old child, take one last whack from the store owner, and gallop back to the base of the tree where Fifi is. I deposit the bucket of popcorn below the tree.

The coach horses cheer my return.

"Get him!" says one of the coach drivers to another. "I'll block this side."

"I'm sorry," I say to Fifi, panting. Hiding my rage, I look up at the tiny bird. I am struck by how small she is, how fragile. A voice in my head, unwelcome but loud and clear, says that back in New York, Fifi did her best to help me and I rewarded her kindness with bile.

I say again, "I'm really sorry." And this time I mean it.

"Better. But I'm headed back to Saratoga Racetrack. Take the caramel and cheese kettle corn there and then I'll help you."

I sigh and pick up the paper bucket of caramel and cheese kettle corn like a delivery driver.

"Don't drop any," says Fifi. The coachwoman is creeping up behind me with a rope formed into a lasso. She throws it. What does any of it matter anymore? All the anger is gone, replaced with regret. I was a jerk, and I'm paying for it, but maybe Penny is paying for it, too. I walk away with the kettle corn and the lasso falls to the sidewalk. The crowd of tourists cheers. I remember how much I hate the taste of cheese.

I am three blocks away, heading east, parting pedestrian traffic on the sidewalk and causing dogs to bark furiously and strain at their leashes when Fifi catches up to me and flies alongside me. "You're really taking the kettle corn all the way back to Saratoga?"

"Yup," I say, the bucket between my teeth. "And then I'm going to Palm Beach to find Arete, if she's still there." I don't say how much time and energy Fifi and the lying mule have cost me. In the end, the delay is my fault, the fruit of my own unkindness. "I shouldn't have been a poo-head to you," I say to Fifi, dodging a corgi in a blue sweater and his very surprised person.

"Was that a . . . pony?" says the man to a doorman in a gray uniform.

"Hold up," says the sparrow. "I think I misjudged you. You're not a jerk, you're just very determined to save this little girl. Do you love her?"

That question again. I start to say no, launch into my explanation of how there is no such thing as love, but I stop myself. There's that voice in my head again. The voice of truth.

I nod. "I love her," I say. I'm shocked by the truth of this. I love Penny. I love her. I'm like those stupid swans, like Caya the hound dog. I should be ashamed, but I'm not. I'm elated. My love for her fills me to the brim and spills over to the point where I dance around and whinny for joy. "I love Penny!" I shout, startling a brace of pigeons.

And in that moment, I feel an intense pain in my chest. "Ow. It hurts so much that I can't find her," I say. "Ow. Ow. Ow. What the heck? This pain is worse than an empty stomach or an ill-fitting saddle.

It's agonizing. It hurts so much not to know if she's okay, or even where she is."

Fifi stares at me with her bird eyes, cocks her head a little, and stares some more. Then she says, "She's here."

"Here?" I set down the bucket of kettle corn.

"Penny is here in Chicago. In a place called the Black Tower of Death."

37

PENNY

AS SOON AS I'm back in the car I look for a listing for Hankins in Springfield, but can't find one. I drive there, but the address Silla gave me is a tanning salon. Dead end. I feel a dull ache in my chest. I will probably never know what happened to my pony or where he is. It was dumb to come look for traces of a pony I haven't seen in twenty-five years. What I'm really looking for, I realize, is the life that was snatched away from me. The confident little girl I never was again.

I DRIVE OUT of Silla's and scan what I can remember of the town I left when I was twelve years old, long before I ever had a driver's license. It amazes me in our rapacious society to see that the little shopping mall with the market and drugstore is the same, all these years later. Tight zoning, I bet. Not like out west where you can basically build anything you want, anywhere. It's beautiful here. Rolling pastures, white fences, stone walls. This is upscale horse country, I realize. It's funny that I didn't see it that way at the time. It was just where we lived. In retrospect I'm amazed that my parents, who were right out of grad school and must have been earning close to nothing as adjunct professors at the local community college, found any housing here at all. Now that I think about it, I don't remember them having any friends here. No wonder they were so eager to move to Chicago.

Things got better for them there. They got hired at good colleges, and then got tenure in their fields: Italian literature for Dad and ancient Greek literature for Mom. Our apartment was filled with books and they were always reading, or talking about Calvino and the theory of lightness or whether *The Odyssey* was really written by a woman.

I miss my parents so much. They're both gone now. Mom had a heart attack. You know how they're always telling us that women have more heart attacks than men? It's true. My mother didn't even know she was having a heart attack. She thought it was a stiff neck. I didn't even get to say goodbye. Dad passed away just last year, in our same apartment in Chicago. He was very muted after Mom died. Rarely left the apartment. They were mated for life, like swans, and everything after Mom was joyless. Laus and I don't really have that kind of bond. Maybe it's better that way. Love hurts so much.

THE HOUSES ON the outskirts of Ithaca seem bigger than I remember, and I assume the last twenty-five years have been good for this place. Less great for me. Being here is bringing up a lot of memories, as expected, some welcome, some less so. I pass the elementary school I attended, getting a memory flash of playing four square and climbing on the jungle gym. There is the ice cream store where I had my tenth birthday.

I blink as I drive past a huge fancy gate that says HIGH RISE FARMS. I pull over, my heart racing.

It's still here. My mind spins. How is that possible?

Alex. Is Alex still here? I quickly google him and find out he's a professional show jumper. High Rise Farms. Ranked number eleven in the nation in show jumping. This is his home base, but from a quick scan of mentions I can see he competes all over the world. Aachen, Rio de Janeiro, Piazza di Siena.

I back up to the gate. I can see a long driveway down to a classic horse farm. Flowering forsythia and stone walls. I push out the bad memories of the last time I was here. Frank is long gone. I don't need to fear him. I focus on Alex. I had such a huge crush on him. It's funny and weird now to think of having a crush on a dorky thirteen-year-old boy with braces. I knew he rode, too. I was so shy. It took me forever to get up the courage to ask him to go riding together. Or did he ask me?

He showed up on that big red mare. So pretty. My pony was so . . . I feel guilty for even thinking the word. Scruffy. He was ill behaved, but I loved him anyway. Or maybe because he was ill behaved. But that day I was a little embarrassed, I remember. I was trying to act cool. I didn't want Alex to know that I liked him, but I wanted him to like me. He said I should come ride the show horses. I was so excited. I should have known. Mom used to say that a thirst for fame is always the precursor to disaster in the old myths. When we got out of the abandoned house, the pony had run off with his horse. Typical. We laughed about it and walked back to High Rise together. I felt like my life was about to change. And it was. Just not in the way that I thought.

I should leave it alone. But I've come all this way. Alex is a horse person. Maybe he will have some ideas about where I should look for my pony.

I get back in the car and drive down the driveway. The stables are beautiful—like something out of a magazine. There are rolling green pastures with split rail fencing, and paddocks with yearlings romping around. These people have Money.

"Can I help you?" asks a voice. I turn and a blond woman of about thirty in a ball cap, polo shirt, breeches, and boots is standing there with a saddled horse on a lead rope, a gorgeous bay. The tack is clean and the horse is spotless.

"I'm looking for Alex," I say.

"Is he expecting you?" She seems tense, but then again, I am a stranger.

"No. I'm an old friend. From childhood," I add. "My name is Penny."

"Oh. I'm Abra. He's riding in the back arena," she says. "Over there. Come with me. I'm bringing him his next horse."

I round the corner and see a man on a black gelding. He's wearing tall black boots and gray breeches and a bulky sweatshirt and a ball cap. He canters the horse up to a red-and-white-striped jump and the horse sails over it, pulling its legs high. He pats the horse and brings it back to a walk.

He comes over to the rail. "He's ready," he says to Abra. "Rub his legs down before you put him away."

He brings his right leg forward over the front of the saddle—a dangerous but flashy way to dismount—and slides off the black horse and tosses her the reins. He takes the second horse and mounts it elegantly in a single leap. Is he showing off for me?

"Alex," I say. It's interesting to see his face again. I sort of recognize the boy in him, but his features are sharp. He's thin and strong, I can see. "You probably won't remember me. My name is Penny." I decide this is a terrible idea and I should probably leave immediately, but I'm stuck in place like a bug on flypaper.

He looks down at me, squints a little. "Sure," he says in a way that doesn't convince me.

"I'd love to talk to you for a sec when you aren't busy," I say.

"This is my last horse of the day. Can you wait twenty minutes?"

I watch him ride the bay horse. He trots her around the arena a couple of times, rating her speed, then puts her into a canter. She tries to bolt, and he lets her out and then pulls her back. He's incredibly confident, I can see, even when she bucks and refuses a jump. He just circles her back and puts her at the jump again. He gives her a kick when they are a stride out and she takes a giant pantherlike leap into the air and clears the fence easily.

"Impressive," I say to Abra when she appears beside me. "I used to ride as a kid. Over at Silla's."

Abra brightens. "You did? I trained with her, too. Oh my God, wait. I remember you. Penny! You were like a goddess to me."

"I was?" I try to remember her, but I can't.

"I was little. Probably six when you were twelve. I remember you and your pony; you were like something out of one of those British kids' books, riding all over the countryside, having adventures while I was stuck on a leadline. Isn't Silla an amazing person? She really cares about horses."

"She does."

"So do you still ride?"

"No. We moved away, so I didn't get very far with my riding."

"You should take it up again. I know a lot of women who start up again when their kids get a driver's license. It's like a thing."

A thing. I could be part of that thing. I hadn't thought about riding. It's so expensive. But I did love it so much. It's like Abra has offhand-edly swung a door open for me.

"You're right," I say, trying to put my thoughts into words as Dr. Resa has taught me, instead of staying silent, which puts people off. "I—I really struggle to connect with people. But with my pony, it was effortless."

Abra shares a wry smile. "We're horse people—that's true for all of us. I've never really had friends."

"Me neither. I try to bond with my coworkers, but somehow I can't make it happen. My husband and I—forget it."

"I've given up on romantic relationships."

I can't believe how I'm opening up to this stranger, and how good it feels. I've been so guarded my whole life. Why? I tell Abra, "Even with my daughter—her anxiety has made our relationship really difficult."

"You definitely need a horse in your life. You want to come ride with me sometime?"

I feel an overwhelming rush of joy, and I can see that she does, too. I just made a friend! I forget that I don't live near here and say, "Yes!"

We trade contact information, and she says, "I'm so glad I met you. Is that weird?"

"It's not weird," I say. "We both really love horses. We're horse bonding."

She laughs and nods.

Alex rides over, dismounts, and hands the horse to Abra. Her smile fades to a frown. There's some tension between the two of them, and I wonder if they're in a relationship.

"I need to change," he says to me. "I'll meet you in the clubhouse. It's right over there."

The walls of the clubhouse are covered with photos and ribbons. It's much tidier and cleaner than Silla's. Way, way more upscale. There are many pictures of Alex riding, but also others who I assume are his clients or horses he bred. For a moment I wonder if this is the life I would have had if . . . I had kept riding, moved from ponies to horses, competed, won things. It's like I am looking at an alternate life. One that was snatched away from me.

But maybe I can rejoin this world. Maybe Abra and I will go riding before I leave. Maybe I will start to take riding lessons again, if I can find a place that will let me muck stalls in lieu of payment.

Alex appears, languidly graceful. He's still wearing the boots and breeches, but the bulky sweatshirt has been replaced with a neat polo shirt. Like Abra's shirt, it has HIGH RISE FARMS embroidered over his heart. He sinks into a leather sofa and gestures for me to do the same.

"What can I do for you, Penny?" he asks.

"I don't know if you remember," I begin, suddenly a little nervous. "I was in the grade below you in middle school. I had a pony."

"Hard to forget," he says. "You murdered my uncle Frank."

38

THE PONY

BLACK TOWER OF Death. This gives me pause. "Why is it called that?"

"Because birds fly into the windows all the time. Very poor design, from our point of view."

"How do you know Penny is there?" I wonder if Fifi is still lying to me.

"All the birds know Penny," she says. "She fills the bird feeders with raspberry jam."

"She's alive, and she's here?"

"Go to the Black Tower of Death and you'll find her."

"Thank you," I say. I leave Fifi fluttering over the kettle corn and trot back into the heart of the city. Fortunately it's late and things have quieted down off the main drag.

Streetlights make circles on the black empty streets. Tall buildings loom all around me. Which one is the Black Tower of Death? I sniff deeply, expecting to catch Penny's unmistakable scent. Sniff, sniffffff. Nothing. But these windows are thick, and she's probably indoors. I hug the edge of the buildings, staying in darkness and willing my hooves to clatter less. I whisper to some moths in the light. "Which one is the Black Tower of Death?" They ignore me. I continue walking, peering upward. A taxi cruises past and I hide behind a mailbox.

And then I see it. A tall black glass tower. The moon shines on it, making it look like a castle. It's eerie.

"That's the Black Tower of Death," says a voice over my head. I look up into the bare branches of a tree that's living in a little box. An owl is sitting there.

"I met your cousin in the forest of the blue butterflies," I say. "How do I get into the Black Tower of Death? I need to get to the roof."

"You could grow a pair of wings."

"Thanks," I say. "For nothing." I'm really tired of bird games.

"Don't be like that. I'm just giving you a hard time. There's an elevator. You know what that is? Box that moves things up and down."

I nod. "Course I do." I don't, but I'm in a mood.

I make my way to the base of the Black Tower. It's very tall. I'm shivering with fear, but I can't turn back now. Penny is here! I stand in front of the revolving door.

"Try the service entrance in back," says the owl. "You're in luck. Someone is moving in tonight."

"Stop following me," I say.

I trot around to the back and open the service entrance door. I find the elevator.

"Push the button," says the owl.

"Go away," I say. I push the button. I gasp as the doors open. I enter the gray box, which has mats like horse blankets pinned to the walls. I wait for something to happen. Then the door shuts. Then the box starts to move! I feel nauseated and very worried. My legs wobble. I sniff the buttons, where I can smell traces of many humans. Underneath all of the other human scents, and a lot of cleaning products, I get a faint scent of her and I almost keel over. Penny! Fifi was not lying.

The elevator comes to a stop and the door opens. There are two men there with big cardboard boxes. They are shocked to see me, and then they frown. "Is that a horse?" one says. I quickly hit the buttons with my nose and the door closes again and the elevator keeps going up. The door opens again and there is a little girl standing there. At first I think it's Penny, but it's not. She's about six and she's in footie pajamas with frogs on them. Her eyes go wide and she stares at me.

"Pony!" she says.

I hear a voice say "Margie! Are you in the hallway again? Oh my God, she's in the hall again." Margie stares in delight at me and just as the doors close I hear her mother say "There was no pony there, honey."

Parents! I think. *Believe your children!*

Finally the elevator doors open and I am on the roof. I can smell traces of Penny everywhere. I walk out onto paving stones and steer around patio furniture and peer out at the city. It gives me vertigo to be high up like this. I am looking out over the world, as if I am on the highest mountain! A light wind is blowing. It's amazing and beautiful, but where is Penny? I walk around the rooftop, inspecting picnic tables and potted trees and attempting to nibble on artificial turf. Yuck! I smell the bird feeders, inhaling recent odors of raspberry jam. Why hasn't she filled these feeders today, I wonder. Why no new jam?

"She's not here," says a voice. That blasted owl again.

"How do you know who I'm looking for?"

"You're looking for Penny."

"Did you talk to Fifi the sparrow?"

"I don't talk to sparrows. I eat them. Penny talked about you."

"You know her?"

"Oh yes. She lived in this building for years and years, and her father lived here for even longer. She had so many bird feeders up here it was like mating season at the wetlands. But she's gone. Her father died a month or so ago and she came and packed up the last of his things. She's not coming back."

A month ago? I missed Penny by . . . days? "She's . . . gone?"

"She grew up. Moved away. Humans do that."

I drop my nose to the artificial turf. Ponies don't really cry, but when it's windy, our eyes water, so let's just say it was very windy.

"I came such a long way," I say. "I just wanted to make things right."

"That was dumb," says the owl.

"I thought owls were supposed to say wise and helpful things."

"Go home," says the owl.

"I don't have one," I say.

"Whose fault is that?"

"What do you mean?"

"We build and feather our own nests," says the owl. "Well, except for the brown-headed cowbird. They're nest thieves."

"Ponies don't nest."

"But you like a nice safe place to sleep and something to eat and companionship, don't you?"

I nod.

"Then make that happen. You've been mean and selfish. Transactional."

"How do you know that?"

"Am I wrong?"

I wobble my head a little, but I can't disagree with him. I have been both mean and selfish on occasion. "Being transactional is normal and necessary in the world we live in," I protest. "Everyone just wants what's fair."

He revolves his head in that unnerving owl way and stares. "Be a generous good friend to all and you will find you have all that you need."

"But is Penny okay? Where is she?"

"She's not okay. You were her friend and you abandoned her in her hour of need. You set in motion a terrible chain of events. Her life was ruined that night. She's never going to be okay. Because of you."

"But. If you tell me where she is—"

"You'll just make things even worse. You're going to have to live with what you've done."

Then, with a flap of his huge wings and a mouse-scented burp, he is gone.

I GET BACK in the elevator and go down. When I get to the ground floor the movers are waiting with a sofa.

"That *is* a horse," one of them says as I exit past them and push open the service door of the building. "But one that got stuck in the dryer for too long."

"Rich people and their weird pets," mutters the other one. "Get a freaking goldfish."

I walk slowly back to the armory. The door is closed so I kick at it with my hoof. *Bang bang bang.*

"Who is it?" says a voice on the intercom.

I neigh.

The door slowly and noisily grinds up.

The guard is standing there. He has a heavy flashlight in his hands and he is hitting his palm with it in an ominous fashion.

"You little f-er," he says. "You kicked me."

He raises his arm and lunges to hit me with the flashlight and I run as fast as I can down the concrete ramp, around the corner and back into my stall. I pull the door closed and drop down into the shavings out of sight. He stomps up and down the aisles muttering curses, but finally the barn goes quiet again.

Penny is gone. I ruined her life. I am filled with feelings I have never felt before. They are not pleasant.

I barely have time to recognize my discontent before a shadowy figure arrives at the stall door. I sniff. It's not the guard, fortunately. It's not Helen or Ines. Where have I smelled this smell before? I struggle to my feet and shake off the shavings. I smell a carrot.

The woman slides a halter over my head. I recognize her scent. It's the red-haired woman who said that Helen ripped her off. Sold her a lame pony.

The woman leads me out of the barn into a back hallway, past some lockers, and then we slip out of a fire door. Outside on the street there is a pony trailer waiting.

"Can you smell the oats?" she says.

I can. I climb into the trailer. She closes the door and it begins to rumble and shake as we pull into traffic. I don't really put it together until I have eaten all of the oats.

I have been stolen!

39

PENNY

I DIDN'T KILL your uncle!" I say, leaping up from the white sofa in shock. "I would never do that. You saw me, I was running away. He chased me into the forest. I was scared out of my mind."

"You could have jumped off and waited for him. Attacked him when he wasn't looking." Alex, too, is on his feet now, and I am super aware that he is very fit, very strong, and I am alone with him. Should I run away? But then he's going to think I'm guilty.

I try to calm myself. I sit down on the sofa. "Alex," I say. "I was a little girl. Twelve years old. Not even five feet tall. I was trying to save your horse from being beaten, and I was scared for my life. All I wanted was to get away from your uncle. Hide from him."

"So what happened out there in the woods?"

"I don't know, but I will tell you exactly what I do know. What I told the police. Please sit down."

Alex stares at me for a second, then exhales and sits down. "Okay," he says, still hostile. "I want to hear your version."

"You saw him hit me across the face with the dressage whip?"

"Yes," says Alex. "And I saw you steal the horse and run away into the woods. Uncle Frank took the quad and went after you."

I am suddenly curious about something. "What did you do?"

"I called the police like Uncle Frank told me to."

"You told them I stole the horse?"

Alex stares back at me. "You did steal her."

I realize this conversation is a huge mistake. "I thought I was saving your horse's life," I say carefully. "You saw him beat the crap out of her."

Alex looks like he's going to protest, then doesn't. "He was a hard guy. He had a temper. But he was very good to me and my mom after my dad died."

I nod. Of course Alex isn't going to say that his dead father figure was a jerk. "Look, I rode like hell intending to go to Silla's, but it was dark by then and I missed a turn in the trail. Plus that mare was bolting. I could hardly steer her." For a second I'm back there. I remember the darkness, the pain in my face, and the sheer terror. "Your mare was so much bigger than my pony, and my feet didn't reach the stirrups," I tell him. "I was grabbing mane to stay on. I really thought your uncle was going to kill me."

"Then what happened?"

"The mare swerved out from under me. I tried to pull myself back up into the saddle but I was half off and hit a tree branch. Fell off, hit my head. That's the last thing I remember before the police found me."

"You didn't see anyone out there? A flashlight? A sound?"

"Like I told the police, I didn't see or hear anything. I was unconscious when Frank was killed. They took my statement at the hospital and my parents came and got me. That was the end of riding for me. My parents basically just kidnapped me and took me to Chicago. I haven't been on a horse since then."

Alex stares at me. I can't tell if he believes me or not. He says, "We thought you killed him but the police protected you because you were a minor. And a girl."

"No. They knew I didn't do it. I was a mess when they found me, all covered with leaves and branches. I had a broken rib and a concussion. I couldn't have hoisted a rock and thrown it hard enough to kill anyone."

Alex doesn't seem convinced. "They never found who did it. They

analyzed the rock for fingerprints and DNA but didn't get a match."
He throws up his hands. "It's very frustrating. For me, for my mom.
His killer has been out there all this time. Loose."

An older woman, very polished, comes rushing into the room, a
stylish linen duster flapping behind her. Her sleek hair pulled back in
a ponytail has gone gray but I recognize her. Melanie Kinsworth, Alex's mother, Frank's sister.

"You little bitch," she spits. "How dare you come back here? You
criminal!"

40

THE PONY

THIS FLAME-HAIRED PONY thief did not perhaps think things through as well as she should have. We arrive at a nice barn a couple of hours outside the city. I am put in a stall that has an adequate amount of shavings and some hay. A horse next door says hi but I am too tired to respond.

In the morning when the woman's horse trainer arrives, things get ugly.

"I am not going to be a part of this," says the trainer. She is a tall, broad woman with black hair.

"I am owed a pony," says the thief. "Helen stole from me. She took my money and so I took a pony."

"I quit," says the trainer. "I cannot be a part of anything illegal. You know what they do, right?"

"No one's going to jail. My husband is—"

"I'm not worried about jail. I'm worried about being suspended from the horsemen's association for life. No more horse shows, ever. They do it to people all the time for mistreating animals. Or for stealing them." And, in case the thief has not grasped the problem, she adds, "You cannot show this pony. You have no bill of sale, no registration, nothing. If anyone sees this pony—like the vet who is coming here later today to give shots—we are in deep shit."

The thief blinks. "What do we do? We gotta get rid of this pony."

"Take the pony back."

"I'm not taking the pony back."

The trainer is angry. "Then we have no choice. He has to go to Canada."

AT FIRST I am intrigued. I have lost track of Penny, and ruined her life, which is bad and apparently according to the owl can never be remedied, but I have heard good things about Canada. It's a place of snow, yes, which makes it kind of a poetic landscape to be exiled to, but it also has universal healthcare, beer (which ponies like but should not consume), and Newfoundland ponies, who are sweet and extra fuzzy. Canadian humans are kind and not as voraciously ambitious as Americans, and they have a good sense of humor.

"So we're going to the Great White North?" I ask as I am loaded into an open-plan stock trailer with a lot of unusually thin horses. This trailer is not at all like the one I crossed the country in with Burnie and the rat. It does not have shavings on the slippery metal floor or windows to keep the cold and rain out. It does not have hay bags or any trace of food at all in it. Still, I try to make the best of things. "Good thing I brought my winter coat!" I neigh.

One horse swings its head around and I see it only has one eye. Its ribs stick out and its hip bones are so sharp it looks like they are going to poke through its skin.

"It's illegal to butcher horses for meat in the U.S.," says the horse. "So we're going to either Canada or Mexico to be slaughtered."

"Wait! What?" I don't want to believe him. It can't be true. "But . . . but . . . I won a blue ribbon," I say. "I have been a beloved pet of many children."

"I won seventeen races," says the horse. "That's two point three million dollars."

"I won twenty-three jumping competitions," says another horse.

The truck echoes with our résumés: barrel racing, gymkhanas, polo, backyard pets . . . none of our accomplishments mattered in the end, once we were no longer useful.

The truck stops and more skinny, lame, old horses and ponies are loaded on until we are so tightly packed that we couldn't fall over if we tried. We can't move, but we can see through the metal slats as the truck rolls down the highway, engine roaring, past carloads of people heading out on vacation, suitcases and camping gear on the roof, kids watching videos in the back seat. They don't even look up as we struggle to stand and strain to breathe as we open our mouths and scream and scream and scream.

PART SEVEN

Terror

41

PENNY

PENNY TUNES OUT the clanging of cell doors and the chatter of the guards' walkie-talkies and recalls how she fled High Rise Farms, Melanie shouting at her and threatening her, Alex standing by mutely. Her cheeks hot with shame, she was happy that the friendly groom Abra was nowhere in sight as she drove away.

She puts down her pen and thinks about Melanie and Alex Kinsworth. Melanie was so furious at Penny for coming back to High Rise. And then, not long after that, Penny was arrested.

What had she stirred up by going back there?

She tries to reconstruct the timeline. When did Dr. Resa lie to the police and say that Penny had confessed? Penny had a session with Dr. Resa a few days before she left on the trip to Ithaca. Were Melanie/Alex and Dr. Resa somehow connected? Did Melanie, incensed by Penny's visit, bribe Dr. Resa to lie? Or was it Alex who was pulling the strings? There must be a connection there, Penny thinks. Who else would frame her for this? She needs to find out more about all of these people, unravel their hidden intersections. But how? She has no cell phone, no access to the internet. Nothing but a pair of opposable thumbs that may as well be hooves for all the good they are doing her.

TWO DAYS LATER she is surprised when Lisa comes to see her. The visit wasn't scheduled. "I'm still writing it all down," Penny tells her. "About my visit to Ithaca. I think we should look more closely at Melanie. Maybe she killed her brother. She inherited the horse farm, after all. And Alex. I mean, if his uncle was abusive to him, which would not be out of character, he had a motive to kill him, too. Also, maybe they bribed my therapist."

"Listen, Penny," says Lisa, looking very serious. "I filed a motion to get access to all the evidence the prosecution is presenting. I was able to look at the video of you and Dr. Resa."

"Video?" Penny didn't remember that their sessions were recorded. Had she agreed to that?

"It's not great for us," says Lisa. She holds up her phone so Penny can see it and pushes play.

The screen is small, but Penny can see it's a recording of their Zoom session. She can see herself, with Dr. Resa very small in the corner.

"Let's do some breath work," Dr. Resa tells her. "Close your eyes."

Penny watches herself close her eyes and begin to breathe deeply the way Dr. Resa taught her as a way to access deep emotions. This isn't how Penny remembered their session going.

"Now tell me about that night in the forest," says Dr. Resa.

"I'm really scared," says video Penny in a small voice.

Penny blinks at this. She has no memory of this part of the session, of saying those words. She leans in, studying herself on the tiny screen. She looks strange, contorted, like Tella when she's dreaming.

"I can hear him coming," says video Penny. "He's going to hurt me." She pants, as if it's happening now.

"You're safe now," says Dr. Resa. "It's okay. Tell me what you see."

"I'm so scared," says video Penny. "I'm shaking. I'm hiding behind a tree. He's coming!"

Her voice in the video sounds high and small as if she *is* a little girl again. Sitting there in the jail's conversation pit, Penny is fascinated by what she's watching, but also mystified. What *is* this? It's her, talking, but it isn't her. Is it artificial intelligence? A fake? But there's a part of Penny that knows this is real. This is *her*, some deep part of her that she kept hidden, that Dr. Resa was able to coax out.

"I can hear his footsteps in the leaves," says video Penny, who is clearly panicked. "I can hear his breathing. I'm trying to be quiet. I'm trying to be perfectly still. But he has a light. I know he's going to find me. So I take a rock and I kill him."

42

THE PONY

THE HUGE STOCK trailer drives on and on, but our panic does not abate. I am pressed between the old racehorse and the slatted side of the truck. The metal digs into my skin. I feel like I'm going to pass out. I think of Burnie and his joy in racing, his copper coat rippling in the sunlight as he crossed the finish line. I think of all of the equines I have known and how hard they tried to please their people, how fast they ran, how high they jumped, how they pranced and spun and danced to the music.

"They sell us because they're always seeking the perfect horse instead of seeing each horse as perfect in its own way," says the one-eyed horse.

"We were never enough," says another horse.

I kick the side of the trailer. At least I still have my anger, I think.

"Neigh if you hate humans," I shout. The truck erupts in neighs.

"Did you ever know a human you liked?" asks a dun-colored gentle giant draft horse whose massive head towers over me. His voice is soft and tired. He could swallow my entire skull, but he would never do that. I position myself underneath him so I get some more room, hoping he doesn't fall on top of me.

"Did you?" I ask.

"Yes," he says. "A man named Henry."

"Then why are you here? Why did Henry let this happen to you?"

"He died," says the draft horse.

"Oh."

"Did you have a special person?" he asks.

I don't really want to go into it, but he clearly wants to talk. "Her name is Penny," I say. "She grew up."

"I knew a Penny," comes a high-pitched whinny from the other side of the truck.

I twist my head but I can't see the horse. "You met Penny?" I call out. I describe her scent pattern: two parts willow, one part marshmallow, a smidge of Ivory soap, denim, nutmeg . . . "and a lot of raspberry jam!"

"Yes," she says. "That's her. That terrible night. That man."

"Arete?" I shout. "Arete, is that you?"

"Yes!" she calls. "My name is Arete!"

I have found Arete!

"Arete! Where is Penny?" I neigh. "What happened in the woods that night?"

At this moment, the truck slows. The horses start to neigh and shift on their feet, making the metal floor bang like a hundred drums. I can't hear anything but that infernal noise. Are we at the slaughterhouse? I try not to imagine what's going to happen next. I hope it will be quick, but I fear it won't be.

"I give up," cries the old racehorse next to me. "Goodbye."

"No!" I shout, and bite him, but it's too late. I watch the light go out of his eyes and his head slumps down. He's pinned between horses so he doesn't even fall, just slides lower, causing the horses around him to panic and thrash. When I bite him again, he doesn't flinch. He's dead. I curse all of the people who owned him along the way, and for good measure the people who bet on him, too.

"Arete?" I call again, but all the horses are neighing now and I can't hear a thing.

I peer out between the slats. The landscape is gray with a light covering of snow. We're at a truck stop. The truck creaks and squeals and finally comes to a standstill. I see the driver's door open and close and watch a dark figure cross the gray pavement to the neon-lit truck stop. He ignores our cries. It's just another delivery for him. Just a paycheck.

I try to press through the truck to Arete, but everyone is squashed together, shivering and crying. Plus, reality check, I am trapped in a semi-load of horses being sent to slaughter. Even if I find out where Penny is, there's nothing I can do about it. I can hear the draft horse's heart beating. "I'm going to die," I whimper.

"Everyone dies," he says. "At least we'll be together."

"What's your name?" I ask him.

"Henry called me Jake," says the draft horse.

So this is it. The end. I must say, I hoped for better than to be made into steaks for French people.

I look back over my life. I am an ordinary pony. Like almost all ponies, I was sold and sold and sold and sold. Except when I was given away. I wanted permanence, and all I got was transience.

"At least death means I will never be sold again," I say out loud.

And then I see movement through the slats. I look out into the darkness and I can barely make out about ten people in black. Skittering like rats across the pavement toward the truck. They are moving silently, staying low. I hear the sound of scraping metal and a whisper: "Fan out and herd them away from the road toward the hills!"

I hear a horse outside, too. No shoes—quiet bare hooves on wet ground.

The horses inside the trailer begin to prick their ears and neigh.

"Who's there?" calls Jake.

Then I hear the creak as the door of the trailer swings open.

"Go, go go!" whispers a human voice.

And then we all start to move. There is a huge clatter of hooves on metal as we begin leaping from the trailer. I have to jump over the body of the poor dead racehorse. "You deserved better," I say to his still form. "Everyone does."

There are two horses and riders in the darkness. One of them takes off, the ridden horse calling to us "Follow me! Come with me! Run as fast as you can!" The trailer horses mill for a second in confusion, some of them limping and in pain, but the other horse and rider get behind them and push them forward, waving a rope. "Get up, get up," calls the rider, and his horse echoes him. "Go go go! Run for your lives!"

Like a river finding the downslope, the horses begin to run, following each other and the horse in front. Even the lame horses find the strength to gallop. There is a thundering of hooves and whinnying as we run along, an unlikely herd.

"Hey! Stop! Whoa!" calls the driver as he comes out of the truck stop.

I race after the horses. "Arete!" I call. My legs are much shorter than the others' and I'm stiff from being crushed in the trailer. There's a break in the fence at the back of the truck stop and we all race through it and up a hill. We drop down through a ravine and some of the older horses are stumbling, but we keep going, racing along. At the bottom we are herded into a pasture and then pushed onward into a pen. Sides heaving, nostrils flaring, we are quickly sorted into groups by size and herded again, this time through chutes into waiting trailers that head in different directions into the night.

Jake the draft horse is loaded into a trailer with an Appaloosa. "Come with me, little one!" he calls.

"I'm looking for Arete," I say. I try to go to another trailer, but a human turns me back.

"I only have room for two," calls the human to the others, and closes the trailer door.

"Arete?" I call into the darkness. "Arete?"

No answer.

I hear sirens in the distance.

"Shoot," says a man near me in a leather jacket. "Load and go! Load and go. Make sure you have the fake bills of sale."

The sirens are getting closer. Jake calls to me over his shoulder as the two-horse trailer he's in pulls away. "Good luck, pony!"

"Can you take the pony?" a woman with long shiny hair asks an older man.

"I'm sorry, I don't have room for him," he says, closing his trailer door. He gets in his truck and leaves.

There are only two humans left. And a little blue car. And me.

The sirens are closer.

"We gotta go," says the long-haired woman to the man in the leather jacket.

"We can't leave him," says the man. He opens the back hatch of the little blue car.

"He's never going to jump in there," says the woman, her hair blowing in the wind. "He's not even going to fit. We have to leave him. We saved all the others."

The sirens are racing toward us.

"Get in the car," says the man to me as if I am a Labrador retriever.

I jump in the little blue car, exactly as if I am a Labrador retriever. This is no time for dignity. There is a dog bed and a chew toy. I have to scooch down to fit in the space, but I drop to my knees and lie perfectly still.

The man closes the hatch and jumps in the car. The woman does, too, and we peel out, headlights off, bumping along a dirt track in the darkness.

"We did it," says the man. He peels off his leather jacket as he drives and tosses it onto me. So now I'm a coat rack, too?

I've never been crammed in such a small space with two humans and I am feeling a little claustrophobic, truth be told.

"I can't believe it," says the woman, pulling her long hair into a barrette. "That was amazing. I feel so . . . alive."

Me too, I think.

"He's really cute," says the woman, reaching back to pet my nose.

With all of the anxiety, I kind of need to poop.

"Do not poop in here," says the man to me, "or my wife will kill me. I'm not kidding. She thinks I'm at poker night."

"My husband thinks I'm at book group," says the woman. "We're reading *Demon Copperhead*. Fortunately it's long, so I can say we talked and talked. What are we going to do with this pony? I usually raid fur farms and pig barns. I don't actually know much about ponies."

"Me neither," says the man. "But we can't keep him. We have to get rid of him right away. We can't leave him where he'll get run over, or eaten by coyotes or dogs."

She nods.

They drive along in silence, and then the woman says, "Wait. I have an idea. Let me look at a map." She pecks at a phone and then says, "Yes!" and shows it to the man.

"Oh," says the man. "I guess that could work."

"It's pretty far. I'll have to tell my husband I drank too much while arguing about fate and destiny in *Demon Copperhead* and I have to stay at Sandy's."

"I guess I could say I had an emergency call. I'm a plumber. It happens. Let's do it."

We drive for several hours. I'm getting a little cramped and I really want to stand up. I shift a little and the guy says, "Please, please be patient and do *not* take a dump. We're almost there." To the woman he says, "The last thing I need is the pony to kick out a window in this thing. It's my wife's car. I didn't want to liberate horses in a truck with my name and phone number on the side."

"Don't kick out the windows," says the woman to me. "Or poop. Please."

I like the "please." I grace them instead with a hefty fart.

After a while I begin to smell the sea, even over my own heavy perfumes. The wind begins to buffet the sides of the car, and I can hear the crash of waves.

Finally, as dawn is breaking, we come to a stop. The two humans open the back of the car. I can see their faces now. They are very innocent-looking middle-aged people. They both smell like shampoo. I jump out and lift my head and drink in the salt air.

"You think he'll be okay?" says the man.

"I hope so," says the woman.

Under a pink sky, I see dunes, a salt marsh, and a white sandy beach. The wind whips around us. I can smell horses faintly, but I can't see any. Where is the stable?

The woman pats me and whispers in my ear. "This is totally illegal," she says. "But I read about this place in a book when I was a little girl, so here we are. You're free, buddy. Free. You can live out your days here. Good luck."

I lower my head and begin eating the grass. It's a little salty, but still delicious, like the French fries Penny and I used to share.

The man laughs. "Go," he says. "Go, before the rangers see us." He waves his arms at me. "Go!" he yells. I keep eating. The woman slaps me on the butt. I still keep eating. "We gotta go," the man says. He gets in the car.

I hear a distant whinny and finally raise my head. I look at the woman. She and the man have broken the law to save me and the other horses.

Maybe all humans aren't bad. But then I think of the killpen truck, the way we were discarded by people who we gave our all for. The way humans treat each other and every species on the planet, not to mention the planet itself.

With very few exceptions, humans are vile creatures, I decide.

I lift my tail and dash in the direction of the whinny. I stop and look back once, and the woman smiles and waves, and then she gets in the car and leaves.

But . . . there is no stall. No barn. No fence. I am confused. I hear the whinnying again. I run toward it.

I crest the dune and see a small group of stunted trees and among them, a herd of . . . ponies!

I stop, shocked. Is this a dream?

One of the ponies catches sight of me and gasps, and they all raise their heads and look at me in wonder.

"Uh . . . hi," I say.

Suddenly the landscape is alive . . . ponies appear out of every bush and hollow. They are all about my size and very woolly, and every color you can imagine; black, white, spotted, palomino, roan, chestnut, piebald, skewbald, bay, and gray. They have leaves and twigs in their hair, and burrs stuck to their fur. They come at me from every angle, like hunters in camo. I am very weirded out. I start running and they follow me, snorting. We make about three laps of the meadow before I'm hot, sweaty, and too tired to run any more.

"Uncle," I say, lowering my head and trying to look as meek as possible.

"Is that your name?" demands the first pony who catches up to me. It's not an entirely friendly question. She's seal brown and very furry, a little larger than me. I feel suddenly shy, and nervous.

"I'm just a pony like you," I say. "You can call me whatever you want."

"Don't talk to her," says a brown-and-white pinto pony stallion coming at me with teeth bared. "We don't use human names here, interloper."

"Ahhhhh!" I say, trying to get away, but I'm blocked by a pair of heels kicking at me.

"Don't hurt me!" I squeal. "I come in peace and friendship."

"Stand still," whispers a little gray colt. "Just stand still."

I do, and all the ponies gather around me and sniff me. I'm afraid they're going to bite me and kick me until I'm food for seagulls, but they just sniff and squeal and snort, and then it's all over and they go back to grazing. I'm trembling, but I manage to walk a few steps and then I lie down and roll. The sand is warmed by the sun and it feels so good.

I see the gray colt nearby and I wander over to him.

"What is this place?" I ask. "When do they come and catch us for pony rides, or pony lessons, or pony races?"

"They don't," he says. "No one rides us here."

"But they feed us?"

"No," he says. "Sometimes we try to steal picnics and handouts from hikers, but no one intentionally feeds us."

"Oh. So we just . . . graze?"

He looks at me and gives a little laughing whinny. "Yes. We're wild," he says, and gallops off, bucking.

"I'm wild?" I say.

I can't believe it. I'm free! Free like my ancient pony ancestors!

THE FIRST FEW days are great. I stay on the edges of the herd, eating grass and nibbling on leaves and bark. Do I miss carrots? Yes. But I cope. I have to get used to the idea of being able to eat as much as I want. The first day, I eat too much.

"Easy there, buddy," says a small palomino. "Don't make yourself ill."

"I've always eaten until the bucket is clean," I say. "I don't know how to stop."

"Just tell yourself there's no bottom to this bucket. Slow down."

I eat plants I probably shouldn't be eating, that make my teeth itch. But then I start smelling what I'm about to eat first. I start to be picky, choosing only the tender shoots to eat. I use my nose to push aside things I don't want and only nibble on what tastes good. Believe it or not, I lose weight. Turns out grazing is actually good for you.

There are downsides. This island is a pony sanctuary, but it is also apparently an unofficial tick sanctuary. It makes me squirm and buck to feel bloodsucking bugs crawling up my legs and under my chin. And the mosquitoes and flies swarm as soon as the wind dies. I long for fly spray.

But I'm free. I'm part of a federally protected herd of wild ponies, I learn. Sounds like a dream, right? Seems that should be where the story happily ends, right?

208

43

PENNY

I TAKE A rock and I kill him.

What the hell was that, thinks Penny as she lies in her bunk. She'd seen frustration and anger and distrust in Lisa's eyes when she'd finished showing Penny the video of the confession.

Penny had struggled to find words. "I . . . I have no memory of that," she'd said at last, knowing how lame that sounded. "I don't know what to say."

"Why don't we take a break and I'll come see you tomorrow," says Lisa. She can see the words in Lisa's eyes.

Guilty.

Plea bargain.

Prison.

Penny will serve at least three years, maybe less with good behavior and if Democrats have enough votes to enact the sentencing reforms they've been promising for years. Three years. It's such a long time to be away from home and family. And everyone will think she killed a guy. And it could be more than three years, lots more, if the judge is in a mood to throw the book at her. In any case she'll be a convicted felon for the rest of her life, even once her debt to society is paid. She'll lose her teaching license, never be able to work with kids again. Her life will never be the same. But has that ship already sailed? She's been here for weeks. Laus can't keep the lid on the truth forever, if he even tried to. What has he told Tella?

Did I kill him?

She has always assumed that the blank in her memory of that night was because she was knocked unconscious when she fell off Alex's horse. Is it instead her brain protecting her from something terrible that she did?

If she was hiding and Frank hunted and found her, and she killed him, would a jury release her on grounds of self-defense? It's not a given, she knows. This jail is famous for being the pipeline to the state prison across the river, a huge cement complex full of women, some of whom genuinely deserve to be there, and some who were fighting for their lives when they killed someone but still ended up serving long or life sentences. Lisa has told her about a woman she tried to help get paroled who was sixteen when she killed the man who was sexually abusing her. She's now in her fifties and will die of old age in prison, never having spent a day outside the walls since her trial. Poor Dawn, who is awaiting trial for killing her husband to stop him from beating their children. "'You could have called social services,'" Dawn says they told her. "I did," Dawn protested, "and they did nothing. So I solved the problem myself." Dawn's likely going to be a lifer, too. Society is still prone to ignore the context and blame the survivor.

She stares at her own hands, tries to picture them hoisting a rock and bashing in Frank's skull.

I'm not capable of it, she thinks. *Even to save my own life.* That's a startling thought in itself, but in this case a freeing one.

If I didn't kill him, why did I say that I did?

Penny tries to objectively analyze the video, based on what she knows from a handful of TED Talks about memory. There was a time when uncovering "repressed" memories was a thing. A scandal involving a daycare. Awful things that people seemed to be remembering from when they were children. People went to jail; their lives were ruined. Suicides. But it wasn't true. It took years to prove that those weren't repressed memories.

"Memory is not a videotape," Dr. Resa has told Penny many times in their sessions. "It's just a story we tell ourselves about what happened. Maybe it is what happened, or maybe it isn't. What matters is why we're telling ourselves that story."

What story was the Penny in the video telling herself?

Who was she afraid of, or who was she protecting?

LISA LOOKS UP from the legal pad. "That's everything Alex and Melanie said to you that day?" she asks Penny. Ever since Lisa showed Penny the video, Penny can tell Lisa thinks she's guilty, even though she told her she has no memory of saying those things, and that they are not true.

"Everything I can remember. I was thinking, what was the amount of time between when Alex called 911 and when the police arrived?"

Lisa flips through the papers in her file folder. "The 911 call came in at 7:16 and the police didn't arrive at High Rise Farms until 7:40."

"They didn't exactly rush over, did they?"

"Well, the call was for a stolen horse. That isn't a national emergency."

"And what time did they find Frank's body?"

Lisa looks again at the police report. "About twenty minutes later, right after they found you semiconscious. Why?"

"Alex or Melanie could have killed Frank and been back at High Rise before the police arrived."

Lisa thinks for a moment. "So you're saying you rode off on the stolen horse, Frank chased you, Melanie and/or Alex chased Frank, killed him, then came back in time to meet the police and send them off into the woods to find you?"

It sounds less believable than it did in her head. Penny thinks some more. "Well, Melanie wasn't at High Rise when Alex and I came back. She might have already been in the woods. She could have killed Frank and gone back to High Rise and pretended she was coming home from somewhere else."

Lisa sighs. "Melanie wouldn't have known you were going to steal the horse and run into the woods with Frank chasing you. If Melanie lived at High Rise with Frank, even if she had a motive, wouldn't that night have been an odd moment and place to kill him? Is there any reason you can think of that Melanie had for killing him in that moment? I mean, they ran a highly successful horse operation together, right?"

Penny nods. "But I think Alex was afraid of his uncle. He—"

Lisa cuts her off. "I tried to contact Alex, but he won't talk to me. We're not police, we can't compel people to talk to us, especially the family of the victim," she reminds Penny.

"But if we go to trial, we can cross-examine him, right?"

"Yes, he's a material witness to the case, so yes, but Penny, going to trial is not always the best option. Juries can be . . ."

"Capricious?" Penny herself had served on a jury only once. A murder trial. A gang member had killed another gang member. She remembered feeling scared in the parking lot leaving the courthouse.

"People have lives to get back to, they don't really want to be there. The judges' dockets are crazy full. The lawyers have giant caseloads. No one really wants to drag it out. It's not like on TV. Trials can go fast, and they can go really wrong."

"That's not reassuring," says Penny. "For me or America as a whole."

"I know, but it's the truth."

"But I'd be confessing to murder."

Lisa looks at her blankly. "You already did."

"That video is me lying."

Lisa blinks. "Why did you lie to your therapist?"

"I don't know! I was in a semihypnotic state. I *was* my twelve-year-old self."

"Can you go back into that state? Can you ask your twelve-year-old self what happened that night so we can all go home?"

Penny can hear a hint of sarcasm in Lisa's voice, and she can't blame her. "I know this seems crazy," she says. "But please believe me. Please."

Lisa says, "Unfortunately it doesn't matter what I believe. You have to understand the effect of that video on a jury. I just need to walk you through what a plea deal would look like. They'll start at second degree murder, but I think we can get it down to manslaughter. I've talked to Steve. We can bring up the self-defense angle for sure. It's already established that he chased you into the woods. He was in a rage. It all happened really fast. You were a little girl, he was a big strong man. He grabbed you, the two of you struggled, you grabbed a rock and hit him."

"Someone else was out there," says Penny. "Someone who wanted Frank dead."

44

THE PONY

ONE DAY I am resting in the shade when something odd happens. I can feel Penny. I can't see her, but it's like she's standing
right in front of me. She's not saying anything, but she's so sad. That's
what I can feel, this whole-body sadness.

"Whatsa matter with you?" asks a bat hanging nearby.

I peer up at him. His tiny black claws are embedded in a branch
of a stunted pine tree. "It's daytime. Shouldn't you be asleep?" I
ask him.

"Insomnia. I was just watching you. Your whole energy changed."

"It's hard to explain. There's a person out there. A human."

"*Ucch.*"

"I know. I hate humans, too. It's my motto: humans are vile. I don't
know why I have this connection to one of them. But I do. I saw her just
now in my mind. She's very sad."

"Come stand closer."

"Are you going to poop on me?"

He laughs. Bats are prodigious guano factories, but I take the risk
and stand under him.

"I can feel her, too," he says.

"You can?"

"Yes. We have a kind of radar. We're good at sensing things. You're right. She's in a dark place, pony. Her courage is gone. It's run dry, like a lake that has lost the stream that used to fill it. She needs you. She really needs you."

And that's when I see it. "Your nose," I say. The bat's nose has what looks like white cotton on it.

The bat coughs and struggles to breathe.

"You're sick."

"I am. So many of us have it. It's bad. Find that girl," he says, coughing. "She's one of the good ones. I can feel it." Then his little claws let go and he falls off the branch to the ground. He's still alive but just lies there panting. I stand over him, worried.

"Hey. Are you okay?"

"I'm fine. The leaves are soft. I just need a minute."

I ponder what the bat has told me.

Penny needs me.

Humans are vile.

She's one of the good ones.

I could end up back on a truck to the slaughterhouse. Or be pony tacos for big cats.

Do I still fear death, after everything? You betcha.

"What's the matter with the bat?" asks a white pelican hovering nearby. "Can I eat him?"

"No!" I say, positioning myself over the bat. "He's just resting."

"I can wait," says the pelican, landing on a picnic table nearby. "I just ate some sunscreen so I'm not that hungry yet."

The bat is gently snoring.

"Humans are vile, right?" I ask the pelican.

"I *love* humans! What other species leaves so much delicious trash everywhere?" With that the bird pecks me on the nose with his big pink beak. I go to bite him and he flies off, chortling as if the whole thing is hilarious.

How much do we owe each other? I wonder.

The bat wakes up and tries to fly but can't flap fast enough.

"Man, it's bright out," says the bat. "I don't feel great."

"Let me help you," I say. "You need to keep your strength up. You need to fight this disease you've got."

I gently grab a tuft of the bat's fur and lay him under the picnic table in the shade. A family of humans comes over the dune and settles on a beach blanket nearby.

"Look at the pony," says the dad.

I want to go over and kick sand on their vile bodies, but I am busy helping a friend. There is a plastic bag full of dead flies hanging from a tree over the picnic table. I climb nimbly up onto the table.

"Wow!" say the kids. The dad starts filming me with his phone.

I grab the plastic bag of flies with my teeth and yank it down. The dead flies spill all over the ground next to and under the picnic table. "Bon appetit!" I say to the poor sick bat.

"Eeew," say the kids, coming closer. "Look. It's a bat. So gross."

"It must be rabid," says the dad. "I better kill it."

That's always your answer, isn't it? *Kill it.*

I charge the humans and they scatter, terrified.

"Thank you," calls the bat, munching on the flies. "I feel stronger already."

I'm thinking about Penny, and about whether any human deserves the affection of an animal. Maybe we all need to rebel, even against the good humans.

"I feel way better," says the bat, flexing his leathery wings. "Thank you. Listen, there's a storm coming. You better get to shelter." And then he lifts off and is gone, carried away on the rising breeze.

I sniff and realize the bat is right—a storm is definitely brewing. I look around and realize that I am the last pony on the beach. The wind is whipping my tail around as I trot after the line of ponies disappearing into the dunes. I follow them across the island. At a steady walk, we skirt a bog, traverse some dunes, cut through the heather and poison ivy, avoid the tangled blackberry thickets, and make our way through a beech forest, and eventually trudge up a very small hill to the highest point on the island. The wind is really picking up and I think we should stay low in the hollows, but the ponies tell me I'm wrong.

We stand under the branches of a huge thick-trunked oak at the top of the hill. Its branches sway and creak. The wind is penetrating even our thick coats—pushing into my ears and whipping my tail sideways. I keep turning my butt to the gusts, but then they change direction, like they're messing with me. Small branches are pelting us, carried on the wind, and there is a blizzard of leaves. Plastic bags left by lazy picnickers fly past. I hear a crack of a tree falling and startle. I huddle close to the other ponies, who all have their heads down, ears flat.

We are joined by other wildlife—deer, rabbits, skunks. When the predators come, we make room for them, too, under the oak tree, however uneasily. Foxes, coyotes, bobcats, a bear family—they pretend not to see us. Everyone is too busy staying alive to eat each other.

The sky goes black, swallowing the light, and the rain comes, sideways and upside down. It feels like little Peacock Lastrigon is beating me with a riding crop. My coat is saturated and I shiver, but more from fear than cold. I look around at the others. A fox lies still near my feet, his face covered by the melting brush of his tail. I nudge him a little and he snuggles deeper into the wet earth. Under my belly, a skunk baby strays from the mama and I push him back to her, letting them all shelter underneath me. The mama gives me a grateful glance. The ponies around me have their eyes closed and their heads low, all pressed together with tails to the wind. We are all just waiting it out. The wind increases, howling like a wild thing. I am terrified, but also excited—I want to see it all. The storm goes on for hours, waves of rain, gusts of wind so strong I think they will blow me over. The noise is just as exhausting as the wind. I have never missed silence so much. I can hear the crash of waves, and as dawn comes I am startled to see that the sea is coming very close to us, rising up the hill inch by inch.

Ponies that are on the outskirts of the circle are pressing in, bands I haven't met before from other parts of the island. Still, the water rises. Rocks disappear beneath it and then it comes to my hooves and the skunk babies climb on their mother's back to escape it. The water rises more and the mom's nose is barely above it. I put my head down to let the little skunks climb up my neck onto my back. The babies burrow deep into my mane while the mama clings to my back, gasping, so tired I can barely feel her heart beat. Bedraggled ravens and sparrows are roosting on other ponies, and a raccoon family clings to each other partway up the tree we're standing under. I feel hot breath and turn to see a cougar panting next to me. I will say, that does make my heart stop. "It's all under water," he says. "I barely made it here." The water is still rising, and ponies and deer are pressing against me as the ones at the outer edge of the circle are pushed uphill to save their lives. The cougar wades through the water to the tree and languidly climbs up only to the first thick branch, the wind ruffling his tawny wet fur. "Can you see anything?" I ask.

"Here comes the eye," he says. I think it's some weird feline reference.

At that moment, the wind suddenly stops. The clouds part, and the sun comes out. "Hallelujah, it's over," I think. I raise my head and neigh with joy. No one else speaks. It is perfectly silent. No one else moves much, either, which I think is odd. I turn and look around. I can see water, nothing but water, around us. Our little hilltop is all that is left of the island. "Wow, look at that," I say. I push my way downhill through the ponies and deer to the edge of the circle of animals to get a better look at the flooding. I stand at the waterline, waves lapping against my hooves. I can see treetops sticking above the water here and there, but no ground, just churning waves. The last ring of ponies and deer in front of me are submerged up to their backs but are still standing. Squirrels and moles cling to them. I tell them the good news.

"It's over," I say. "Look, the water is receding." It is in fact rushing past, so "receding" might be a tad premature.

The ponies and deer and one large moose stare at me, too tired to speak, and then a tiny mouse says from between the ears of a black-and-white pony who has water up to his withers, "It's not over."

At that moment, the wind starts up again and the sky darkens. "The eye is just the middle of the hurricane," shouts the mouse in a high squeak. I turn and look for a path back uphill to the oak tree, but the animals have moved into the space I occupied. The animals in the water push past me uphill, so that everyone is now crunched together, wet, shivering, and terrified. I am now on the very outer edge of the circle, and the water is still rising. I try to turn and face uphill again, press my way toward the trees at the top, but there is no room. The rain comes, and more darkness, and now lightning and thunder. I hate thunder and lightning. A wave crashes over me. I try to scramble with my hooves to hold on. The skunk family is washed off my back. In the flash of lightning, I see them swimming, and I neigh to them. At the next flash I see them again, safely atop another pony. "You made it," I shout, but the words are washed out of my mouth by a wave that knocks me over.

I claw my way back upright, which is impressive given my lack of claws. I stand there panting as the storm intensifies, water swirling around my legs. Then I hear a voice.

"Help!"

Some of the animals look toward the voice. I prick my ears and listen. A human. I stare into the driving rain, trying to see where it is coming from.

"Help!"

I see it. A small human hand is clinging to a branch. I neigh to it, willing it to kick hard and swim toward us.

"Help!" The cry is getting fainter.

I take a step toward the human. The mountain lion shakes his head. "They hunt me with dogs."

The squirrels shake their heads. "They hunt us with guns."

The mice shake their heads. "They trap us and poison us."

The deer say, "They put our heads on their walls."

I look to the other ponies, the only domesticated species under the oak tree. They avert their eyes.

I owe humanity nothing, I decide. *Vile. Vile. Vile.*

The cry of the human is getting fainter. I take a deep breath. Then I jump into the water.

45

PENNY

A GUARD DELIVERS A message to Penny that she is scheduled
to receive a phone call at three p.m. She will be escorted to the
phone room at the appropriate time. She wonders if Lisa has found
something. The hours until then drag.

Finally, the guard comes and takes her to a room with a row of pay
phones. Each one has a woman at it, talking, laughing, crying, twirling
her hair, or shouting. There is no privacy whatsoever. In addition, the
line of phones has a large sign above it that says ALL CALLS ARE RE-
CORDED.

Great, Penny thinks. Isn't the American system supposed to assume
that you're innocent until proven guilty? Everything Penny has expe-
rienced has shown her that the opposite is true. If you are rich and accused of a crime, you hire a great lawyer, you get out on bail, and you
await what will no doubt be a fair trial, maybe even one skewed in your
favor, given how many cases district attorneys have to handle.

If you are poor, as Penny is now, her middle-class life having been
sacrificed to Tella's treatment, then you get locked up until your trial,
which could take a long time, given the backed-up caseloads in the system. You get an overworked, underpaid public defender who probably
just graduated from law school, has about five minutes to prepare your
case, and is eager to move on to greener pastures. The scales of justice

are heavily tilted against you. She's angry, which is good, actually. It's energizing. She feels like the pony, about to buck someone off.

The pay phone in front of her rings. Penny answers tentatively. "Hello?"

"Pen. It's me."

"Laus." She's so happy to hear her husband's voice, she almost chokes on the lump in her throat. She hasn't spoken to him often since she was arrested, between the time difference, his work schedule, and prison rules.

"Is it terrible, Pen? I'm so worried about you. They're going to let you out soon, right? You'll write a book about this. How crazy it all was."

"Is Tella still okay?"

"Yes. I don't like lying to her, Pen. But I really don't know what to say, so I said you're on a silent retreat. You know, like a Buddhist thing."

This is kind of a dumb lie, since Penny has never been a Buddhist and Tella knows this. But Laus is trying. Penny can't control this. "That's good," she says. "Yes. A silent retreat. She knows I love her, right? She doesn't feel abandoned by me?"

"I don't think so."

That's not super reassuring.

"Laus, did you think anything was weird about Dr. Resa? Like, did she seem sane to you? Did she ever come on to you?"

"No. I mean, we talked a couple of times but you know I don't like therapy much."

"Yeah. I'm sorry I made you do that."

"I'm sorry for a lot, Pen. You did everything for Tella. I felt so useless."

"It's okay. We're all just doing our best," Penny says. "They're going to cut us off soon, Laus. If you remember anything strange about Dr. Resa, tell me, okay? You could google-stalk her a little, you know, if you feel like it. See if she has any connection to Ithaca, or horses. Any reason why she would say that I did this."

"Sure. I will. Pen, about Ithaca—I thought I should tell you about something that happened. It might be relevant to your case."

"What?"

"Right around the time you got arrested, Susan saw someone steal a package off our front porch." Laus had moved back into the house, Penny knew. Yes, they were separated, but it didn't make sense to have the house sitting empty.

Susan was their neighbor. She had a thing about porch pirates. Susan'd had a bunch of packages stolen herself and had become something of a vigilante, following the cars that followed the UPS and FedEx trucks. When someone tried to steal a package, she sounded an air horn and took pictures of their license plates. Ed the sheriff's deputy had warned Susan that she was going to get herself beaten up or killed.

"Well, it's not like I'm going to be wearing that new sundress anyway," said Penny.

"It wasn't from Amazon."

"What was it?"

"I don't know. Susan said there was a fight between the porch pirate and an animal for it. She was far away and she couldn't see that well. She thinks it might have been a bear."

Penny can't help but laugh. On purpose she never orders food online because where they live, up in the mountains of central California, any food left lying around is fair game for bears, raccoons, coyotes, even neighborhood dogs.

"Did someone send us a fruitcake or something?" she asks Laus.

The phone beeps and a message says, "Ten seconds left."

"I asked Phil the UPS guy and he checked his records and it was from someone named Abra. In Ithaca."

PART EIGHT

Hollow Detachment

46

THE PONY

THRUST MY nose up, paddling, trying to get to the human and the branch to tow them back to safety, but the current has me in its grasp. It pulls me away from the other animals, out into the ocean.

"Help!" I hear the human scream.

"Heeeeeellllp!" I scream. I can do nothing but swim among the giant waves. Branches and logs litter the water, battering against me. I try to climb onto a floating tree trunk, but it sinks under my weight. The water is moving fast in all directions—up, down, and sideways. It's dark and loud and I tumble again, going under, choking on salt water. I am so wet and tired, and only my nostrils and eyes and ears are above water. Still, I paddle, not knowing if my hooves will ever feel solid ground under them again.

"Help!" I hear from close by.

With my last bit of strength, I swim to the voice. The human's face is just above water. I swim past, and it grabs my tail.

The extra weight pulls me down, and we both go under.

Of course.

47

PENNY

I GAVE BIRTH to my youngest while I was incarcerated," says Dawn. They are chatting through the grates before the guards come and close them for the night. "The father was a guard. Really nice guy. That's why once you're convicted they move you from prison to prison all the time, so you don't make attachments."

There's so much to unpack in this conversation. Penny's head spins. She sticks with what seems like the safest part of Dawn's casual revelation. "How does giving birth while in prison work?" she asks. "Do they take you to a hospital?"

"If you're lucky. I heard about a girl in one of those Alabama hellholes who had to give birth on the floor of the shower with no anesthesia. But yeah. I was induced. They take you to a regular hospital, but a guard is always with you. They shackle you to the hospital bed by one ankle until you're actually in labor. Then as soon as you give birth, you get chained up again."

"And then you come back here?"

"I was in a state prison, but yes. They put a crib in your cell. Takes up most of the floor space, but that way you can nurse."

"And then what happens? They take the baby away?"

There are some sniffles before Dawn speaks again. "Yeah," she says. "My mom came and took him. I'll never get to see my kid getting on the school bus, never get to see him on the jungle gym."

"When will you get parole?"

"Been turned down every time I've asked," Dawn says. "Sure wish I could see my kids."

It hits Penny again, as it does many times a day, that she hasn't seen Tella in so long, that she hasn't heard her voice, hugged her. The last time she saw her was the day she dropped her off at the boarding school. That was so bad that she tries to focus on happier times, the hike they did in the giant sequoias, the picnic by Emerald Lake. They were always at their best out in nature together. Tella liked to get above the treeline, up where there was nothing but granite as far as you could see. She said her head got quieter up there. Penny loved it, too, sitting up high on Alta Peak, cloudless blue skies, nothing but the gentle sighing of the wind and those stunted alpine flowers that clung to the tiniest patch of dirt, making the most of the few weeks a year they weren't covered by snow. Tella was so calm up there—they could laugh and sing together. Penny can hear her singing *"Valderi, valdera, valdera ha ha ha ha!"*

She desperately wants to ask Laus to go pick up Tella and bring her here on visiting day, but that seems so selfish. Tella is better off where she is, focusing on getting better. Hopefully eating more vegetables than Penny is. *Why is all the food here beige,* Penny wonders. She would kill for arugula. Okay, not kill. Pay handsomely.

"Besides your kids, what do you miss most?" Penny asks.

"Decent hair care products," Dawn says.

WHEN THEY ARE locked down for the night, Penny's mind spins and turns all the facts of her case, as it does every minute she is not talking to Dawn.

In the nine seconds they had left after Laus told her about the package from Abra, she'd asked him to call High Rise without giving his name, ask for Abra, and find out what the package was.

"It's like detective work," said Laus with a chuckle. He sounded excited and onboard with helping her, which was cheering.

"Thank you," she said.

"Honey, I know we were in a rough patch when this happened, but I am here for you," he said. "Anything you need."

She had cried a little at the relief of that.

"I miss you," he added. "When you get out—"

And that was when the call cut off.

THEY ARE ALLOWED snail mail, the most exciting moment of the day, according to Dawn. Of course all of the mail is opened and read by the jail staff, and you're not allowed to enclose photos, but it's still a moment of connection with the outside world. Dawn has told her if you want your mail to get through the system quickly, use postcards.

Three days after her call with Laus, Penny gets a postcard from him. On one side is a picture of a breaching whale that she bought on their trip to Baja six years ago and taped to the kitchen wall near the fridge. It's yellowed and a little dog-eared from people brushing past it. She turns it over.

Abra is dead, it says on the other side. *What should I do next???*

48

THE PONY

WE RESURFACE. THE human is still clinging to my tail, so I assume it's still alive. The lightning is flashing, and the wind howling. I swim for what seems like hours. I am exhausted and ready to give up, but if I stop swimming, we're both going to die. Water keeps sloshing into my nose and ears. Ponies may have a slippery side, but we are not fish, and we can only swim for so long. Cassandra the cat told me back in Ocala that I was going to drown. If this is my fate, so be it. I feared death in the slaughter truck, but now I don't. I think about carrots, and I think about Penny, and I think about all of the humans and ponies and dogs and cats and bats and other people I've known in my life. I think that all in all it's been a pretty good life, though to be honest it does feel a tad unfinished. But probably everyone who is about to drown thinks that. Then I hear a voice in the darkness.

"Hey," it says.

At first I think it's the human, but then I realize it's an animal voice. The wind is still roaring and I think my ears are playing tricks with me.

"Hey, hairy mammal," it says. "You look really silly from this angle. Little legs going like crazy under that fat tummy, and that skinny tail—all hair! Useless."

I gurgle a little. That's the best I can do.

"There's land that way. I'm going to give you a push. Don't kick me." I feel movement under my belly and find myself being supported from underneath. I start to panic at the strange feeling—but then as my head and neck come up out of the water, I have a crazy realization.

"I'm riding!" I say. "I'm riding you! This time pony's on top!"

The human is still holding the tip of my tail, though in silence.

The sea creature carries us forward through the waves. It's an incredible feeling—the power of the animal underneath me, the sense of being lifted up to the sky. No wonder people like riding us. It's amazing.

The crashing sound of the surf gets louder, and I can smell land. The sea creature drops down under me into the depths and I am swimming again, but I can feel my hooves scraping sand. To my left, the sea creature makes one leap into the air and then disappears.

"Thank you!" I call. I have a moment of panic as I scramble with my hooves in the sand and the waves pull me back out again, as if they are being cheated and angry and not going to give me back to the land, but I swim harder, refusing to give up. Then the waves carry me forward again fast—too fast. I slam into rocks and feel pain but push myself again to swim toward the sound of the surf and the smell of wet sand. Three times the waves drag me out and then throw me back.

Finally, I give several hard kicks and pull myself up the beach, stumbling over the giant piles of trash the storm has washed up. Every object you can imagine, natural and human-made, is on that beach—parts of boats, endless plastic bottles, splinters of wood, leaves, grass, boards, a washing machine, a car seat, fishing nets, tennis racquets, Styrofoam, seaweed, and dead fish. I make it up to the dunes and sink onto the sand, exhausted. I look back and the human is there, still holding on to my tail. It is a sandy lump, its face turned toward the sky, eyes closed. I don't even have the energy to sniff it to see if it's still alive. I fall asleep.

"WE'RE GOING TO need to put a winch on the truck for that," says a voice. I awaken slowly, blinking. The sun is warm and I can hear flies buzzing with glee about laying their eggs all over an entire dead pony.

"I'll cut it up with a chainsaw and we can feed it to the dogs." At this I leap up. The flies scatter.

Two startled men stand in front of me. They're wearing shorts and sunglasses and T-shirts with words on them. And baseball hats.

"It's alive," says one of them with a particularly excellent grasp of the obvious.

I shake the sand off me. I look around for the human I saved, but whoever it was is now gone.

"Let's catch and it sell it," says the taller of the two. He takes a step toward me.

I let him get close enough to almost touch me, and then I turn and gallop off down the sand.

49

PENNY

HOW DID YOU know this person?" Lisa asks when Penny tells her that Alex's groom is dead. They're back in the conversation pit, getting ready for Penny's trial. Unfortunately at the next station in the conversation pit is a woman who is screaming at a man Penny assumes is her lawyer at top volume. "He says I stole his French bulldog?" the woman shouts. "That's *my* dog!" The lawyer steps away from the glass and the woman stands and pounds on it. "You tell the police that I am ready to tell them everything they want to know about that SOB right down to the size of his—"

"I only met her once," Penny says, trying to focus on Lisa. "When I went to High Rise to talk to Alex. Abra was very nice. We kind of bonded. But it's weird, right? She was young and apparently healthy."

"Maybe she fell off a horse." Lisa has never warmed up to the idea of the horse world, and Penny can't exactly blame her. Alex's world of international show jumping is even more ridiculously rarefied than Silla's pony lessons. "What did she send you?" Lisa asks.

"I don't know. Someone stole the package off my front steps. A person . . . or an animal. My husband is trying to figure that out. He called High Rise and they just said she passed away."

"He should not be calling High Rise," says Lisa sharply.

"He didn't give his name."

Lisa opens her notebook. "Let's not get sidetracked. Our trial date is getting close. We need a coherent defense."

"Is Steve coming to talk to me?" Penny has barely heard from her actual public defender since her pre-trial hearing.

"He'll try, but I will prepare him thoroughly. We're going to focus on our cross-examination of Dr. Resa to try to get her to say that the confession might have been planted or coerced in some way."

"Can we hire an expert to say she could have planted the idea, even inadvertently?"

Lisa frowns. "It's too close to trial now for that."

Why do the rules always seem to work against her, Penny wonders. She hopes Laus is digging into Dr. Resa and will come up with something Steve can use on the stand. She has a brief fantasy of Steve turning to the jury and waving a hotel bill and saying "Dr. Resa, is it true that you and Alex Kinsworth are having an affair?"

Lisa is talking. "But we need more—especially character witnesses. I've scheduled depositions for your colleagues in California so they don't have to fly across the country. Is there anyone here who can speak to the little girl you were back then?"

"Silla," Penny says.

IT'S PENNY'S ONCE-A-WEEK turn at the pay phones. Laus put money in her jail account so she can make calls, which are ridiculously expensive. She has thirty minutes before she must give up the phone to another inmate. It feels like a wild freedom to sit on a warped plastic stool and punch numbers into a dingy pay phone that smells like someone else's chin. Thank God she memorized Laus's number—about the only one she actually knows.

"I talked to Dr. Resa," he says. "She was sympathetic to me and asked about Tella, but she was kind of offended at the suggestion that she might have coerced a confession."

"Yeah," says Penny. "I expected that. Did you google-stalk her?"

"I did, but she doesn't have much of an online presence. A graduation picture, some volunteer awards. No connection I could find to Ithaca or the Kinsworths. She didn't go to school in New York, or ever ride horses as far as I could tell. I looked on Ancestry to see if maybe she was a distant relative of the Kinsworths or the Rosses, but no luck."

"You're still a great detective," says Penny. "How's Tella?"

Laus says that Tella doesn't reveal much on their weekly calls, but that reading between the lines, he thinks she's doing well at Arcadia, and that the staff agrees. "Every time I say the name of the school, I think of that show you made me watch," he says.

"*Brideshead Revisited*," she says. "I can still hear Jeremy Irons say in his plummy voice 'Et in Arcadia Ego.'"

"Ten insufferable hours of British people and their teddy bears," Laus laughs.

"Thirteen," she says. "Thirteen heavenly hours. The best miniseries ever. Except maybe the Colin Firth *Pride and Prejudice*. You must have really been hot for me to sit through that."

"I was. I am," he says, startling her. "I miss you. This time apart, it's made things clearer for me. I think—and I know it's been torture for you—but having to take charge of talking to Tella, talking to the school, it's been good for me. I should have been doing more all along. I'm sorry about that."

"I miss you, too," she says through tears. Neither of them uses the *love* word, though, which worries her. Can flames of love be summoned from the ashes of their marriage?

When they hang up, she has a few minutes left and tries to call Silla, who only has a landline. It rings and rings, not even an answering machine. She should have asked Laus to keep trying to reach her, let her know about the trial and what Penny needs from her so she doesn't hear it first from Lisa. Next time.

50

THE PONY

MUST LOOK like a sea monster. I'm covered with wet sand and have green seaweed tangled in my mane and tail. I assume I can find my way back to the wild ponies, but I can't seem to get my bearings. I trot down the beach until I come to some houses. That isn't right, so I trot back the other direction. People are starting to appear—peering over the sea wall by the road, coming out of boarded-up buildings. I hear pounding and a piece of wood falls away, revealing an old, old man. His house is half torn away. He waves at me and smiles. "We made it!" he says.

I'm confused. Where is the wild part of the island? Where are the ponies? I head for some trees and find myself trotting down a road. I pass boarded-up restaurants, a gas station, and some half-submerged cars. There's trash everywhere, and downed power lines. The street I'm on ends in a flooded area, motor oil slick on the surface of the water, so I turn back. I'm walking down a street past a row of silent, boarded-up houses, the trees in front of them stripped of leaves, when a fire truck rolls up behind me and two people in yellow suits get out.

"Found him," says the man into a radio.

"He looks okay," says the woman.

"Hey, pony," says the man. "Come here. Everyone's talking about you."

I stop and assess the situation.

"Careful. Could be dangerous. One way to find out." He fishes into his pocket and holds out some Life Savers. I'm interested. I haven't eaten in a long time, I suddenly remember.

I let him walk closer. "This is not a good place for you, buddy," he says. "Let me take you someplace safe where we can look at those cuts and get you some food."

I look down and see I do have cuts on my legs.

"You think he's one of the wild ones from the island?" asks the woman.

"He doesn't have the brand," says the man. "So he can't be one of them. Plus, if he'll take Life Savers, he's not wild."

O caustic irony! I, the domesticated beast, do not have the human-made imprimatur of the wild animal. This burns more than any brand could have. *Aren't we all wild?* I want to shout at them. *Do we not all have a right to live free?*

Somehow I know my life as a wild pony is over.

I reach for the Life Savers and he puts the rope over my head.

51

PENNY

LISA IS WEARING a black suit that Penny hasn't seen before. It's nicely fitted and she looks powerful in it, Penny thinks. A good sign.

"Hey," Lisa says, sitting down and picking up the gray phone. "That groom at High Rise? Abra? She died when the brakes failed on the pickup truck she was driving."

"That's so sad," says Penny.

"And also a little suspicious," says Lisa. "The police are actually looking into it. That's good for us. But we need to find that package she sent you."

"Wow. Do you think maybe she found something that proves that Melanie or Alex killed Frank?"

"It's a long shot, but who knows. Can your husband find the package?"

"He's trying. I'll ask again. Did you talk to Silla?"

"I haven't been able to get hold of her. Her phone rings and rings. How does someone who runs a business not have a cell phone?"

"You'll know the answer to that when you meet her. She's . . . old-school. As in old."

"But she will tell the jury that you were a sweet and lovely little girl, right? That's really important."

52

THE PONY

HAVE MY picture taken by the local newspaper. The human I saved is alive, and I am a hero. Apparently he was washed off a boat that got caught in the storm. He tells everyone how I saved his life. He's very weak, and in the hospital, and they bring me there to see him, right into the hospital. It's all white and shiny and smells like the vet's. I go up to the bed where the human is lying and he pets my nose. "Thank you!" he tells me, and gives me a sugar cube. The cameras whir and click and flash. I am a celebrity. I am Instagram famous.

Not for long. For my heroism in saving a life I'm "adopted" by a man who tells the Animal Control officers that he runs a livestock rescue in another state. Frankly, he has a truck and trailer and the pound is overwhelmed with animals, so I think they are a little lax with the background checking. In any case, the "livestock rescue" turns out to be a run-down gas station with a petting zoo/pony rides out back (add your own exclamation points and blinking neon to the sign). The landscape is flat prairie with a mountain backdrop, the tall grass leveled by the wind. The gas station sits at the intersection of two poorly paved county highways, with no other human habitation or sign of life in sight. It is best described as "downwardly mobile." There's a wind-chipped FOR SALE—COMMERCIAL PROPERTY sign out on the highway. Winter comes, snow falls, snow melts, and the cycle begins again, the FOR SALE sign still creaking in the wind.

I have given up on my quest to find Penny. It's been about a year and a half since I said goodbye to Caya and Circe and hit the road to look for Penny, twenty-five years since I saw her last. I saved the human in the ocean. Even though that person wasn't Penny, maybe the karmic balance has been restored. I tell myself so, anyway. The owl said Penny is better off without me. Even if she's in a dark place, what could I, a pony, do to help?

Despite the miles of grass all around us, the petting zoo owner doesn't own pasture land, and he doesn't give us much hay to eat. Winter is hard on an old pony like me, especially when rations are light. There are eight of us ponies sharing an occasional flake of hay, and we have nothing but a rickety piece of tin under which we have to huddle together for warmth and protection from that razor-sharp wind. Yes, ponies have thick coats, and yes, we are built for that kind of weather, but that doesn't mean we enjoy it. Try telling a woman screaming in labor that she is built for childbirth.

There's a certain look that seeps into our eyes as the rain pelts us and the snow begins to pile up on our backs, and our empty tummies rumble, and the wind blows our tails sideways across our bodies. I call it "going away." You see it in animals in pain, too. I have seen it in humans. The light fades from the eye and it becomes slightly opaque. You just stare for long periods. Days on end. Months. It's not death, or even the longing for death, though I've seen that, too. It's just a leaving, a necessary departure from the body. The mind goes numb.

I've always feared this numbness, because I'm not sure you can entirely come back from it. I've met a lot of ponies who have spent years in this state, living without enough food or in mud up to their knees, untrimmed hooves grown into terrible slipper shapes that make it painful to move. Even when the authorities come in and remove them from the horrible places and take them somewhere safe and dry, feed them and trim their feet, the spark doesn't really come back into the ponies' eyes. They know the bad part might come again, so they can never quite trust themselves to inhabit the good. They end up living in a kind of limbo. Because pain no longer matters, neither does pleasure. It's a living death.

At the gas station, there's a pony like that. Buttercup. Mostly when you get tossed into a new herd, everyone perks up for a few minutes and establishes a pecking order. Things get dusty as we churn and dart like a flock of very hairy sky-dancing birds. I like to pin my ears back and threaten to kick any newcomer, in a friendly sort of way. That way they know I'm the boss, and I get primo access to the food. The day Buttercup arrives, we all start circling the pen in the usual way, tiny hooves in motion, getting ready to show her who's top pony. Let me stress this is normal pony behavior, and that when Snowball says, "I think I can take her," she means it in a mostly nonhostile way. Snowball, hardly larger than the ball of ice she's named after, always eats last, getting the "broccoli stalks"—the tough, thick pieces of hay the rest of us don't want to bother chewing.

Mr. Alcinous drops the ramp on the old horse trailer, kicking it into place. I wish he would get that trailer fixed—a pony could plant a hoof through a floorboard in that deathtrap. You have to straddle the rotten boards as he drives along at ninety, the battered metal box of the trailer jumping around, engulfed in the clouds of diesel fumes spewing from his ancient truck. On a hot day the damn thing is an Easy Bake Oven.

Buttercup backs down the ramp. She's cute—yellow, as you would expect, with a white mane and tail. Little dished face a pony could lose his heart for. Mr. Alcinous leads her to the corral as the seven of us prance and snort.

"Get back, you, get back from that gate," says Mr. Alcinous. His tone is gruff, but his threats are empty. He's at heart a nice man, though also a sad man. Money is perpetually tight at the gas station, hence the various get-rich-quick schemes he cooks up and the lengths to which he goes to get free animals. The petting zoo is a particularly ill-advised venture. One spring day he trucks in three sheep, four rabbits, a cow named Daphne, and a garter snake named Lester who lives in a heated cage he can easily escape from. Do you call that a zoo? Not that I want lions or tigers around, no no no, but if you're going to lure tourists to pull over and plunk down a few bucks, you should probably give them a thrill or two. Children in the electronic age are not that interested in petting live animals. From what I can tell, they hardly pay attention to the dogs in the back of their station wagons and SUVs. But their parents drag them over to the sheep and say, "Look, touch it." Then, "I paid twenty bucks for this, touch it." Then, when the kid still just stands there, the parent adds, "Touch it and you can get back in the car and play more Game Boy." The kid reaches out a hand toward the thick greasy fleece of the sheep, and the sheep (Snoozy, Doozy, or Floozie) lowers her head and threatens to butt the kid. The kid runs screaming back to the car.

The littlest tots plunge their fingers into the fur of the rabbits, grinning at how soft it is, then get a thump from those hind legs and start crying. The braver kids pretend to want to touch the snake but scatter when Mr. Alcinous lifts him from his cage and he flicks out his yellow tongue in greeting. Daphne the cow genuinely likes children—I give her a lot of credit for that kind of patience. She tries to wash their hands and faces with her sandpaper tongue. Unfortunately mothers these days are not so keen on their kids being drizzled in cow saliva like an ice cream sundae, and they shriek and produce antibacterial wipes from out of nowhere. I always want to tell them that cow saliva is the original antibacterial wipe—and loofah—but no one listens to me.

Mr. Alcinous unsnaps Buttercup's halter. Snowball charges her but comes to a dust-spewing halt as she realizes Buttercup is not going to flee. I trot over, trying to look menacing and friendly and handsome at the same time. I pin my ears back. No reaction. Buttercup is a statue of a pony. I stare into her face and I see it. The look. We all back off, and Buttercup walks over and stands in the corner, head at half mast, eyes unfocused. She has "gone away."

I'm starting to feel myself "going away," too. I'm old and feel older than I am. Life is either bone-chillingly cold or baking hot, but always monotonous. Kids are not that interested in the pony rides, though Mr. Alcinous continues to saddle us every morning. We stand there all day, tied in a circle, waiting for something to happen, and then he comes and unsaddles us at the end of the day. The hay portions get smaller. The wind never stops blowing across the treeless landscape, whether it's twenty below zero or a hundred above zero. The FOR SALE sign creaks like an angry ghost. I forget my past, let go of the present, and live in a kind of mindless limbo. Am I always hungry or never hungry? Baking or freezing? We ponies stop the daily bitching at each other and fall into a collective silence. I feel lost in the vastness of the universe, but also disinterested in it, as it is disinterested in me.

53

PENNY

"GOOD NEWS AND bad news," says Lisa as she picks up the phone. They're back in the conversation pit. The trial is going to begin in three days, and both Lisa and Penny are on edge. "Just before Frank died, someone sued him for wrongful death when their kid died falling off a drugged horse."

Penny is startled by this image of a child being crushed under a staggering, doped-up fifteen-hundred-pound animal. "That's the good news?"

"It's a gap in their armor," Lisa says. "It's something I can ask Melanie about in the cross-examination, get her to admit that Frank had enemies who wished him dead."

"Great," says Penny.

Lisa is flipping through her list. "The bad news is that I still haven't been able to reach Silla—and we really need her. I'm just going to drive over there."

"Thank you," Penny says. "Sorry you have to do that."

"Part of the job. On that note . . ." Lisa says with a sigh. "I have to be honest with you. Our case is not rock solid. We will try to introduce reasonable doubt, the self-defense angle, but juries can be tough."

"You think I should take a plea deal?"

"It's up to you. But it's the safe choice, if you want to see your daughter on the outside someday soon. I think the judge will give you a lighter sentence, given that you have led an upstanding life since the crime, though of course I can't promise. Some judges are hardasses."

Led an upstanding life since the crime. But there was no crime, at least none that she committed, other than maybe stealing a horse, and no one ever pursued that. Penny feels caught.

"You don't have to answer now. Think on it overnight."

PENNY LIES IN her bunk, unable to sleep. Admitting guilt to a manslaughter charge—if Lisa and Steve can get it down to that—will guarantee that she will never teach again, but she will see her daughter sooner than if she is convicted of second degree murder. But isn't there a chance that the jury will see that she didn't kill Frank? That justice will be served?

She had another postcard from Laus today. He has been sending one every day, taking the postcards down from the wall in their kitchen that memorialized their travels and mailing them to Penny with messages of encouragement. A lighthouse on Prince Edward Island was the postcard today, a squat white spire with a red top, shining its light out over the sea. That was a pretty good trip. Tella was just a baby, and though she cried a lot, making it hard to eat in restaurants, they had had picnics on the bluffs, put her in the stroller, and taken long walks along the waterfront. She remembers holding hands with Laus, their cheeks red from the wind.

The last road trip they took together was a lot less fun. They drove Tella out to Arcadia. Even though it was the school Tella herself had picked, and they had all agreed this was the best plan, as the miles ticked by Tella had become agitated in the back seat. The energy in the car had shifted, like a change in the weather that brings a storm.

They were driving down a long, straight highway, wheat fields on either side, mountains in the distance. The view outside the car was so serene and beautiful . . .

54

THE PONY

ONE AFTERNOON A car pulls into the gas station. I can see it from far down the road. We used to take bets on whether cars would stop, but that has ceased. Without pricking my ears, I let my eyes follow the white sedan as it pulls up to the pump. I hear an angry voice as the passenger door opens. "It's none of your business," says a girl of about thirteen as she unfolds skinny legs and strides away, clenching a phone. The dad waits in the car, on his phone. These humans and their phones! They may as well live in separate cages. I see the mom—short, dark curly hair—get out of the car and reach for the gas pump. She rests her arms on the hood of the car, and her chin on her arms, a worried look on her face. There is something familiar about her.

The daughter is madly pressing her phone with her thumbs. The mom calls out, "We gotta go," but the daughter frowns and looks over at us ponies. "I want to see the animals," she says.

She comes over to our pen and all of us except Buttercup raise our heads and look at her. The girl doesn't look at us, though; she just keeps her face in the phone.

"Tella," calls the mom.

"I'm busy," she says, and then adds, "Can I have ten bucks?"

Mr. Alcinous wanders out of the gas station office. "Want a ride?"

he asks. The girl seems at least five years too old for a pony ride, but he's a hopeful man.

The mother says, "Honey, there's no time. We gotta get going. You're supposed to be there at five for orientation." She's crossing the parking lot toward us, a short figure walking briskly. I feel a quickening of my blood, a shiver, though it's hot as Satan's armpit. The wind is blowing the wrong way, and though I flare my nostrils, I can't get her scent.

"Yes," says the teenage girl to Mr. Alcinous. "I want to ride."

"Come on, this is not . . ." The mom looks around at all of us. "Good." She's upset, I can tell, and the daughter knows that, and is trying to get her goat.

"I want to ride that one," says Tella, pointing to Buttercup.

"Little small for you, but okay," says Mr. Alcinous. He drops a bridle over Buttercup's head and she takes the bit gently, not like me—you need pliers to get my mouth open.

The mom reaches the corral. I move out of the herd toward her, drawn like a magnet.

Mr. Alcinous leads Buttercup out of the pen and into the riding area. It's a kind of track, about ten feet wide and about a hundred yards long. I believe it was actually built for dog racing a couple of generations ago, but it works as a chute to keep people and ponies contained as they make a couple of laps before getting bored. Toddlers get led around, but the older kids are set loose in there. Mr. Alcinous has removed all of the grass, but we can usually find an occasional weed to eat, yanking the kids down over our heads.

"Sign this," says Mr. Alcinous, producing a clipboard and a waiver.

"Are there helmets?" asks the mom, signing.

Both Mr. Alcinous and the girl ignore her as the girl climbs on Buttercup.

The mom audibly winces. The girl's legs hang long down Buttercup's sides.

"How do I make it go," the girl says.

"Press *her* gently with your heels," says the mom. "And cluck a little, like this." She makes a clucking sound with her tongue. I gasp.

The girl and Mr. Alcinous look at the mom, surprised.

"I used to ride," the mom says.

"I didn't know that," says the girl.

"Well, it's been a long time. I loved riding. It saved me."

"What do you mean?"

"I . . . was really unhappy. To be honest, I hated my life. Animals were the only things I could connect with, the only . . . ones who understood me." She shakes off what she's remembering and forces a smile. "That was a long time ago."

The girl kicks a little and clucks, but Buttercup doesn't move. Finally Mr. Alcinous gives her a swat on the rump with the clipboard and she ambles slowly down the chute.

I sniff the mom's hand where it lies on the corral fence. I feel like I'm awakening from a long slumber. I nicker involuntarily, and then again, intentionally.

The mom looks over at me and our eyes meet. Is it her? The eyes are the same, even though most everything else is different. She looks so sad. She's got that hollow detachment. She's gone away.

"Ow, shit!" Buttercup is slowly but firmly dragging Tella's leg along the splintery boards, crushing it against the fence. "Jesus," says Tella, jumping off the pony.

"Stop cursing," says the mom. "I'm sorry," she says to Mr. Alcinous. "It hasn't been a great day."

"And it's not getting better," says the girl, stalking back to the car, phone in hand. *Slam* goes the car door.

"I'm sorry," the mom says again, and hands Mr. Alcinous money.

"You're taking her to the school over there?"

She nods.

"I hear they do good work," he says. "I had teenagers once, too."

The mom starts to walk away, then stops, turns back. "Did you ever think you . . . didn't always like them?"

"All the time."

"Did you think you failed, somehow?"

He nods again.

247

"Did it get better?"

He stares out toward the mountains. Then he says, "The only thing you can do is to be a good person yourself and hope they notice."

"What if all they notice is that selfish, greedy people get rewarded in this world and terrible things happen to good people all the time?"

He shrugs.

I nicker as she starts to turn away. She stops and looks at me, then takes in the whole scene. Her eyes sweep the corral, the other ponies, the gas station. I see pain in her face. A loud horn blast comes from the car. She turns and walks away.

I give a long shrill neigh as the car pulls out. I neigh again, loud and high-pitched, a scream I don't think I have ever made before. The other ponies look at me in worry and surprise.

The car drives off. I stand there for a moment, watching its outline fade into the misty distance. Then I back up and run forward, jumping over the lowest part of the fence. I don't have quite the spring I used to, so I take out a good portion of the fence as I land, stumbling. I don't stop, though. I trot in the direction the car went. The other ponies pour through the gap in the fence, heading for the nearest clump of grass.

Mr. Alcinous, who's leading Buttercup back toward the corral, stares at me in shock as I trot past him.

"Hey, wait. Thor!" he calls.

I didn't even know my name was Thor.

"Come back! Supper, it's suppertime," he calls. He grabs an empty bucket with his free hand. "Come on, pony, come back, pony."

I don't even look back. I break into a gallop and head off after the car.

55

PENNY

PENNY LIES ON her bunk thinking about that awful day. When they'd left that weird David Lynchian petting zoo and those sad ponies, Tella had just exploded. "I'm not going! I'm not going!" she was screaming, and trying to open the doors of the car while they were moving. Penny was absolutely terrified.

"Jesus! Make her stop!" Laus was shouting. He sounded so angry, which just made things worse.

"Tella! Let's just look at it!" Penny said.

"This is insane!" Laus shouted, slowing down. "I don't know what to do."

"It's okay!" Penny said. "Just keep driving!"

"No!" Tella wailed. "I don't want to go! I want to go home!"

Home. The same home Tella had labeled "hell on earth" in their last family therapy session with Dr. Resa. The place Tella had said she never wanted to see again. Had threatened to end her life in if she had to stay one more day. Their own family home. Why was it so awful for her? Why did it make her so anxious? They had asked Tella so many times to try to tell them what she was bothered by, what felt so overwhelming to her. Should they repaint her bedroom? Should they move? "It's not the house," said Tella. "It's my head! I want out of my head!" Laus and Penny were living in a state of terror. Their baby girl, their beloved daughter. Every day was hell for them, too. They were terrified she would follow through on her threats to end her life. Getting her away from home, paradoxically, seemed to be the safest choice, although that itself was agonizing to Penny and Laus. Tella had gone through the brochures herself, picked Arcadia, said it looked like a good place to try to get better.

Tella was now shouting obscenities at Penny and Laus from the back seat, even trying to take a swing at her mother. "I hate you!" she shouted. "I hate you both!"

Penny climbed into the back seat while Laus sped along the rural highway. Penny grabbed Tella's arms, tried to hold her still, tried to convey all the love she felt for her. She thought of the pony at the gas station, how much he looked like her own pony, lost so long ago. An eerie coincidence that made her connect with Tella more deeply—she'd had all these feelings herself, twenty-five years earlier, in the backseat of the family car as her parents drove away from Ithaca on the way to Chicago. The rage, the powerlessness, the grief.

The grief.

They got to the turnoff, saw the sign. ARCADIA.

"See? It looks nice," Penny says.

"I'm not staying here," says Tella.

And then Laus, who has promised to stand united with Penny, has promised in front of Dr. Resa that he will not do what he always does, leave Penny to be the bad guy, the adult in the room, says to Tella, "We don't have to go in." He turns to his wife. "It's up to you, Penny."

56

THE PONY

PENNY! I CAN'T believe it's really her, but it is her. She's different, yes, a little taller, though not much, with shorter hair and wearing different clothes. But it's her. I know it's her. Every animal on earth, even the human animals, has a unique smell. And ponies never forget a smell. It's Penny. She didn't recognize me because humans have a terrible sense of smell. They are really pathetic in that arena. She was so close! I have to get to her, make her see it's me. I have to save her from the terrible sadness that envelops her, the gone-away-ness.

All lethargy is gone. I gallop down the road in the direction her car went, my hooves clicking on the pavement. I haven't galloped in ages, and it feels pretty good, despite some arthritis in my old bones. I think of that summer with Penny all those years before. I was young, and I felt so good in my own hide. Penny would lie in the grass as I ate and talk to me, pick flowers and festoon my mane and tail with them. I liked being a pony then. I wouldn't have been anything else. I forget about everything that has happened in between.

I pick up the pace, following the white line around a curve. I see Penny's car ahead. The blinker comes on and turns left. I start to follow her car across the highway but I hear a loud horn and I shy as a dark blue pickup truck comes toward me. I hear brakes screeching and tires skidding on the wet road.

57

PENNY

I'S PENNY'S TURN at the line of stinky pay phones. Today hers smells like maple syrup. How does someone have syrup? All the other inmates seem to have things Penny doesn't—nail polish, candy, books. And there are apparently places she's never seen—a store, a library, a gym, something called the Loom Room. It's like the jail is modeled on Dante's map of Hell, and that Penny as a "nonconvicted" inmate is sequestered in Purgatory, a place of no torture but also no luxuries, while others are living on different levels with different attributes. Is there a basement where people are held in ice, she wonders? Is the Loom Room where you are doomed to weave and unweave the same Thanksgiving tablecloth for the rest of your life?

The woman next to her is crying hysterically into the receiver. It's hard not to overhear that her daughter has a new boyfriend. "Not a drummer!" the woman sobs.

Motherhood, thinks Penny. It tests us in every way, whether we are ready or not.

She calls Laus but it goes to voicemail. Has he found the package Abra sent? Is he even trying to find it? Does he really care? Doubt creeps in. She had said terrible things to him after they dropped Tella off. *I hate you. You're weak.* She tells herself now to keep it together.

She tries to call Silla again. No answer.

There is no one else to call.

That is her own real failing, she thinks. Her inability to truly connect with other humans. With Laus, with Tella. She is like this battered pay phone, its keys half worn off to the point where you have to press the six really hard just to get it to beep. She hasn't worked hard enough on communication. She hasn't told Laus and Tella who she really is, shown them, so of course they have not done that for her either. She has fed them, clothed them, kept the house neat, scheduled their dentist appointments, but she hasn't been vulnerable with them. What did Dr. Resa say to her? That she was "emotionally distant." They had started doing the breath work to try to get her to open up, to be real, to be "authentic," a word that Penny hates.

"So you think I'm uptight or something?" Penny had asked Dr. Resa.

"I think you feel like you need to be in control at all times," the doctor had said. "That's very normal under the circumstances, with a child who flies off the handle at any moment."

Dr. Resa had taught her to close her eyes, to breathe deeply, repetitively, in and out. To feel safe visiting scary things, scary places in her mind. Scary feelings.

Anger. Sadness. Grief.

She had scheduled a session with Dr. Resa when they got back from dropping Tella off. She had so much to say, but she started off telling her about seeing the pony at that roadside petting zoo near Arcadia.

"He was like a vision from the past," Penny said.

"Sometimes life does that, it sends us signs," said Dr. Resa.

Penny wasn't sure she believed that, but she nodded politely into the camera on her computer. "It made me think," she'd said. "About how it felt to be so sad, so angry. I think I need to let myself feel those things more often."

"Does that scare you?" asked Dr. Resa.

"Yes."

"Why?"

"What if people don't like me? What if they prefer polite Penny?"

"Penny, you're creating a dichotomy that doesn't exist, because other people don't actually know you. So the choice is letting people know you, all of you, or none of you. Because that's what you're doing now. Hiding. Why don't you trust people?"

"I don't know. I'm afraid to."

"Because you don't trust yourself? Because you feel like a bad person?"

Tears sprang to Penny's eyes. "Yes."

"When did you start to feel like a bad person?"

"When I let my pony down." She could feel the truth of this. "I'm so afraid something terrible happened to him. Ponies' lives can go so wrong. They can end up in such terrible places." She couldn't suppress a sob, and didn't try to.

"Is there a way to find out what happened to him?"

And then the tears really came, along with a hefty amount of snot. "I'm worried he's dead."

PART NINE

Anxiety

58

THE PONY

HAVE TRAINED many children to fall safely. Just FYI, duck and roll is your best bet when a pony launches you skyward. This is also the technique I use as the blue truck catches me with the corner of its front fender. Fortunately I'm already leaping away, so it just increases my velocity. I tumble into a ditch. The driver keeps going, either unaware that he has just hit someone with his massive pickup truck, or . . . you fill in the blank. I mean, I'm not a squirrel, dude. I hope I dented his chrome.

The upside of rolling into the ditch is that I am invisible when Mr. Alcinous goes racing past. I'm free to continue my pursuit of Penny. Penny! Clearly the universe did not agree with the owl that I should leave her alone. She has landed in my path and I intend to go find her and make things right between us. She's all grown up now, like the owl said, but she still radiates the Pennyness I remember. But the sadness! It hangs on her like a wet winter coat, and I can feel how it's eating at her. Sadness can be deadly, and Penny has that kind of sadness.

I climb out of the ditch, covered with mud from head to toe, and continue trotting down the road, only slightly askew after my accident. Penny's car is long gone, but I follow the faint scent of her for a few hours until I lose it. I backtrack, sniffing, and make a few more wrong turns. Finally I come to a dirt road. I can't smell Penny anymore, but I do smell farm animals, and the road feels promising. Plus, darkness will be on me soon. This is a coyote zone, and I don't want to risk being caught out here by myself.

I make my way to where a driveway turns off to the left. There's a sign. Unlike the rat, I'm not much of a reader, but I learn a lot from a good long sniff. This place is full of nervous girls. Nervous is one smell I'm deeply familiar with. In the past when I carried little girls toward large jumps, they emitted a certain . . . perfume that is indelibly stored in my brain. Dogs, of course, are masters at smelling anxiety on people, but ponies aren't far behind. Free-floating worry is a cloud on this place, as if it's a factory spewing anxiety out of a smokestack. I walk down the long driveway in darkness. I come around a corner and in the moonlight I see below me white fences, a barn, some paddocks and pastures, a main building where some cars are parked, and a set of cabins.

I trot straight to the parking lot, but Penny's car is not there. I'm crushed to realize I missed her. But right away I pick up her scent! I follow it through the parking lot, down a pathway to the farthest cabin. There are no lights on, and I move slowly through the darkness. I get to the cabin. I know Penny is not here, but I can smell her child. The child, Tella, is inside this cabin!

I peek into the window but it's dark inside. I snuffle around the edge of the screen door, reading what I can from the scents within.

At that moment, someone in the cabin screams and shouts, "Bear! There's a bear! Ahhhhh!"

I am afraid of bears, so I spin around looking for where the bear is. There's clattering and lights come on all around me in the cabins. Small faces appear at screened windows. A woman I can't see says, "Damn it, I was just getting to sleep. Hey bear, hey bear . . . Shoo! Go away."

I am still looking around for the bear when a flashlight finds me. I blink in the sudden light. "Not a bear," the woman says cautiously. "But what is it?"

"A beaver?"

A beaver? Really?

"A badger?"

"A really big raccoon?"

"A swamp monster?"

A spritz of worry jets around the camp, and voices call from cabin window to cabin window.

"It could be rabid!"

"It could bite!"

"It's going to eat us!"

"I see claws!"

"Be careful!"

Finally a screen door slams and a small child in polka dot pajamas holding a phone flashlight walks up to me.

"Noooooo!" shout the others.

"Suzy, stay back!" the woman calls. "Oh my God!"

"You're going to die!" chorus the girls.

I stand still as Suzy shines her light all over me. "It's a pony," she says at last. "I always wanted a pony. Can I keep it?"

There is audible relief from all the cabins, and clutches of pajama-clad girls emerge, all holding phone flashlights. They chitter and chatter like songbirds, and little hands reach out to me and then squeal at the mud that encrusts my shapely form. Only my muzzle is clean, and that is what they pet.

"It tickles," giggles a little girl in pink pajamas.

Then one of the adult women arrives in a bathrobe and fuzzy slippers with a bucket of oats. She holds it out, and I dutifully follow her. As I move through the crowd, I note there is one person missing. Tella. I follow the oat bucket and enter a paddock.

"Sleep well, pony," says Suzy, the little girl in the polka dot pajamas.

BY MORNING I have the lay of the land courtesy of a donkey named Ike. "These girls are as wound up as a Thoroughbred on race day," he tells me. "It's like a barnful of Arabians."

"Usually you put nervous equines with calm ones," I say. "Why are all the high-strung humans grouped here where they're just going to set each other off?"

He sighs. "Another stupid human idea."

"Or maybe not," I offer. "Creatures can change. I watched a rat turn a nervous horse into a champion."

"That's good to hear, because I'm sick of these females. I'm done. You're the therapy equine now. There's also a therapy hamster and a therapy sheep and several therapy dogs. Good luck."

"I don't have training to be a therapy pony," I say.

"Are you cute under all that mud?"

"Naturally."

"Then you're hired. I'm retiring." He goes to the far corner of his pen and closes his eyes.

First thing in the morning, a squad of girls ranging in age from about ten to sixteen arrives to bathe me and brush me and feed me. They get out the hose and the scraper thing and the brushes and combs and towels. Several of them are afraid of me, and I try to stand very still and not make any sudden movements, as if they are fawns. Still, one cries and has to be comforted by another, who in turn starts chewing her fingernails.

Once the mud is off me, they dry me and groom me and even blow-dry my forelock into a fluffy halo. Then they stand back to admire their handiwork.

"Do ponies have diseases?" asks one girl.

"What about funguses?"

"He's probably full of parasites."

"He is cute, though." On this they all agree. Except one. I spot Tella hanging back, outside the fence.

I stare at her and put an idea into her head. *Come closer.*

"I don't want to," she says out loud. "Ponies are mean."

I'm not mean. Well, I can be mean, but I won't be mean to you.

"I don't trust you. That other pony tried to scrape my leg off."

"Who are you talking to?" Suzy asks Tella.

"No one," says Tella, frowning. She stares at the dirt and kicks up clouds of dust instead of joining the others in the pen with me.

Stop kicking up dust, I command.

She kicks harder. Suzy starts choking and coughing.

Please stop kicking up dust, I ask.

Tella stops kicking and looks at me. Can she understand what I'm saying? I try something more difficult. *Stand on your right foot.*

She looks at me and stands on her left foot. Then she flips me the bird and walks away.

"THERE'S NOTHING WRONG with these girls, they're just very sensitive," I say to the donkey later, when the girls are in the main building for their classes.

"I can spell crazy," he says, though I doubt he can.

"That's both unkind and not true. I thought the racehorse I lived with was crazy, but he was just grief-stricken and deprived of the things that calm horses down, like friends and room to run whenever he felt like it. And he was fed all kinds of high-energy food that made his stomach hurt."

"Cra-zy," he brays in a passable imitation of Patsy Cline. "You can call it whatever you want, but this place is chock-full of girls nuttier than a fruitcake."

I'm done with this donkey and his dismissive attitude toward mental health.

"Dogs!" I call.

A border collie, a Labrador mix, a Jack Russell terrier, and a pot-bellied pig gather around me. "Dogs reporting for duty," says the border collie.

I peer at the pig. "Are you a dog?"

"Yes," says the pig. You want to make a thing of it?"

I shake my head. "Dogs. I refer to your superior understanding of humans and how they work. What do you know about the girl called Tella?"

"She doesn't like us," says the border collie. "Tells us to stay away."

The Jack Russell pipes up. "I think she can understand us when we talk. Usually it's just really little humans who have that ability, but they all grow out of it."

The border collie shakes her head. "Conspiracy theory. Humans can't understand animal conversations after the age of three."

"I'm telling you, that one can. I've heard about people like her," says the Jack Russell.

"They exist?" I ask.

"No," says the border collie in the firm tones of a dog who has completed all the levels of obedience school. "It's physically impossible. Once they reach full humanness at around age three, their brains eliminate the synapses that can understand animal speech. No one knows why. It's an evolutionary thing, probably having to do with empathy. Humans don't like to kill things they can talk to, so one theory is that evolution selected for humans that lose the ability to talk to animals."

"My grandmother belonged to an adult human who understood her," insists the Jack Russell.

"Unproven," insists the border collie.

"Hearsay," says the pig. "A spider maybe, but a human? No way."

The little Jack Russell continues to bark. "All I know is, my mother told me what her mother told her."

Outside the barn the adult woman calls, "Doggos! Time for grooming!" The border collie herds the Jack Russell away from me with a nip and a growl.

I lean over the fence to where the sheep is napping. "Stanley," I call.

"Resting," he says.

"Have you ever been convinced that a nontoddler human could understand what you're saying?"

He shakes his head. "They get the basics, distress call versus happy grunting, but they're functionally illiterate in terms of communication. It's sad, really, how they lose that essential language skill. Gentleness often disappears at the same time, replaced with ambition and a thirst for power and control."

"But there could be one or two older humans who do understand us?"

"Not that I am aware of," he says. "That would be pretty life-changing, but on the other hand, what would you really say to them? Thanks for turning my hair into sweaters and leaving me naked and freezing? Thanks for eating my family? Baaaaa . . ."

He has a point.

A COUPLE OF days go by and I charm the other little girls and let them climb on me, but Tella doesn't appear. She's avoiding me. One night, I open the latch on my paddock and creep up to the screened window near her bunk.

Tella.

"Leave me alone," she whispers. I hear her bunkmate roll over and fart in her sleep.

Do you understand how rare and wonderful it is that you can hear me?

"It's terrible. I can hear everyone."

So can I. Even the worms I'm standing on right now. Sorry, worms.

"I can hear all the animals, all the insects. I can even hear the plants cry when we step on them. I can hear way more frequencies than most people. No one believes me. It's excruciating. I can't take it."

Can you tune some of it out?

"I'm trying to tune you out right now."

"Shut up. You're talking in your sleep," says her bunkmate.

"Leave me alone," says Tella as she puts on headphones and rolls over so she can't see me.

Tella? Tella?

No response.

59

PENNY

THE NEXT POSTCARD from Laus is of Yosemite Falls, a huge cascade of water. It's from their honeymoon, when he splurged on a night at the Ahwahnee. He was so handsome. Still is. She was working at an athletic shoe store while finishing her last year in college and he came in to buy running shoes. She'd measured his feet and looked up at him and thought, *This is the man I'm going to marry.* He had felt the same bolt of lightning, asked her out, and three months later they were married. Maybe they should have dated longer, she thinks. Tella came along so quickly. They'd hardly had time to get to know each other.

When I got home from work I went door to door in the neighborhood, asking about the missing package, the other side of the postcard says. It comforts her to see his square handwriting. She thinks how they never handwrite notes to each other anymore. It's nice. His writing gets smaller as he runs out of space, and she has to squint to read it. *Get this. On that day, the Moores' Ring camera had pics of a pony on it. The guy down the street with the pet chicken is out of town but I'm checking with other neighbors to see if a pony stole your package.*

A pony? It couldn't be, she thinks. That is a *really* weird coincidence.

Maybe Dr. Resa is right. Life is sending her some big signs. But what does it mean?

LISA LOOKS GRIM as she sits down. She is wearing jeans and a black T-shirt, so not coming from court. "Listen. I just watched the video deposition of one of the teachers you said would be a good character witness. Linda Janson?"

"Yes. I've worked with her for years. She teaches fourth grade."

"Well, she said some nice things about you, but then she said she felt obligated to add that you had confided in her that you wanted to kill your neighbor."

Gobsmacked, again. "What?"

Lisa checks her notes. "Someone named Glenn?"

Glenn. The neighbor with the pet chicken.

"Oh my God," Penny erupts. "I was kidding! Glenn shot a bear and I was really upset about it. I like Glenn. We wave."

"But you said to people that you wanted to kill him?"

"I said 'kill,'" Penny says, using air quotes. "Not actually kill. He could electrify his chicken coop to keep the bears away, but he chose to just shoot the poor bear instead. It was infuriating."

Lisa sighs. "The prosecution is going to use it to show you're a dangerous sociopath, you know that?"

Penny blinks. "But . . . I'm not."

"We can't seem to prove that, can we?" Penny can tell Lisa is fed up with her, with what seems like a pack of lies, with ponies, with all of it. Who can blame her?

Lisa goes on, "The people who sued Frank over their daughter's death were on a cruise the day he died, so that's a dead end for us."

"They could have hired someone to kill him."

Lisa frowns. "I will try to introduce that possibility, but the judge is not going to like it. Oh, and your husband asked me to show you this picture. Someone's Ring camera."

Lisa holds up her phone to the chicken-wire plexiglass. Penny can see a slightly blurred photo of a pony's rump. And then one that shows part of its head. Penny gets a chill.

"That's my pony. But it can't be."

60

THE PONY

ONE DAY I catch Tella as she's standing at the edge of the pond. In the water are some girls playing a cautious game of tag. Tella is shivering slightly, even though she hasn't gone in yet.

I stay quiet, exuding amiability.

"I hate cold water," she says at last.

Hey, can you tell me where your mom is?

Tella stiffens. "Why do you want to know?"

I know her. We're old friends. Is she coming back here soon?

"No. Not for a long time." She sounds irritated. I realize I should be more sympathetic, more helpful. Not just use her to get to Penny.

I can help. Let's go for a walk. I'll introduce you to all the creatures. There are some toads you're going to love. Word to the wise: be nice to the swallows. You know, the world isn't so bad when you get used to it. Your mom and I really enjoyed being outside together. Let's go into the forest together.

I wonder if that sounded creepy.

Tella swivels around and looks at me, then screams and calls to the lifeguard, "Ow! Jesus, the goddamn pony bit me! It broke the skin!"

What? I did not!

An adult woman comes over. She is concerned, frowning. She examines Tella's finger, which is indeed bruised, though not by me.

"Let's get you to the nurse," says the woman.

"There's something wrong with him," Tella says, pointing to me, her voice high and full of rage and fear. "Why did you take in a wild animal like that? He's vicious. Why is he loose like this? It's not safe." She feigns tears and runs back to her cabin.

The woman grabs my halter. "I'm sorry," she says to me.

Why are you doing this? I shout at Tella as the woman drags me away. *I want to help you!*

I AM EXILED to a chain-link pen on the far side of the property. Even though it's off-limits for the girls, Suzy comes and cries, her tiny fingers clawing the wire fence.

"It's so unfair," she wails.

I feel terrible that Tella is so unhappy, but clearly I am not the right person to help her. It seems like she's in good hands here. I feel guilty about it, but I need to go. I need to trust that these humans will help Tella, and I need to find Penny.

That night, the Jack Russell slinks out of the darkness.

"Don't tell the border collie I'm here," she says.

"Thank you for coming. I didn't really bite that kid," I say.

"I know. She has an anxiety disorder. Takes one to know one," says the Jack Russell. "Hang on. I have to chase my tail for a sec." The dog spins around, chasing its tail. "Okay. Better. Are you judging me?"

"Not in the least. Everyone is wired differently. We're all just figuring out how to get through the day."

The dog stares at me for a full minute, then finally says, "True."

"Listen, I need to find Tella's mother. Is there anything you've smelled on Tella that would help me find her? An indicator of a location?"

The dog shakes her head. "No. All I can smell on her is anxiety. It's overwhelming, like the smell of dog biscuits. You need to find another human to help you find Penny. I only know one other human who can understand what animals are saying."

"Who?"

"Okay. It's far from here, though. There's a forest with blue butterflies in it, and—"

"Are you kidding me?" I interrupt. I pin my ears back. "That's not funny!"

The Jack Russell cocks her head. "What are you talking about? I'm just telling you where my grandmother lived. That's where the person is who can help you."

I NEED TO get back to the forest of the blue butterflies. Fortunately luck is on my side. Suzy's time at the facility for nervous girls is up. She has gained confidence and learned to manage her anxiety. She is going home, but not alone. I have planted the idea in her head that I must accompany her. She won't be safe without me. I feel sort of bad about this, because thanks to the good human therapists and healthy lifestyle at the school, Suzy has learned to manage her anxiety and has gained a ton of confidence. And here I am planting doubts in her head. *The world is scary. You need me. I will always be here for you. Pet me and you will feel calmer.* I justify this by saying life on the outside is going to test Suzy. I'm just the first test, gaslighting her and undermining her confidence in herself. If she can learn that I am a charlatan and she doesn't really need me, then she will never fall for anyone like me again. Icky, right? But I have to get to Penny, who really does need me.

"Honey, we live in the middle of New York City," says Suzy's mom when she arrives to accompany Suzy back home.

"This pony is the reason I am able to reenter the world," says Suzy. "I'm not coming home without him. I can't function without him."

Gulp. I am a bad pony. But the upside of being a bad pony is that I am on my way to New York and thus in one day will be much, much closer to the forest of the blue butterflies than I am now. That's because Suzy, Suzy's mom, and I have first-class tickets on an airplane. Yes!

The night before I leave, Tella appears at my pen.

Hi, I say cautiously.

"Say something," she says to me.

What do you want me to say? I hope you're feeling better. I'm going to find your mom and try to help her be less sad. Can you help me find her? Where is she?

Tella starts to cry. "I can't hear you. I can't hear anything," she says. "It's gone. I can't hear any of the animals anymore. I can't hear the plants, either. Only a tiny whisper from the oldest trees."

She puts her fingers through the wire and pets me. I put my nose to the fence and she kisses it.

"It's so quiet," she says, sobbing. "All I wanted was silence, but now I feel so alone."

I lick her tears away. *You're going to be okay,* I try to tell her. *It will be okay.*

"IS THAT A—?" asks the flight attendant as Suzy leads me onto the plane.

"Emotional support animal," says Suzy. I have been groomed to a high shine and my hair is fluffier than it has ever been. Even my hooves are polished and trimmed.

While I strike an aloof pose like a movie star, Suzy's mother hands over a sheaf of documentation that I assume is forged, but it's enough for the flight attendant. I am given a pillow, a blanket, a glass of champagne, and a seat. I know the drill, so I stand in front of the seat and only nibble on the seat cushion when no one is looking. Old habits die hard, after all. The flight is uneventful except for when I poop and the humans all panic and hold their noses. I mean, really. Why is poop such a big deal to them?

We collect our luggage and head to the curb. When the taxi driver looks at me, Suzy's mother starts peeling off bills from a wad in her purse. I ride in the wayback of a minivan (quite pleasant after my hatchback experience) and before I know it I'm standing in front of an apartment building on the Upper West Side. Yes, there is pavement underfoot, but I like the look of the leafy trees and green grass in the park next door. Focus, I remind myself. This is just a means to an end. But a pony's gotta eat, right?

I ride in an elevator (another thing I have learned to do in my travels) and arrive in a lovely three-bedroom apartment with a view of the Hudson River. Nice, if you're a human. But I'm not. I'm a pony with places to go. I need to peel Suzy off me and convince her she can function in the world without me. Unfortunately I have done a really good job of convincing her she needs me, and she spends all of her time with her fingers entwined in my mane, including while we're asleep.

So, in the grand tradition of men who need to break up with women but don't have the courage to say so, I become Bad Pony. I trot around on the hardwood floors, making noise and scuffing the walnut finish, and make some choice poos in proximity to some very expensively upholstered midcentury modern chairs. I ignore Suzy and start sleeping in her parents' room. I snore. A lot, and scratch my itchy butt on everything in sight.

"Absolutely not," says Suzy's mom, the president of the co-op board, and every other tenant in the building. I have achieved what no presidential candidate or pizza place ever has: a unanimous vote. Against, but still. I am a uniter.

Send me to an animal rescue in upstate New York, I command Suzy. *I will be happy there. You can come visit me whenever you like.*

The communication I have with Suzy is not like the communication I had with Tella before she lost the gift. It's imprecise, like smoke signals. But my suggestion is also the obvious answer. Except I end up at an animal rescue in New Jersey. Oops.

It's a tall fence with a locked gate, but fortunately they do not expect a pony to tunnel *under* the fence, and I am on the lam once again before the day is out. I stay in the woods whenever possible, travel by night, look both ways before crossing roads or train tracks, and within a short time I make my way back to the forest of the blue butterflies.

Once again I stand under the gnarled beech trees at the intersection on the trail where Penny and I met Arete the red mare and her boy. One path leads to the abandoned house. One leads to High Rise Farms, where Arete lived. The third leads back the way Penny and I came.

To Silla.

When the Jack Russell at the school for nervous girls told me her grandmother belonged to a woman who could understand animals, it took me a while to figure out who she was talking about.

"Ribs?" I asked her. "Are you talking about a dog named Ribs?"

"Yes!" she yipped. "That was her name."

"Silla is the human who can talk to animals?"

I run my mind back over all of my encounters with Silla. Had we conversed? She had certainly shouted nonstop at her fellow humans, but I couldn't remember her shouting at us ponies. I remembered her *asking* me to do things, and yes, I guess I did understand what she was saying. I thought back to when she was training me. It was all in silence, but she did seem to respond when I had concerns. *I know it feels weird, but pull the cart calmly and you will start to enjoy it. No, that tree is not going to eat you. Yes, he's a brat, but let this kid ride you and I will give you a carrot. Be nice to Penny, she's special.*

Silla! She had the gift and I never even realized it! That must have been what she recognized in Penny. Another person who listened to animals!

I trot down the familiar trail. As I get closer to Silla's barn, I begin to pick up a scent I recognize. It can't be, I think. But it is. Penny. A fresh scent. Penny is here! I gallop around the corner into the barn.

The barn aisle is empty. No sign of Penny. I sniff the floor. She was here, though, and not that long ago. When I pass the barn office, a voice drifts out. "It's you. Of course."

I stop and stick my head in. It smells like dust and cats. Silla is very old now, her wiry gray hair standing up like a nest of snakes. Her skin is lined and her eyes a little bloodshot. She looks like she's snarling, her face in a kind of grimace, but I finally realize it's a smile. I've never seen Silla smile before.

She starts laughing. It sounds like a cross between a cackle and a cough, and her eyes run and she slaps her knees. "You two really are something. Come with me," she says.

61

PENNY

THAT CAN'T BE my pony. He's not in California. Penny, hands shaking, punches Silla's number into the pay phone again. She has told a guard that there's a family emergency and the guard has taken pity on her and let her use the phone even though it's after hours. It rings and rings. After fifty-eight rings, Penny hangs up.

Back in her cell, she lies on her bunk. Her thoughts are flying all over the place like bats, diving and swooping, so she grabs a piece of paper and the wobbly pen and begins to write in an attempt to make sense of them. *I was really upset when I drove out of the gates of High Rise...*

I JUST DIDN'T expect to get screamed at and accused of murder by Melanie and Alex. In retrospect, maybe they already knew the police had reopened the investigation. It must have been shocking to them that I just appeared there like that.

I didn't know any of that then. I drove back to Silla's, to tell her that Hankins was a dead end and to find out what she knew about why Alex and Melanie would react that way to my appearance. I guess I thought she might know something about what happened after I left when I was twelve. She knew Melanie and Frank. I think they were old friends or something, at least colleagues in the horse world.

Silla was giving a lesson when I got there, a little girl of about ten. She was bobbing along on top of a black-and-white pinto pony with shaggy legs and a huge fluffy mane. I waved at her and she waved back and I pointed to the woods to indicate that I would be back when she was done. I headed down the path that my pony and I took a quarter century earlier, the last time I saw him.

PENNY PAUSES AND thinks about that moment. The walls of her cell dissolve and she is back there again, on the bumpy trail that winds into the woods, the gnarled arms of the huge beech trees arching overhead, their roots underfoot.

THE TRAIL IS the same. It's weird how I can remember it so clearly, even after all this time. I follow the twists and turns under the elm and ash trees, hearing the leaves sigh and shift overhead. I lift my feet to avoid roots and jump small puddles.

I don't want to think about the last time I was here, the terrifying panic I felt in the darkness, the feel of the red mare's mane in my fists. The taste of blood in my mouth.

Instead I think of my pony. His smell when I buried my face in his mane. The way he made me laugh, every day. The way he swished his tail when he was irritated because the carrots were late or I lost my balance over a jump, and the way he flipped it high in the air when he was happy, when we jumped in sync, flying as one being.

A blue butterfly floats past me. It's so fragile and beautiful. I have come to a crossroads in the trail and I sit down on a rock. The sunlight is dappled on the ground around me, the moss green on the trees.

What is wrong with me that I have never been as happy with anyone as I was with that pony?

I hear an owl hooting somewhere nearby. It sounds so mournful and lonely.

Maybe there's nothing wrong with you, says a voice in my head. *Maybe we find love where we find it, and we shouldn't question it, just treasure it.* I sigh.

The butterfly dances around me, its wings flashing blue and silver in the light.

I loved that pony more than I have ever loved anyone. I've known that for a long time, but I felt guilty about it. My husband, my child. I love them, of course. But it's so complicated. I never feel like I'm doing it right.

Every time I looked at the pony, my heart would swell and lift and sing. I loved everything about him, even his naughtiness and bad moods and little tricks. I loved the little black tips of his ears, and his prickery whiskers, and the feathers on his fetlocks. The silly frizz of hairs that stuck up around the base of his tail. He wasn't the tallest or most athletic or most beautiful. It didn't matter. He gave me courage, he made me laugh. I loved him intensely, with a connection that I have never felt since then.

I start to cry. Something huge and painful wells up in me and I can't stop it. It bursts out of me in great gasping gulps.

Grief.

I am making a noise that is very much like a donkey, and I really hope a dog walker doesn't go by in this moment. I take a deep breath, and try to stuff the grief back down inside me. I don't have a Kleenex, so I wipe my tears and blow my nose on the cuff of my shirt, then roll it up like I did as a kid.

And that's when he appears.

PART TEN

Love

62

PENNY AND THE PONY

WE STARE AT each other. Neither of us can believe the other is real.

You, Penny says.

You, says the pony.

We actually sort of circle each other warily, disbelieving our eyes. And then Penny reaches out and touches the pony's nose, and in a nanosecond, she has her arms around his neck and, with a little scream, her face is buried in his mane. He gives a little screaming neigh and snakes his nose around and shoves it in her armpit.

The smell of him warps time and sends Penny pinging back and forth from past to present, feeling every emotion she has ever felt, all at once. She's laughing, she's crying, she's braying like a donkey again. And she doesn't care—all she cares about is being here, with this little furry creature who she has worried about, pined over, ached for. She's had so many nightmares in which she was searching for him and couldn't find him, nightmares where she knew he was in danger and she couldn't get to him and she would wake up shouting. So many times she imagined him dying somewhere starving, alone, neglected, and it was all her fault. And now she's awake, and he's here, and he's fine, and she can feel his heart beating strong against her hand. He's alive! He's alive! After twenty-five years—the sheer shocking joy of it, the relief, leaves her weak in the knees.

The smell of her does the same for him, as if he is living all of the moments of his life simultaneously in a wild orchestral crescendo. So many miles, so many dangers, so much heartache to find her. He was so afraid she was hurt, or lost, or dead. So afraid it was his fault, because she was his one true person and he abandoned her. But she's here. She's alive, and he can feel her heart beating under his nose. How could he have ever doubted her? How could he have ever thought she was anything but wonderful, wonderful, loving, kind Penny?

We stay that way for a long time. Birds sing around us. Fifi the sparrow appears with her whole flock and they warble a lilting chorus of exultation. The owl hoots. One particular bat circles our heads, darting back and forth in glee. Even the seagulls mass overhead, squawking like rowdy soccer fans whose team just won the championship. The trees sigh with happiness, and crickets and beetles come together to form a small band and play celebratory tunes. Earthworms wiggle and shimmy. The sun beams with joy, and the wind kisses our hair and tickles our ears.

Finally, the sun gets tired and begins to drop low in the sky. The partygoers disperse. As with all moments of emotional overload, the wave recedes from our bodies, and small details come to the fore. A mosquito whining out of tune near an ear. Goose bumps on an arm. A rumble of hunger in a tummy. We untangle our limbs and face each other.

"I can't ever be apart from you again," says Penny. "But how do I get you home to California?" she asks. "You won't fit in my carry-on luggage. What are we going to do?"

We head back to Silla's, together, the way we should have all those years ago, if the pony had stayed tied to the tree, and if Penny had not followed the boy down the trail to the fancy show barn. Fate ripped us apart, but love has reunited us at last. If this were a different kind of story, we would fade to black here, but we both know that keeping a pony is not like keeping a dog or a cat, and Penny's circumstances haven't allowed her to have even those lower-maintenance pets. And she's broke. Shipping an equine from New York to California? Fuhgeddaboutit.

Silla is waiting for us in the barn, with the daughter of Ribs, also called Ribs. Silla has prepared a stall for the pony, with a manger full of hay. Grass hay, delicious but low cal, which is thoughtful of her.

"I will keep him for you until you can make a plan," Silla says.

"My daughter . . . It's a difficult moment," Penny begins.

Silla waves her hand. "I didn't say you could never find a good home for a pony," she said. "I just said it's a rider's responsibility to make sure their pony has a good retirement. Food, friends—"

"Freedom," says Penny. "Thank you. I'll come back to visit as soon as I can."

"He's an old pony," says Silla. Her implication is clear. This might be the last time Penny and the pony see each other. "Make sure you tell him everything he needs to hear."

Penny's eyes fill with tears. She throws her arms around the pony. "I love you," she says.

I love you, too, says the pony.

Silla smiles at the pony. "He knows," she tells Penny.

Penny's phone beeps and she says, "I have to go, but thank you. Thank you." She goes to hug Silla but thinks better of it and hugs the pony one more time. She's halfway to the car when she turns back.

"You knew Frank Ross?" she asks Silla.

Silla is standing in the aisle of the barn, backlit, so Penny can't see her expression. "Of course I did. Small world, horses. He and I grew up together."

"They never solved his murder?"

"Lots of people wanted him dead. He was a charmer, but a real bastard." Silla grabs the broom and gives the floor a vicious sweep.

"Yes," Penny says. "But his family wants justice." Penny is about to tell Silla that Melanie and Alex think Penny killed Frank, but it feels too shameful.

"Justice? Far as I can tell, justice was served the day that man went

281

to hell. He was cruel to horses, cruel to people. I doubt many people cried over the death of Frank Ross," says Silla.

"I feel responsible that I set the whole thing in motion," Penny says. "If I hadn't taken the horse—"

"Don't waste a second thinking about it. You did the right thing." Silla sweeps harder.

Penny starts to walk away, running late for her flight, but Silla calls after her. "Of all of my students," she says, "you were my favorite."

Penny's eyes fill with shocked tears at this—Silla never pays compliments or shows affection. She nods gratefully, knowing Silla doesn't want more response than that.

"I knew you would come back," Silla says. "Both of you."

PENNY LIES ON her bunk in the jail, suffused with feelings and worries. That pony on the Ring camera in California can't be her pony. Her pony is safe and sound at Silla's, isn't he?

But also . . .

Silla has always put horses first. Frank was a horse abuser. The night Frank died, the pony would have come back to the stable without Penny. Silla would have seen him and gone looking for Penny. Silla would have protected Penny. Silla would have protected the horse. Protected all horses.

Was Silla in the forest that night?

63

THE PONY

IT'S STRANGE AND kind of wonderful to be back at Silla's. I imagine this is what it's like for humans to sleep in their childhood bed again. Silla turns in early, but I stay up, lying in the fluffy shavings and realizing that I am no longer on the run. No longer hunting anyone or anything. Not seeking revenge or love. I found my person. I am safe and happy and while Penny is not a hundred percent happy, in her complicated human life she at least knows there is one person out there who loves her fully and completely: me. I have given her back what she lost all those years ago: courage, love, laughter.

I sleep the deepest sleep I have slept in twenty-five years. The sun is coming up when I awaken to a voice in the barn aisle. It's a young blond woman I don't know, but her energy is worried.

"Silla?" she calls.

Silla emerges from her office looking like a chewed-up dog toy. "Abra," she says. "I haven't seen you in a while." Silla sounds guarded. "How is life at High Rise? Must be very exciting to be working for an international show jumper like Alex."

Abra sinks onto a hay bale and puts her head in her hands. "You were right when you told me not to take that job. It's a nightmare."

Silla frowns. "Is Melanie still drugging horses? I'd hoped she learned her lesson."

"It's Alex. He's using electrified spurs."

Silla's hair pretty much stands on end at this news. "What the hell does that even mean?" she asks. "Stay. I'm pouring us both some coffee."

I can smell burnt strong coffee and Silla emerges from the office with two chipped mugs. Abra winces when she takes a sip. "Do you remember what you made me promise?"

"I made every rider promise it. To never hurt a horse. It's fundamental to the sport."

Abra nods. "That was an easy promise for me to make," she says. "But Alex . . . He's very careful about it, but I've seen the wires. They go from the spur through a tiny hole in his boot and up through his breeches to a battery pack under his shirt. He hides it under his clothes, but I've seen it. It's totally against the rules, of course, on top of being totally unethical. He has a button in his glove and he zaps the horses as they go to jump, and it makes them jump bigger."

Silla just stares at her, a pot about to boil.

"I don't know what to do. I mean, if I tell the FEI—"

"He'll be banned from the sport. He should be. That's why the FEI exists, to set rules for the entire world, every country, every rider, every competition. Rules like not zapping your horse."

"I like Alex. He's a good boss. In every other way he takes great care of his horses. But I can't . . . I just . . . I don't know what to do. That's why I came to you."

"Have you tried to talk to him?"

"Yes. He told me to mind my own business. Now he and Melanie are watching me all the time. You know what it's like over there—I live on the property, my phone is on their plan, same for my internet. I think they search my room when I'm not there. I told Alex I was sorry and he was right, it wasn't any of my business, but . . ."

"Well, you've got to get another job for starters," Silla says.

"I'm worried if I try he'll trash me. You know what the top levels of show jumping are like."

"A distant memory for me, actually."

"It's still a small world. His word carries a lot more weight than mine."

Silla takes a kind but firm tone with Abra. "You know he can't be allowed to keep doing that. Electric spurs?"

"I wish he would just stop," says Abra. "I mean, I get that it's a multimillion-dollar business for him, but aren't we all in it for the love of horses?"

Silla snorts. "Not everyone. Why do you think I stopped competing?"

Abra blinks. "I guess I always assumed you didn't have the right horses, or the money, or that you got hurt."

Silla shakes her head. "I didn't like what I saw. People drugging hunters so they fit the judges' standards of robotic behavior, and the judges pretending not to see it. Halter classes with horses getting blue ribbons who had crooked legs and backs too flat to carry a rider. Tying their legs together with rubber bands to get higher action, or putting chains on their fetlocks. And they all call themselves horsemen, and think it's fine, because they never ask the animals what they think about it."

Abra blushes. "You think all riding is corrupt?"

"No. Not at all. There are good people—lots of them—taking good care of their animals, and horses that love to compete. They love it. You can see it in their eyes. Lots of horses love to run and jump, they love to perform, they love the feel of connection with a rider. But it's hard work, isn't it, to get that level of athleticism from horse and rider? Ethical riders don't take shortcuts. They put in the time, they use patience and kindness to bring out the best in their animals. I love to watch them. But people who don't care about the horse's well-being . . . Alex's uncle was the same. His mother doesn't give a crap about the horse's well-being. She cares about winning, period. What kind of evidence do you have? It can't be Alex's word against yours or you're right, he'll say you're lying."

"I could steal the boots and the wires. Bring them here. I'll take photos of him using the spurs. When we have all the evidence, we can send it to the FEI. And the press."

Silla thinks. "They know you trained with me. That we're friends. They'll come looking here." Silla retreats into the office for a minute, then returns holding a piece of paper. "Mail it to this address. She's not in the horse world. But she'll keep the evidence safe until the time is right."

Abra looks at the paper and frowns. "Penny? I met her yesterday. Isn't she an old friend of Alex's?"

Silla gives a mirthless laugh. "Penny's always on the side of the animals. But be careful. The Kinsworths are dangerous."

Abra nods. "I better get back. Let's keep this between us for now, okay?"

Silla nods.

Abra gets back in her truck and drives off.

Silla leans on my stall door. "The plot thickens, doesn't it, pony?" She rubs my forehead and I nudge her pockets to see if there are any treats in them. "Not packing," she says. I nibble on the stall door to show her I would like to go out to graze.

"Let's wait until the dew is off the grass. Safer for a gentleman of your size. Can you be patient for a little while?"

I toss my head in reluctant agreement. She heads off and I circle a couple of times, then sink down into the shavings for another lovely nap . . .

"Silla?"

I stagger to my feet, shake off the shavings. How long was I asleep? I stick my head over the stall door. A large woman in jodhpurs and black shiny boots is striding down through the barn like she owns it. She has gray hair pulled back and red lips. I don't like this woman. Her energy is very dark. I don't like her at all.

"Melanie Kinsworth," says Silla, coming out of the barn office. "It's been a while. How are you? I see Alex's picture in *Chronicle of the Horse* all the time. He's a superstar."

The Melanie person is impatient. "Alex had a visitor yesterday. That girl."

Silla pretends like she isn't bothered, but I can feel her rage rising. "Sorry, it's feeding time," she says. "You know how it is. I don't really have time to chat." She grabs the wheelbarrow in her gnarled hands and pushes it up to where some hay bales are stacked. I have seen Silla do this a thousand times. She reaches up to where a box cutter hangs on a piece of baling twine on a post. She grabs it and slices through the three pieces of twine that hold the bale together. At this point she always replaces the box cutter on the nail, but I notice her slip it into the pocket of her jacket.

"She was asking questions about the day Frank died. Claims she didn't kill him. The DA is a friend. You know the police reopened the investigation into Frank's death just last week?"

"It wasn't Penny."

Melanie frowns. "Don't you care who killed him?"

"Of course. You know Frank and I—"

"Childhood sweethearts. When you and I were in pigtails winning the pony classes. But later you were rivals."

Silla snorts. "Melanie, your brother's barn outclassed mine by a mile. So does your son's. I run a different kind of operation here, for a different kind of rider. I admired what you and Frank built. The trophies you won. But I didn't like your methods."

Melanie is studying Silla, I realize. She looks like a cat deciding whether to pounce.

Silla takes three flakes of hay and places them in the wheelbarrow and pushes it out the door of the barn. Melanie follows her. I let myself out of the stall and follow Melanie.

When they see me, the two ancient horses in the field prick up their ears. "Good morning," the chestnut gelding calls. There's a llama who hangs back, playing it cool.

"Hello," says the palomino gelding, pushing on the fence.

"Watch out," I say, "that's electric, isn't it?"

"She never turns it on," says the chestnut. "It's not like we're going to run off."

Silla tosses the hay over the fence to the horses. They step back from the fence and drop their heads and start to eat the hay. "Yum," they say to me in between mouthfuls.

Silla reaches down to turn on the spigot to fill their trough. I notice she has one hand in her pocket, the pocket where she put the box cutter.

"Abra came to see you this morning," said Melanie.

"She's an old student of mine. Came to check on me."

"I don't trust her," says Melanie. "Grooms . . . they always get ideas."

"Abra is completely trustworthy," says Silla.

"No, she's not, as a matter of fact. She's making up lies about Alex. Things that could hurt him. End his career. I told him to fire her."

Silla doesn't respond, just watches the water slowly filling the trough. It's black, and there's a stick tied in it so that squirrels don't drown when they lean down to get a drink.

Silla, be careful, I say.

Silla glances over at me and says silently to me in perfect clarity as if she's inside my head, *Protect Penny.* Then she turns and stares Melanie right in the eye.

"Frank got what he deserved," says Silla to Melanie. "And so will Alex if he doesn't stop. Try running a clean barn, Melanie. Your victories will be a lot sweeter."

Melanie stands there for a second in silence, not moving. None of us moves. Then Melanie turns and walks two steps away. I think she's leaving, but she flicks the switch that turns on the electric fence. I hear it crackle to life. Then, with surprising speed for a woman her age, Melanie runs back and pushes Silla into the electric fence.

64

PENNY

T'S THE DAY before her trial is set to begin. Penny is in the conversation pit. Lisa has a big folder of documents and notes and looks very preoccupied. She has also brought Penny some clothes to wear to her trial—a boxy blue dress with a white collar and a pair of sensible heels.

"Maternal, nonthreatening," Penny notes when the guard brings her the clothes.

"An air of innocence," says Lisa.

"Were you able to find Silla?" Penny asks. She has so many questions. If Silla did kill Frank, would she have let Penny stand accused of the crime? Penny trusted her with the pony. Why hasn't Silla come to see her in jail? She must know Penny is here.

Lisa frowns and looks up from her files. "I'm sorry. I don't know how to say this. I'm afraid Silla passed away."

Penny sits there in shock.

Lisa starts to say, "But I found your sixth-grade teacher. She said she remembers you—"

"Wait. Silla is dead?" The plastic of the gray phone presses into Penny's cheek.

"Yes. I'm really sorry. I drove over there. A neighbor is looking after the two horses while the probate goes through."

"What happened?" Silla was old, it's true, and had a lifelong drinking problem, but she looked so . . . vital.

"Apparently she fell onto an electric fence. Stopped her heart. She must have stumbled. The neighbor said it was probably instantaneous, so she didn't suffer. Now this teacher of yours—"

The hair on Penny's neck goes up. "Silla didn't keep that fence electrified. She told me herself she hadn't turned it on in years. She was murdered," Penny says.

Lisa frowns again, and sighs. "Penny. The trial begins tomorrow," she says. "We really need to focus."

"Where's my pony?" Penny begins to panic. "Was there a pony there? Did you see a pony?"

Lisa stares at her like she has lost her mind. "I didn't see any ponies. There were two normal-sized horses. And a llama. The neighbor said that's all the animals that were there."

My pony is gone. Lisa is talking about Penny's sixth-grade teacher, Mrs. Roberts, and how she remembers Penny fondly and even can produce a report card saying she was a very good girl. "We're not allowed to coach witnesses," Lisa is saying, "but I really hope she says 'shy' and not 'loner.' And also . . ."

Lisa keeps talking, but Penny isn't listening. She's thinking about how happy she was when she found her pony in the forest. How it was like a missing puzzle piece was put back into place, making her whole self come alive again after years of dormancy. How good she felt from that moment on, how optimistic, all the way up until the day she was arrested.

She remembers driving home after school. It had been a great day in the classroom. They worked on fractions and read from *Misty of Chincoteague.* The kids were light and full of laughter, probably because Penny was. She'd even had a message from Tella saying she liked the school and was feeling more able to navigate the world. She and Laus had planned a dinner date at the local taqueria and she planned to have a margarita, something she hadn't allowed herself to have in a long, long time.

Since finding the pony and coming back from the trip she'd felt like a new person. She found things funny again. It made her so joyful to think that her pony was safe and sound with Silla. She didn't feel the need to have the pony right in front of her, even if she could have afforded to ship him to California, which was out of the question—he wasn't a possession she needed to look at and covet or control, he was a family member she needed to know was safe and happy.

"I guess that's what love really is, just caring. Caring is hard, and heartbreaking at times. But it's life."

Penny realizes she has said this out loud. Lisa is staring at her through the chicken-wire plexiglass. "We can ask for a postponement," Lisa says at last. "If you're not ready for this."

65

THE PONY

RIBS IS HOWLING over Silla's body. The sounds coming out of the ancient little dog are so mournful, a terrible keening that vibrates the hairs inside my ears. The two old horses are standing at the far end of the pasture in shock. Melanie is gone.

Ribs lies down in the crook of Silla's elbow and gives a little whimper. She takes a last breath, licks the cheek of her human, and I watch the life leave her, the dog and the woman united in death. I stand there in shock as the two bodies grow cold and stiff.

Protect Penny.

I need to get to her. I know from the scents I smelled on Penny's clothing that she lives far, far away from Silla's. Not so far, in fact, from where I was when I lived with Caya and Circe in the old man's backyard. Close to the fairgrounds. Oh, the irony.

I leave Silla's and head back to Saratoga, retracing the path Fifi took me on, though bypassing my paddleboard adventure this time.

When I get back to the track, there is a different set of racehorses there. No Burnie, no rat. But there are other rats. There are always rats.

"Hi." I introduce myself to one of them who's scurrying along an electrical wire in the barn, a large egg in her mouth. "I need to get to the fairgrounds that is about five months' walk from here. Where it smells like manzanita."

"That's a big word for a little pony like you," says the rat, holding the egg in her paws.

I can see from the curve of her belly that she's pregnant, and I'm hoping that means she's in a generous, caring, maternal mood. "I met my dear friend Dr. Rat there, and we had many adventures together," I say. "Ah, dear old Rattie."

The lady rat brightens. "You're the pony."

"Indeed."

"The doctor thought there was something special about you."

"I'm just a regular pony," I say. "Who needs to get to California as fast as possible."

"Yes, I can see you in Hollywood," says the rat. "You do have a star quality. More *Chucky Meets Misty* than *Black Beauty*, but still. There's a horse hauler heading for Santa Anita with a load of Thoroughbreds. Think you can stow away in that?"

A WEEK LATER, courtesy of the oblivious driver of *Bob's Racehorse Transport*, I'm back in California.

Now I just have to find where Penny lives. Though birds are the most expert navigators, ponies are not far behind. We map the world according to edible things, as I've said, and Penny's scent contained some key markers. Manzanita, as I told the lady rat, but also poppies, redbud, buckbrush, tarweed, fairy lanterns, and a host of other plants in a specific combination that I used my nose to find.

A few days out from Santa Anita, I'm staying out of sight of humans while also cautiously following a country road, sniffing for Penny's scent. I think I can sense it getting stronger, but I'm an old pony. What if my sense of smell isn't what it used to be? I hope this is where she lives . . . I hope Melanie hasn't gotten here before I have . . . it all seems so flimsy now, all this hope . . .

I'M LOOKING AT a house. It is small and gray and has pansies out front. The whole place is suffused with the scent of Penny. She lives here, I know that for sure. I've found her! Penny! I have scent images of her here, tending the flowers, playing with her daughter. Penny. At last. I am so tired from my travels I could fall down and die.

I circle the house and look in the windows. No one is home. I hope she'll be here soon. Penny.

I hear a rumble and hide in the bushes. The last thing I need is to be grabbed by Animal Control now, when I'm so close. A big brown truck comes into view.

I relax a little. I've seen these trucks before—they drop off cardboard things for humans. Not interesting to me, but all the dogs love them because the drivers carry biscuits. Now, if they carried carrots, that would be different.

The truck stops in front of Penny's house.

The driver gets out and deposits a package on Penny's doorstep. I stay hidden nearby.

I watch the brown truck drive off.

The truck is barely out of sight when a little white car drives up, like it was following the truck or something.

I stay hidden in the bushes. *Please be Penny*, I think. The car slows and stops in front of Penny's house. I'm ready to spring forward. A woman gets out. But it's not Penny. It's an older woman. Dress, pearls, city shoes. I know her. It's Melanie, the woman who pushed Silla into the electric fence. The murderess!

She looks around, then furtively walks up to Penny's house. I watch her, waiting, thinking. I've thrown kids off my back, nipped plenty of people, and delivered the occasional gentle kick. But I have never seriously hurt anyone. That is an ironclad part of the equine code. It's just a given that horses don't attack humans unless they are afraid for their lives, and even then we do everything we can to escape. We're not predators, we're prey. We don't fight, we run.

Attack a human, get shot. That's what my mother told me back at Happy Pony Farms, and that's what I've heard in every stable I've ever lived in. *Run if you can, otherwise it's better to submit.* That's the code horses have lived by since the first ancient human dropped a grapevine over a horse's neck and climbed on. It's paid off pretty well for many of us, as the array of horse blankets, horse booties, molasses-flavored feeds, personalized vitamins and skin care products for horses, and organic horse cookies will attest. But how do I solve a problem like Melanie without violence?

She studies the house, then quickly grabs the package and picks it up. Her eyes narrow and her mouth settles into a firm line. Anger. But also relief. She puts the package under her arm and heads for the car.

I burst out of the bushes like a quarter horse chasing a steer. I hurtle toward Melanie and catch her from behind, knocking her and the package to the ground. I can't harm her, but I have to get her out of here before Penny comes home. I grab the edge of the package and bite down on it, taking hold, and gallop off, hoping Melanie follows.

Melanie gets up, shaken, and sees me with the package. "Here, pony," she says. "Good boy. Whoa. Stand still."

I trot off a few yards and turn to stare back at her, willing her to follow me, to leave Penny's house.

Melanie grabs a handful of grass and holds it out. "Here, pony," she wheedles. "Good pony. Just stand."

When she gets close, I trot a few yards farther down the road. Melanie follows me, spewing her lying sweet talk in an attempt to get me to come close enough so she can grab the package.

I stop opposite a house where a man sits on the porch petting a chicken who roosts calmly in his lap.

"Having some trouble there?" he calls to Melanie, laughing.

Melanie is startled to see him but composes herself and flashes him a big smile. "Yeah. My pony got loose," she says. "Do you have a carrot by chance?"

He puts the chicken under his arm and disappears inside the house, returning with the biggest carrot I have ever seen. I mean, that thing is the size of my foreleg. The man hands it to Melanie.

"Thank you," she says. "Here, pony. Look." She cracks the carrot into two with a loud snap.

I start to trot away but I find myself slowing against my will. I stop. I am powerless to resist. I don't even know what's in this package, after all. All I know is it belongs to Penny and that murderous Melanie wants it, badly. But that carrot smells so good. All thoughts of flight flee my brain—even thoughts of Penny, I am ashamed to admit. I fix the carrot with a stare. Generations of equine ancestors tell me to run, to lift my forelegs and flee the lions and pterodactyls and murderous humans, but I can already taste the carrot on my tongue, the crunch of it between my teeth, the little bitlings that will float around my molars all day, delighting me anew. I stay where I am, hypnotized, and Melanie comes near, carrot in hand. *You are a pony*, says a voice in my head that sounds a lot like Circe's. *You can't escape your fate. You am what you am.*

Melanie reaches for the package as she puts the carrot right under my nose.

Her fingers start to close around the package. I am about to open my mouth and release the package and take the delicious carrot when a memory floats into my brain like a blue butterfly. Penny's laughter. *O pony*, she says, her voice tinkling like a harness bell. *You'll do anything for a carrot, won't you?*

No. This time I won't.

I dash off, the package in my teeth. Melanie runs back and jumps in her car, and begins chasing me through the streets.

66

PENNY

THE COURTROOM IS disappointingly basic. Not that Penny was expecting white wigs or Perry Mason, but at least a little walnut paneling would be nice. There are unflattering fluorescent lights, a portrait of the governor that looks like it was done using paint-by-numbers, a beige tile floor, a limp American flag that has seen better days, and heavy wooden tables, one for her, Lisa and Steve, and one for the prosecutor and his team. The audience sits behind a low metal dividing wall in hard plastic seats that are nailed to the floor.

"All rise," says the bailiff, and the judge comes in. Male, probably in his forties, Penny thinks. Her first thought is that he looks like the kind of guy who pretends to like women but doesn't. He looks like a fraternity, men's club, cigars, you-did-a-great-job-in-the-interview-but-Bob-is-a-better-fit kind of man. *Stay positive*, Penny thinks as she smiles innocently at him.

Penny also smiles at the pool of potential jurors in the jury box as Lisa has instructed her. Not too wide, and not at any one person for too long. *I am like you*, the look is meant to convey, not *I am going to kill you.*

Penny spots Laus and gives him a genuine huge smile. He gives her a little "go get 'em" wave like she's in a tryout for a remake of *Ally*

McBeal. He's wearing jeans and a polo shirt. Penny also spots a stone-faced Alex and Melanie Kinsworth and avoids their eyes.

Penny is wearing the boxy blue dress. It's not her style, but it's nice to be out of the dark green jail uniform. Nice to be out of her cell, too.

Lisa leans over to Penny. "I talked to your husband in the hall. Unfortunately, he hasn't been able to find the missing package from Abra."

"Oh," says Penny, her heart sinking a little. "And the pony?"

Lisa shakes her head.

Steve and the prosecutor get into some back-and-forth with the potential jurors about their jobs, size of their families, whether they've ever been accused of a crime or not, and how they feel about horses. Steve is clearly looking for women who are moms and animal people, and the prosecutor is looking for angry old men who have a "hang 'em high" approach to criminal justice.

Finally the jury is empaneled and opening statements begin. Out of the corner of her eye, she sees Laus look at his phone, then get up and leave. *I'm sorry*, he mouths.

What is more important than this, she thinks in annoyance. No one else apart from Lisa and Steve is there for her. Couldn't he stay for one whole day?

The prosecutor outlines how he is going to prove that Penny, although a child, was strong enough to hoist a rock and easily kill a man she wanted dead by hitting him from behind. "Not in self-defense," he says, "but out of malice." He says he's going to show the court that Penny harbors deep anger toward men and is capable even now of terrible violence. He says that Frank Ross was a beloved local hero whose loss harmed the community and devastated his family.

She catches herself half believing the prosecutor, which is not good.

Steve, on the other hand, is not as impressive as Penny hoped. He refers to her as "Pammy" at one point, and when he removes his jacket it's clear he has sweated through his shirt. He drills down on the concept of reasonable doubt rather than obvious innocence. "My client is not an animal" is his strongest line.

There's a lunch recess that seems to last forever. Lisa offers to get Penny something from the vending machine, but the guard takes her to a temporary cell instead. When they come back into the room, Lisa leans over to Penny.

"Um, listen. I don't want to distract you, but I feel like there's something you need to know. I had a voicemail from your husband. He's very sorry but he can't be here."

"Why? Is it Tella?" Penny's heart is in her mouth. She's already running the scenario in her head. Tella is dead. It's all her fault. Penny left her at Arcadia.

Lisa nods. "She ran away from the school."

"When?"

"Apparently she ran away once before but they found her immediately. All was fine until last week, when she disappeared again."

"Last week?!"

"Laus said he didn't want to tell you, with everything going on, and he was hoping they would find her quickly like they did last time, but he wants you to know why he's not here. He wants you to know he's doing everything he can to find her."

PART ELEVEN

Storge (Rhymes with Corgi)

67

THE PONY

DASH DOWN a bank and across a river and successfully evade Melanie.

I stay near Penny's house for a couple of days, hidden. Melanie's car passes a few times, but she doesn't see me. I survive on grass stolen from some nearby lawns.

A man comes and goes from Penny's house, sometimes putting a card in the mailbox and putting up the little red flag, but Penny does not return. Where is she? I can't protect her from Melanie if I don't know where she is. And I have this package. I study the man from a distance. His energy is not scary or aggressive, but he seems agitated. I can't tell if I can trust him or not. He doesn't have the vibe of an animal person. I need to find Penny.

In the animal world, one of the most powerful forces is storge, or love of family. If Penny isn't here, she is probably with her offspring.

Tella.

I pick up the package in my teeth and start walking.

68

PENNY

ON DAY TWO of the trial, Lisa tells her there is no message from Laus, but he has promised to call Lisa immediately if there is any news of Tella.

Where is she? Penny wonders. How long has she been on her own? Where would she go? Not knowing where Tella is, the thought of her in danger—Penny is in physical pain. Laus was right not to tell her before, she grasps. There is nothing she can do to help, and this is torture. Her stomach burns and her lungs ache. "Love hurts" is right.

But the trial must go on. As the witnesses are called, Penny begins to realize why Lisa encouraged her to take a plea deal.

Alex takes the stand to talk about his uncle Frank, the trip into the woods with Penny, and her theft of the red mare. Alex looks very handsome, with his dark wavy hair and chiseled physique. The prosecutor makes sure the jury knows that he is a respected equestrian who rides for the United States in international competitions.

"You wear the flag when you ride?" the prosecutor asks.

"Proudly," says Alex.

Most of the jury members look like they want to sleep with Alex.

"Ms. Marcus invited you to ride with her in the forest?" says the prosecutor.

"Yes, she did," says Alex. "I didn't know her well. She didn't have friends at school."

"What was she like?"

"I was a little afraid of her. I didn't really want to go to the old house, but she was pushy. She insisted. She had an energy about her that frightened me."

"And how did she end up coming home with you that night?"

"She didn't tie her pony up properly and it ran home."

"Did that strike you as odd?"

"Yes. She seemed like a very good rider who wouldn't make a mistake like that."

"Did you get the sense that she was executing a plan? A plan to get your uncle into the forest so she could kill him?"

Jesus. Is Steve *ever* going to object, Penny wonders. Can she object? Lisa kicks Steve under the table.

"Objection," says Steve, looking up from his phone.

"Whose idea was it to go back to your farm?" the prosecutor asks Alex.

"She said she didn't have a flashlight," said Alex. "I couldn't leave her out there alone in the dark, so I invited her back to High Rise."

Steve's cross-examination of Alex is brief and ineffective. "Is it true you might be going to the Olympics?" he asks Alex at one point.

Penny wants to bite Steve, hard.

69

THE PONY

STILL CARRYING THE package in my teeth, and after a week or so of skirting towns and fortifying myself on lawns and golf courses, I make it back to the school for nervous girls. I got kicked out of there once already, so I stay out of sight and wait until darkness, then slide stealthily into the camp.

Tella, I whisper outside her cabin. Given our history I'm ready for an argument, but in a flash, she comes out of the cabin and hugs me. She smells like cotton pajamas and strawberry shampoo. It feels so good to have her face buried in my neck, her arms tight around me, as if Penny has returned to me in child form. When Tella finally releases me, I drop the package in front of her and tell her that her mom is in danger.

"I can't understand you," she says, starting to cry, but at the same time I can feel the anger rise in her. She zaps and zings. Her energy is so powerful that I take a step back. Then I see her take control, breathe. She's changed since I saw her last. Like a young pony, she's learning how to control her feelings. "I know something is going on. I can tell everyone is lying to me. Mom hasn't called me in weeks and weeks. Dad says she's at a Buddhist retreat, but I know he's not telling me the truth. I'm afraid something has happened to her. Why isn't she calling me? Then I got a postcard from her today. An effing postcard! She said she's really enjoying the retreat and she's so sorry she hasn't called. Sorry? It's all bullshit." She kicks a tree, and then apologizes to it. "What is this thing?" Tella asks, picking up the package.

The brown paper wrapping got a bit torn up in my trip here, and Tella squints at the label, smoothing it with her fingers. "Abra Smythe. Ithaca, New York." She frowns. "Mom grew up in Ithaca. Are you telling me she went back there?"

I do my best version of a shrug.

Tella opens the package and takes out a pair of riding boots and some wires. She reads the note inside. "'Afraid for my life' . . . "

"Holy crap," she says. "I need to steal a phone." Then, a beat later. "I think my mom is in danger!"

I nod vigorously. I'm hoping Tella will talk to the other adults, get them to help her.

"I have to go," says Tella.

Okay, I think. We could go solo on this. I position myself next to her so she can get on my back. I can picture us galloping off to the rescue, our hair streaming behind us, a modern day Alexander the Great and Bucephalus. A girl and a pony save the day. A pony and a girl. I deserve top billing.

"No offense," she says. "But I think it might be faster to steal a car."

I AM STANDING in the road when Tella climbs into a small green car holding a set of keys she stole from the school office. She is a lot more bold than Penny was at her age, which scares me a little. I try to get in the car with her, but she pushes me away.

"Sorry, pony," she says. "I think that a thirteen-year-old driving a car with a pony in the back seat might attract attention, and I gotta get to the bottom of this." I neigh in alarm as she backs up without looking. "It's okay," she says through the window as I jump out of the way of the shimmying car. "I've seen all the *Fast & Furious* movies." She comes really close to removing the door handles of another car as she exits the parking lot in fits and starts.

With a screech of tires, the car rockets off down the road in a terrifying zigzag, and I am once more impressed with this very ponylike teenage girl. But also frustrated and worried.

I start galloping down the road after her. It's a long way to Ithaca from here, and I am an old, old pony, but I have to follow her.

I am partway down the road and already slowing to a trot when a familiar old truck appears alongside me. It's Mr. Alcinous, the owner of the pony rides/petting zoo. He seems just as surprised to see me as I am to see him. He rolls down his window.

"You broke my fence, you little bastard!" he says. "All the damn ponies got loose that day. I've caught all of them but you. Where have you been all this time?"

You have no idea, I think.

I dart left, then right, then left, but so does he.

And a lasso lands around my neck.

70

PENNY

MELANIE KINSWORTH TAKES the stand on day three. With her chignon, cashmere sweater, and pearl studs, she's polished and cool and she gives off a clear air of authority and old money.

"It's very frustrating for little girls when they don't have ponies that measure up," she says as the jury listens, rapt. "I have seen them cry when they lose at horse shows, but I've also seen them lash out. Little girls can be very, very devious. I mean, they're really capable of anything."

You should know, thinks Penny, remembering Melanie's exchange with Silla at the horse show that long-ago day.

Day three ends early because of mysterious reasons that Lisa says have to do with the judge's dental work schedule. They will resume the next day. As with every day of the trial, when Penny leaves the courtroom, the pretense that she is a free citizen dissolves. She changes back into the green uniform and is handcuffed and returned to her jail cell. She becomes, once again, a number.

71

THE PONY

M R. ALCINOUS HAS no intention of keeping me. He just wants a return on his investment, which you'll recall was zero, given that he adopted me after the hurricane. He delivers me to a livestock auction yard. This is not a place you ever want to be. There are large pens of cattle, horses, burros, sheep, and goats. Some of the animals are healthy—the steers look pretty good, fat and shiny. I don't tell them that the Hungry Cannibal awaits them.

The horses, on the other hand, are not looking their best. This is the place that is the last stop before the trucks to Canada and Mexico like the one I ended up on, and many of the horses are just as old, sad, confused, and brokenhearted as the ones I met there. Many are old draft horses who have spent their lives pulling a plow. They tower over me as I sink into the morass of mud and manure and piss up almost to my belly. What's even more humiliating is that I have a number on my rump. 13.

"That doesn't bode well," says a very thin old horse standing in the corner. She's bigger than I am but smaller than the Belgians and Clydesdales. There's something familiar about her. I wade through the muck over to where she's standing, one foreleg stretched out in front of her in the telltale sign of lameness. The stench here is unbelievable. It chokes you. I can see all of her ribs through her thin, coarse chestnut coat. There's no gloss or shine to her, no copper highlights. Does she have white socks? It's hard to tell under all the mud.

"I used to be beautiful," she says. "You'll have to take my word for it."

"I know you," I say. "Arete."

She turns her head to me. Her face is flecked with gray, which has fuzzed the edges of her broad once-white, now grimy blaze. Her eyes are sunken in deep hollows.

"I won horse shows. I used to be a contender," she says.

"Penny saved you from Frank."

She snorts. "I saved *her*. They sent me to Florida. I was a show jumper, a polo pony, then a lesson horse, then . . . you know."

"I do."

"People said they loved me. But girls sold me when they went off to college. Trainers sold me when I bucked in lessons. I tried to be a good girl. Sometimes. You know how it is." She rubs her bony head on the chewed-up fence.

"You're a redheaded mare," I said. "They knew what they were getting."

"Spoken by a true pony," she says.

"What happened that night?" I ask. "What happened in the forest, after you took Penny away from High Rise?"

"I saved her life," Arete said.

"Yes, Frank slashed her across the face with the whip and you went to her and let her get on and jumped out of the arena and carried her safely away into the forest."

Arete blinks. "Yes, but then I really saved her life."

72

PENNY

PENNY SITS BOLT upright in her bunk. She has been dreaming. But was it a dream? She was back there in the forest. It was so clear, like she really was there.

Arete is under her, galloping. Penny is trying to hold on, but her feet can't reach the stirrups. The saddle is slipping. She can hear Frank's machine behind her. She has never been this scared in her life. She's holding the mare's mane as tight as she can, hunched over her like a jockey, gripping with her knees. But she's getting tired.

She can't see in the dark the way the horse can, and when Arete rises and jumps over a log, Penny is thrown off. She lands hard and rolls, and for a second, everything goes black.

She comes to with Frank standing over her. "You little bitch," he says. He's holding a big branch, and Penny can see what he's about to do. He's going to hit her as hard as he can. It's going to look like she hit the branch when she fell off. It's going to look like the branch killed her.

But Penny sees something else. In the ATV's headlights, she sees the horse. The horse is thrashing, trying to break the reins he's tied her with. There's a rock on the ground she's dancing around, tripping over. And as Frank begins to swing the branch, the horse takes a hind leg and kicks the rock as hard she can, with the aim that only a redheaded mare has.

73

THE PONY

"YOU KILLED FRANK," I say.

"I know we're not supposed to hurt the humans, but why are they allowed to hurt us?" asks Arete. Her cloudy eyes are bright now, her nostrils flared in anger. "And each other? Why is that okay? Why do they, of all the species, get to set the rules?"

"Welcome to the Homer County Auction Grounds," says a loudspeaker over our heads. "Whether you're here to ride it, shear it, or eat it, it's a great day to buy livestock!"

We are herded toward the arena.

74

PENNY

NEED TO TALK to you," Penny says to Lisa as soon as she sits down at the table in the courtroom the next morning.

Steve is on his phone, as usual, working out a plea deal for another client. "We won't take a day more than ten years," Steve says. "My client wants to be out and find herself a new husband before she gets wrinkles."

The trial is about to begin. It's day four. Friday. Lisa thinks they will wrap up today because no one wants this to drag out into next week, into the holiday season. The jurors will want to get back to their lives, their families.

It's not going well for Penny.

"Are you ready to make a deal?" Lisa whispers. "We can do that all the way up until the verdict, but then it will be too late."

"The horse killed Frank," Penny says. "I remembered last night."

Lisa's face is blank. "The horse?" she finally says.

"Yes. It was the horse. I remember it clearly now. I was protecting her. I knew they would put her down if they knew. Horses that kill people—they get shot. I knew that, so I didn't tell anyone what I saw. I knew they would put her down. And she saved me. She saved my life."

Lisa blinks like she can't believe what she's hearing. And not in a good way, in the way that means she thinks Penny is crazy. Gaga.

Nutso. Off her rocker. Round the bend. "I read the coroner's report," Lisa says. "They would have seen if he was kicked by a horse. There was a rock next to his body with his blood on it, and a matching mark on his skull."

"The horse kicked the rock. Like a soccer ball, but backward. With a hind leg. I saw her do it. He was about to hit me with the branch. She saved my life."

"Court will come to order," announces the bailiff. "Silence, please!"

I don't think the jury will buy that, writes Lisa on the legal pad in front of them. *Sorry.*

Penny draws a picture as best she can. Lisa stares at it, then passes it to Steve. Steve stares at it for a beat.

"May I approach the bench, Your Honor?" says Steve.

75

THE PONY

ALL OF US are herded into a chute made of battered metal corral panels. As we pass through the chute one at a time, a human in blue jeans and an orange vest runs a scanner over our necks. Beep. Beep.

"What's that?" I ask Arete, who is right in front of me.

"They're checking for microchips. It's a new requirement, instituted because people have been stealing horses to make money selling them at auction."

"People are vile," I say.

"No argument from me," she says.

I vaguely recall someone sticking a needle in my neck at one point. "What if you have a chip?" I ask.

"The name on the chip has to match the name of the owner who put you up for auction," she says. "Otherwise they contact the person on the chip to find out if you were stolen."

Did Mr. Alcinous register me? I have no idea.

Beep. Arete is scanned and sent forward.

The guy in the orange vest has to lean way down to reach my neck. "Frickin' ponies," he says, almost losing his balance.

Boop, says the scanner.

76

PENNY

THE COURT HAS granted a ten-minute recess.

Steve and Lisa and Penny are huddled together at the table.

"How am I supposed to prove this?" Steve whispers. Penny can see that the prosecution team is staring at them, wondering what this is all about. The jury is not in the room; they have adjourned to the hallway vending machines. No one wants this to drag out. Except Penny.

"I don't know," she says. "But it's the truth. You can put me on the stand—"

"Never a good idea," Steve says, cutting her off.

"I have an idea," says Lisa.

77

THE PONY

CAN'T BELIEVE it. Caya the hound dog and Circe the goat are staring at me. And so are eight puppies.

"You're back!" says Caya with joy, thumping her tail but not getting up to greet me. The puppies swarm around my legs, tickling them with little teeth and tongues and tails.

Moments before, I was unloaded from a truck and deposited back in the backyard from whence I fled all those many moons ago, in the company of the rat.

"You're back," says the goat, with notably less enthusiasm than the puppies.

"Microchipped," I say. "This is the address I'm registered to, so the auction house had to send me back here."

"That's the surveillance state for you," says Circe.

"You've been gone a long time. What happened?" Caya asks. Really, that's all us storytellers want. That one question. And boy do I have an answer.

Slowly, embellishing only a little, I tell them the whole story of my quest to find Penny: my life with Burnie the racehorse and his rat life coach, pony racing with Robbie, horse shows with Helen and Ines, being stolen, the slaughter truck, being wild on the island ... all the way to Mr. Alcinous, the boarding school for nervous girls, New York City.

"But here's the most important thing: I found Penny! She was in the forest of the blue butterflies, right where I left her. She wasn't mad—she hugged me and kissed me and cried."

"That's amazing!" says Caya.

"Gross," says Circe.

"She retired me to the stable I grew up in. It was heaven, at least for one night. Then I witnessed a murder."

"Oh no!" says Caya. "Is Penny okay?"

"I hope so. I have to save her." I've said that so many times, but this time it's really true. "The woman who murdered Silla is coming for Penny."

Caya lifts up her head and howls. I was going to say "mournfully," but is there any other kind of hound dog howl?

"And her daughter is trying to find her, too. She thinks Penny is in Ithaca. That's near Saratoga, the racetrack I went to with the rat."

"I seem to recall that's a very long way from here?" asks Circe.

"Yes," I say. "But I'm actually an expert traveler now. Lotta frequent trotter miles. I think I can get there. I just hope I'm in time."

Caya is more excited than I have seen her since I arrived in this godforsaken backyard. She says, "Think of how big the world is, and how unlikely it was that you and Penny would see each other again, but you did. Twice! That shows there's a magical connection between you."

And this time, I agree with her.

Caya is the happiest I have ever seen her. Her usually dull coat glows with pride. The fat little pups splayed out around her are of all different colors, some spotted, some white and brown, some black and brown and white, and some brindled.

"Caya, either you had a visitor a few months back or you went out," I say. "Fess up."

Caya sits up and talks to me as she licks her puppies, which warps her words a little. "It was while you were away. I—lick—got out—lick—when the old man left the door to the garage open."

Caya says she intended to get as far as she could, as fast as she could.

"I was outta here," she says. She was halfway down the alley behind our yard when she met a charming canine named Nick.

"Pathetic," says Circe.

"Nick was sweet. Really good at humping. And aren't these little darlings adorable?" sighs Caya, licking her puppies.

"You're going to rub the fur right off them," I worry.

"Silly," she says, and keeps licking.

I give the breeze a sniff. "It's been great to see you two again, but I'm leaving tonight," I say.

"To go find Penny?" Caya thumps her tail.

"Gotta protect her from Melanie," I say.

"Well, then we should all go," says Circe sarcastically. "Who would notice a pony, a dog, eight puppies, and a goat traveling thousands of miles on a Greyhound bus? Maybe we could get a big overcoat and stand on each other and hide under it." She sniffs superciliously and curls up on top of the doghouse. "And good luck getting out of here, Masked Avenger," she adds. "The old man wised up after you escaped last time. The gate is latched with a metal chain that's padlocked."

"If only you were a bird," says Caya. "Can you turn him into a bird?" she asks Circe. "I've heard goats can do that." Caya is so sweet and dumb. As much as dogs frustrate me, I can see why humans keep them in their houses. Except the ones they toss into the backyard and ignore, of course, like Caya. It's so mysterious—to my eye, she's not any less worthy of love and attention than any other dog, yet here she lies in a barren backyard, instead of on a sofa where she belongs.

Circe says, "You're not getting out of this place. Just accept it. The only way any of us is getting out of here is slathered with barbecue sauce, on a bun."

I try the gate. Circe is right. It's impregnable.

The raven on the telephone pole above us laughs and laughs at me, then flies away.

I slump down in despair. "I have to get out of here," I say.

Circe says, "Admit it. Sometimes you wish you had never met Penny, right? Right? Right? I mean, all these unnecessary *feelings* . . ."

Circe is trying to break me, dominate me, her favorite game. Pecking order is everything to her, and according to the laws of hoofed mammals, pony outranks goat every time. But she is cunning and persistent, a pony of a goat. If anyone could break the laws of nature, she could.

I rouse myself from staring at the gate trying to make it open and turn to face her where she stands on the doghouse, which gives her a view of the neighborhood beyond the fence. That view, tracking the comings and goings, keeps her alert, I think, while Caya and I can see nothing but the monotony of bare dirt and lawn implements. I toss my head and pin my ears. "*A friend is one to whom one may pour out the contents of one's heart, chaff and grain together, knowing that gentle hands will take and sift it, keep what is worth keeping, and with a breath of kindness blow the rest away.*' With a breath of kindness, Penny would blow all this away," I say. "And that's a question so dumb only a goat with a tin can for a brain would ask it."

Her slitted pupils glare at me, her thin lips tight. "I see a silver Buick in the alley," she says. "I see an orange cat. I see another cat. I hope they fight."

I have to get out of here tonight. If I don't, if I can never get back to Penny, I can imagine myself withdrawing, becoming like Buttercup. Once I really go away like she did, I know I will never come back. I'll forget Penny. Forget everything. Forget my whole story.

Finally, it's dark enough, and the neighborhood is asleep. I think about everything I've learned about doors in my travels.

"Goodbye," I say to Caya and Circe. I use my teeth to twist open the door to the garage and then I hit the button for the automatic garage door opener. It creaks and groans upward, revealing the alley and the world beyond bathed in moonlight.

The man's bedroom light clicks on.

"Hurry!" says Caya.

"Remember, you're microchipped," Circe says. "They're always going to bring you back here. You'll be picked up by Animal Control, scanned and sent back here again and again in a Sisyphean circle."

I stare at the alley. My body hums with electricity. I sniff the air. Navigating such a long way will be dangerous. If I stay here I will be fed every day. If I leave, it's very likely I will be hit by a car, or starve to death, or be killed by another animal. I stop in the doorway, take a deep breath. Not caring what the sarcastic goat will think, I say, "I'm trusting the magic of love to guide me," and then I walk through the door.

"Goodbye!" calls Caya. I can hear the happy squeaks of sleeping puppies. I take a few steps out and breathe in the night air. Only three thousand miles to go. But first I have to get out of this city.

"Wait up," says a voice behind me.

I turn to look at Circe as she trots through the open garage door. "You?" I ask.

"Someone has to be the brains of the op this time."

And with that, Circe and I step out into the wide world.

PART TWELVE

Nostos, Which Sounds Like
a Crunchy Road Trip Snack

78

PENNY

"YOU WANT TO do what?" says the judge. He looks like he is very late for his first martini of the night and has plans to jet off to Florida for the weekend for some golf once this annoying trial is behind him. "Absolutely not."

"It's been done before," says Steve, using the words Lisa gave him. "There are precedents."

Penny holds her breath. She sees that Lisa is holding hers, too.

The judge looks extremely dubious, then turns to the prosecution. "What is your view of this idea?"

The prosecutor (who really does look like Steve's doppelganger) thinks for a moment. Penny can tell he and Steve are archrivals, like identical fighting roosters. Lisa has muttered about "the dark side over there," but clearly the prosecutor thinks that he is saving society from murderous Penny. *God help us when everyone thinks it's an existential battle and they have the moral high ground*, Penny thinks.

Finally the prosecutor looks at Steve and says, "I think your stunt is just going to show the jury even more clearly that your client killed Frank Ross in cold blood. It's going to totally blow apart your whole self-defense claim. I think it's the stupidest thing I've ever heard. So I'm all for it."

79

THE PONY

SAY WHAT YOU will about goats, and I will not censor you, but I must admit they are masters of deception and disguise. Circe leads me down the sidewalk and into some bushes at the end of the road. "Stay low," she says. "Lower."

"Any lower and I'll turn into a lizard," I say.

We head for the fairgrounds where I met Burnie. I'm really hoping for a ride to Saratoga. That would be ideal. I'm relieved to hear a voice from the telephone wire above my head. "Well, I'll be!"

I look up and see the rat there. "Dr. Rat!" I say. "Just the person I was looking for. How are you?"

"Great. Burnie's been winning all over," he says. "In fact we won a stakes race here today. And Mike and Joel got married. Joel's divorce was ugly, but Nancy hooked up with Larry, so it all shook out in the end. How's the quest going?"

"More urgent than ever," I say, "but you were right about so many things I didn't understand at the time. Thank you."

"That's what friends are for," he says.

"Can you get me and my friend here to Saratoga? I'll pay you a lot of grain. Bags of it. That nice flaked corn that crunches in your teeth."

He shakes his head. "Mmm. I love a good crunch, but we're spending the summer in California. Our anniversary is coming. Don't tell Burnie, but I got us matching ear warmers for chilly nights."

Circe snorts and I shoot her a look. "Love that," I say.

We'll have to go on foot, I realize. Three thousand miles. At a run.

"You still owe me six oats from our last bet!" calls Circe to the rat as I urge her onward.

Circe and I move through a housing development, munching on lawns and shrubs as we go to keep our strength up, but never stopping. We keep moving toward the ridge of hills in the distance. As dawn begins to lighten the sky we are almost to the safety of the hills when some kids on bikes see us and whoop and yell. "Hit it," says Circe, and we run as fast as we can across an intersection. Brakes squeal and the kids chase us up a road that runs between two rows of houses. "Faster!" I call to Circe as she falls behind.

The kids are closing in on her. I turn and dart across a yard and behind a house, hoping she will follow. She does, and we scramble up some rocks where the hillside climbs sharply. She's better at this than I am, and I stumble a few times and nick my fetlocks. At least the bikes are useless here, and the kids stop in frustration. I'm panting and sweating but I keep going. We keep climbing up the dry hill until the houses peter out and we are over the top.

"Where are we?" I ask as I look out over a huge valley below us. I see row after row of houses, and another mountain range far in the hazy distance. "Are we there yet?"

Circe looks at the grid of streets filled with cars, the buildings poking up to the sky. Airplanes glide past through the smog and helicopters hover. Barely any trees or grass.

"That is still Los Angeles," says Circe. "We've hardly begun."

WE TRY TO skirt the sprawling city and head toward the rising sun, which my pony sense tells me is the way to Ithaca. But passing through giant metropolitan areas without being seen is not easy. We hide out in some dense bushes on the edge of a park and wait until night falls again to go through a viaduct underneath a highway, but we still have to dodge cars that honk and swerve. We keep going, climbing and descending and climbing again, eating whatever grass and scrub we can find, drinking from bird baths and swimming pools.

On the second day we have made it out of the city; and we stop on a mountain trail to grab a bite to eat. Circe likes the crunchy leaves and so do I. What is it about being on the road that makes you want to crunch something?

"I can't reach that branch," says Circe. "Hold still." She jumps up onto my back. Her hooves tickle, but I stand still.

"Are you going to share?" I ask.

"Sorry," she says. "I ate it all."

At that moment two hikers come around a bend into view, probably a father and son. They stop at the sight of a pony with a goat on its back.

"What the—" says the kid.

"Stay back," says the father. As if we're dangerous—we're cute enough to be on a birthday card.

"They look nice, and they might have food," I say.

"Nononono," shouts Circe, jumping off my back. "Not nice. Stay away. Run!"

I pause and the man and boy stare at me, and then I turn and bolt down the hillside away from them. I finally catch up to Circe.

"Never ever go near a human again if you want to stay alive," says Circe.

"You won't say that when you meet Penny," I say. "She's different."

"We'll see," says Circe.

DAYS LATER WE are on another mountain trail. It's beautiful. There's a wide variety of plants, yellow monkeyflower and purple fiesta flower and orange poppies. I say hi to the lizards and the ladybugs. We keep moving all day, stopping to grab mouthfuls of grass as we go.

We run into lots of deer who stare at us in fear and surprise.

"It's okay," I say. "We're just moving through." We climb up to cattle country and ask some condors for directions. I don't like the way the condors look at us with those dark little eyes in their naked orange faces surrounded by manes of fluffy black feathers, like maybe they might be interested in sending us the wrong way and then eating our dead bodies.

EVENTUALLY WE MAKE it across the mountains and hit the next valley. It's broad and I can smell farms. But in the distance is yet another mountain range, this one capped with snow, even though it's summer.

"I didn't sign up for snow," says Circe.

Before we even get to the snowy mountains, we have to cross a vast expanse of roads, dry riverbeds, and desert.

"I'm thirsty already," Circe says.

"We're traveling an old Pony Express route," I tell Circe, sniffing the ground. "Like pioneers in reverse. I can smell the history."

"Except instead of a new pony every fifteen miles I'm stuck with the same one for the whole three-thousand-mile trip."

We travel through huge cattle ranches without seeing a sign of human habitation outside of an occasional fence that I am able to lie down and slide under or find a way through or over. In one case Circe has to chew through the wire for me, a job I am amazed that she is quite able to perform. My fur is drenched in a full-body sweat all day, hardening into stiff white salty swirls at night. There is no water to be found.

"I don't know if I can go any farther," I say one day. It feels like my mouth is full of sand.

"You can," says Circe, panting. "You have to."

We follow the tracks of small mammals to a dry riverbed where Circe orders me to paw. I do, and eventually I hit a damper layer of dirt. Circe encourages me, and I keep digging. Eventually I hit a brackish puddle of water. Her Goatness and I drink big gulps of it. I feel drunk afterward, and stagger. Circe manages to caper a little bit. A shadow falls over us and I see a turkey vulture overhead. "Not yet!" I call to him.

We lie down when we need to rest, but not both at once. One of us always keeps watch.

FORTUNATELY WINTER IS still a ways off and we make it up and over the tall mountains. We're now crossing a high desert studded with sagebrush and chemise. The ground is flat and sandy. Despite the fact that there is no moon, it's not difficult going, and Circe and I are in a good mood. The air is cool and our bellies are full of water and grass we found earlier on the outskirts of a golf course. Overhead I feel sheltered by the big arc of what the humans call the Milky Way. I think of it as a racetrack for stars.

"What's your favorite thing about being alive?" I ask Circe as we walk along, our hooves making no sound in the sand.

"Not thinking it all adds up to anything," she says.

"Ha! That's funny, because my favorite thing is that it does feel like it all adds up to something," I say.

Circe stops to drop her head for a moment to grab a bite of sagebrush.

At that moment, a shooting star explodes over us, then another, then another. "Wow!" I say. It's a sign. I know it.

Circe lifts her head and looks around. "What?"

The sky is once again still.

"Nothing," I say, and we walk on.

WE CLIMB, WE descend, and we traverse, for months. We always head for the direction the sun rises from and angle toward the north star at night. We stay far from people. We pass through forests and over plains and past huge lakes. We go past cornfields and wheat fields and soybean fields that seem to last for days. We avoid distant cities, easy to spot from far away by the light that pollutes the night sky.

"Did you know that for millions of years there was a tiny horse species named Nannippus who roamed this continent?" Circe says. "I ate a book about it once. Nannippus had three toes."

"That would come in handy for vending machines at truck stops," I say.

Like our ancient herd ancestors, Nannippus and his ilk, we always keep moving, even though we are very tired.

The landscape rises under our hooves, carrying us into massive rolling forests of oaks, beeches, and pines. It's wetter and colder here. We pass deer and songbirds as we go. Word of our coming precedes us, thanks to the birds, and soon huge flocks of chickadees and grackles and cardinals and robins gather in the treetops to cheer us on.

"Honk if you love ponies," I call to some migrating Canada geese, and their serenade sounds like a New York traffic jam.

One morning we are walking along through a wet woodland, crossing creeks and nibbling on dried grass. The air is cold and crisp. A light snow begins to fall.

"Did I mention I don't do snow?" Circe says.

I sniff and then stop in my tracks.

"Hang on. I can smell something. Come on!" I run through some boulders and into some trees. The snow is beginning to stick and I'm sliding a little as I canter across the cool blanket of white.

"Slow down. I have to pee," complains Circe, trotting after me.

Though I'm old and tired and we've been traveling for what feels like forever, the snow fills me with energy. "We're almost there," I call to Circe, breaking from a canter into a gallop.

"Slow down!"

I slow to a measured trot so I don't leave her behind, but lift my knees and my tail in excitement and flare my perfect nostrils.

We follow a road through the whitening hills, leaping into the bushes when the occasional car comes by, its tires sighing in the deepening snow.

"We could just stay here," Circe says, munching on some grass sticking up through the snow.

"We're so close," I say.

The light is fading as we climb up a hill. The elevation is higher and the air thinner. I sniff deeply. Woodsmoke. Pine. Oaks. And Penny. "I can smell her," I say, making a right turn at an intersection and trotting down a rutted road.

"You brought me thousands of miles to this godforsaken place?" Circe bleats. "You know what I can smell? Humans. A lot of them. I don't like this."

I can also smell disinfectant, and sadness, but I don't tell Circe that.

"I think maybe Penny lives nearby. Down the road from here."

Circe sighs with fatigue. I can see that all of her ribs are showing, and her hip bones are sticking up under her fur. I know mine are, too. "Is it safe?" she asks plaintively. She can smell it, too, I realize. Penny is in a bad place.

"We're almost there," I tell her.

We're a few hundred yards farther down the road toward a huge red castle in the distance when I see a shadow move out of the corner of my eye. I snort in alarm as I realize that a pack of coyotes has silently come out of the forest and encircled us. I count seven of them. Their pointy black noses and ears and teeth are all I see at first, and then their gray and brown bodies materialize, skinny legs half hidden in the fallen leaves. Black-tipped bushy tails hang low. Their caramel eyes, rimmed with black mascara, glimmer even in the dusk, and their white chins drip with saliva, sandy-colored cheeks pulled back to reveal white teeth.

"I don't know what you're having, but I know what *we're* eating tonight," snarls the leader.

Everyone on the whole planet likes a good meal, which never fails to keep things interesting. We are the crunchy snacks on this coyote family's road trip.

Circe lowers her horns, ready to butt, and I turn my back, ready to kick.

We don't stand a chance. There are too many of them.

"I'm sorry," I say to Circe. "You came all this way to help me. We should have stayed where we were. You were right."

"No," she says. "That was a slow death. This one will be fast and likely very bloody. But this trip has been . . . magic."

As the snow falls harder, the first coyote darts in, and I hear a crack and a yelp as Circe connects with him. But then another comes at me, and I kick, kick, and another comes at her, and then they are on us, snapping, snarling, that unholy screaming they do. *Yip yip yip*, they laugh—it freezes my blood.

I feel something nip at my neck, and I fear I'm going down, but then there's a different, louder bark, a baying, a loud baying and a wild snarling and a massive form appears out of the swirling snow.

"Caya!" shouts Circe, fighting off a coyote with her horns.

Caya grabs a coyote in her huge jaws and flings it. The others leave us and go at her. I've hardly ever seen Caya move at all, but now she is a wild churning thing, tan and black, white fangs snapping, breaking bones. The wind screams, cheering her on.

The coyotes outnumber her but they are not brave, and as two of them run away, the others join them, howling and yipping in anger and shame, outraged at their lost meal.

When they are well and gone into the dense woods, Caya comes to us. Circe and I are shivering, in shock. She has blood streaming down her neck. I can feel pain in my hind leg. The snow is scarlet and trampled around us. One of Caya's lovely long velvet ears is torn, but she ignores that and licks our wounds.

"Normally that would make me very nervous," I say. "But what about . . . your puppies?"

Caya shakes her head sadly. "The man took them away. I don't—I can't talk about it."

Circe is quiet. I don't like that. I nudge her, but she is silent, standing still as if frozen. I lick at some blood on her jaw and she lets me do it.

I'm very cold and wet. We're all shivering.

"How did you find us?" I ask Caya.

"I'm part bloodhound, aren't I?" she says. "I tracked you. We've got to get out of here. The coyotes will be back. Which way is Penny?"

The wind masks the sound of the vehicle, and the three of us are standing in the road when the Animal Control truck comes around the bend.

80

PENNY

THE WEEKEND DRAGS by. Dawn has been transferred to state prison. Without Lisa, Penny is cut off from all news of her family. She sits in her cell staring at the cinder-block walls with no updates about Tella. Presumably Laus and the police are looking for her, but where has she gone? Penny doesn't know of any friends or family Tella might seek out.

She's a loner like me, Penny thinks. *Why did I let that happen?*

Penny wants to batter the walls of her cell with her fists, scream in the night as others do. But what good will that do?

Tella is intelligent and resourceful, it's true, but she's just a child, and painfully sensitive one. Penny thinks about a camping trip when Tella, age ten, insisted on carrying her own pack up a ten-thousand-foot-high mountain, but then collapsed in tears when she realized she had forgotten her plastic goat. Also—what kid has a toy *goat*? Not a cuddly teddy or a bunny or a pony. A realistic, molded plastic nanny goat. With actual tiny horns, mind you. Sharp ones. "Where's Goatie?" she had screamed so loud it echoed off the mountainsides. "I want Goatie!"

Penny looks out the window at the upturned arms of frozen apple trees in the distance and focuses all of her energy on Tella. *Be safe*, she tells her. *Call Daddy. Go home*. She pictures Laus opening the door of their home in California to Tella, enfolding her in his arms.

I can't live if something has happened to her, Penny thinks. *I can't do it.*

She berates herself. *I should never have sent her away. I shouldn't have left her there. I should have weaned her sooner, or later. I should have raised her in a city, or on a farm. I should have been a different kind of mother, or sent her to a different school, or camp, encouraged her to play sports, or draw, or fed her a different diet. More leafy greens? Or fewer leafy greens, because of oxalates? Did she eat enough fish (omega-3s)? Or too much (mercury)? I should have eliminated all screens. Or not restricted them, but taught her how to use them better. I should have had no plastics in the house, or no cleaning products, or a cleaner house? I should, shouldn't, should, shouldn't . . .*

81

THE PONY

BEHIND BARS, AGAIN. Animal Control. I smell orchards from my cell. Frozen apple trees. Because I tried to bite and kick the Animal Control officer who was lassoing me, I was labeled as "dangerous" and put in high-security lockdown in this dog kennel. Me!

The facility is chock-full of unwanted and lost pets, and we are in the annex, outdoors in a row of cages under an overhang—it's windy and cold, and the wide world is tauntingly close but unreachable.

On one side of me is a Labrador named Rusty who growled at a kid who stepped on his tail. On the other side is a desert tortoise under a heat lamp. He was in the process of retracting his head into his shell to avoid a child who was bothering him, but the finger of the kid got caught between the shell and his head and the kid yowled. Guess who got blamed? Have you ever heard of a killer tortoise? Me neither. That would be some horror movie.

"Owner coming for you?" asks the tortoise, munching ever so slowly on a leaf of romaine.

They did scan Caya and me for chips and called the old man, but he said they could do with us what they would. No "return to sender" for me this time.

"No," I say.

"Not from around here?"

"Nope."

"Me neither. Why'd you come here?" asks the tortoise.

"To prove to a goat that love is real," I say.

The tortoise rolls his tiny eyes and retracts his head into his shell.

CAYA IS TWO cells away from me. She is depressed and just sleeps all the time. I can't blame her. I try not to think about poor Circe.

There's another thing I'm trying not to think about. Caya has been taken to two consecutive Saturday adoption days at the pet store in town. Each time I heaved a huge sigh of relief when she returned at the end of the day, but that's a problem. If Caya is unadoptable, she will be put to sleep. Killed in cold blood. The clock is ticking.

"She's so sweet," says the volunteer who feeds us and cleans our cages. She's talking about Caya to another volunteer who sweeps the aisles and walks the dogs.

"Caya," I shout to her. "Wag your tail! Lick her hand. Look adorable. Maybe she'll take you home herself and foster you."

"I don't care anymore," says Caya, refusing to even lift her head.

I have tried to break out of the cell I'm in, but it's securely latched, damn them. A couple of prospective adopters have come to see me. Families with little kids. Apparently there's a cute picture of me on the Animal Control website and it is almost Christmas, aka Wishing for a Pony Season. But when the parents hear that I bite, they head to the kitten aisle.

"It's so sad," says the nice volunteer, whose name is Anna. "I can't believe they're going to put this cute old pony down. Some horse person must want him."

Put me down?

I am vastly cheered when I hear a bleat and Circe is led past my cell.

"You're alive!" I shout. She has a lot of stitches, but her yellow eyes are bright and reassuringly mean.

"Look, the pony knows her," says the volunteer. "They were found together. Let's put them in the same cage."

They open the door and Circe strolls in.

"Love what you've done with the place," she says, looking around at the bare floor and water dish.

"The pony's on Petfinder but no one's claimed him," says the other volunteer. "And it's a shame about the goat since they worked so hard to save her life. But I'm afraid we're out of options and we need the cage space."

"I'm on a lot of painkillers," Circe says, butting me gently. "Do I know you?"

I lick her ears.

"They're so cute together," says the volunteer sadly. "It's really a shame. Well, at least we'll give them a good last day." She puts a little extra hay in our cage.

"Caya," calls Circe, spotting the dog in the cage just past the tortoise. But Caya barely lifts her head. Circe says, "Thank you for saving my life!"

"Goodbye," howls Caya. "They're putting me down today."

"Us too," I say.

IT STARTS TO rain sleet outside our row of cages. I'd like to think the world is crying because we're going to die today, but I know the world is not that concerned with one pony, dog, and goat. Meaning doesn't come down from the sky, or in the form of a blue ribbon or a trophy; it comes from within us, in our bonds with each other. I know that now.

It's dark outside. Caya and Circe and I are quiet, listening to the pelting ice on the tin roof of the kennels. I think about what Caya said about magic. Is there any magic left in the world?

And that's when the fire alarm goes off.

82

PENNY

THE CHARTERED BUS gives a loud screech as the doors open
and the jurors begin to file out holding little bags of chips. The
judge gets out of a black car nearby and looks angrily at the sky and
then at Steve. It's December twenty-third and despite the novelty of a
road trip, it's obvious that none of them wants to be walking into a forest under glowering skies that are about to open up and dump snow, or
worse—sleet—on them.

Penny is standing next to a white van that says CORRECTIONS on
it. Steve and Lisa argued that Penny is not a flight risk and that having
her cuffed to a guard is prejudicial, but the judge was unmoved, so
Penny is wearing her green jail uniform and her right hand is cuffed to
a guard.

"The crime scene is all taped off," says a uniformed police officer
to the judge. "It's a bit of a hike down this trail."

The judge rolls his eyes. "This better be good, Counselor," he says
to Steve.

83

THE PONY

THE TWO VOLUNTEERS on duty are running around in a panic. "We can't leave them to die!" says Anna, the one with the kind voice. "All this hay . . . and the sawdust!"

She's right, I think. This place is a tinderbox. The fire alarm is blaring. I neigh in distress. "Let us out!" All the dogs are barking.

I am aware of the irony that they were about to euthanize us, but happy that they don't want us to burn to death.

The two volunteers quickly open all the cages. Most of the animals bolt into the darkness. The tortoise doesn't so much bolt as lumber. Some of the more brainwashed dogs stay close to the volunteers, who are standing in front of the facility waiting for the fire department to arrive.

"Come on," I say to Circe, and hightail it outside the circle of light before I pause, panting, for her to catch up.

What's interesting is that I don't smell smoke.

But I do smell . . . I turn and there is a small, slim figure standing in the darkness on the edge of the trees, her eyes glittering like a fox's.

Circe and Caya find me in the dark. I can smell Circe's medicinal smell, her wounds still in the process of healing. Caya's hound dog tail is up and she's sniffing audibly.

"Who is that?" asks Circe, staring at the human. "She has a strange vibe."

Tella, I say. *Did you pull the fire alarm?*

I know she can no longer understand animal speech, but the left side of her mouth turns up in a little curl. This kid . . . she is a piece of work. I can see why Penny is so tired. But there's also something amazing about Tella. Something that reminds me a lot of Penny.

How did you find me? I press her, willing her to understand me, trying to break through. *Magic?*

"Sort of," she says. "The internet."

I stare at her, amazed. *You can communicate again*, I say.

"A little," she says, squinting at me. "Or maybe I'm just guessing what I think you're saying. You're very expressive. Some might even say manipulative."

I give a little shrug. *Some of us just have a gift*, I say.

I walk up to her, and this time she gets on my back.

84

PENNY

ENNY HAS TO hand it to Lisa. She knows Steve was not on board with this idea of transporting the jurors to the crime scene, but Lisa convinced him it was their last chance to free Penny. Lisa has given it her all. There is a life-sized palomino fiberglass horse, an ATV, and the actual rock in its evidence bag. There are large maps on easels shielded with plastic wrap. There are red markers to indicate the path that the mare took as they galloped into the forest, and blown-up crime scene photos of the tracks of Frank's ATV.

There is a red duct tape outline on the ground where Frank's body was found. The jurors are just supposed to view the crime scene in silence. If they have questions, they're supposed to submit them in writing to the judge, who will answer it after a consultation with the two attorneys out of earshot of the jurors.

In reality, everyone can hear everything.

"The question, and it's a good one," whispers the judge to Steve and the prosecutor, waving a piece of paper that the jury foreman has handed to the bailiff, and the bailiff has handed to the judge, "is why the hell we're here."

"So that everyone can see clearly that it's not just perfectly possible that the horse kicked the rock at Frank Ross as my client attests, but it is the easy-to-grasp and only obvious truth. Your Honor," booms newly confident Steve.

"To create a distracting, time-wasting sideshow that only proves his client is guilty," says the prosecutor, who pulls his fur-lined parka closer around him.

"Take a look around and draw your own conclusions," says the judge to the jury.

"Are we almost done?" the judge asks the lawyers. "Because it is colder than a witch's ice chest out here."

Penny glances at the members of the jury. They look frozen, and very dubious. This was a waste of time.

The prosecutor, though, is loving it.

"Don't rush on my account," he says to the judge and Steve. "When we get back, I still have witnesses to call. Penny Marcus's phys ed instructor, who will tell us that she was the best shot putter he ever saw for her age. She could throw that heavy piece of metal harder and faster than any child he'd ever seen. Boom."

"They could hear that," says Steve. "I smell a mistrial."

"Oh hell no," says the judge. "Disregard that remark," he tells the jury. "Even if you can't disregard the fact that your nose is frozen."

Penny thinks it was nice to see the forest one last time. She will probably never see it again. It's so beautiful, the way the snow is falling on this place that she loved so much, and yet was where everything she loved was ripped away from her. The clean white snow is covering it all up, covering the paths, their tracks, each individual leaf. Each person.

In this light, you might even say it was magical.

85

THE PONY

"SLOW DOWN," SAYS Circe, trotting along behind us. "I'm busting my stitches."

Caya is panting, too, and I know she needs to rest. But we can't stop. Still, I slow my pace to a fast trot.

"We need to get into the forest before it gets light out," I say. "It's not safe, especially leaving tracks in the snow like this. We're sitting ducks."

"I am no duck," says Circe. "An eagle, maybe. But not a duck. And never a guinea fowl."

"Can we trust this child?" asks Caya, nodding at Tella.

Tella is astride me, her legs dangling, her fingers curled into my mane, her jaw set. A tangled mop of hair falls over her eyes. "I hope so," I say.

BUT TELLA DOES guide us safely back to the forest of the blue butterflies. As dawn breaks, I trot down the familiar trail. Not to High Rise, not to Silla's. Back to the old abandoned house. The snow sweeps clean the tracks behind us, nature's housekeeper.

"Home sweet home," says Tella as she steps over the broken glass in the doorway. I see she has set up a small blue tarp in a corner of the old living room. The ring of rocks has been reassembled to make a small fire pit. It's okay for animals but on a cold winter day like this it seems pretty cold and lonely for a human. I'm impressed. Tella is not the scared, anxious child she was when I first met her. She has found strength, and confidence. Fortitude.

"Hmm," says Circe. "I like the ventilation here. And the proximity of snacks." She munches on the dry sticks of a wild grapevine. "But where is the Penny person I've heard so much about?"

I can smell her. She's somewhere close!

I don't think Tella can fully understand me anymore, but she still knows who I am looking for. I nudge her and look into her eyes.

"If you want to see my mom," says Tella. "This is your last chance. But don't get us caught. They'll be here soon. I read it in a news story online."

We leave Caya and Circe to rest, and Tella leads me through the forest to a thicket of bushes.

"Wait here," she says. "And don't make a sound."

86

PENNY

I THINK WE'VE seen enough," says the judge. The jury turns to head back to the bus. Penny is shivering in her green uniform. Even she is looking forward to being back in her warm cell.

"Wait," says Lisa. "Look!"

That's when Penny's pony comes trotting out of the bushes.

He's alive! she thinks. Her heart soars. He's been hiding in the forest this whole time, of course. Smart little pony. There was a part of her that wanted to believe that the pony on the Ring camera who stole the package was her pony, but that was three thousand miles from here. It was just such a weird coincidence, though . . . But here he is. In the forest. Their forest.

The jurors stop and stare like a gaggle of wild turkeys.

"What is this?" says the judge. "Some kind of animal act? Bailiff, get that thing out of here."

But the pony dodges the bailiff and trots over to the exact place that Penny remembers Arete standing in. He wasn't there, she thinks. How does he know?

The pony pushes the fiberglass horse aside and takes its place next to the ATV.

"What's going on?" demands the judge. "Whose animal is this? Jurors, disregard this."

The jurors are very much regarding it, though. They watch as the pony walks up to the rock, encased in a plastic bag.

"Hey, that's evidence," says the prosecutor. "He can't . . ."

The pony turns his back to the rock, looks over his shoulder, and with one deft movement, kicks the rock with his hind leg straight at where Frank Ross was standing that night.

Unfortunately, that's where juror #1 is standing.

The crowd gasps, and fortunately the juror ducks. The rock goes whizzing past his head and thwacks against a tree, dislodging a large piece of bark.

"Jesus," says the juror. "I could have been killed!"

87

THE PONY

AS THE HUMANS chatter in their ridiculous way, I disappear back into the forest quickly before someone catches me. I pause to take one last look back at Penny, who gives me a big smile.

88

PENNY

"SHOULD WE CALL Animal Control or something?" asks the bailiff. It's starting to snow harder, and the jurors are already on the trail back to their bus. Penny's hair is wet and dripping but she can't wipe the snow off her face because her hands are cuffed to the guard.

"He's gone. Just let him be," says Lisa. "We've got enough people locked up already."

89

THE PONY

WIND THOUGH the forest, making sure no one is following me, then make my way to where Tella waits in the old abandoned house.

"The news says they're going to convict her," says Tella glumly, shivering under the tarp and eating a purloined energy bar. She takes the phone and throws it into the trees. "I'm never going back to their stupid world. Never. I'm going to live in the woods forever. Alone."

THE NEXT DAY is clear, blue skies and no wind. Tella has somewhere along the way acquired a camera with a very long lens. I wonder if she stole it. I don't care if she did, though I worry about her. She has a very good heart, I have discovered, though she has as dim a view of her fellow humans as I do. Except for Penny. I can see she misses her mom. We all slept in a warm ball under the tarp, Tella in the middle. Circe snored and Caya farted, but it was nice to be together.

After breakfast Tella ties us all up. "Don't follow me," she tells us. "I have to do something." She heads off, a small figure with a backpack melting into the trees.

"I'm worried," I tell Caya.

"Me too," says Caya. "She's an amazing kid, but she's a little feral."

"I like her," says Circe. "A lot."

———

A COUPLE OF hours later, Tella comes back. She pulls treats out of her backpack for us. I can see that the big camera is still in there. "I stole some grain for you guys," she says to me and Circe, "and some biscuits for you," she tells Caya.

"I'm good with squirrels, really," says Caya. "But I won't say no to a biscuit."

But before Tella can untie us, another human steps uninvited through the broken front door into our home.

Melanie!

90

PENNY

PENNY IS IN the little holding cell in the courthouse. They brought her here this morning. The staff is a bit resentful to be there, because it's Christmas Eve. They were supposed to get the day off, but the judge made everyone come in. Penny is sure he has plans to go to Florida and doesn't want the trial to ruin them.

The lawyers made their closing statements, each trying to use what happened in the forest to his advantage. The prosecutor called it stupid pony tricks that the jury should ignore. "Penny Marcus killed Frank Ross in cold blood. There is no right choice except to bring back a verdict of guilty."

Steve did his best, but Penny can tell from Lisa's face that she's not sure it was enough.

Then the jury went to their room to deliberate. They've been there for four hours. Penny was brought here, to this cell.

The guard outside the door is spending the day on her cell phone catching up with distant friends and family. Her ringtone is "I'll Be Home for Christmas."

Lisa told Penny that Laus is looking for Tella. "He said he loves you," said Lisa. "I'm pretty sure he meant it."

"He's a good man," Penny says. "He made some mistakes, but so did I."

"We all do," says Lisa. "Isn't that the point? That we can change?"

Change. The word plunges Penny back into that horrible conversation with Tella where Penny admitted she wanted Tella to change. *Why, why didn't I just tell her she was perfect as she was?*

Tella, thinks Penny. *Come home.*

91

THE PONY

"ARE YOU LOST?" Tella asks Melanie. "I'm camping here. Girl Scouts. Solo sleepout badge." Tella is sitting on the ground, her backpack between her knees. Melanie towers over her.

I'm ten feet away pulling at my lead rope. Tella has knotted it so I can't get loose. I neigh. Caya, also tied nearby but not close enough, barks. She can't get loose either.

Circe appears to be asleep under the tarp.

"I saw you spying on my son Alex," says Melanie. "Taking pictures. Why?"

I don't like the way she's looming over Tella. I strain at my lead rope and paw the ground, squealing.

"I'm a fan," Tella says. "He's so handsome. And famous. I kind of have a crush on him. Doesn't every girl?"

Melanie looks around the old house, peeks under the makeshift tent. "I followed you. What are you, homeless? A runaway? Drug addict? I think you're a thief. And a rat."

I am offended for many reasons. Rats are some of the nicest creatures I know.

"I think you need to leave." Tella tries to inch away, but she's hemmed in by vines and walls.

"You're trying to ruin my son's life." Melanie's tone is harsher, and her fingers are curled.

"I don't know what you're talking about," says Tella. "I'm just camping here. I'm not homeless. I have a family. They love me. I like to take pictures of handsome men on beautiful horses. I didn't know that was a crime."

Melanie lifts another of the blue tarps. Sees the package from Abra. My breath stops.

Quick as a flash, she pulls a gun from her pocket and aims it at Tella. "I knew it. How did you find that?" she asks. "Who are you?"

Tella puts her hands up in the air. "Calm down. Put down the gun, lady."

"Who are you? Some animal nut? Are you from PETA or something? Where did you get this?"

"It's mine. Penny Marcus is my mother. It's her package, so it's also my package."

Melanie nods. "Of course. The murderer's daughter."

Tella's face reddens. "She's not a murderer and you know it. But your son is for sure a douchebag who deserves to lose his riding license. Effing horse abuser. He makes me sick."

"Shut up," says Melanie.

Circe jumps up and bleats loudly from where she's tied, startling Tella and Melanie. Melanie swings around and I'm afraid she's going to shoot Circe, but fortunately she doesn't.

"Make them all shut up," says Melanie. "I can't think."

"Quiet, you guys," says Tella.

With that, we all fall silent. I can smell Tella's fear, and Melanie's. And the metal of the gun.

I hate guns.

Tella says, "Let's be reasonable. What are you going to do, shoot me? So you go to jail for murder? Just put the gun down and I'll give you the boots and the pictures I took. You want the dog biscuits I took from your barn? You can have those, too."

Caya sighs.

"Really?" I say to Caya.

"Squirrels just aren't as satisfying as you think they're going to be," she says.

Melanie says to Tella, "I will *take* what belongs to me. And go home. But you, sadly, were shot and killed by some random maniac in the woods. Happens to pretty little girls all the time. And my son will keep riding. I expect he'll win the gold medal in the Olympics next year."

Caya is straining at her rope, teeth bared. If only she could get free!

I'm working furiously, trying to chew through my rope. Circe is butting the air with her horns.

"It's risky. They might catch you. Better to just take the package," says Tella. "I won't say anything. I won't have any proof of what Alex did, so what would be the point? You won. Let me go. It'll be your word against mine and we both know how that's going to go." Tella is smart and persuasive, but Melanie is vicious. She cocks the weapon.

The rope between my teeth finally frays and breaks and I leap toward Melanie.

And the gun goes off.

92

PENNY

LISA AND STEVE are still out in the hallway. Penny passes them on the way in. They look grim. Penny sits down at the table. The guard with the Christmas ringtone who brought her back to the courtroom hovers near the door, clearly wanting to get home soon.

Lisa and Steve file in, wordless. The judge hasn't called the jury back in yet, but he asked the bailiff to bring everyone else back into the courtroom. He'd said if they didn't reach a verdict by three p.m., they would all reconvene on the twenty-sixth. It's now almost five. It's dark out, Penny guesses. She hasn't seen a window all day.

No one wants to come back the day after Christmas.

Does a jury rushing to a verdict seem like a good thing or a bad thing?

"A bad thing," Lisa said when Penny asked. "It's way easier to get everyone to agree to convict. No one wants to think they let a murderer go free."

"What about jailing an innocent woman?"

Lisa shrugged. "It's hard for people to put themselves in that position. Everyone assumes that they will never be where you are."

Penny knows this is true.

Laus isn't in the courtroom, of course. He's trying to find Tella.

Hardly anyone is here. A couple of reporters. A janitor waiting to mop up and go home to his family before the snow blocks the roads.

She's surprised that Melanie and Alex aren't there. She'd expected them to be front and center when she was convicted.

"Court is in session," says the bailiff. A door opens, and one by one, the members of the jury file back into their seats. Penny tries to make eye contact with them, but not a single one of them will look at her. Her heart sinks.

They think she's guilty. She pictures tomorrow, Christmas behind bars. Probably the first of many. She will probably be moved across the river to the state prison, to a bunk in a group cell. She will have a few square feet to call her own.

At least Penny will be safe from weather and hunger. Tella will spend Christmas out there on the street somewhere. Laus . . . Penny wonders if she is strong enough to take what is coming. She will do the kind thing and divorce Laus so he can remarry, start a new life. Tella will be raised by someone else. If they can find her. If she's in danger . . .

I would do anything to protect the people I love, she thinks. Anything. When she got to Sticks River, she thought she was different from the other women here. But now she sees that she is just like a lot of them. She understands Dawn, and the others whom the system failed. Given the choice of respecting the law or protecting their family, they made what now seems to her like an obvious choice.

Tella. Please be safe. Please be okay.

Penny holds her breath. Lisa slides over next to her and puts a hand over hers.

"Members of the jury, have you reached verdicts on the two counts?"

"We have, Your Honor."

"Have you filled out the verdict forms?"

Oh, for God's sake, Penny thinks. *Forms? Can't they just say it?*

The foreperson of the jury hands the envelopes to the bailiff, who hands them to the judge. The judge takes an agonizingly long time to open the envelopes and read the contents. Then the judge gives a little sniff and hands the envelopes to the clerk of the court. She fumbles interminably for her glasses as Penny feels like she's actually going to commit a murder if someone doesn't say something soon. Finally the clerk speaks.

"State of New York versus Penelope Marcus. Count one: We the jury in the above entitled action find the defendant Penelope Marcus not guilty of the charge of second degree murder of Frank Ross."

That's good, but not good enough. The clerk picks up the second sheet and reads.

"We the jury find the defendant Penelope Marcus not guilty of the lesser included offense of manslaughter of Frank Ross."

Penny exhales in disbelief. Opens her eyes. Lisa is grinning.

The judge raps the gavel. "Case closed. Penelope Marcus, normally you would be returned to Sticks River for processing, but guard, can you tell them she'll complete the paperwork after Christmas?"

The guard brightens, her workday shortened, her ringtone coming true. "Yes, Your Honor."

"Then Ms. Marcus, you are free to go. Merry Christmas."

On TV, the courtroom always erupts in noise. But in this case the few people who are there just stand up and leave quietly, pulling on coats and hats and gloves. The jurors file out without looking back, their civic duty done for this year.

Lisa hugs Penny. "Thank you," she says. "Thank you."

Steve is already out the door.

Lisa and Penny walk together out the front door of the courthouse. Penny has always been brought in through the back and now looks down the broad marble steps for the first time. There are huge stone lions on either side. They convey a sense of justice and fairness and solidity that she knows is more fragile than this sturdy building implies. The principles of the justice system are perfect—justice for all, equality under the law. It's the application of them that needs some work.

Still, she's free. It's snowing, and the light from the streetlamps makes cones of blowing snow.

"It's beautiful," she says.

"Glad you think so," says Lisa, pulling the hood of her overcoat around her. "Do you want a ride somewhere?"

"No, thanks," says Penny. She breathes in the cold winter air. It smells so good. Not at all like fruit cup or despair.

"Do you have a place to go?" Lisa asks.

"I'll figure it out," says Penny. "It just feels good to be out."

"Well, I didn't want to say anything before, but I have more good news. I passed the bar exam." Lisa is grinning. "I'm now a Public Defender Grade One."

"Congratulations!" says Penny, and gives her a hug. "You're going to be great because you already are."

"Thanks," says Lisa, then adds, "I'm sorry but I kinda gotta bounce. You know, Christmas and all."

"And things to celebrate. Is your mom . . . home yet?"

Lisa smiles. "Yes. She got out last week. It's going to be a really nice holiday."

"I know you have to go, but I want to . . . help. I don't know how, and I need to get my life back, but I want to help make the justice system more . . . just."

"That's a good goal," says Lisa. "There are lots of ways to help. Change is possible."

Lisa walks down the steps and away into the snow. She turns back just before she disappears from sight. "It was the pony, you know," she calls out. "The pony saved you." And then she's gone.

Penny walks slowly down the steps on her heels, her sneakers leaving perfect little half moon prints on each stair. Pony prints.

As she reaches the bottom stair, she is shocked to see two figures appear out of the snow and come toward her at a run, as if they have been released from a snow globe, or into one.

"Mom!" the smaller one calls out.

"Tella!" Penny screams. "Oh my God, you're alive." She grabs her daughter and holds on tight.

"Of course I'm alive," says Tella. "I'm fine."

"Are you?" Penny says. Tella does in fact seem fine. Great, in fact, with flushed cheeks and a big smile.

"I think she is fine," says Laus. He opens his arms and enfolds both of them. Her lips find his and his kiss is electric, like when they first met. A little zap.

"Where have you been? Why did you run away from school? Was it awful?" Penny asks. "I'm so sorry I left you there."

Tella waves a mitten. "Don't be, it was great. They're amazing and nice there."

"I don't want you to change. I love you exactly the way you are." Penny hugs her tighter.

"Mo-om," groans Tella. "That's too bad, because I *have* changed."

"You're better?"

"I hate that word," says Tella. "I'm changed in a way that makes it easier to be in my skin. In my head. On a daily basis."

"Oh my God. That's amazing. I'm so happy to hear that." Penny is suffused with relief, relief and love for this small person who is so, so large in her heart.

"I mean I'm not quote unquote normal, okay, so don't expect that—"

"I don't want that—" says Penny, but Tella is still talking, so strong and clear and confident.

"—and I still pretty much hate everyone but you and Dad, but I'm working on that. I'm sorry I blamed you for the way I felt. It wasn't your fault. I wanted to tell you that. I was scared to change, but it's okay. I changed and I'm still me. And I didn't leave the school because I hated it. I came because you needed me."

Penny decides they'll explore that one later. "I'm so happy to see you I could scream," says Penny.

"Please don't," says Tella. "I still hate loud noises."

Penny has to laugh, because Tella may have changed, but she is still clearly very Tella.

"Can we go home now?" says Tella.

"To California? It's late and I'm really tired," says Penny. "Can we get a hotel?"

"No room at the inn," says Tella, smiling in an impish way.

"Didn't you hear?" says Laus with a twinkle in his eye, taking his coat off and putting it over Penny. "The only place that has room is a stable."

Penny looks from Laus to Tella and back. They grin at her. "What are you two talking about?"

Laus and Tella each take one of Penny's arms. "You remember Silla?" says Laus.

"Yes," says Penny. "I heard she passed away."

"A probate lawyer called me. It turns out she left you everything in her will," says Laus. "Home, barn, property. The whole shebang. A very crabby llama, too, I think."

"Oh my God," says Penny. "Wow. I love that place."

"Me too," says Tella. "It's perfect."

"But . . ." Penny looks questioningly at Laus, who has always prized neatness and modernity over dust and disorder, who loves California, who has never owned a pet.

"It's growing on me," says Laus.

THEY ARE STANDING in the doorway of Silla's barn. Penny breathes in the deep dusty, woody, horsey smell. "Shouldn't we start in the house?" says Laus.

"No," say Penny and Tella simultaneously. A large dog comes toward them down the barn aisle.

"This is our dog," says Tella. "I rescued her."

The dog, which is of no discernible breed, but is black and brown and has one blue eye and one brown, gives a funny roll of her eyes that makes Penny laugh. "I didn't know you liked dogs," she says to Tella, leaning down to pet the dog, who bangs her tail against Penny and looks up adoringly.

"I love this one," says Tella, giving the dog a hug. "And this is our goat."

To Penny's surprise, a goat steps out of the shadows. It looks like a toy that has been torn apart and sewn back together again, and gives off a sour odor that is not unpleasant now, but could be in closer quarters.

"We have a goat?" laughs Penny. "I have been gone a long time, haven't I?" She kneels in front of the goat, who stares at her with yellow eyes.

"She's much friendlier than she looks," says Tella.

"At times," says Laus. "She did eat my mittens."

The goat looks unrepentant and gives Laus a little head butt with her horns. To Penny's surprise, Laus laughs and rubs the goat's ears.

"Dad is her favorite," says Tella.

Penny looks at the row of stalls and sees the two old horses with their heads over the doors and gives a little sigh. "Did my pony come back?" she asks. "From the forest?"

"Well," begins Laus, a shadow passing over his face.

"There's something you don't know," interrupts Tella. "It's a little scary. And sad. Something happened in the old abandoned house in the woods . . ."

Penny's heart sinks and a lump forms in her throat.

WHEN THE STORY is over, in one leap, Penny has Tella in her arms again. "Oh my God, oh my God," she's saying. She is crying and Tella is crying, but Laus, bless his heart, is still trying to explain.

"A hiker heard the shot and called the police," says Laus. "They found Melanie, subdued by the dog. This dog."

Penny stops hugging Tella and hugs the dog.

"And by the goat," says Tella. "The goat was standing on Melanie's head."

Penny turns to the goat and kisses her on the nose. "Beautiful, wonderful goat!" she says. "Thank you!" The goat blinks at her and waggles her ears.

"When the animals jumped on Melanie, I was able to get the gun from her," says Tella.

"The hiker helped and then police came and took Melanie away."

Penny and Laus share a look of terror and relief.

"I mailed the evidence Abra sent to the International Federation for Equestrian Sports," says Tella proudly. "Alex will never hurt another horse. And Melanie—they arrested her for murdering Abra. She cut the brake line of her truck."

"Oh my God. What a story. Thank God you're okay." A shadow passes over Penny's face, like she doesn't want to know the answer to the question she's about to ask. "And the pony?"

Laus and Tella look at each other.

"That pony took a bullet for me," says Tella. "Literally."

93

THE PONY

'M LYING DOWN and napping in deep shavings in my stall, the last one at the end of the aisle. I can hear the wind outside and I know it's cold out there, but it's nice and warm in here. Tella has decorated my stall with twinkle lights and tinsel and a garland made of olive branches, which is a shame, because I don't eat olives or their branches. Maybe that was the idea. The manger is full of sweet-scented hay, but alas, I am no longer hungry. I never thought I would say these words, but a pile of carrots sits uneaten at my feet.

The bullet seared into me, and the vet came, and I am preparing to die.

I have said my goodbyes to Caya and Circe. They will take good care of this family. They will be part of it.

I don't know what awaits me on the other side of all this. Maybe nothing. Maybe I will be fertilizer for a tree, which is not a bad thing. I have always liked trees and I would enjoy being part of one, looking out over the world with my arms outstretched, soaking up the sun and waving at the moon, dancing with the wind. At least I am reasonably certain I'm not going to be food for tigers, even though, let's face it, those barn cats were right and tigers gotta eat, too. If there is something after this life, and if there are rules there, I hope they're set by the ponies. I hope it's a place where everyone's well-being is taken into account, from the salamanders and ants to the bats to the birds and the whales and the plants. It's really such a beautiful world when you go out and trot around and talk to the other creatures. If the ponies are in charge, you can bet there will be snacks, naps, and a lot of fun. Won't everyone else be surprised when they get there and find out that the great writers like Homer and Dante were wrong, and that it's nine circles of spring grass and carrots?

My eyes are half-closed and I feel again like I did in the ocean, connected to every kind of creature in the world. I'm neither hungry nor afraid, but there is one more thing I want before I go, one thing I need to say, one person I am waiting for.

I catch a whiff of a familiar scent and the stall door swings open. With a rush of air, Penny kneels down in front of me without touching me. She closes her eyes. I lift my head and reach out with my nose and lay it against her cheek. We breathe in and out together. Her tears drop into the shavings below, each one a tiny mirror reflecting our love for each other.

You, she says. *You. Here. You saved me. You saved Tella. It's a miracle.*

I feel her energy. Even through her sadness, I can smell raspberries and marshmallows and joy. The brave and kind little girl I loved has come back and I know she will never leave again.

Welcome home, I say.

And she answers me in return. *Welcome home.*

Okay, I guess I can die now, I think, and lie down flat in the shavings. I close my eyes. I wait solemnly for Death for a few seconds, but . . . well, the thing is, I can smell those darn carrots, and there's one *really* close to my nose. Maybe there's time for just one more treat before the Grim Reaper takes me away. I did always plan to die with a full belly. With my eyes closed, I reach out my extremely dexterous nose and lips and grab the carrot.

I hear laughter. I open my eyes.

Penny, Tella, Laus, Caya, and Circe are all looking down at me.

"You do know you're going to be fine?" says Penny. Her eyes are warm and twinkly.

"The bullet hit you in the rump," says Caya. "A flesh wound."

"Your giant butt saved the kid's life," says Circe. "Congratulations. A medal of honor from the Order of the Huge Derrieres is on its way."

"Wait. I'm not dying?" I ask the goat. Surely she will not sugarcoat the diagnosis.

"Unfortunately we're all stuck with you for the foreseeable future," says Circe. "Merry Christmas."

"Merry Christmas," says Caya. "And many Happy New Years."

"Well, in that case," I say, leaping up and shaking myself off, creating a snowstorm of cedar shavings in the stall that blinds everyone else, "Let's eat!"

As Penny scratches my withers, and Tella rubs my ears, and Laus no doubt calculates how much all these animals are going to cost to feed, I tuck into the pile of carrots and feel like what I am, the luckiest pony in the world. That's how every pony should feel, I think. We deserve it.

ACKNOWLEDGMENTS

Like Odysseus returning to Penelope, this pony had a lot of help on his journey home. In the role of Athena, goddess of wisdom, was Claudia Cross, who heard me say I was going to write a Christmas movie about a pony and said, "Write it as a book instead!" Jen Monroe and Candice Coote at Berkley were the goddesses of metamorphosis who came up with the idea that I turn what was then an unpublishably dark novella for kids into a full-length murder mystery for adults (what intrepid writer could pass up that challenge?).

A core crew deserves blue ribbons for reading many drafts: Barbara and Robert Schwan (Pony's #1 fans), Charlotte Sommer, Kathleen McCleary, Lynette Cortez, John and Jennifer Brancato, Loren Segan, Keri Hardwick, Martin Velasco Ramos, Laurel Wood, John Paulett, Jamie Moore, Landon Spencer, Stacy Brand, Karen Bodner, Andromeda Romano Lax, John Kiley and Cathy Van Poznak.

Peggy Blanchard patiently explained the justice system to me, even after I said it was a book about a pony who solves a murder.

Sally Brady and the Stone House crew cheered me through both creation and revisions, and Anna Kovel named the novel one chilly March day in 2022.

At Berkley, I would like to thank Claire Zion, Loren Jaggers, Tara

ACKNOWLEDGMENTS

O'Connor, Jin Yu, Hillary Tacuri, Megan Elmore, Vi-An Nguyen, Amy J. Schneider, Craig Burke, and Jeanne-Marie Hudson.

Thank you to the estate of Pat Schneider for the use of lines from "Instructions for the Journey."

The quote about friendship on page [TKTK] is from nineteenth-century writer Dinah Maria Mulock Craik.

Though this book is dedicated to all ponies everywhere and the people who don't just love them but also make sure they have good homes, good lives, and good retirements, notable equine inspiration was provided by George, Sabrie, Siena, Yippie, Patsy, Cody, Pi, and their humans. The dog muses know who they are.

Of course my own pony, Floraa, will claim most of the credit.